ALL OUR
YESTERDAYS

Also By Erik Tarloff

Face-Time
The Man Who Wrote the Book

ALL OUR YESTERDAYS

a novel

ERIK TARLOFF

CL PUBLISHING

All Our Yesterdays

Cover Design by Natanya Wheeler
Interior Design by Frank Wiedemann
Published by CL Publishing
First Edition
10 9 8 7 6 5 4 3 2 1

Paperback ISBN: 978-0-9914478-0-0
Ebook ISBN: 978-0-9914478-1-7
Printed in U.S.A.

Library of Congress Catalog Number: 2014907028

For Scott Johnson and Zachary Leader,
fellow Uglies

One

1968

M y oldest friend, Stanley Pilnik, insists he feels no connection with his younger self, denies any continuity between the Stan he was and the Stan he is. We disagree about this. I once said to him, "If only Adolf Eichmann had thought of that defense, he might have been acquitted." Another time—we have these arguments a lot—I said, "So I guess I'm not the guy who borrowed twenty bucks from you last week." Both cheap shots, I admit. And I admit it can be difficult to recapture how you felt in an earlier phase of your existence, when your body functioned differently, the state of your knowledge and experience was different, the world looked different and smelled different and came at you through a different set of filters. When your life was still poised to take a decisive direction instead of having passed the point of no return. But I insist on believing the links are there if you dig. No need to dip a madeleine into some undrinkable tisane, either. Reminders are everywhere.

This isn't just a matter of personal conviction, it's also professional bias. My work more or less forces me to believe in the integrity of every personality, the relevance of memory, the value of excavating the past.

Like many shrinks, I now incorporate aspects of cognitive therapy into my practice, helping clients get over their symptoms before delving into all their mysteries. But I still have faith in the talking cure. In recalling the past and discovering the origins of one's self within it.

But this is probably a good place, right here at the beginning, to say, *don't get me started.* My wife frequently takes me to task for…not talking too much, exactly, but *explaining* too much. "People don't need pocket biographies of every person you mention," she'll admonish me. "They don't need to have key words defined. It isn't necessary to tell them every idea you rejected before you reached a conclusion. If you use more than one subordinate clause per paragraph, they'll stop listening."

My wife's a professor of English. You ignore her at your peril in matters of this kind.

Her hypothesis is that I do this because I spend my days wordlessly listening to people explain their lives to me, at exhaustive, voluptuously narcissistic length. She thinks this enforced silence coils up in me tighter and tighter, and when the pressure is finally permitted an outlet, it bursts forth in an explosive torrent. Well, maybe. But it's possible she's being generous. It's possible I've been this way since I first began to talk.

Mind you, Molly is a shrewd observer, and she knows me awfully well. We go back a long ways. To college, in fact, although the history of our relationship is a lot more tortuous than that might suggest.

You could call it love at first sight, although that ennobles my motives beyond what the traffic can honestly bear. Still, the night we met, we ended up spending together. Not untypical of the mores of the era. It wasn't just us; that sort of thing was happening a lot back then. For all I know, it still is. My son rarely tells me stuff like that. Neither, thank God, do my step-daughters.

But anyway. Stanley Pilnik—we've been friends since elementary school in Los Angeles, we'd once even had an actual furious flailing fistfight over which of our Davy Crockett coonskin caps was the more authentic and as punishment we were sent home from school in disgrace, our embarrassed mothers had to come fetch us, that's how far back we go—Stanley and I were giving a party. This was early in our sophomore year, it must have been October, I can still remember the autumn chill in the air, the damp wind off the bay, the trees getting bare, the fact that it was markedly darker earlier than it had been only weeks before. Sophomore year, and Stanley and I were renting an apartment off-campus. Almost everybody in our year was (except the foreign students holed up at International House), it was finally allowed, the first time any of us were permitted to live somewhere without adult supervision or rules. Our place was just awful in every respect, a cruddy little stucco two-bedroom on Arch Street, but it had some prestige because it was on the north side of campus where Berkeley's grown-ups tended to live, the professors and doctors and lawyers and so on. Not in our building, of course, but within hailing distance. In case we needed a lawyer or a professor on an emergency basis. Besides, prestige didn't depend on our place being habitable. The address was respectable; location, location, location. Just having our own apartment was an astounding novelty to Stanley and me, and things like acceptable furniture or adequate maintenance, let alone keeping the refrigerator stocked or the place clean, were utterly beyond our ken. No one teaches boys those things. Or didn't back then; Stan and I took shop classes at Bancroft Junior High while the girls were given Home Ec. We fashioned little wooden boats, they made cinnamon rolls. Both equally indigestible.

We shared the apartment, but the party was Stan's idea. He was eager to start celebrating his independence as soon as possible. I briefly resisted, sensing how much work it might entail and how many ways things could go wrong (I'm always worried things will go wrong, and I'm often right), but then let myself be swept along by his enthusiasm.

I hope I'm not giving the impression that Stan was some sort of party animal. The idea, to anyone who knows him, would be preposterous. He's chubby and earnest and shy with everyone but his closest friends. Was then, is now. One of the most socially awkward people I've ever known, and believe me, I know socially awkward people; they troop in and out of my office one after another. Besides, Stan wasn't just socially awkward; Stan was awkward period. In the seventh grade, in PE class, we were given some sort of national fitness test—JFK's initiative according to our gym teacher, a disappointed Republican who no doubt hoped to deflect our annoyance onto the new president—and Stan was unable to perform any of the assigned tasks. Couldn't do a push-up, couldn't do a single sit-up, couldn't climb a rope, couldn't balance on one leg, nothing. By the end of the test, even that hard-ass Japanese-American PE teacher was laughing, something we rarely saw him do. I wasn't much of an athlete either, but next to Stan I was Jim Thorpe. Well, regardless. It was 1968, the world was changing, we were nineteenish, people were behaving in extraordinary ways. Stan included.

So we were giving a party in our grotty apartment on a chilly Saturday night in late October. A couple of days before Halloween. A week or so before that year's presidential election, about whose outcome we all professed indifference. And by and large meant it, although it was also a fashionable stance at that time, to scorn orthodox politics as a corrupt game arranged to maintain the oligarchy's grip on power. But fashionable or not, for the first time since I had become conscious of politics (in 1956, Adlai's second doomed run against Ike), I honestly didn't much care who won the election, and neither did anyone else I knew. One of the two candidates was self-evidently the quintessence of evil and the other had metamorphosed in recent years into a eunuchoid buffoon. The people I might have supported—and as I say, it would have been unfashionable in some circles to support even them, but I might have done it anyway—but of the people I might have supported, one lost the California primary and with it any dim hope of getting nominated, and the other won the California primary but got gunned down in a hotel kitchen pantry the same night. After that, there wasn't much left to excite one's rooting interest.

But I'm letting myself get waylaid here. I was talking about Stan wanting to throw a party. Stan probably wanted to throw the party because he never got invited to any. And it was an excuse to approach girls—he was predictably queasy in that department—a pretext to phone them up, a way to maneuver them past our front door. And for all his awkwardness, Stan wasn't stupid: He also made a point of inviting a few people who were over twenty-one, to ensure that someone would bring some jug wine. A number of other people, or maybe the same people, were also bound to bring pot. Who could say what might result? It was 1968. Lightning might strike. We had unseated Lyndon Johnson in March, and having accomplished that one miracle, now maybe we could top it by getting Stanley laid.

What ultimately happened to Stan that night is lost in the mists of history. Obviously, nothing happened. Things didn't happen to Stanley at parties. Except I saw him get sick a couple of times. He vomited on a couple of carpets, pretty much wearing out his welcome in the process. Too much wine, too much dope; he wasn't good at handling those things, although he wasn't easily discouraged. When he finally got married, more than ten years later, it was impossible not to think he was lowering his expectations and settling. Carla was overweight and not pretty and had the grating voice of a New York yenta, a genus I had thought extinct until Stan introduced me to this sole surviving specimen. He probably found her in a diorama behind a glass case in some museum. But it just goes to show, because theirs was one of the more successful marriages in our circle. But I'll get to all that.

Molly had caught my eye the moment she arrived. Not her in particular, but as part of a sudden surprising influx. I didn't know her. She came in late, eleven or so, when the party was already in full swing. She arrived with a group of three other good-looking girls. Girls like that always seemed to hunt in packs. These were all attractive, all poised, all out of our league. Not just Stan's league—the girls out of Stan's league were a numberless horde—but mine too, an ever so slightly smaller group. Could he have invited them? It was remotely possible, but unlikely. Word must have just gotten out somehow, because our apartment was already crammed with people, most of them total strangers. The old college grapevine. When Molly's group arrived, something about the matter-of-fact way they made their entrance gave me the impression we were just one stop on a crowded itinerary. This strategy of party-hopping never appealed to me, not then, not now, but some people consider it a splendid way to spend an evening. Drop by, sample the vibe, move on. It may be a defect in my character, I don't know, but going on a party crawl never resonated with me. Once I get somewhere, I prefer to dig in and find out what's on offer.

Anyway, Molly and her friends arrived, said hello without much ceremony, obviously assuming they were welcome wherever they happened to alight, gave the room the once-over and probably wondered why they'd bothered. Our apartment was a hovel—I'm sure I've suggested as much already—with that dusty, moldy, seen-too-much-life smell you find in old apartment houses. Miserable ratty furniture, dirty carpets that hadn't been replaced in a decade at least, walls down on their knees begging for a fresh coat of paint. And right now the apartment was jammed with people, many of them cigarette smokers. People still smoked cigarettes back then. And music was playing; the white album had recently come out and the splendid side two was blaring from the stereo, making conversation difficult. But having crossed the threshold...the girls must have felt it constituted a commitment of sorts. They proceeded to drop their coats in Stanley's bedroom, on top of everyone else's, they poured themselves some Almaden Chablis in our cramped little kitchen, and then blended into the living room fauna.

Understand, during this whole arrival business Molly didn't particularly register on me. These four girls were, all of them, very cool in that ethereal way girls aspired to be cool in those days. Tight bell-bottom jeans, peasant blouses, hair worn straight. Some sort of cheapish, Indianish hand-crafted jewelry around the wrist or neck. Smooth skin, clear eyes, calm gaze. A floating gait. *Berkeley angels*, Stanley used to call the type. It was an intimidating type. The style in those days was to scorn artifice and aggression—which had its own extravagant artifice, of course, the most flagrant kind, and was often offered with its own sanctimonious aggression—but it made girls seem flirt-proof. You could tell you weren't allowed to play the old-fashioned boy-girl game. Lust was out, even though sex was mysteriously, tauntingly in. A paradoxical business, one whose rules were almost impossible to decipher. The best practitioners seemed to rise above any carnal agenda, that being the best way to achieve their carnal ambitions. And for some reason, pretty people were able to intuit the rules better than the rest of us. They always are.

No complaints, though. Not that night. I felt the familiar pang at being so lost within the prevailing zeitgeist, so unhip when hip was the only way to be, but I was still glad the girls were at our party. Having them in our living room definitely added to its lustre, their presence a sort of benediction, even if they planned to stay for only a few minutes before moving on to greener social pastures. Of course, it was also all too easy to imagine the air escaping from the party the moment they made their getaway.

My window of opportunity was narrow. I pretended to myself I was trying to come up with a way to approach one of these lovely new arrivals, but on some level I knew better. Once I thought about it, I was dead. With all acts of courage, you basically need to move on instinct, without thinking at all. Thought is paralyzing; courage requires willed stupidity.

When a joint was suddenly passed my way, I just passed it along. Even back then, dope made me self-conscious, confounded my ability to read social signals. In a situation like this one, that was the last thing I needed. Just by chance—well, maybe not just by chance—I was positioned near Molly at this particular moment, so I chose her as the recipient of the joint. A little transient contact, a consolation prize I awarded myself. She took it from me and immediately passed it on without taking a toke, and then said, "You don't smoke either?"

No joke, it took me a moment to realize she was talking to me. Of course, she had to shout in order to be heard over Paul wanting to do it in the road, so she might have been addressing someone across the room. I leaned in closer to answer. "Sometimes," I said. "When paranoia doesn't conflict with my other plans."

She smiled at that. A small victory. "What are your other plans?"

"Oh, just to survive the night with my dignity more or less intact. What about you?" It would have been unforgivable not to follow up. "You don't smoke this stuff?"

"No." Flat. No explanation.

"Is there a reason?"

She shrugged. "I'm not sure. Maybe I'm a goody-two-shoes, although I'd hate to think so."

"You've never even tried it?"

A short hesitation, then, "Not really." And then, "No." And then, "Friends have blown it in my face a couple of times, but nothing happened. Except I coughed."

"Hmm. Any other vices?" I was starting to feel emboldened, as you can see.

She held up her plastic cup of wine. "Well, this. In moderation. And anything from Sara Lee. Not in moderation." She smiled again. "But I'm guessing that isn't what you had in mind."

"I suppose I was angling for something a little more titillating."

"I figured." She sighed.

"Not that I have anything against Sara Lee. Nobody doesn't like her."

"I'm sorry to be disappointing." Before I could even protest, she went on, "No, really. It's not only you, it happens a lot. I must look more interesting than I am."

She looked so mournful when she said it. As if all of a sudden we weren't engaged in party banter, but rather a probing analysis of a deep flaw in her character. It was at this moment, I think, that I started to fall in love with her. I could feel it happening, too; I wasn't sure what it was—I probably thought it was too much Almaden—but something within me lurched. I briefly feared I might pull a Stanley on the carpet, but nevertheless had the presence of mind to instruct myself, Do *not* misplay your hand, Zeke, this isn't just about scoring anymore.

So I didn't blurt out anything that might alarm her. Instead, I said, "You're doing fine so far." Pretty brazen all the same: As if it were up to me to judge.

"Meaning—?"

"Meaning you're the most non-disappointing thing tonight."

"Yeah?" She ran a hand through her long, straight, dirty-blond hair. "Maybe you have a problem with expectations."

"No question about it. Can I get you some more wine?"

"Are you trying to get me drunk?"

The ground had shifted under us, you see. Suddenly we were flirting. Or rather, suddenly she was flirting back. I felt like pinching myself.

8

"Not exactly," I said. "It's just, we're out of Sara Lee at the moment."

"This is your apartment?"

"Does that ruin everything?"

"It doesn't help."

"No…I can see that." We were both smiling. "Well, where do *you* live?"

"Unit Three."

"You live in a dorm?"

"Have to. I'm a freshman."

"Ah." An interesting datum, occasioning a rapid reappraisal of the situation. Was she a virgin? Or maybe feeling homesick, or lost in the alien new world of college? Did my one-year seniority confer any advantage? I could sense a gentle shift in the atmosphere; her telling me she was a freshman altered things. And she must have known it would; she'd conceded the fact reluctantly.

"Where are you from?" I asked.

"Wyoming."

"Oh my God."

"I know."

"With horses and everything?"

She nodded. "'Fraid so. My folks even own a ranch."

"Oh my God."

"I know. But it's a small one. Not the Ponderosa or anything."

"So…I'm just guessing now…you're probably not Jewish?"

"It's that obvious?"

"Plain as the nose on your face."

She smiled, then frowned. "Are you allowed to say that?"

"I am, yes. But you aren't."

"Doesn't seem fair." And then she added, "But then, I guess the Holocaust wasn't fair either." She laughed. I stared at her, and after a moment, she looked chagrined. "Uh oh, was that over the line?"

"From anyone else. From you, on the edge."

"Why do I get an exemption?"

"'Cause I'm starting to like you a lot."

"So there isn't some larger philosophical principle at work?" She slid right past the content of what I'd said.

"Nope. Liking you overrides everything else." Giving her a second chance.

"Where are you from?" Not taking it.

"LA. Let's go somewhere we can talk. It's very noisy here."

"LA? So you're like…a Hollywood boy?"

"Fairfax. Let's go somewhere we can talk."

"What's Fairfax?"

"Sorry. Fairfax High. It's a high school, the main rival to Hollywood High. It was a stupid inside-LA joke." Despite this small stumble, I still sensed some momentum, so didn't let myself get confounded. For the third time in a row I said, "Let's go somewhere we can talk."

"Meaning your room?"

"Is that a problem?"

She was looking down into her empty plastic cup. She had a broad forehead, I noticed. In the nineteenth century, phrenologists would have concluded she was very intelligent, and for different reasons I was thinking the same. When she looked up and spoke, her tone was thoughtful. "See…I just got here in September. And, you know, it's the first time I've been away from home. And not just away from home. I mean, it's not like this is Cheyenne or something. It's *Berkeley*. The commie-beatnik-drug-sex capital of the world. My parents freaked when I decided to come here. I mean, they freaked when I applied, they freaked when I was accepted, and they *really* freaked when I chose Berkeley over Smith and Radcliffe. Do you understand what I'm saying?"

"I don't have a clue."

She smiled wanly. "Despite my impressive cogency?" She took a deep breath and started again. "I guess what I'm saying is…" Another silence. Then she blurted, "What I'm saying is, I don't trust you."

"You think I'm capable of violence?"

"No, no… It's not what you'll *do* that worries me, it's what it *means*. What it means to *you*, I mean. See, the thing is, I can't tell if you're like a slick operator or just an interesting nice guy. I don't know if Berkeley is full of guys just like you or not. Maybe you're the kind of predator who waits at the train station for the innocent young ingenues from the mountain states to disembark, you know?"

"You think I'm an interesting nice guy?"

She looked both exasperated and amused. "You're missing the larger point."

"To me, that *is* the larger point. Let's go to my room."

"I'm not going to fuck you," she announced.

This was 1968. It was still a novelty to hear girls say "fuck" like that. As a synonym for sexual intercourse, not a meaningless epithet. Especially this girl, who had just been protesting her innocence.

"Okay," I said. What else *could* I say?

"And listen, sometimes when girls say that to guys, it actually signals the opposite. But not in this case, okay?"

"Why are you arguing? I said okay."

"I don't want to find myself in a wrestling match."

"You mean you're not gonna wrestle either?"

"Best of three falls and that's *it*."

"You're actually adorable," I said.

"Can we get some more wine?"

"Of course. Anything you like. It's my apartment, I make the rules." I was feeling pretty cocky all of a sudden. As I led her through the press of bodies into the kitchen, I caught a glimpse of Stan looking my way, and the look on his face…it was hard to tell whether admiration or hatred had the upper hand. Story of our friendship in some ways. Back then, anyway. Things between us have calmed down a lot since he met Carla, despite the occasional zig or zag. "Listen," I said as I poured Molly a cup of Almaden, "there's something I need to ask."

"Okay." She visibly braced herself.

"You don't support the war, do you?"

She was briefly startled. Then she asked, "Is a lot riding on my answer?"

"Uh huh."

"No, I hate it. I organized a teach-in last year at my high school. I was working for Bobby Kennedy until…even though I was a Goldwater girl four years ago. Believe it or not. Everyone in my high school was. Well, not the boys, but you know what I mean. My parents are for the war, but I'm not. And I think my mom has started to waver. Finally." She took the cup from me. "Thanks. What would have happened if I'd said yes? Would you have stopped talking to me?"

"Uh uh. But I might have spent the next hour haranguing you."

"A fate worse than death."

"There are those who say I harangue with panache."

"Are you like one of those political types?"

A tough question. I was interested in politics, and active in anti-war protest, and could be a monumental bore on the subject if you caught me in the right mood. But in Berkeley terms, I didn't qualify. I didn't call myself a Marxist, for one thing, which pretty much put me out of contention. In the circles I moved in, being a Marxist was a minimal requirement if you wanted to be considered *serieux*. And I had no interest in, or sympathy for, violent protest. It's not only that violence scared me, although it certainly did; it also offended me, morally and aesthetically. It seemed sloppy and adolescent. And doctrine bored me. I found it hard to bear the company of those guys—they were mostly guys in those days, although that would be changing soon enough—who saw it as their mission to make you think exactly the way they did. Who couldn't conceive of such a thing as an honest disagreement, but assumed, if you didn't unquestioningly accept whatever they were telling you, that you hadn't understood and needed to have it all explained again. Who hectored you and spewed at you and wrapped everything up more neatly than the real world could ever allow. Domineering commissars who never stopped to ask themselves where their ideology ended and their testosterone began. Who sounded so certain of things they were making up as they went along. Later, in graduate school, a similar repugnance kept me from self-identifying as an orthodox Freudian.

Besides, I didn't have a beard. I couldn't be a political type. I sometimes let my moustache grow—it was a definite look in those years, Zapata moustache, bushy sideburns, Jewfro—but I never had a beard.

Now, in a funny way, Stan *was* a political type, certainly more than I. Of course, he did have a beard. A sad, scraggly thing, making him look more like a yeshiva student than a revolutionary. But come to think of it, a disproportionate number of Bolsheviks probably also looked like yeshiva students. I don't mean to suggest Stanley was any sort of bomb-thrower; his relationship to violence was very much like mine, except maybe even more so. But he did consider himself a Marxist back then—if I remember correctly, he was a self-proclaimed Trotskyite, and he considered such distinctions meaningful—and was fluent at explaining fundamentally inexplicable things, and defending fundamentally indefensible things, all according to his understanding of some abstract theory. And now he's a lawyer, so I guess he's still explaining the inexplicable and defending the indefensible. Our friendship survived our political differences—we've always had a lot of differences about all sorts of things, from coonskin caps to the dictatorship of the proletariat, and our friendship survived them all—but there were times when he called me a capitalist lackey and I called him a horse's ass and neither of us was kidding.

"Not to a political type I'm not," I said now, to this pretty girl at our party. "Political types consider me what Lenin used to call a useful idiot."

"You're useful?"

"Ha ha." I was liking her more and more. That little white ball kept coming back at me across the net, and always had a fresh bit of english on it. "Maybe we should tell each other our names. Or is that premature?"

"I'm Molly."

"Hi, Molly." As I shook her hand, not sure whether the gesture was appropriate, I said, "Most people call me Zeke, and a handful of very old friends call me Easy, even though I wish they wouldn't."

"So you're Ezekiel?"

"Shrewd deduction."

"I've never met an Ezekiel."

"Me either. It isn't one of those Old Testament names that've caught on."

"So that makes you unique."

"How kind of you to say."

"Unique isn't necessarily a compliment. Are you going to take me to your room now?"

"Fine idea." I then did something I had no right to do: I grabbed a half-full jug of Almaden from the counter and carried it away with me. It wasn't mine. Someone else had brought it, and it was supposed to be for the guests. At that point, I didn't care. If the person who brought that bottle of wine is reading this, get in touch with me and I'll buy you a gallon of something cheap and nasty to make up for my dereliction.

I led Molly down the corridor to my room, a squishy plastic cup of wine in my left hand, a heavy greenish jug of the stuff in my right. When I kicked open the door, I smelled marijuana, and could make out in the darkness a recumbent couple on my mattress over in the far corner. They were visible only as silhouettes, and unknown to me, or at least unrecognizable. It was impossible to tell whether they were dressed or undressed, and what level of intimacy they'd attained. When I pushed through the door, they both jumped, and looked my way, startled. Molly was behind me, peering over my shoulder. I heard her suppress a laugh. I wasn't nearly so amused. In fact, I found the situation damned annoying, almost a personal violation, but I wasn't feeling spiteful enough to switch on the light.

"Sorry to intrude," I said, keeping my voice even, "but this is my room, and I need it."

There was a brief silence, and then some movement. "That's cool," said a male voice. I heard a zipper being zipped.

I hadn't actually been seeking his approval. I was, in fact, affronted that a couple of total strangers apparently thought it okay to come into my room, lie in my bed, and engage in sexual activity. But you couldn't express that sort of indignation back then. You would have been branded uptight. Territorial, censorious, unspontaneous. Those were all bad things to be. So I tried to think benign thoughts while Molly and I waited for the couple in my bed to make whatever adjustments to their clothing they saw fit to make, get up, and leave. The girl never uttered a word. The guy muttered, "Peace," as he exited.

Well, this could have been awkward. But Molly sniggered again, and that made it all right. "Love is in the air," I said.

"So that's what it is. Smells a lot like marijuana."

"I hope they weren't at any decisive phase yet."

"I didn't get that impression," Molly said. "I think she was on the verge of giving him a blowjob, though."

This was even more startling than when she had said "fuck" earlier. Doing it was one thing, and amazing enough, God knows; saying it right out loud was something else altogether. But I tried to roll with the punches. "Yeah?" I said. "He'll probably never forgive me."

She snorted. "Tell me something. Seriously. What is it about guys and blowjobs? I mean, I'm sure they feel terrific and everything, but I get the impression there's more to it than that. The way you guys talk about them…it must have some significance beyond simple sensation. Is it the girl-on-her-knees business?"

"Let me guess. You're a psych major. Or is it sosh?"

"English, smarty-pants."

"Whatever. You've devoted some thought to this."

"Well…you know, giving a blowjob, the mind's free to roam."

Another provocative datum. I didn't follow up. Too timid. I went over to my desk and turned on the lamp, twisting the gooseneck toward the wall so that it wouldn't be too bright. A dramatic chiaroscuro effect. Long shadows, film noir. Rembrandt. Very atmospheric, except my room suddenly looked even crummier to me than usual, seeing it through Molly's eyes. A mattress (at least the bed clothes were still in place, albeit a little rumpled), a desk constructed of an unstained board and gray bricks, a straight-back chair, some shelves also made of boards and bricks holding books and LPs. A KLH stereo on the floor, the turntable flanked by two speakers. A couple of posters affixed to the wall with scotch tape: One of those psychedelic Fillmore Auditorium things with the crazy lettering, and an Escher print. Bare floors. Lots of dust everywhere.

"Love what you've done with the place," she said.

"It's not me. I had a decorator in."

"Very creative use of negative space."

"I let her know I don't like clutter."

"But you evidently have a thing for dust-puffies." Then she said, "So look, here's what I'm thinking," and her tone was suddenly and subtly altered. "If I sit on the chair, that might send an unfriendly signal, and I don't want to do that. But if I get on your mattress that sends another type of signal. And those are the only choices."

"You could stand."

She harrumphed humorously, and then crossed to the mattress and plopped herself down.

I went over and sat on the chair. That made her laugh. "Don't be a jerk," she said. "Come here."

As I was crossing to the mattress, I noticed a small green glass ashtray on the floor with a joint in it. The joint was almost pristine; someone had taken perhaps one puff on it before letting it go out. "Look at that," I said as I picked up the ashtray. "Poor guy. Didn't get the blowjob *and* forgot his dope."

"You could go find him and return it."

I sat down beside her. "Or I could give him a blowjob myself. But the chance of either happening is very remote."

"Do you want to smoke it?"

I was seated beside her on the mattress, my back against the cold wall, and now I turned to face her. "Are you serious?"

"I've gotta try it some time."

"But—"

"Look, I can't go home at Christmas and say, Yeah, Berkeley's neat, but no, I never smoked any weed. That would be *so* lame. My reputation would never recover. But I don't want to do it in a crowd. What if I disgrace myself, you know? You seem like a nice guy. Not a loser. Someone I can probably trust. Up to a point."

"Your logic is impeccable."

"But listen, if it's going to make you paranoid…"

Now my manhood was on the line. "I was just kidding back there," I said. Which was a lie. I really didn't like being high; sometimes just the smell of marijuana drifting in from an adjacent room was enough to induce incipient panic. It had a way of confounding my carefully-constructed defenses, maybe even my carefully-constructed identity. All the conflicts and anxieties I thought I had laid to rest not only in adolescence, but going right back to infancy, from toilet-training and language-acquisition on, loomed large and ominous. I would be overwhelmed by a whirling chaos of memories and disturbing thoughts and random impressions, and I disliked losing control; at a time when being cool was the most desirable quality going, dope undid whatever slight purchase I had on cool. But as I say, my manhood was on the line. So I found a book of matches in my shirt pocket, steeled myself, lit up, and took a toke. "The trick," I said, in that talking-while-trying-not-to-exhale way, "is to hold it in your lungs as long as you can."

"Gimme." She held her hand out.

"I think we have to kiss first. In case things get weird, I want to make sure I've got a kiss deposited in the bank. Okay?"

"Sure. Good thinking."

Again, we were smiling at each other, broadly, unselfconsciously. That feeling you rarely get after adolescence that you're in perfect emotional sync with someone else. Well, maybe you still get the feeling when you're older, but you've learned not to trust it. I put the joint in the ashtray, leaned in toward her, and our lips met. At first it was a sweet chaste kiss, and then it wasn't. Wasn't chaste, I mean. It stayed sweet. We kissed for several minutes, and a certain amount of unemphatic groping took place as well, and then, when we broke for a second, and I was preparing to whisper a cajoling suggestion about maybe reconsidering her earlier resolution, she got there first, saying, "Let's smoke that thing."

It didn't feel like rejection exactly, just a change of subject, so I shrugged and got the jay relit. And we smoked, and she got stoned for the first time, and she was amazed by the experience, and I was enjoying her company so much, and we were getting along so well, that I didn't get weirded out and had a great time too. We giggled and talked, in both cases without restraint. I told her—I thought this might turn out to be my ace in the hole—that the three things pot was best for were music, food, and sex. She told me she wasn't hungry right just then, and she added good-naturedly that she still wasn't going to fuck me so I could forget about that, but she admitted that she wouldn't mind listening to some music. Putting some rock on the stereo seemed too obvious, a generational cliché, so instead I put on *Kind of Blue*. Good choice; it made an original impression, and by God it sounded incredible. At one point she whispered, "The music's so *big*!"

While we reclined on my mattress side-by-side, lost in the sounds, not talking, eyes closed, holding hands, there was a knock on the door. Startled out of my trance, I called out, "Come in." The door opened and one of Molly's friends stuck her head into the room. She made a little face, probably in response to the smell of dope. Then she said to Molly, "We're going, hon. Grab your coat."

There was a brief pause. Miles' ice-cool trumpet picked out a thin scattering of notes, just the right notes, a glittering constellation of notes. I looked at Molly. She looked at me. Then she looked up at her friend and said, "I'm gonna stay. You go on without me."

The girl looked at me with a glance that came very close to being insulting. "For *him*?" it seemed to ask, with transparent incredulity. Or so, in that sensitized state, I interpreted it. As I say, marijuana can make me paranoid. "You sure?" is what she actually said.

Molly looked at me again, seeking a cue. "Do," I murmured very quietly. I didn't want her friend to be privy to this conversation. "I can take you back to your dorm whenever you want."

"Yeah," Molly told her friend, "I'm sure."

The girl stared hard at me for a moment—was it intended as a warning?—and then said, "Okay, have fun." And left. Didn't thank me for the party. But I hadn't really been much of host, had I? In fact, I knew I'd be hearing from Stanley on this very subject the next time we spoke. Right now, I didn't care.

But it was impossible to slip right back into that hypnotic music space again after what had just happened. I had admired Molly's ability to listen closely, not to need to interrupt the music's flow with conversation, but now the intrusion had shattered our concentration, and besides, her decision to stay seemed momentous. So I did what anyone would have done. I kissed her. Her lithe little body melted against mine and we began kissing in earnest.

"I haven't just made out since high school," I said a couple of minutes later. As if that was a lifetime ago.

"It's underrated," she whispered back.

"Like a dinner consisting exclusively of hors d'oeuvres," I suggested.

"Don't ruin this, Zeke. It's nice."

And it was. "Don't ruin this" is often a phrase used by women to discourage sexual advances, but in this case Molly intended it at face-value. What was happening *was* nice. Lovely. Everything felt heightened: The pliant fleshiness of her full lips, the sweet smell of her breath, with its hint of Mountain Chablis and smoke, the warmth of her face against mine, the pertness of her breasts and the complex texture of her small nipples, bare under her coarse cotton blouse. She had looked delicate, but her body felt firm under my hands, toned and sculpted. I didn't try to push things; it was clear that would destroy the mood. You have to respect mood even when it interferes with your grand designs.

We kissed a lot, we talked endlessly, we killed the bottle of Almaden, we finished the joint, we listened to more music. The Gould Goldbergs, another inspired choice; she had never heard them before, or even *of* them. She asked what else Goldberg had written, and she wasn't kidding, and for a second it felt like I was talking to Gracie Allen. But once they got underway, she was transfixed, she was more than transfixed. "I never want to listen to anything else," she murmured at one point. We finally stripped down to our underclothing and got under the covers and slept a little.

When I woke up with a start at about five, I was surprised to discover Molly awake next to me, lying on her left side, staring at my face wide-eyed. I wasn't used to waking up next to somebody, and it was a little disconcerting to see that searching gaze the moment I opened my own eyes. She was one of those rare people who look good first thing in the morning: That perfect face with its regular features, the high forehead, the straight blond hair, those frank, guilt-free green eyes.

"Well," she said. And then, a moment later, "Good morning, stranger."

I smiled at her, and said, "I don't think we're strangers anymore."

"No," she agreed. Then she rolled into my embrace, and a few seconds later, without any ceremony, she reached for my cock, in those days dependably erect each morning upon awakening regardless of circumstance. "My goodness," she said. And a few minutes after that we closed the deal; maybe I had passed some test the previous night by letting things ride, or maybe the inevitability of this happening was so obvious there was no reason to delay it any further. It was all over fairly quickly, but it was indescribably sweet. And it didn't seem she was a virgin.

About fifteen minutes later, when she tiptoed back into my room from the bathroom down the hall, I asked her if she was feeling energetic. The question puzzled her, but she said she felt okay. I told her to get dressed, and then I led her outside to my Earl-Scheib-candy-apple-red-painted Plymouth Valiant (trying not to notice the appalling mess left in the apartment by the previous night's party), and we drove up Hearst Avenue to Gayley Road, above campus, headed south, and then turned east on Derby. I parked next to what was then the California School for the Deaf and Blind (subsequently taken over by the university and re-styled the Clark Kerr Campus). "There's something I need to show you," I told her. "I've been saving it for the right person. It's a steep walk, though."

"I'll manage."

So we entered the forest-like area just off the road. We climbed the dirt path dog-legging up the side of the hill, like a ski trail, the sharp, complex smell of eucalyptus in our nostrils—I could hear her breathing laboriously beside me as we walked, her hand in mine—until we finally reached the narrow crest, with its panorama of the entire bay. The crest is small enough and the drop steep enough so you can't get too comfortable; the best you can do is take gingerly steps over to the large tree that occupies most of the limited flattish space and lean your weight against it. But the view is magisterial, and we watched in silence for a while as dawn broke and the darkness receded toward the west, and the bay, glittering silver, and the Bay Bridge and the Golden Gate Bridge and the skyline of downtown San Francisco each caught the light from the morning sun as it rose behind us. And then it was suddenly morning everywhere. The sheer immensity of the vista, its breadth, its crystalline clarity, left us speechless for a few moments.

"Wow," Molly finally said, drawing a deep breath. And then, perhaps realizing how inadequate that universal hippy response to every experience could be, added, "This is...grandiose."

"Worth the climb?"

After a brief pause, she asked, "Have you really been waiting to share it?" Her voice oddly timorous, a tone I hadn't heard from her till now.

"Almost a year," I confirmed. "You don't show something like this to just anybody."

So we kissed a bit, although kissing in so precarious a spot gave me vertigo, made me fear for my balance. I don't mean either of these observations symbolically, by the way. But it felt necessary somehow, it seemed appropriate that we signify the occurrence of something so momentous. And then, after a few more minutes, we retraced our steps down the hill to my car—it was almost as strenuous in this direction as the other way, and harder on the hamstrings—and I drove us the short distance to the old-time aromatic glories of Dream Fluff Donuts, which always opened early (it was a favorite stop for people coming down from a long night's acid trip, and it was no surprise to see a few such people there that morning, with their drawn faces and haunted eyes), where we got some donuts and coffee. I thought she might decline the donut, but she selected a glazed one without hesitation and tore into it with gusto. Then I drove her back to her dorm. As I walked her along the cement path to the front entrance of that hideous glass and concrete box, I said, "I want to see you again."

"Well, yeah. Of course."

"I mean soon. I mean tonight."

"Okay." As simple as that.

She moved her stuff into my apartment less than a week later. Stan was okay about it, a lot better than I expected.

Two

NOW

Molly's cell phone was ringing. The traffic on Warring Street was so slow she was able to dig inside her purse on the passenger seat beside her and fish out the phone without endangering herself or others.

The caller I.D. told her it was Zeke. "Hey, Easy," Molly said into the phone. "I'm on my way to get Ashley. Stuck in traffic. What's up?"

"Nothing much," Zeke answered. "I've got a client in a minute. But I had a cancellation this afternoon, I can take care of dinner. Go by the Cheese Board and grab a couple of pizzas."

"You're already hungry, aren't you?" She was smiling fondly as she framed the question, but he wouldn't know that. Or maybe he did.

"Ravenous."

"I can tell. But you're too late. I got us some salmon."

"Shit."

Molly didn't exactly laugh, but she exhaled with amusement. "Trying to sneak some cholesterol in by the back door?"

"It was worth a shot."

"This is better for you."

"Exactly."

"It'll be delicious."

"I'm so fucking sick of fish. It's against my nature. I come from a long line of hunter-gatherers."

"You come from a long line of push-cart peddlers. All of whom thought fish was a great delicacy."

"Only when it was smoked."

"You'll thank me when you're a healthy eighty-year-old." She was almost at Derby. With luck, after she made the left turn, traffic would ease up. There was one annoying, and equally pointless, traffic light to contend with after the series of stop signs, but that was the last serious impediment.

"Do we get potatoes, at least?"

"Brown rice." Zeke groaned. Molly laughed. "You'll survive."

"Barely."

"No, I meant it literally. You'll survive, and this'll help."

"You make it sound like I'm at death's door. Dr. Penman says I'm in excellent health."

"Except for the cholesterol."

"The Lipitor's brought it down."

"And the couple of extra pounds."

"Holding steady."

He didn't mention that she too was no longer as slender as she'd once been. She noticed, and filed it away for later appreciation. Zeke had a certain gallantry about him, a courtliness toward her, even after more than thirty years, and even after more than a decade of marriage. On the other hand, she still looked pretty good if she did say so herself, despite the slight albeit mortifying thickening around her waist and hips. It wasn't catastrophic, that thickening. All those miserable hours of weight-training and yoga classes and aerobics hadn't been wasted. She looked more womanly than a few years ago, no doubt, but she still turned heads. And every semester at least one of her male students usually made it known he was interested in something beyond pedagogy.

"You're in okay shape," she said. "But you're not nineteen anymore. Me either. We don't have a lot of room for error."

He groaned again. "Thanks for brightening my day. First salmon, then intimations of mortality."

"Pick up a nice cabernet, why don't you? You can look forward to that."

"Right," Zeke said. Glumly. "It would go better with beef or lamb. Or, you know, pizza."

"You should consult someone about this oral fixation of yours, Dr. Stern."

"First time I've heard you complain."

She laughed again, affectionately, and said, "Is this a promise?"

"An oral contract," Zeke said.

"See you tonight," she said, then clicked the phone closed and slipped it back into her purse. She had made the left turn at Derby, but the traffic was still crawling. As she drove along the southern edge of Clark Kerr Campus, she didn't give a moment's thought to the walk she and Zeke had taken up into the hills to her left some thirty-five years before, the first morning they had spent in each other's company, the morning they'd first had sex, the morning they'd fallen in love. She'd been past this spot so many times since, at so many different periods of her life under so many different circumstances, any specific memories associated with it had been sanded smooth ages ago.

When he was starting out, Zeke used to feel obliged to listen closely to his clients, later berating himself if his attention wandered. Which it always did, sooner or later. The clients, more often than not, were full of gratitude for his help, assured him how much difference he had made, how useful their therapy was, but Zeke wasn't sure. Most of them talked about the same thing over and over, re-visiting the same painful events from childhood, rehearsing the same adult grievances. Not exactly evidence of progress, surely. And after the fourth repetition of some egregious parental malfeasance or romantic embarrassment or professional frustration, it became hard to focus with the same intensity. Especially since a strategically-placed "Hmmm" or "Yes" or "I see"—almost invariably prompted by some intonation or pause suggesting an expression of sympathy, or maybe merely a bit of conversational punctuation, would be welcome—usually was enough to keep the kvetching on track.

More difficult still was when he found himself either disliking or, alternatively, envying the client. This seemed to be happening more and more these days. The latter especially. Like right now. Samantha. Lovely young woman. Senior at Cal. (Did she know his son? That could be awkward, if true. But even awkwardness could be put to good use, a way of examining transference issues. Uncomfortable for both of them, but that was the nature of the work.) Pleasant, slightly seductive manner. Probably automatic when she dealt with older men, nothing personal. Affluent parents. No genius, but smart enough to be doing okay at school and to make a good career afterward. You don't have to be a genius to be a success. Sometimes brains just get in the way.

Not to deny her her pain. People's unhappiness is real enough to them, and why they come for help; deciding to see a shrink can be a brave and difficult step. But still...Jesus, Sam had her whole life in front of her. It would probably be quite a good life as lives go, barring some unforeseeable catastrophe. So what if her father often went away on business trips when she was growing up? So what if her mother liked her better than her somewhat less attractive sister and she felt guilty about it? So what if the young men she dated seemed more interested in her breasts than her mind? Things are tough all around. I'm into my sixties, and nowhere near where I hoped to be. I'm not especially discontented, but what remains to me is more or less predictable and nothing to get excited about. I have to eat salmon when I want pizza, and I'm never going to be on Oprah or write a best-selling self-help book, and even though an hour ago I was flirting with my wife on the telephone about performing cunnilingus, the truth is we'll be feeling tired by ten tonight and it probably won't happen, we probably won't even make the sort of quick dutiful love that's become our normal sex life, not till the weekend at the earliest. So you want to stop complaining for a minute and change places? I mean, Christ, your parents obviously loved you and took good care of you. Your guilt is nothing compared to the distress your sister must experience on a daily basis. Those breasts of yours are the best friends you have, and, frankly, *are* more interesting that your mind. You have sixty or seventy years left, and there will be nice surprises and unpleasant surprises and that's just the way it is.

Did any therapist ever quote the Eagles to a client? "Get over it!" No doubt, in one form or another. But it wasn't Zeke's style.

His mind was drifting to dinner. He was starving. Lunch had been some Mexican-style chicken soup brought back from the Cactus Cantina just around the corner, eaten quickly in his office out of a Styrofoam cup with a plastic spoon. Not bad, and quite virtuous from a nutritional point of view—Dr. Penman and Molly would both approve—but it wasn't what you'd call filling. Or even satisfying. And he'd thrown away the corn chips uneaten. Untasted, in fact, since he knew if he had one, the whole bunch would be mindlessly consumed before he could stop himself. Life in his fifties was proving to be one protracted exercise in self-abnegation. Could it possibly be true that he had eaten cheeseburgers for lunch more days than not when he was in his teens? Amazing. Weight wasn't an issue then. He'd been a slender kid. With no notion of any kind of cholesterol count at all, good or bad.

Salmon tonight. Fucking salmon. Fucking Omega-3 fatty acids. Molly had been clever, beating him to the draw. She worried about his health far more than he did, and she knew him well enough to know his appetite for fatty foods was an insistent, unruly craving requiring constant policing. He'd have to figure out some way to make the salmon at least marginally more appealing. As the attractive, self-absorbed girl droned on about her current boyfriend—she felt attracted to his roommate, how astonishing, how unprecedented—Zeke's stomach rumbled. He hoped she didn't notice. Apparently not, she didn't change expression as she continued, "...he's sweet, but sometimes he seems kind of immature, you know?"

Was this her boyfriend or his roommate? Or someone else entirely? Christ, who knew? She seemed to expect some sort of reaction. A sidelong glance at the clock told Zeke that the fifty minutes were just about up. Phew! "I'm afraid we have to stop here," he said, with a hint of regret, a tone he'd mastered decades ago.

"Oh," Samantha said, momentarily nonplussed, as his clients always were at this juncture. On some level, they expected him to be as interested in them as they were in themselves, far too interested to care about the time. And then, almost apologetically, as she struggled with feelings of rejection along with awareness that such feelings were inappropriate, "Okay."

"We can pick up again at the same place next week."

"Or whatever," she said. "But this has been great, Dr. Stern. It means a lot to me to be able to talk to somebody who really *listens*."

Ashley, unsurprisingly, didn't touch her salmon. She wasn't a vegetarian, and as far as Zeke could tell—and he was professionally attuned to the warning signs—she wasn't suffering from any eating disorders. But she almost never ate what was served at the family dinner table. She ate, however sparingly and fastidiously, when they went to a restaurant, and she seemed to eat with her friends, and, judging by her conversation, she had the typical Berkeley teenager's sophistication about and interest in nutritional issues; she preferred organic, liked fresh, respected raw, scorned packaged and preserved. But at the family table, she moved her food around her plate with her fork for a brief interval and then asked to be excused. There was, Zeke was sure, something punitive about this: It wasn't food per se she had a problem with, it was the parents who provided it. Zeke couched this to himself as "the parents," but she probably didn't consider them a unit. It wasn't clear to Zeke which of them she regarded more definitively as the enemy, but regardless, her mother and her stepfather certainly occupied different regions on her emotional map. She had adjusted to the marriage less well than her sister or step-brother, which was odd, since she was the youngest of the three, and her memories of the time before Zeke and Molly had married figured to be the vaguest and least vivid. They'd been living together for almost two-thirds of her life by now.

"The salmon is delicious, Zeke," Molly was saying. Zeke, in a forlorn attempt to make it more enticing, had barbecued it in the Weber with moistened mesquite chips. And then, to Ashley, "You ought to try it."

"I have," Ashley lied, without energy or conviction. "It's fine. I'm just not that hungry."

Olivia, Molly's elder daughter, was looking on silently. Hard to know what she was thinking; Molly and Zeke both found her a bit of a puzzle. She was smooth and poised where Ashley was all sharp edges and raw emotion. There had been a few storms a couple of years ago when she was Ashley's age, but in retrospect—assuming no recurrence—they had been mild. She was a good student, but she didn't display any particular brilliance in conversation, no noteworthy originality, no special area of curiosity. Attractive, but unlike her younger sister, not really a beauty. Adequately popular; she was busy most weekend nights. The question Molly often posed to herself was whether there was any sort of depth to the girl, emotional or intellectual, that she somehow kept hidden. It was hard to believe anyone so manifestly competent could exist so exclusively on the unperturbed surface of things.

Well, at least she was eating her salmon.

"What's the homework situation?" Zeke asked. Molly understood: Precisely because his feelings were a little hurt about Ashley's refusal to eat the salmon, precisely because he wanted praise for his handiwork, he was pretending it was a matter of indifference to him, and moving on to the next subject. She wondered idly if Zeke could read her as well as she could read him. In theory, reading people was what he did for a living, and he could be sharply intuitive when engaged. But he didn't always seem to pay much attention at home. It was probably different at the office.

"Some reading," said Olivia. "*The Great Gatsby*. I'll probably finish tonight." She added, "It's really good."

"You like it?" Molly was pleased. She'd always wanted her daughters to be readers. Readers for pleasure. There was a time when it looked like neither would be.

"Love it."

"I've got a math set," Ashley said, by her standards almost pleasantly. "In fact, if I can be excused, I probably should get to it."

Molly pursed her lips and looked over at Zeke. He made a small gesture, signifying it was Molly's call. They had handled the potentially tricky business of step-parenting with a tacit deference; the biological parent cast the deciding vote if there was a disagreement, although they also tried to maintain some sort of consistency from child to child to avoid accusations of bias or unequal treatment. Especially, Zeke would occasionally say, twenty years from now, when they were on some analyst's couch somewhere rehearsing their grievances. The need to keep track of precedents sometimes seemed worthy of the Supreme Court, but there was no avoiding it. The kids could be relied upon to remember if they didn't.

"Go ahead," Molly said resignedly, after a short pause. "But this is to do your homework. I don't want to hear you talking on the phone up there till it's done."

"Right." An easy point for Ashley to concede. She could maintain multiple conversations with friends via IM while sitting silently at her keyboard. One of the many mischievous ways technology had changed every parent's life. Molly and Zeke had no way of knowing what Ashley was up to once she disappeared into her room. Especially since the sounds of hip-hop music blaring from her stereo speakers, those jump-rope chants of sexual braggadocio, drowned out every other sound anyway.

After she left, conscientiously taking her plate into the kitchen and rinsing it before heading upstairs, the atmosphere around the dinner table felt flat. That was the interesting thing about having a family member who was a source of turbulence (and who was a disquieting presence even when she wasn't actively turbulent, since you knew the potential always existed, you were always waiting uneasily for the next eruption). Without all the drama, one's sense of relief was offset by a vague sense something vital was missing.

And of course, Molly reflected, Zeke probably felt something vital was missing anyway. Something vital *was* missing: The presence of his son, Owen, now a freshman in college. At Cal, only a mile or two away, in a dorm on Durant Avenue, but there were times, Molly could tell, when Zeke felt as if Owen had sailed off to the antipodes. He was gone. He would be back in the house at holidays—even though his bedroom had now become Olivia's, whose own room had in turn become Ashley's—he would certainly visit periodically, but in the most fundamental way he was gone and never coming back. The dynamics inside the house had altered accordingly. Zeke must be feeling these changes keenly. He was the only male now, and the only one of his bloodline. He never said a word about it, and Molly was gratefully conscious he'd always been a dutiful, even a loving, stepfather, but still, it must have been hard on him.

"I really like the salmon, Zeke," Olivia said a few seconds after Ashley left the table. A good girl, not exactly deft, but sensitive to emotional nuance. Molly often wondered whether she'd acquired that quality during her parents' rancorous break-up. That must have been a tough period for her. "How'd you get it to taste like this?"

The question may not have been enough to make Zeke feel okay again, exactly; he sighed before launching into his explanation. But launch into it he characteristically did.

The next night, Friday night, was Zeke's regularly-scheduled poker night. It was Stan's turn to host, in his big hacienda-style house up on Grizzly Peak, the one with the magnificent view from his living room. It was the same view as everyone else's, of course—that view was a Berkeley bourgeois staple—but since the vantage point from Stan's living room was higher than anyone else's and his windows more numerous and larger, the view was even more panoramic, with the Golden Gate Bridge to the northwest and the Bay Bridge to the southwest, the ugly bare dot of Alcatraz, the cowering green porcupine of Angel Island, man-made Treasure Island, the reclining Indian maiden silhouette of Mount Tamalpais, the Oakland docks with their horse-like cranes, the dense downtown San Francisco skyline, all laid out like some sort of Imax presentation. Even after forty years of familiarity, the vista made you catch your breath if you took the trouble to notice.

Stanley had bought this big old handsome house, with its exposed beams and terra cotta floors, five or six years earlier. He was doing all right for himself. Had been for a long time now. He was always identified as "left-leaning lawyer Stanley Pilnik" in the *San Francisco Chronicle* when his name appeared in a story, and there was no question he usually represented good guys and victims, and he did plenty of pro bono work, death-penalty appeals and so on, he had kept faith with his political ideals more than most of the people Zeke knew. But somehow, somewhere along the line, he had also managed to become satisfactorily rich.

Stan had kept faith with Carla too, or at least had stayed married to her. Fidelity, or indeed anything to do with sex, wasn't something they talked about anymore, hadn't for decades, so Zeke didn't know about that side of Stanley's life. But at an age when many men who had achieved his level of success jettisoned their first wives and upgraded, Stan had remained loyal. Which could be regarded as a mixed blessing if you found Carla a trial, as almost everyone seemed to, Zeke included.

Still, if it was a mixed blessing, it wasn't an unmitigated curse. And one of its advantages was on display whenever it was Stan's turn in the poker rota to host. Carla was a great old-fashioned Jewish cook, the sort of *bolla bosta* that was widely believed to have gone the way of the stegosaurus (a creature, Zeke sometimes ungenerously thought, Carla vaguely resembled), and she produced delicacies—rather indelicate delicacies— Zeke had rarely eaten, had barely even laid eyes on, since his paternal grandmother had entered an old people's home some forty years earlier. Food not merely alien but defiantly antithetical to Berkeley's foodie culture. If Dr. Penman knew Zeke was eating this stuff, she would go into instant cardiac arrest herself. Chopped liver, egg salad, gefulte fish, stuffed cabbage, pickled herring in sour cream, pastrami, corn beef. Great coarse fatty dishes, ethnographic relics you were unlikely to find in most dining rooms these days. There were never many leftovers by the end of a poker night.

The cast of poker-playing characters had remained steady for almost ten years. Liam was an old friend from Stan and Zeke's early days in Berkeley, but most of the others Zeke didn't really know socially, they were men he encountered only at these games. Three were lawyers Stan dealt with professionally. One of these, a very smooth, elegantly-dressed, suavely humorous African-American lawyer named Mike Bond, had been named to the bench by Gray Davis before his recall. The handful of others…well, it was hard to remember how they'd first found their way to the game. In many cases, Zeke didn't even know what they did for a living, barely recalled their last names. He had some sense of their betting styles, and a feeling for who gloated when they won and whose tempers flared when they lost, but he knew next to nothing about their private lives. It wasn't like that awful men's group he and Stan had joined once upon a time, when everybody knew everything about everybody.

They played Texas Hold'em, mostly. It wasn't a forbiddingly high-stakes game, the big winner rarely left the table with more than two or three hundred extra dollars in his pocket, no one's life was changed as a result. Still, going home to one's wife having either to lie or to explain away one's bad luck was a prospect without appeal, and enough losing sessions in the course of a year could get expensive, and in any case, even when playing for matchsticks, it always feels better to win than lose. Tonight, Zeke had been losing steadily. No big hands, no huge pots, no great disasters, just steady attrition as his pairs refused to improve and his would-be straights and flushes refused to complete. Along with a lot of junk he wasn't even tempted to play. Cards were like love; when things were going well, you assumed they were conforming to natural law, but then when they weren't, you were reminded how little control you have over your fate, how dependent you are on circumstance and luck.

Zeke was a conservative—some would say cowardly—player disinclined to chase will o' the wisps. He sometimes thought he simply didn't have a clear enough conscience for the game, didn't believe he merited good luck and good hands, the benign bounty of a friendly cosmos. Tonight he rarely had occasion to stay in beyond the flop. But still, what with putting in his antes and occasionally securing a look at the first three communal cards, and once or twice finding himself with the second-best hand, his stake had been gradually eroding, forcing him to buy a second $200 worth of chips before an hour of play had finished. Never a good sign. The false feeling of being flush again with all those chips in front of him was an additional danger.

Stan, to his immediate left, had the deal, and gave Zeke an ace of spades and a ten of diamonds. After the two blinds, there was a raise from Liam, a couple of calls, a couple of folds, and then it was up to Zeke. Given his luck so far, his first impulse was to toss in his cards, but his position was good, what he held was playable, so he took a WTF and called. Stan folded, and the two blinds did the same. Stan then dealt out the flop. Heart ten, spade eight, heart jack. Liam bet quickly, his lips thin and tight. He was gambling, Zeke was sure of it. Betting on the come. The set of his mouth told him so, and the feigned decisiveness. Could have tripped, of course, but was much more likely working on a flush or a straight. Might be holding two hearts, or possibly a nine. Mike, to Liam's left, raised immediately. Already had the chips in his hand. A discouraging sign. Not just the raise, but its alacrity. He was feeling cocky. The other player still in the hand folded. Zeke was pretty sure he ought to do the same—ten pair, ace kicker—but this was one of those annoying situations where he would feel like a wuss for folding and an amateurish clod for staying in. The sort of situation that made you wonder why you bothered to play cards at all. Unless you were a gambler by temperament, in which case it was your reason for living. To his dismay, Zeke found himself calling. More an expression of frustration than anything else. Not the smartest way to play the game.

The turn produced another ace, of diamonds. Liam checked to the raise, Mike bet, and Zeke was again in a quandary. In a way, the turn card was the worst kind of good news. Two strong pair, often the most disastrous kind of hand to hold onto. Well, in for a penny. With a sinking heart, already reconciled to losing, he called. Liam instantly raised. He'd been lying in wait. Christ. He wasn't usually so sly. Mike glanced at Liam appraisingly for a moment, and then called. Zeke, feeling like a condemned man being marched to the scaffold, unthinkingly moving one foot in front of the other because he couldn't envisage an alternative, did the same.

Stan dealt the river card. Ace of hearts. Holy shit. Zeke's own heart started to pound, but he did what he could to keep his face impassive. Years spent listening to a variety of dumbfounding first-person accounts from his clients came in handy. If you reacted in any way, you might break their flow; he'd learned to keep a poker face not from poker, but supplying psychotherapy to people who had done appalling things and harbored unspeakable urges. He made a conscious effort to keep his body still as well. The tell could come from anywhere. It was often easier to control one's face than hands or shoulders or feet. Liam bet, not meeting anyone's eyes. Usually a sign of strength, paradoxically enough; bluffers forced themselves to make eye-contact to reinforce the bluff. Mike, with a brief but theatrical show of I-must-be-crazy reluctance, raised. Zeke waited for one moment to assess the possibilities a final time; even given his own habitual expectation of bad luck, he saw there was no way he could lose this hand. He re-raised, and for the first time all evening wished they were playing table stakes.

Foolishly—probably figuring Zeke for trips—Liam also re-raised. There were no caps in their game; Mike also raised. Zeke was sure he knew the table now; he was up against two complete hands, Liam's almost certainly a flush, but neither capable of beating his. Zeke raised again. Calls all around. When he laid down his boat, Zeke was gratified but at the same time almost offended by the surprise of the other two players. What did they take him for? He raked in the big pile of chips with both hands. Suddenly, life was looking a heck of a lot better.

It would be bad form to count his winnings, but he was sure he was in the black for the first time that night, solidly so. This was the kind of big hand you dream about. He imagined he could even feel his luck changing, a palpable thing. Which is why he was annoyed when Stan suggested they break to eat; luck is a fragile commodity, it doesn't necessarily wait around while you occupy yourself elsewhere. And Zeke, being Zeke, tended to feel its visits were rare enough and brief enough in the best of circumstances. But again, it would be bad form to balk after winning a big hand, and nobody else offered an objection. They all rose and made their way across the spacious tiled foyer, through the grand dining room, and into the kitchen.

Stan's fabulous newly-renovated kitchen, which had already been featured in *Sunset Magazine*. Tile floors, granite surfaces, big windows, huge gleaming steel appliances. The biggest refrigerator Zeke had ever seen outside of an industrial kitchen. A cozy family room dominated by a state-of-the-art home theater console was just off the kitchen, open to it, but that room was empty. Zeke had expected Carla to be there, watching TV and knitting (she was one of the few women Zeke knew who knitted, as her mother must have done before her). There was no sign of her, but there were plenty of her handiwork. On the kitchen's imposing central island, she had laid out one of her signature buffets, along with wine and beer, crockery and silverware and paper napery.

"Help yourself," Stan said, and stood off to the side to let his guests go first.

The men made sounds of appreciation and anticipation and bovine greed as they jostled their way to the buffet. Zeke held back for a moment, slightly put off by the press of bodies. He secured a plate and then waited next to Stan. A second later, Liam, having grabbed a small bottle of Calistoga water—he had become sober several years ago, after a painful, ugly intervention—joined them.

Zeke regarded his two old friends. Sometimes, with a jolt, he found himself considering how they looked now. The changes had been gradual, and God knows he didn't have their young selves constantly before his eyes, but still, there were times when it was a shock to see these two old codgers and realize they were his boyhood chums. Of the three of them, Stan had aged the worst, even though he'd arguably had the shortest distance to fall; he was moon-faced, rotund, sloppily-clad, with a wild gray halo of hair on his head, and a perpetual squint behind those damned granny spectacles, always sliding down his nose. In any American city other than Berkeley, he would have excited disquiet on the downtown streets and perhaps even risked arrest as a vagrant. Here, though, he was instantly recognized as a pillar of the community. Liam, once a handsome and romantic-looking young man, a lady-killer in his prime, was still passably attractive for a fellow of sixty, but everything about him had softened and coarsened; his hair, once a thick mane of sandy blond, was thin and wispy, his body doughy, his chest oversized and droopy, his belly almost a pregnant woman's protrusion, and his features without their former poetic fineness.

"That was a hell of a hand," he said to Zeke.

"Got lucky on the river," Zeke said off-handedly, not making a big deal about it. "Almost folded on the flop."

"Those always turn out to be the big ones. The ones you should fold."

"Not when I play them. Not normally."

"Well, I'm gunning for you now," Liam said, and his tone wasn't quite as light as it should have been, and the big grin he flashed was vulpine rather than comradely. Those yellowing teeth. Then he took a swig of sparkling water and turned to Stan. "Hey, I heard a rumor, Stan. About a, a former client of yours. Any truth to it?"

Stan shot a quick, furtive, concerned glance toward Zeke before replying. Then he shrugged and said, "Who can say?"

Zeke's antennae quivered with a sense Stan was trying to cut the conversation short. "What's the rumor?" he asked.

Another covert glance from Stan toward Liam, but although Zeke noticed it, Liam didn't. "You haven't heard? Corin wants to come back. He's supposed to be in negotiations with the Feds." And then, to Stan, "You must know something."

"I can't talk about it," Stan mumbled.

Zeke managed to remain impassive, still maintaining his poker face. But he felt a sick loosening in his gut. His appetite for Carla's rich fare disappeared on the instant. And he knew with something approaching certainty he wouldn't be dealt another good hand tonight. His luck had once again deserted him.

He got home a little after one, exhausted and oppressed. Climbing the steep stone stairway to his front door, something he did unthinkingly several times a day, usually two steps at a time, now seemed to require intense physical effort. He stopped half way up, leaning his weight on the iron railing, gripped tightly in his right hand, and caught his breath.

Not for the first time, he was wondering why he continued to play in the game. If somebody asked him whether it was fun, he would have been hard-pressed to answer affirmatively. He probably ended up losing more than he won over the course of a year. He had a couple of good friends in the game, but he could see them anytime, and more than half of the players he never saw in any other setting. Was the appeal merely habit?

He pulled himself the rest of the way up the stairs. The house was dark except for the porch light Molly had left on. He stuck his key in the lock, turned the dead bolt, and stepped through. He remembered to flick off the porch light, and then, standing in the darkened foyer, he heard a noise coming from the kitchen.

A small jolt of adrenaline. It was unlikely to be anything worrisome, but still, he proceeded stealthily through the dining room toward the kitchen. And saw, through the open archway separating the two rooms, a silhouette illuminated only by the light pouring from the open refrigerator. A tall, thin figure with bad posture. His son Owen, standing obliviously in the dark, head back, drinking orange juice from an upended carton.

Zeke found himself smiling. "Owen?" he said.

Owen wasn't startled. He must have had heard the front door. He turned toward Zeke. "Hi, dad."

Zeke flicked on the light. Owen, tall, lanky, with a shaggy head of rich black hair, was wearing baggy jeans and an oversized flannel shirt over a Gap tee. Nothing tucked in. The prevailing impression was one of easy-going looseness. A deceptive impression: Owen was a lovely boy, but he wasn't easy-going. Zeke took a step toward him, and at the same time Owen crossed to Zeke in a couple of long strides. The two embraced warmly. It was still a novelty to Zeke that his son was several inches taller than he was, it probably would always remain so, but his pleasure in the physical contact was unaffected by that.

"I hope this is okay," Owen said, stepping smoothly out of the embrace. His accompanying gesture seemed to encompass the open refrigerator, the orange juice, the room, the house, himself.

Zeke felt a great wash of the old familiar tenderness, but kept his tone casual and conversational. "Of course. It's still your house, Owen. I can't tell you how pleased I am to find you in it."

"Thanks, dad."

"Everything all right?"

"Everything's fine. I couldn't sleep. My roommate's pulling an all-nighter, trying to finish a paper."

"On Friday?"

"I know." Owen shrugged humorously. "I lost the roommate lottery. Some lucky bastards get babe-magnets and scoop up the discards and rejects, some *really* lucky bastards get drug dealers. Don't look at me like that, it's a joke. Me, I got a grind from Seoul. So I was wondering…is it okay to crash in Ashley's room?"

"Of course." He was secretly pleased at what he assumed must be a slight case of homesickness. Some small, no doubt unworthy part of him hoped it would always be there. "Stay the weekend, why don't you?"

"I might, if that's okay. Or at least hang out for a while."

"All you want." Zeke hazarded another quick hug. He never wanted to let go of his son. Then he said, "You need anything? Toothbrush? Towels?"

"Brought a toothbrush," Owen said. "I know where the towels are." He looked around the room. "It's nice to be home." And then laughed self-consciously. "I sound like I'm living on another continent, not just across town."

"It's okay, Owen. The truth is, finding you here has made my night."

Owen became subtly more alert at that. "How'd the game go?" He'd taken an avid interest in Zeke's poker nights since he was very young.

Zeke felt a sudden unpleasant return of a bad emotion, and hoped it didn't show. "Fine."

"You lost." Not a question.

"As a matter of fact, wiseguy, I came out the princely sum of $9 ahead."

"Hey dad! Way to go!"

"Yeah, now I can retire with peace of mind." He gave Owen's back a quick light pat. "See you in the morning, pal. When you come up, come up quietly."

Owen abruptly pulled him over and kissed him on the top of his head, which was sweet and disconcerting in about equal measure. Zeke smiled, left the room, padded back through the dining room, and climbed the carpeted stairs. He went past the kids' bedrooms, through his own study, and into the master bedroom. It was very dark; he could see Molly's shape in the low Scandinavian kingsize, just a lump of something indeterminate in the prevailing darkness. She was breathing heavily and regularly, her familiar not-quite-snoring, and didn't stir. But as he began to undress, she said, in a voice clotted with sleep, "Hey, Easy. How'd you do?"

"Won a little," he said.

"Goody." Her voice still sounded as if it was coming from somewhere far away.

"Owen's here. He's gonna spend the night. Maybe the weekend." He waited without moving in order not to miss her reaction.

"That's nice," she said. He exhaled. She and Owen had gotten off to a rocky start all those years ago, but lately Zeke had begun to trust the affection each now professed for the other.

"And—" And then he stopped himself.

"What?"

"Nothing. Carla wasn't there tonight, that's all I was going to say." It required a small internal struggle, but he had decided at the last moment not to tell her the news about Corin. She was the only one he wanted to talk to about it, but he didn't dare.

Three

1968

Our first conflict, a minor one, came a couple of months after we first met, as Christmas approached. Molly's folks expected her to go back to Wyoming for the holidays. I was urging her to join me in LA. I always liked Christmas in LA, and my parents, eager to meet my new girlfriend, were applying some pressure. Molly was my first official college girlfriend, and they were curious. And maybe relieved.

But Molly had lots of arguments on the other side. "It isn't really Christmas in LA," she said more than once. "Even the song 'White Christmas' is about how it isn't Christmas in LA. You can't call it Christmas if you're sitting by a swimming pool." We rehearsed these arguments repeatedly during that period, sometimes acrimoniously, sometimes jocularly. We argued on a bench in Sproul Plaza while eating lunch, on my mattress before and after sex, on line at movie theaters. "The sun will be shining," she'd say. "There won't be snow."

"First of all, the sun won't necessarily be shining." I kept assuring her of this, but it never seemed to sink in. Maybe she found my frustration alluring; it always seemed to provoke a fond smile from her. "Sometimes it's overcast in December," I would insist. "Kind of noirish. To me, that's what Christmas feels like."

"Because you've never known anything else."

"And even when the sun is out, the light is different, it comes in at that winter slant. And anyway, snow is overrated, at least after the first few hours. After that it's mostly just a hassle."

"Very romantic," was her standard response to that. "This would be my first Christmas away from home. My folks wouldn't like it. I'm not sure I would either."

"Gotta happen sometime."

"But not my freshman year, Zeke. This is already the longest I've ever been away."

"Is that so bad?"

"It is for me, yes. Just because I disagree with them about stuff doesn't mean I don't miss them."

I finally noticed she never countered my invitation with one of her own. It took me longer than it should have, but I got there eventually. And it gave me a clue. "They wouldn't approve of me," I said one afternoon. It hit me all of a sudden. We were in the North Berkeley Co-op, shopping. "Do they even know I exist?"

"They know I have a boyfriend. Sort of."

"Sort of know, or sort of have a boyfriend?"

"Definitely know there's someone I sort of spend time with."

"Do they know my name?"

"Your first name."

"Which is probably bad enough," I said. I was catching on. "It's the Jewish thing, isn't it?"

She hesitated. "My parents aren't bigots," she finally said.

"Of course not."

"And besides, they wouldn't even know 'Stern' is a Jewish name. I mean, it isn't necessarily a Jewish name."

"No, but if the name is *Ezekiel* Stern, the odds are pretty good. Anyway, you seem to be having it both ways. Is it they wouldn't know or they wouldn't care?"

She stopped right there in the narrow aisle, blocking a woman who was pushing her cart behind us. At that point, she didn't even notice. She was considering the question; Molly was incapable of answering tactically. "Ordinarily, I don't think it would be a big deal," she ultimately said. "A mild novelty, vaguely noteworthy, but not a big deal. At Christmas, though...look, if I spend my first Christmas in college with a Jewish family in LA instead of at home...well, I don't guess it would bring out their most broadminded impulses. Okay?"

"Excuse me," the woman behind us said, with a touch of asperity in her voice.

As we pressed up against the jars of olives to get out of the woman's way, I said, "So they *are* bigots is what you're saying."

"Have it your way." And then she said, "Would your parents like it if you spent Hanukkah with a Christian family in Wyoming?"

"They wouldn't give a rat's ass about the Hanukkah part. I haven't been inside a synagogue since my bar mitzvah. Neither have they, as far as I know. And they wouldn't care about the Christian part. They might have a problem with Wyoming." And then, before she could respond to that, I added, "Am I invited?"

Which flustered her. She hadn't considered the consequences of her argument in advance, and now she was trapped. She had no answer for a moment or two. Then she said, a little helplessly, "Noooo. I don't think it would be a good idea. Yet." I started to say something, but she cut in, "Not for religious reasons, if that's what you're thinking. Just because... oh, because of everything."

"They'd hate everything about me, that's what you're saying?"

"Oh please, let it go, Easy." And then she said, "Which, by the way, may be the most inappropriate nickname in history." And then quickly continued, "When they meet you, they'll like you, I'm sure of it. My mom'll fall in love with you. Unless you start trying to provoke them the way you sometimes do. But...I need to prepare the ground a little first, okay? You're...you're..."

"What?"

She pouted. After a second or two, she said, "They'd consider you a

Communist. Don't tell me you aren't, I know you aren't, but the distinction would be lost on them. You're from Los Angeles, which they don't consider an American city. You've got long hair. You dress like a hippy. You have a sardonic sense of humor, which they might like when it's Morey Amsterdam but not when it's their daughter's boyfriend. You sneer at a lot of things they value. We're fucking and sucking, which they'd suspect even if they'd do everything in the world to avoid knowing it. You represent all the reasons they didn't want me to go to Berkeley in the first place."

"Besides, I'm a rootless, money-grubbing, Christ-killing cosmopolite."

"Fuck you. It isn't that. I doubt they spend any time at all thinking about things like that. The only person I know who ever brings up stuff like that is you."

"I only started recently." Which was a sort of concession, although admittedly a graceless one.

It was Stan, of all people, who provided the basis, or at least the occasion, for a compromise. We needed to be in a situation where compromise wouldn't feel like surrender, and Stan provided it. This must have been the same night, since that day in the Co-op was about as contentious as the argument ever got; neither of us had ever said "Fuck you" to the other before that, even if it had been said half in jest. That same night—I remember now, it was a Friday night—the three of us went to LaVal's for pizza, which had become a sort of Friday ritual for us. We went, I think, in order to feel superior to the frat-boy types, otherwise largely invisible in Berkeley, who noisily frequented that dingy basement. In those days, downstairs at LaVal's was an isolated pocket that managed to reflect traditional collegiate life in the midst of the changing mores and violent social upheaval inescapable everywhere else. Anyway, while we waited for our pizzas and looked covetously at the pitchers of beer on nearby tables (we were all still under-age), Stan quite innocently asked Molly and me about our holiday plans.

We looked at each other warily and didn't answer.

"I'd love to stay up here," Stan said, filling the silence. "See what the town is like when the students have left. And to avoid going home, of course."

"You don't want to?" Molly asked. The attitude was incomprehensible to her. Not necessarily obnoxious, just impossible to understand.

"I've been waiting to get away from my parents my whole life," Stan said. "I've finally managed it. And so far, it's lived up to expectations."

I knew the Pilniks well, having spent lots of time in their house, starting in the first grade when Stan and I watched Pinky Lee together in the afternoon on their old round-screen Philco. They had a wooden playhouse in their small backyard that I considered the coolest, most desirable possession imaginable; Stan and I would often hang out there for hours on hot summer days, reading comic books and talking. His mother would sometimes bring us lemonade. I never understood Stan's detestation of his parents, which began sometime during junior high. They seemed like perfectly nice people to me. His father was an accountant, an undeniably unexciting guy with thin shoulders and a thin chest but a big belly who wore his trousers too high and compensated by making lots of bad jokes and then laughing at them loudly. Irritating, but surely there are worse sins. Maybe not for a son, though. And Stan's mother was…well, she was maternal in a way that my mother, for example, had never even tried to be; she was a good cook, she kept a spotless household without the assistance of any cleaning lady, she was always hoveringly concerned with Stan's health and well-being. Especially of a digestive nature.

Writing about them now, I'm beginning to see his point of view. What took me so long?

Anyway, Stan was saying that while he didn't think he could skip LA entirely, not if he wanted to avoid hurt feelings and acrimony—to his credit he was never overtly rebellious, he didn't take pleasure in confronting his parents with his distaste, he just preferred to avoid them—he still hoped to keep his visit as brief as possible.

"The whole gang will be there," I said, by way of counter-argument.

"See, that's the thing," he said. "You miss the gang. I don't. They were only my gang by default, because I was your friend. They just put up with me. Barely. Getting out of high school was the best thing that ever happened to me, and I have zero interest in going back."

That's when I had the idea. "Look, let's all drive down together. That part might be fun, at least. And afterward, Molly can fly to Cheyenne out of LA instead of SF." I turned to her. "Spend a couple of days with the lovable, laughable Sterns, then fly home for Christmas. Your parents don't even have to know where you've been."

Then I addressed Stan. "You can go back to Berkeley whenever you decide you can't take it anymore, go back however you like."

Molly looked thoughtful. "I could just say I'm spending a couple of days with a college friend. I don't have to mention your sex."

"Except with reverence and awe."

She gave me a sharp nudge with her elbow, which suggested we were no longer mad at each other. I found out why later that night, when we were alone in my room, getting ready for bed. "Listen," she asked, "did I understand Stan correctly?" I was on my knees on the floor, pulling back the covers from my mattress—with no box springs, making and unmaking the bed was an arduous undertaking—and she had already begun undressing. "Were you friends with him even though your other friends thought he was uncool?"

"Oh, I don't know. In a way. You know what high school's like. It wasn't a big deal."

"Did they ever give you grief about it?"

"Not really. Maybe. I don't remember."

She suddenly kneeled down, grabbed me, and gave me a big kiss. Her blouse was off by now, and as usual she was wearing no bra. I was pleased, as goes without saying, but also puzzled. "What?"

Her hands on my shoulders, she pushed me back onto the mattress, straddled me, and then was smiling down on me, her face inches from mine, her hair tickling my face. "It's just...you're a good person, Zeke. Which is lucky for me. Because frankly, it wasn't your goodness that initially attracted me."

"No? What was it?"

"Never you mind."

45

"Was it...*this?*"

Her smile broadened. "Uh uh. I didn't know about that yet."

"Well, so what could it have been?"

"It doesn't matter. Your being a nice guy is why I've stayed."

She leaned down a little farther and kissed my nose. We were lying there, she on top of me, grinning at each other. I said, "All this because I befriended a nerdy schmo in high school?"

Her smile faded, her face became thoughtful. "No. Well. It's more than that. You stood by him. You noticed there was a valuable person beneath the nerdy carapace. It's taken *me* a while to see it."

"It didn't take profound insight. We'd been friends since kindergarten."

"Yeah, that's another thing. Loyalty. Lots of kids jettison their uncool friends in high school. It's a price they're willing to pay to be popular. You weren't."

"No one asked me to."

"No one does. It isn't necessary. The message gets conveyed. I'm sure the message *got* conveyed. You ignored it."

"What can I say? I'm a prince."

I was being facetious, but the truth is, I hadn't been such a prince. There were many occasions when I'd been willing to ditch Stan to spend time with the cool kids. There were plenty of times when having him around was an embarrassment I just had to grit my teeth and endure. I always loved Stan, and I always valued the friendship, and it survived, but I'd walked a very narrow line and occasionally stumbled; my behavior hadn't always been exemplary. We had had our share of feuds during those years, and even some extended rough patches, and there were times when he felt like a lodestone around my neck, and I'm sure there were times he felt betrayed.

But Molly wanted to think the best of me. Saw the best in me. Sometimes she even made me believe it. Lying there, looking into each other's eyes, we smiled at each other some more, just happy to be near each other. That's how it was back then.

Over the next few days, we toyed with the idea of taking Route One, devoting a couple of days to the journey, seeing some of the sights like San Simeon and Big Sur, camping out on the beach. It was Stan who nixed the idea. When we were alone one morning, at the breakfast table, sipping our instant coffee, he announced, "Listen, I've thought about it, and I don't want to spend a night on the beach."

"Why not? It could be fun."

"I don't want to have to hear you two fucking."

I hadn't thought of that. "That won't happen, necessarily," I said.

"Of course it will. You can't help yourselves. It's bad enough here in the apartment, but at least there's a wall between us, and I can crank up my stereo. The sound of the surf isn't going to do it."

I could have argued further, or made a solemn vow, but...well, first of all, he was right; as soon as he said it, I recognized that fucking on the beach would be irresistible, urgent and romantic and novel. Hell, a few years later they even named a drink after it. In those days, our sex life, Molly's and mine, had a life of its own. We'd been together less than two months. And we were so young. Sex was a gleaming new toy train we were amazed to realize we could take out of the box and play with anytime we wanted. So we might promise Stan that we'd forbear, but as soon as we thought he was asleep, the revels would begin.

In the end, we took the opposite tack, speeding down the old 99, the fastest route available back then, stopping for one quick meal about half-way down, in Tulare. In those *Easy Rider* days, we felt vulnerable in the agricultural regions of Central California, and obtrusive in the restaurant where we stopped to eat. Being young, having long hair, one of us sporting a scraggly beard, two of us easily identifiable as ethnically alien, we didn't feel especially welcome among the cowboys and farmers at neighboring formica booths and tables, and we ordered fast, ate fast, and got out of there fast. But we were treated fine. It was just our imagination.

Molly and I dropped Stan off at his parents' house in the Hollywood flats, south of Melrose, midway between Fairfax and La Brea. The same dinky house he had been born in, the same one we'd played in as tots. And then, after bidding him goodbye as he stood forlornly on the sidewalk with his suitcase at his feet, warily contemplating his front door like the returning soldier in that Norman Rockwell *Saturday Evening Post* cover, I suddenly felt a little apprehensive myself. For the first time, the prospect of introducing Molly to my own parents didn't seem like a simple matter; the gulf of mutual incomprehension figured to be vast. Why hadn't this occurred to me before?

Molly had never been to LA. I therefore had an excuse to delay our arrival by giving her a short but no doubt thoroughly boring guided tour: *Ezekiel Stern, the Early Years.* The small house less than a mile from Stan's in which I had grown up and which my parents had sold only the previous year, after I'd left for college. My grade school, junior high, and high school. I showed her the Fairfax District, that little piece of the lower east side planted smack dab in Hollywood, pointing out Canter's and CBS Television City and the Farmers' Market and the new, counter-cultural *LA Free Press* bookshop. She was a good sport, but none of this could have interested her much, and she must have been feeling a fair degree of apprehension on her own. Only when I had exhausted all my youthful venues did I surrender to the inevitable and aim for my parents' new house, off Doheny, just above the Sunset Strip, not far from the Whisky a Go Go and the Roxie and two short blocks from the house in which Igor Stravinsky still lived and breathed.

I came to a stop in front of the low white picket fence surrounding my folks' front yard. The house, a wide, low ranch-style, was in the hills, but the street on which it stood had been terraced, and so the front yard was flat while the grounds behind the house fell away dramatically. I had stayed there a few times by now, but it still felt alien, distinctly not mine. It was unsettling when my parents had moved the previous year, so soon after I'd left for college. There had been no hint they were planning anything of the kind. Not that they owed me an explanation, but when you leave home, some part of you relies on its being there when you go back, no matter what Thomas Wolfe says. And to make matters worse, they had bought a smaller house, as if to celebrate my absence.

Smaller but nicer. My father's business—he owned a couple of clothing stores, one on Beverly Drive in Beverly Hills, just below

Wilshire, the other on the Strip less than a mile from the new house—had been making good money for almost a decade now, and especially in the last few years. Early on, he had seen the potential of mod fashions and hippy ersatz-homespun and designer jeans, etc., and had added that sort of merchandise to his stock. He considered it ugly and badly-made and over-priced, but hell, give the people what they want. Which brought him a whole new class of clientele, rock musicians and some of the younger movie stars. Mick Jagger was in once, and George Harrison, and Tommy Smothers. Tony Bill. Peter Fonda. Stephen Stills, although one of the clerks had to tell my father who he was. Anyway, business was booming. The store was even considered hip, a ridiculous notion if you knew my father. Previously, he had catered to the sort of people who wear golf togs around town. So by any objective measure, it was time he and my mother upgraded. I just would have preferred the upgrade to have more capacious guest quarters.

"Nice house," Molly said. Not casually. As if it required a major reassessment of the situation.

"Yeah, I guess it's okay."

We climbed out of the car and got our suitcases out of the trunk. It was late afternoon, after five o'clock by now, and chilly. Getting dark, too. Christmas in LA, not the tropical idyll Molly had envisioned. "Okay," I said, "brace yourself."

Molly smiled uneasily. I led her up the flagstone path to the front door. I had a key, but somehow didn't feel right just letting us in. I guess because, as I said, I didn't feel I belonged in (or to) the house. I rang the doorbell.

I assumed my mother would be home and my father at work. This was a reasonable assumption, not just hope springing eternal; my mother could be a cipher, but fine in situations requiring little beyond superficial graciousness. That she possessed in abundance. My father, on the other hand, could be a handful. But he always worked long hours, that was part of his ethic. His stores stayed open till six (nine on Thursdays), and he was generally at one or the other of them at closing time, keeping an eye on things.

But it was my father who opened the door. He had a glass of whisky in his hand, never a good sign. And his color was high, also ominous. "Welcome!" he said expansively, and too loudly. "We were starting to worry!" He offered me a hand to shake, but he didn't hug me. We never hugged. "Mom was getting into a state!"

"This is pretty much when I said we'd arrive," I pointed out as I shook his hand. "We're not late."

His eye fell on Molly. I could see him assessing her prettiness, her slim body. I registered him taking note of her small shapely unsecured breasts, her nipples visible through the thin cotton of her blouse. This assessment had less, I think, to do with its direct sexual effect on him than what it might say about his son. If she were insufficiently attractive, he would feel both embarrassed on my behalf and Oedipally triumphant. If she were *too* attractive, well, he wouldn't like that at all.

He leaned toward the second response, was my impression. But Molly's self-presentation, at least by LA standards, was simple and unglamourous, and he could just about manage not to feel competitive, despite her angelic face and her small, beautiful breasts. No make-up, simple clothing, nothing fancy about the hair. The girls he saw every day in his stores looked like models and starlets. Many of them *were* models and starlets. And frankly, it wouldn't surprise me—today, that is; the thought didn't occur to me at the time—if he'd been screwing some of his salesgirls.

"Molly," he said. "Nice to meet you finally." And then he kissed her on the cheek.

"Nice to meet you too, Mr. Stern."

It was at this point I noticed my mother, standing a few steps behind my father. The house was dark within, and she was hidden in the shadows. We were still standing on the doorstep.

"*Mr. Stern?*" my father bellowed. "My name is Seymour! You can call me Sy!"

I saw Molly pull into herself. She wasn't used to being bellowed at, even in an ostensibly friendly manner.

"Come in, come in," he went on, the decibel level not much reduced.

He reached for her suitcase and led us into the living room. They had put in a small Christmas tree—not for Molly's benefit; we were a secular family, we usually had a tree—but otherwise, it hadn't changed since I'd been here last, the same beige carpeting, the same Scandinavian furniture. My mother approached. She gave me a kiss, gave Molly a kiss, and told us she was glad to see us. "I was starting to worry," she then said.

"You were starting to panic, is what you were doing."

"Show them to their room, Sy."

Molly gave me a look that could almost be described as alarmed. It wasn't their little contretemps, good-natured by their standards (although Molly didn't know that), but rather my mother's use of the singular form of the word "room." It hadn't occurred to Molly we would be sharing a bedroom. I hadn't been sure myself.

"You'll be comfortable, I think," my father said. "It's nice and private." In case we had missed the point.

We followed my father down the corridor, past the kitchen, and came to the guest room. "Here we are," he said. "I'll give you a little time to freshen up. Then we'll have a drink." At least he didn't wink.

After he left us alone, Molly and I stood there for a moment, looking at each other. She smiled hesitantly. "Your parents are a lot more liberal than mine."

"And proud of it," I said. "Eager for the world to know and celebrate the fact." Noticing her hesitation, I said, "Does this make you uncomfortable?"

"Not exactly. I just…"

"Feel like we have an audience?"

"No, that's not it. I just…my parents would be horrified. Even more horrified by your parents' attitude, I think, than by the fact we're having sex."

"Better not tell them."

"I don't plan to tell them *anything*. As far as they're concerned, your name is Rachel."

"At least you picked a Jewish name."

She smiled at that. "Easing them in. One shock at a time."

That night, my parents took us to Scandia, one of their favorite restaurants and a traditional family venue for celebratory dinners. It was close enough to where they now lived we could walk over. Which was for the best, considering my father's condition.

Scandia had a dress code, most grown-up restaurants did in those days, so Molly had to hunt around in her suitcase to find a dress. Fortunately she had packed one for when her family went to church on Christmas Eve. I wasn't so lucky; I hadn't thought to bring anything but jeans and cords, and my one suit was either in storage somewhere or had already been donated to Goodwill when my folks cleaned out the old house before moving. It probably wouldn't have fit me anyway. I ended up borrowing one of my father's sports jackets, which was more or less the right size (just about perfect in the shoulders, a little roomy in the middle), and one of his ties, and paired them with the least ratty pair of corduroy pants I had brought. I just about passed muster, at least after we were seated at our table and the cords weren't visible. Molly, who I'd never before seen in a dress, looked resplendent.

Right after we were seated, my father ordered a scotch. I saw my mother react, although she didn't say anything. She ordered a glass of white wine. Molly and I, underage, contented ourselves with water. Ordering Coke in Scandia seemed too infra dig to contemplate.

"So," my father said, "what's the story? Are you two living together or what?" He looked directly at Molly when he asked this question.

Molly looked startled, so I jumped in. "No," I said, "freshmen have to live in a dorm. University rules." No need to mention she spent almost every night in my apartment and kept most of her stuff there. It would just encourage him. Not that he needed encouragement.

"Because I think it's a good idea," he proclaimed, as if I hadn't said anything. He had a piece to speak. "Young people shacking up, I mean. Lots of kids are doing it now, I understand. There was less of that when mom and I were your age. More of a stigma attached. Now, it barely raises an eyebrow. And that's good. Gives you a chance to get to know each other before you get married."

"Dad, I'm only nineteen. Molly's eighteen. No one's getting married."

"The good, the bad, and the ugly. Spares you nasty surprises, you know?"

The waiter arrived with drinks. My father reached over and grabbed his off the tray and took a sip. Then he went on, "And besides, all those rules, all those constraints, all that old-fashioned Victorian bullshit, what good did it do? Where's the advantage in keeping kids horny right when their hormones are at their peak?"

My mother, as she accepted the glass of wine the waiter put in front of her, said, "Okay, Sy."

"No," my father said irritably, "I'm serious." As if she had been questioning his seriousness. "What's going on today, challenging convention, challenging authority, it's an excellent thing. This marijuana business too. What do they call it? Pot. You two smoke pot?"

"Not really," I said.

"You ought to," he said. "At least try it. It isn't addictive, you know."

"Sy!" my mother said. She sounded alarmed and not a little fed up. "I can*not* believe you're urging your son and his friend to take an illegal drug!"

"Oh, legal schmegal. Those drug laws...total crap. It ought to be legalized."

"Besides, they're still minors."

"Big deal. From what I read, marijuana's a lot less bad for you than alcohol."

A longish silence followed. We were all of us, I daresay, contemplating the damage alcohol can do. Was doing. All of us except my father.

And then he broke the silence. "Can't you find pot in Berkeley?"

Molly and I looked down so as not to smile.

"Well, have you tried it, at least?"

"Yes, dad, we've tried it."

"What's it like?" my father persisted.

"It's..." I found myself shrugging. "I mostly don't like it very much."

"Does it heighten the senses the way they say?"

"I guess so."

"It's a whole new world," he said, shaking his head. "We were brought up to believe one puff of a marijuana cigarette and you'd turn into a dope fiend. Now there's marijuana, there's that LSD. That Huxley thing, what's it called? Mescadrine or something. He took it right near here, you know. Just down Kings Road. What don't you like about pot?"

"Makes me feel weird."

"Isn't that the whole point?" And then, "You don't have much of a sense of adventure, do you, Zeke? You've always played it safe."

"Right." I'd learned long ago not to rise to this sort of bait, especially when my father was drinking. You weren't going to win, and you weren't going to have the last word.

But this was Molly's first exposure to Sy Stern, and she was offended on my behalf. "I don't think that's true at all," she said firmly. "Among our friends, Zeke's always the leader." I don't know where she got this; she was just being loyal in whatever way fit. I didn't want to be a leader any more than I wanted to be a follower. "No one thinks he plays it safe. He's led the way on all sorts of things."

My father stared at her, almost pop-eyed. Because he had just met her, and because she was a pretty girl with an ethereal sort of manner, he hadn't expected to be directly contradicted like this, and was, I think, flummoxed about what mode of bullying would work with her. None offered itself. When he spoke again, it was to change the subject. "Have you seen *Hair*?" he asked. "Mom and I went. We even bought the album. We love it."

I prayed Molly wouldn't argue. She didn't, thank goodness. "You like it?" she said politely. Admirable restraint on her part. I knew she believed *Hair* to be a calculated, cynical, contrived exploitation of everything we valued.

"It's great. A lot of our friends, they tut-tut about it, the nudity and so on, they don't get it, but it's their loss. I tell you, the world is changing, either you change too or you get left behind. We even broke down and bought *Sergeant Pepper* a few weeks ago. Zeke was playing it all last summer and I couldn't stand it, it was driving me nuts, all day every day, 'Good morning, good morning,' 'I get by with a little help from my friends,' Christ. But damn if after he left I didn't find myself humming it. It grows on you, you know? Some of those tunes are very catchy."

"Glad to hear you came around," I said.

"Gotta change with the times."

"I liked it from the start," my mother offered. "Some of it, anyway. The quieter songs."

"That's true," my father agreed. "Fanny was ahead of me on this one."

"What's your favorite song on it?" Molly asked. I could have kissed her. She was pretending this was a normal conversation, not a grotesque travesty of a normal conversation.

It was only later, after dinner, when we were back in the guest room, that she said to me, "Look, I know your folks drive you crazy—"

And I interrupted to say, "Please don't tell me you're going to defend them."

"No, no, I wasn't going to."

"Or say how cool they are. Anything but that."

She looked at me levelly. "I wasn't going to say anything of the sort."

"Good. That would be exactly what my father wants you to say."

"Yeah, I know. Give me some credit, Zeke. Listen, everybody's parents get some latitude, these situations are impossible and other people's parents always seem so lame. Meeting the girl friend or the boy friend or even the roommate, trying to figure out what's been going on with their kid while he's been away, trying to be friendly and welcoming to a stranger, not knowing how to talk to them, not wanting to seem like a jerk, all of it. But I can see why your folks drive you nuts. I don't even know if that's what you want me to say, but your father, at least, can be a real pill. And as far as I can tell, it wasn't your fault. At all. In fact, you were incredibly forbearing. I just took my cues from you."

"Of course. I've always been a leader."

She smiled at that. "Well, I wasn't going to let him put you down without an argument." And then she went on, "But what was going on back there was interesting in other ways. Ways that didn't have anything to do with you and your dad. You did notice, didn't you?"

"Notice what?"

"Well, of course your parents are different from mine, but…did they always ask so many questions about…not your life so much, but your world? Your music, your experiences, drugs, the movies you like, that stuff?"

"No," I said, "that was unusual, now that you mention it. They mostly used to treat my enthusiasms like kid stuff, uninteresting to grown-ups."

"Exactly," she said. "My folks too. And they don't even have enthusiasms of their own. But, I mean, take the Beatles…they thought it was funny how excited I got when they were on Ed Sullivan. Like it was a passing fancy."

"That's how my parents usually are."

"Not tonight."

"No. You're right."

The next night, we met Stan at the Beverly Hills Hamlet, and then drove on to a party at Wendy Larner's beach house in Malibu. The Larners' main house was a big old mansion in Hancock Park, but they also had a house in Malibu for weekends and in summer. From about the tenth grade on, they'd let Wendy give parties there. Unchaperoned parties. You can imagine. Against all odds, there were no fatalities.

At the Hamlet, while Stan and I ate our burgers and Molly had lobster bisque, she asked him how his visit was going. He sighed. "My mom keeps asking me about laundry," he said. "I told her we have a washing machine in our building, but she can't absorb the information. My dad keeps asking whether I smoke dope."

"Mine too," I said. "It's like they all got the same notice in the mail."

"What'd you tell yours?"

"I told him I had, but I don't like it."

"He must've been relieved."

"No, it's just one more way I'm a disappointment to him. What did you tell your father?"

"That I hadn't. It would have freaked him out if I said yes. Of course," he added with a laugh, "I was stoned when we had the conversation. It was the only way to survive my first night home."

Have I mentioned Stan was a major pothead in those days? He was high most of his waking life. It was as if, after almost two decades of being an obedient, well-behaved boy, he'd finally discovered an activity that let him rebel without requiring him to put himself in any obvious danger, and he threw himself into it with abandon.

"Are you sure he'd disapprove?" Molly asked.

He gave her a funny look. "Of course he'd disapprove. He's my dad."

"I don't know. Something weird is going on."

When we got to Wendy's beach house, the party was already underway, if not quite in full swing. A bunch of people were out on the deck—the back of the house was on stilts, with a deck looking out over the Pacific—and a few people were in the living room, playing records. Molly, Stan, and I made a beeline for the kitchen, which was just off the entrance foyer, to get something to drink. I was surprised to find Wendy's father, Bud Larner, in there, pouring drinks and holding court. He was wearing Levis and a tight red sweater. Jeans were still a relative rarity on adults, but Bud could carry it off. And the tight sweater just showed what good shape he was in, lean and muscular. As I said, in high school Wendy's parents had let her give these parties without feeling the need to be present. Was it misplaced confidence, or simple indifference? Regardless, I didn't expect to find either of them in the house this particular night.

Bud was an actor; he had been in a number of films in the '50s, part of that group of wild upstarts that included Dennis Hopper and Russ Tamblyn and Nick Adams and Steve McQueen, and then he'd been the co-star of a TV detective show for a couple of years when we were in junior high. The hero's handsome but essentially comic sidekick. Which probably cost him points among his acting cohort, but made him very cool to us, and lent Wendy serious reflected glamour. Even cooler was the fact he had starred in a second-season episode of *The Twilight Zone*. That was beyond cool. He was a tall, handsome man with a big, vivid personality; when he turned up at school events, or put in an appearance at one of Wendy's parties, or picked her up from somebody else's, it was always exciting, although, as LA kids, we did our best to act blasé. He was past leading-man age now, in his early fifties, but he still appeared frequently in character roles, mostly on TV.

When our little threesome entered the kitchen, Bud gave me a big companionable greeting, clapping my shoulder, and then said hello to Stan with less ceremony—although he remembered Stan's name, which was impressive under the circumstances—and then looked expectantly toward Molly. I made the introductions. It was hard for me to tell whether Molly recognized Bud from TV or not. She wasn't the type to act impressed. Almost as a point of principle.

"You be nice to him, now," Bud said to Molly. "Zeke is one of my favorites."

"I'm doing my best."

"I always hoped you and Wendy would end up together," he said to me.

"Me too," I said. And then, recalling there were conflicting sensibilities in the vicinity, I added, "For a while. At Fairfax." I'd taken Wendy out a few times in our junior year, but it soon became clear that while she enjoyed my company, and didn't consider me completely hopeless or self-evidently unworthy, she just couldn't work up any romantic interest. Still, Bud had always managed to convey, when I showed up at their house, that he approved of me and, insofar as it was within his power, supported my cause. It wasn't within his power at all, of course.

"Looks like you landed on your feet, though," he said now. This was intended as a bit of gallantry toward Molly.

"Oh yes," I agreed. "In clover."

But Bud still had more colonizing to do. He peered closely at Molly and then said, "Have you ever done any acting, sweetheart? Or modeling?"

She colored. "No."

"Ever thought about it?"

"No!"

"Because you have the face for it. Great eyes, great mouth, cute shiksa nose, elegant cheekbones. You ought to consider it."

"Really?" She was flattered, of course; it would have been impossible not to be, even for someone as mistrustful of vanity as Molly. And Bud's charm, when he chose to exercise it—as he clearly did now—was a compelling force. But even before he could reiterate the compliment, as her "Really?" invited him to do, she pulled herself out of the spell—you could see her doing it—and said, "I don't really see that happening. I mean, thank you and everything, but I don't have the time, not with school work and whatnot."

"Your school work's important to you?"

"That's why I'm there."

"Do you have a major yet?"

"Not officially. It'll be English lit."

He took a second to process this. "Modeling could pay your tuition," he suggested.

"Even still."

Bud handled the rejection with his customary smooth grace. "Well, give it some thought. In the meantime…what would you guys like to drink? We have wine and beer in the fridge. Which of you is driving? Zeke? Too bad. No booze for you."

Molly took wine, Stan a beer, and I made do with a Coke. I led Molly into the living room, although we somehow lost Stan en route. Otis Redding was on the stereo, perched unhappily on the dock of the bay. I found Wendy. She'd finally had her nose job the previous summer, and she was looking good. She'd always been pretty, and she had a killer bod, and now she was a knock-out. Wearing heavy eye make-up which gave her an almost Egyptian look, and dressed in a blue blouse and designer jeans with some sort of rhinestone ornament on the left butt cheek (she probably bought them at my father's store), she looked flashy. I said hello, kissed her on the cheek (feeling very grown-up for doing so), and introduced Molly. An interesting moment; Wendy, smiling politely, making all the right noises, slowly looked Molly up and down, her eyes cold and appraising, and Molly, always self-contained, seemed to withdraw into some sort of Zen version of herself.

Wendy asked Molly a couple of pro forma questions—where was she from, how did she like California, was this her first visit to LA?—and then turned to me and said, "I like her, Zeke." And then turning back to Molly, said, "You're really pretty. Zeke always had high standards."

Molly thanked her demurely. But after we'd disengaged, she murmured, "So glad she approves," her tone oozing disdain.

"Aw, she meant well," I said. Actually, I didn't have a clue whether she meant well or not.

"I don't think so," Molly said. "Patronizing bitch. You sure you two weren't a couple?"

"I'd remember."

"I'll tell you one thing. She wasn't born with that nose."

One of the few catty things I ever heard Molly say.

We spent the next hour or so moving around the house, greeting people, catching up. It couldn't have been fun for Molly, who had no catching up to do. She was a good sport about it, though, taking part in conversations when she was able. The rest of us were scoping each other out. What had happened to us since high school, and had the pecking order subtly altered? Who had become more or less attractive than we would have predicted, more or less confident, successful, poised? Who had had more adventurous experiences than we might have expected? Who appeared to have interesting secrets they chose not to divulge? No definitive answers, just intimations these would remain interesting questions over the years. There were no obvious Widmerpools among us, but you never can tell.

Later, when Molly went to use the bathroom, I went out on the deck, where a small group of other kids had gathered. I didn't know where Stan had gone; he'd disappeared while we'd been in the kitchen with Bud. It was chilly, but the night was beautiful, with a big fat full moon and only a few gauzy wisps of cloud. A couple of couples were making out on chaises longues, a few people were talking quietly. Molly appeared a few minutes later, looking a little lost. She lit up when she saw me. "I've been looking for you," she said.

"And now you've found me. I'm like amazing grace."

We leaned against the railing, not saying anything for a minute or two, staring down at the moon's reflection in the water as it shimmered and writhed in the waves. We were trying to re-group a little—the past few days had been unrelenting, as had the past few hours—and then Bud stepped out onto the deck and, after a moment's hesitation, approached. Had he been looking for us? He had a joint in his hand, and was extending it in our direction. "Want some?" he asked. "Zeke? Be my guest. I don't believe it affects your ability to drive."

One of the myths of the era. Healthy, natural, youthful marijuana versus corrupt, poisonous, grown-up alcohol.

I shook my head. It was startling to see anyone's parent with a joint in his hand, but since acting unfazed was a vital aspect of one's personal presentation in those days, I chose not to comment. Especially since I could tell he wanted me to. And then Molly, to my surprise, accepted the proffered joint from him, toked, and passed it back. This made me slightly uneasy; there's something intimate about sharing a joint, Bud was obviously taken with Molly, and I sensed she wasn't completely immune to him either. Not that I was actively worried; Bud was a parent, for God's sake, and besides, I trusted Molly. But that involuntary territorial instinct we males all seem to possess was bristling just a little.

"Used to smoke this shit back in the '50s," Bud was saying. "You kids didn't invent it, you know." He took a deep hit, gave his lungs a few seconds to deal with the intake, and then continued, "There was a big jazz scene here fifteen, twenty years ago." Smoke issued from him as he talked. "Started back in the war years. Fabulous players. Legends. Kicking around the local clubs, trying to make ends meet. Jackie and I used to be part of that scene. Through Bob Mitchum. No one talked about marijuana then, not in public, this was the fifties, McCarthy, witch-hunt stuff, we were all paranoid, the squares thought it made you a sex fiend, it led straight to heroin, you know the drill. But it was around. In that circle, I mean. Our people, our secret. We called it 'boo.' As in 'Don't say boo,' maybe. That just occurred to me. Anyway. There were jazz guys, some young actors, some film-maker wannabes, the young Hollywood scene. Some of the guys fresh out of the service, hot to start living, some too young to have served, sorta feeling defensive about it, had something to prove. There were pansies around too, rejected by the draft boards. That's show biz. But all of us were what we used to call hipsters. Sounds so quaint now. Yesterday's slang always does. You watch, someday you'll hear the word 'groovy' and it'll set your teeth on edge. Anyway, after-hours, when the music stopped and the club doors closed, we'd turn out the lights and sit around one of the tables and toke up. Felt terribly wicked and avant garde. Blacks and whites together, getting wasted, feeling transgressive. Lots of flirting, lots of laughing. You kids smoke it like it's drinking a beer, mild recreation. For us, there was sex and danger in the air. 'Course, we didn't have LSD. And only the hardcore messed with horse, some of the musicians mostly, but they kept it among themselves."

He'd never been so chatty before, not in my hearing. Nor so indiscreet. Our crowd had always suspected he was cool—aside from being in a TV show, he just had the aura—but his guard was usually up, he had a parental role to play. Tonight he was a different guy. He suddenly shrugged, passed the joint back to Molly, momentarily turned away, briefly registering the necking couples, peering at them a second or two longer than strictly necessary, and turned back again, toward the water, leaning his elbows on the wooden railing and staring out at the ocean. The tide was in, you could hear and feel the waves as they glided in below the deck on which we were standing, crashing against the wooden stilts supporting the rear of the house and the rocks beyond. I put my arm around Molly's shoulders, half afraid she might shrug it off, I don't know why. She didn't. It was cold out there, and getting colder, and she pressed against me as she took another puff off the joint. Bud suddenly and loudly sighed. I'm tempted to say "theatrically," but that might be unfair; he was an actory guy, no question, but actors can have real feelings too. Molly inclined her head toward me and caught my eye; even in the moonlight, I could read the amusement there. That was reassuring. At least she wasn't entirely, uncritically entranced by him. I hadn't been sure.

"Tell me something, Zeke," Bud said softly, breaking the short silence. He was still gazing out at the water. "Do you know what you're going to do with your life? Do you have things mapped out?"

"Uh uh. Not a clue."

"You aren't planning to be the Jewish Jack Kennedy anymore?"

I felt myself smiling sheepishly. I probably even blushed. That had been a long time ago. It sure wasn't something I'd mentioned to Molly. "Ask not."

He smiled and nodded. "Well, are you enjoying yourself? Having a good time at college and so on?"

"I think so."

"That's something you should *know*." Another sigh, quieter, less ostentatious than the previous one. "The worst thing that can happen to you, maybe, aside from never having been happy, is only realizing that you were happy afterward."

"Isn't it always like that?" Molly suggested, a little timorously. She'd been quiet for a while now.

He turned his head—not his body, still leaning against the railing—toward her. "You might be right. It could be we're mostly happy when we're not paying attention. When we're paying attention to something else, I mean. Concentrating on it so completely that we aren't thinking about happiness, or ourselves. Even when it's our own career, we're thinking about *it*. And then, later, when that period of our life is over, we look back and think, 'Gee, those were great times. I've never been happier than I was then.' But it's too late. They're gone forever."

"You're really cheering us up here," I said.

He smiled crookedly. "Yeah. Sorry. Merry Christmas. This time of year always makes me melancholy. Especially now, with Wendy grown. All that Santa Claus shit over for good." He snorted. "Perfect example. Raising a kid, you're too busy to notice much of anything, it just seems like a hassle, and then later you see those were great times. But by the time you do, they're history."

With one hand, Molly was handing the remnant of the joint back to Bud. With the other, though, she took hold of one of mine and squeezed. I took the squeeze to be her way of saying, "Get me out of here!" Till a couple of minutes before, I'd thought she was in Bud's thrall.

"We should probably look for Stan," I said.

"Okay," said Bud. I think his feelings might have been hurt by my ending the conversation so abruptly. "Good to talk to you, Zeke. It's nice, the way you kids have stuck together. I remember you from first grade. Miss Kato, right? Probably recently released from an internment camp." He smiled at Molly. A little mournfully. As if he recognized that somehow or other, somewhere or other, he had mishandled the conversation. "And you, young lady. A pleasure to meet you. Hope I didn't drone on too much." He flicked the roach into the incoming tide.

On the drive back to town, Molly said, "Can we stop for a bite? I'm starving."

"The vaunted munchies?"

"Maybe. But all I had for dinner was a bowl of soup."

Stan proposed Wil Wrights, a small chain of ice cream parlors now as extinct as the dodo. The Beverly Hills branch was very near where we had had dinner, which meant it was near where Stan had left his car, so it was a sensible choice.

Wil Wrights was a quintessential LA institution: Decorated like the set of an extravagant movie musical version of a Middle American turn-of-the-century ice cream parlor, re-imagined by the gayest gay designer the studio could hire. In garish pastels, with a little cherub head-and-wings motif popping up here and there ("It's heavenly" was the slogan). On the back of the menus was a list of all the famous people who had ever consumed Wil Wrights ice cream. Including my parents' current neighbor, Igor Stravinsky.

Molly's eyes widened when we entered. And after we sat down, she said, "This is pretty weird."

"You're still stoned," I pointed out.

"Maybe, but it would be weird regardless. Like that party we just left, although that feels like a week ago. That was weird too."

"What was?" Stan asked.

"I guess I'm mainly thinking about that guy, Wendy's father. Mr. Larner."

"Oh jeez!" groaned Stan. "Bud Larner!" He turned to me. "You got stuck with him again?" Back to Molly. "He always had a thing for Zeke.

When I saw him glom onto you two in the kitchen, I made myself scarce."

I felt I had to offer a protest, out of some vestigial sense of loyalty. "Aw, Bud's all right," I said.

"Mister Hipster! The grand thespian! Lenny Bruce's pal! Gerry Mulligan's gin rummy partner!" And then, to Molly, "Now you maybe have some idea how fucked up our childhood was. Zeke and I actually knew kids who auditioned to be Mouseketeers. Little Bud Larners in the larval stage."

I laughed along with Molly, but I had a slightly bad conscience about it. I *liked* Bud. He'd always been nice to me, talked to me as if he were interested in what I had to say, and he had a lot more to offer than most of the other parents we knew, more to offer in the way of interesting personal experience and provocative conversation. And besides, I mistrusted Stan's scorn; if Bud had shown more interest in Stan, Stan would probably have been more respectful in return.

The waitress came. We ordered. Simple dishes of ice cream, nothing fancy. It was too late in the evening to grapple with a sundae.

"I think Bud was coming on to Molly," I said after the waitress left us. Disliking myself for it, but I said it anyway, just to get the roll of laughter going again.

Molly flashed me a sharp glance, while at the same time, Stan said, "Really?"

"Well, he was *flirting*, at least." I turned to Molly. "Don't you think?"

She shrugged uncomfortably. "I don't know. Maybe it's the only way he knows how to talk to a girl. Maybe he was trying to, to…to show we aren't from totally different worlds. That it isn't completely foreign to him. They've all been doing it this trip. The grown-ups. It's kind of sweet and kind of pathetic. Zeke's folks. Even yours, Stan, from the sound of it. This Larner guy. It's like…like it's suddenly occurred to them that they're missing something. After years of paying no attention to the stuff that interests us, or treating it with amused disdain, they've started to think they should have paid attention. And it just seems to have *happened*. In the last few months."

"I wonder if it's peculiar to this generation, though," I said. "Or is it the way of things? Your kids go off to college, they're sort of adults, of *course* you start to envy them. They're young, the slate's clean, they're free to do grown-up things without grown-up obligations. No career, no marriage, no kids, no mortgage. What's *not* to envy?"

"Uh uh," said Stan. Flatly. He had thought it through in the few seconds I was speaking and had reached a conclusion. Very Stan. "Molly's right. It's different this time. It's been an incredible year. People are going to look back and compare it to 1848 in Europe. And the media are all over it. Spiced up to make it sexier. So even our folks know something is afoot."

There was a long silence, and then Molly spoke quietly. So quietly that Stan leaned forward, across the table, to be able to hear her. "The thing is…I mean, they say—we do too, it's not just them—we say it's about music and politics and cosmic consciousness and all that *Hair* stuff. But it isn't, really. It's about sex. Just like *Hair*. Nudity on stage, 'free love.' Not sympathy and understanding. Getting laid. Everything else is window dressing. Or metaphor."

"You're stoned," Stan said. We seemed to be pointing that out frequently.

"Yeah, I am, but I mean, here's this guy, and say what you like, he's been around, right? He might be a poser, but it's not *all* made up. He's almost a movie star—I recognized him right away, Murray on *Bailey's Law*, my family used to watch that show every Friday night—and he probably did hang out with all those jazz guys and people. And you could tell from the way he was describing it, even though he didn't say so, everyone was fucking everyone else back then. Hollywood, right? And the way he casually dropped Robert Mitchum's name, calling him 'Bob?' So, my point is, why should he feel he has something to prove? To people like us, especially? Nobodies. Kids."

The waitress arrived with our ice cream and complimentary little macaroons in wax paper wrapping with the little cherub-head logo on it. As we dug in, I said, "Well, we are his daughter's friends."

"So why should he have to prove anything to us?"

"I'm saying maybe that isn't what he was doing."

"Of course it is. To show us he's been through what we're going through, even if he actually hasn't. He must be feeling left out. Left behind. He wants us to know he's groovy too. He probably thinks we're all having sex all the time."

"You mean we're not?" said Stan. A little joke. It had been a while since he'd had sex. And a while before that since he'd had sex before that.

Molly reached across the table and put her hand over Stan's, a sweet gesture, suggesting, "Your time will come." And then she said, "Look, I don't know who is and who isn't. But *they* all seem to think *we* are. At love-ins and happenings and be-ins and all the shit the media are talking about. 'You've lost your kids! They're taking drugs and fucking like rabbits and having bizarre kinky experiences and you're powerless to stop them!' And even worse, we don't feel guilt about it or fear retribution. So they're outraged and they're envious, sometimes burying the envy under the outrage. And that nonsense sells papers and stops people from switching channels. Fear and titillation are great selling tools. But…*be-ins*! Have you ever been to anything you'd call a 'be-in?'" She snorted. "They're jealous. That Bud guy needed to let us know he'd been there, to his own 1950s-style be-ins. With Bob Mitchum, no less. It was sort of competitive and sort of wistful. It's probably a good thing he has a daughter instead of a son, or he'd be challenging the poor kid to arm-wrestle every fifteen minutes. I mean, honestly, a guy that age bragging to a couple of college students about how hip he used to be."

"I was under the impression you liked him."

"That's neither here nor there," she said, which wasn't a very satisfying reply.

"I still don't get your point," Stan said.

"It's simple. Our folks can't be interested in any gathering-of-the-tribes stuff, can they? Age of Aquarius? They must think it's bullshit. I doubt they think our music is better than theirs, better than Frank Sinatra and Nat King Cole and Ella Fitzgerald. They don't wear hippy clothing, obviously, and they don't have long hair. Except for a handful who look like idiots. Aside from agreeing about the war—some of them anyway, not mine, of course—they must regard our politics as naïve. So what does that leave? What can they relate to? Why do they care? It's gotta be drugs and sex. They missed out. They're missing out."

"I never knew you were so cynical," I said.

Molly shrugged. "I don't think it's cynical. Just something I noticed tonight."

Later, after we dropped Stan at his car, on a side street off Beverly Drive, and headed back up toward my parents' house, Molly broke the silence by saying, "See, the thing is, Zeke…" She hesitated, then said, "I don't know if I should even tell you this, and please don't get upset, but…" She sighed. "That Bud guy *did* come on to me. I didn't want to say anything in front of Stan."

I felt my heart rate accelerate. "What happened? What did he do?"

"He got me alone in the hall and asked how he could get in touch with me. Said he wanted to see me again. Said he could come up to San Francisco."

I was shocked. Naïve of me, no doubt, but I was shocked. Shocked and hurt. The father of my good friend. The guy who had taken such an approving, avuncular interest in me. A guy old enough to be Molly's dad. All I could say was, "Did you agree?" I already knew I'd be working through his perfidy for a long time, and already knew I'd probably never figure out how to come to terms with it.

"Oh, no," she said. "No, no, no."

"I really need to say something to him, don't I?"

"Oh, you mustn't. Please. That would be awful. I took care of it. It's fine. And you mustn't say anything to, to Wendy."

"No, of course not. I wouldn't do that." And then, "Were you tempted? Tell me the truth."

She hesitated for a fraction of a second. "Look, he's an attractive man, I can't deny that, and he's…I mean, he's very seductive. Practiced at it, I'd almost say. Smooth. Insinuating. But it was also obnoxious. In about a thousand different ways. So no. I can see how someone might have said yes, but I wasn't tempted."

"So what did you say to him?"

"I said no."

"That's all?"

"I told him I didn't think it was a good idea."

"You didn't tell him he was out of line, asking? Or let him know you thought it was obnoxious?"

"I just said it wasn't a good idea. I figured that was enough."

"And then he came out on the deck and joined us like nothing had happened. And delivered his poignant monologue. That took a lot of brass. I guess he was relying on your discretion."

"If so, he was mistaken."

"Right. Good. But I wish he knew it. Jeez, what an asshole. I can't fucking believe it."

We were silent for the rest of the drive. And silent while getting ready for bed. As she was climbing into bed—wearing only panties, so she had me at a disadvantage—she finally broke the silence, saying, "Don't take this the wrong way, but it's going to be a relief to leave." She was scheduled to fly on to Wyoming the day after next. "I'll miss you, but this place is creeping me out."

"Because of Bud Larner?"

"Because of everything."

Typical Molly. No sugar-coating. It saddened me, because some part of me still felt an LA sabra's loyalty. But I could tell her mind was made up, she was never going to give the city a second chance. And it got to me. On some level I'd been feeling uneasy since we'd arrived in LA, but the feeling had simmered below the level of consciousness till now. Something just hadn't felt right.

I discovered the cause on Christmas Day. My folks and I had always exchanged presents at Christmas, never Hanukkah, and Christmas morning I took a quick, very cold swim in the pool, showered, dressed, and then crossed the house to the living room. It was a tradition, the family opening presents together first thing, before breakfast. I had bought my mother a sweater from Magnin's and my father a copy of *The French Lieutenant's Woman* at Pickwick. As I was placing them under the tree, my mother came into the living room. She was still in her housecoat, and looked wan and unrested.

"Hi, mom," I said. "Merry Christmas."

She didn't return the greeting, didn't smile. Instead, she said, "Sit down, Zeke. There's something your father and I need to tell you."

Four

NOW

There was the familiar argument over the check. Zeke had laid down his Visa gold, Liam put his impressive platinum American Express on top of it, and the young African-American waitress, when she picked up the little tray with the check and the two credit cards, asked rhetorically, "Fifty-fifty?"

She no doubt expected a quick affirmative. It must have come as a surprise when Zeke said no at the same time Liam said yes. Melanie and Molly exchanged an exasperated glance, as if this were some testosterone-fueled game that had nothing to do with them.

They were upstairs at Chez Panisse, the less formal, café-style part of the restaurant. For celebratory occasions, or when entertaining guests from out of town, they might eat downstairs—universally acknowledged Ground Zero for the classic Berkeley foodie experience—but for casual dining among townsfolk, the more rollicking upstairs venue provided the pleasanter setting. Liam sometimes called the downstairs area "the Sistine Chapel of food," and he didn't mean it as a compliment. A certain hushed solemnity seemed mandatory in that venue, and devoting a disproportionate segment of table conversation to praise the various dishes as they were delivered and sampled was obligatory. The food might merit the praise, but the exercise could become tiresome.

The waitress stood by their table now, uncertain what to do, not even sure if she was being joshed.

"Look," Zeke said, "it's unfair for you to pay for half the wine." He noticed that Melanie was favoring the waitress with an apologetic glance. Rank treachery!

"Aw, let it go, will you," said Liam. "Honestly. Do we have to do this every fucking time? Melanie had wine even if I didn't. My hors d'oeuvres was more expensive than yours. The entrees weren't priced equally. I don't know who actually drank the most, and I doubt you do either."

"*I* did. I don't think Melanie had more than one glass. Molly and I did the rest of the damage." He quickly added, "I did a lot more than Molly, of course." Molly wouldn't want to be dragged into this.

"Aw shit, it doesn't matter. It'll all come out in the wash." He looked up at the waitress. "Down the middle. Please. Fifty-fifty. Ignore this guy. Go, now, quick, before he opens his mouth again."

She laughed at that, and hurried off.

Zeke shrugged. He had given it his best shot. Anyway, they weren't altogether out of the woods yet. There was still some competitive maneuvering about the tip to get through. It was tricky here; the check included a service charge in the European manner, but higher than any European restaurant would dare impose, and a notice at the bottom of the check specified that no additional tipping was expected. Still, most people felt compelled to leave something anyway, and some, having started down that path, felt compelled to leave a full 20%. And if you were splitting the check, you didn't want to be the one leaving the lesser amount. Zeke suddenly grinned at Liam, sitting diagonally across from him in the wooden paneled booth. Grinned broadly, barely suppressing a laugh.

"What?" demanded Liam.

"I honestly don't know," said Zeke. The grin refused to go away. "Maybe…I'd have to free-associate to be sure. Don't give me that look, it's an effective technique. Maybe it's just, we've known each other so damned long. And here we are having dinner, like we've done about a thousand times, and we're having the same ridiculous argument about the check. How long has this been going on?"

"This particular argument?" said Liam. "Since I've been sober, I guess." He never showed any discomfort talking about it.

"And how long has that been?"

"Four years, eight months, eleven days." He wasn't joking. He was one of those alcoholics who *knew*. The date was as significant to him as his birthday or anniversary. More. He sometimes forgot his anniversary.

"Right. And is either of us surprised by the other's arguments? They're always the same, and it bores and annoys our wives to tears, which may be part of the fun for us without our admitting it. And we both act like it matters when we know it doesn't. It's the sort of thing we would have sneered at when we were young, the grown-ups' quadrille. For some reason, the phenomenon suddenly tickled me."

"We're codgers, Zeke."

"So why haven't our wives aged?"

While Molly and Melanie both rolled their eyes at this labored bit of gallantry, Liam said, "Mine's Chinese, you can't tell with them. Yours must have good genes."

"If they think this crap'll get them laid tonight, they're dreaming," said Melanie.

Which broke up the table and provided a smooth exit.

A few minutes later, walking home along ill-lit Walnut Street, Zeke said to Molly, "That was nice."

"Mm. Usually is. They're low-maintenance, as our friends go." And then she added, "These days."

"Interesting you should say that. I was just thinking how I still sometimes expect Liam's sobriety to be a bummer, like it's going to have a chilling effect on the evening. But it never does, does it? He's completely at ease about the whole thing. Doesn't need to talk about it, doesn't mind talking about it. Which is interesting, since excess was such a big part of his persona in the old days. With drugs, drink, sex, ideas, pretty much everything. He *cultivated* that persona, too, it didn't just happen.

73

And now…well, I suppose his ideas are still kind of excessive. But I was also wondering… do you notice anything different about him since he got sober?"

"God, I haven't thought about it for a long time. I mean, I never think about it. Why do you ask?"

"No reason. Just…that awful intervention, remember, with the screaming and crying and the curses and the threats, and I'm wondering if it was really necessary."

"Well, he seems happier, and proud to be sober. And we don't see much of it, but Melanie says he's active in the whole recovery thing. Goes to meetings, counsels people who are struggling. It's a big part of his life. A part we're not part of."

"But did he act all that differently before? I don't remember many really grotesque episodes. Or is that early-stage dementia on my part?"

"Besides the roaring Celt thing? 'Cause he still has that, or at least an attenuated, middle-aged version."

"Yeah, besides that."

"He used to get sloppy. It wasn't grotesque, just embarrassing. But it made everybody tense, waiting for the shenanigans to start. And he always insisted on driving, insisted in that truculent way drunks have, you know, where it's almost impossible to say no unless you want a fight. It used to scare the hell out of Melanie. And…I think it got kind of ugly at home. In ways we don't know."

Meaning in ways Zeke didn't know. Molly clearly did; Melanie must have confided in her. Now that he recalled it, Molly was the one who insisted Zeke take part in the intervention. Pleading on Melanie's behalf. He initially wanted no part of it. Molly finally persuaded him not only by telling him how desperate Melanie was, but implying his refusal stemmed from professional snobbery, shaming him into it, forcing him to demonstrate he wasn't one of those elitist shrinks who thought his guild controlled all the keys to mental hygiene. He had been aware Liam and Melanie were having *some* marital trouble, since, at Liam's request, he had recommended a counselor a year or two before. But no explanation for the request had been offered, and Zeke, professionally discreet

74

as always, even with close friends, *especially* with close friends, hadn't sought any, merely supplied a couple of names.

"It's funny how Melanie confides in you," he said now, as they walked along the darkened street. Walnut sloped upward here, and after the big meal he'd just eaten, Zeke found his breathing labored. Or was it age rather than satiety? Would the same thing have happened five years ago?

He felt Molly's glance on him. "What?" he asked.

"What makes you think she confides in me?"

"I just do."

"You oughta be a shrink, Easy." And then, "Why is it odd?"

"Oh, I don't know. Maybe 'cause I've known her all my life. Since, jeez, first grade." A smart, cute little Chinese cookie, who always wore neat crinolines to school, and who took to reading with the same facility as Zeke, even though English was hardly spoken in her home. They were academic rivals during their secondary school years, and frequently faced off against each other when it was time to elect a class president. Melanie's parents ran a laundry on La Brea in those days, the family living in cramped quarters behind the shop. Zeke could remember attending her seventh birthday party and feeling disturbed by the squalor. By junior high, though, the Lee family owned a small chain of laundries, and had moved to a pretty little house on a tree-lined street in West Hollywood. The birthday parties there were much jollier. The squalor was a brief interlude before acculturation and affluence. But the acculturation had inevitably been more thorough for the second generation than the first; Zeke remembered Melanie's parents unexpectedly coming home one afternoon during the eighth grade and finding an impromptu kissing party in progress, and the attendant furor had rivaled the contemporaneous Cuban Missile Crisis for trauma.

"So," Molly said, interrupting these ruminations, "you're saying you got there first?"

Zeke laughed, hoping his laughter didn't sound defensive; he and Melanie shared a very old secret, irrelevant to anybody else, but still best left unrevealed, its very existence best left unsuspected. "I don't think it's as territorial as that," he said. "It's just, I didn't think you two were especially close back in the day. Not that Melanie and *I* were super close either," he hastily added. "But, I don't know, somehow she's always sort of…*been* there. Whereas you and she…" He shrugged.

"You're right, it happened later. Snuck up on both of us." She didn't appear to want to talk about it, and Zeke was willing to let it ride. He knew from professional experience that patience—even apparent indifference—was a better tool for eliciting information than overt curiosity. But he did suspect there might be an interesting story there, if Molly ever saw fit to tell it.

Of course, he had his own store of interesting stories.

"Well, anyway," he said, "she's good people. I undervalued her when we were kids. Too well-behaved, maybe. And she and Liam…their marriage has worked out. It's one of the success stories."

"Like you and me, Easy." She took his arm. "You okay? You sound winded."

"That's just lust, gathering force for the fireworks to come."

"Oh yes?" She laughed, a low-pitched chuckle. "Dinner didn't do you in?"

"I ordered light. My eyes were focused on the distant connubial horizon."

"I'm flattered."

Even in the dark, each could sense the other's smile. Zeke put his arm around her shoulder. "You think we're a success story?"

"Don't you?"

"I like hearing you say it."

She stopped walking, and he stopped beside her. She leaned toward him and kissed his cheek, nuzzling him. "I consider myself the luckiest woman I know," she said, and there was an interesting undertone of earnestness in her voice. "I don't take it for granted."

"Aw, taking it for granted is one of the perks of a good marriage," he said. Keeping it light. "It isn't like having a hot affair, where it's all you ever think about."

"And how do you know about that?" Her suspicious tone was playful.

"From about 70% of my clients," he answered.

"Really? That many?"

"By conservative estimate. Whereas a good marriage, it frees you to pay attention to other things. It's like maintaining a healthy bank balance, you know? When you have it, you can stop thinking about it."

"Such a romantic."

"Hey, I'm as romantic as they come. I'm gonna fuck you tonight, ain't I?"

"You have a way about you, Easy. No denying it."

When they got home a few minutes later, the house was dark. "Could the girls really be asleep?" Zeke whispered as they climbed the stairs to the second floor.

"Could be. It's a school night."

"Seems too good to be true."

"They both had homework. Maybe they tuckered themselves out getting it done."

"Or they just want us to be happy."

"That must be it."

Molly took longer in the bathroom than usual, which was frequently the case when lovemaking was on the agenda. It wasn't clear to Zeke why; contraception was no longer an issue, and elaborate beautification rituals, hygienic procedures, and the application of unguents and scents were all unnecessary. They'd known each other for almost forty years, they'd been married for over ten; there was no need to make a stunning impression. But this wasn't a mystery he chose to examine; in marriage, the romance of your partner's body was already sufficiently compromised simply through the rough-and-tumble intimacy of daily life. A little ignorance was beneficial.

Zeke lay in bed in the dark, waiting for her to emerge. A quick self-assessment. Didn't feel too full or sluggish, no digestive problems to speak of. Good. A slight residual buzz, but he wasn't drunk. Good. Some preliminary stirring. Good. He was beginning to feel a certain anticipatory eagerness about what was to come. Not always the case anymore. Sometimes in advance it just felt like duty, although there was invariably pleasure once the Rubicon got crossed.

And then he had a disturbing thought, seemingly from out of nowhere: Someday, somehow, a time would come when he would have engaged in the last act of sexual intercourse of his life. A pesky little notion he'd never entertained before. Presumably he wouldn't realize it at the time, unless it was one of those death-in-the-saddle horror stories, but who could say with any confidence? Maybe he'd go in for a routine physical the next day, feeling energetic and chipper, and emerge having received a medical death sentence. Or maybe he'd be walking down the street and suddenly collapse, from a stroke or a coronary or an aneurysm. Who knew? And who could predict when such a thing might occur? It could be next week or decades away. He remembered his first sexual experience, of course—everyone does—but the last was going to have the same sort of reality someday, whether or not he knew it.

He could only hope it would be in the distant—the unimaginably distant—future. The other book-end to his active sexual life. A sexual life that began some sixteen years after his actual life started. What sort of interval would divide his final sexual act from his last breath? Would there be an equivalent span, but this time of decrepitude and decline rather than growth and maturation? Of course, now that chemical assistance was available, age by itself needn't dictate a cessation of potency. At some point, let's hope a decade away at least, he might find himself embarrassedly asking Dr. Penman about Viagra or Cialis or whatever pharmacological miracle might then be available. Not a prospect he found enticing, but lots better than not having the option. Still, while that sort of technological progress wasn't to be sneezed at, it didn't alter the fundamental proposition: At some point, everything was going to stop. At some point, his sexual history would be precisely that: History. The fuck preceding that point would be his final fuck. And at some point thereafter—long thereafter or shortly thereafter, who could say?— his heart too would undergo its final seism.

So much for that preliminary stirring. Nothing like death to provide handy instantaneous cock-shriveling. Did I do that to myself on purpose, he wondered, his therapist's instincts perpetually on the alert. Sabotage my own desire for some obscure reason? If so, was it to punish myself or Molly? I'll have to examine that question later. But now...he tried to summon up some image that might get the old hormones secreting again. Not so easy to do when you're under the gun. When you're sixty-something and under the gun. The age thing isn't purely physical, either. When you're sixteen, it doesn't take much more than, say, the thought of a bra strap to spring you into action. Everything's fresh, everything's novel. By your fifties, you're a little jaded.

Well, he thought sourly, this is certainly turning into a night of lubricious extravagance. Maybe I should put the Britten *War Requiem* on the stereo to really get us in the mood.

After another minute or two, he heard the running water shut off, saw the light go out behind the bathroom door, and then, a couple of seconds later, the door itself opened. Molly, naked, emerged in shadow, a dark shape against the general darkness. Quite a nice dark shape, however, if memory served.

"So," he said. "You finally made it."

"Getting impatient?"

"Ridiculous, isn't it? It's only been...what? A couple of weeks?"

He felt rather than saw her smile. "Yeah, I know," she said. "There's always so much else clamoring for attention. This is the thing that gets sacrificed. We shouldn't let that happen." She crossed the room quickly and climbed into bed beside him. "Brr!"

"Cold?"

"Mmm. Warm me up, Easy. If you can stand my cold feet."

"I worship the ground your cold feet walk on." And thought, cold feet, cold ground, massa's in the cold, cold ground.

Stop it!

Meanwhile, she had rolled over toward him, onto her side, and his left arm went across her hips. Her feet were indeed freezing. He did his best to ignore them, and kissed her.

She sighed, and said, "Sometimes I forget how nice this is."

"You do?"

"Not *that* it's nice. Just *how* nice. It's so easy to get caught up in other things, and suddenly time has gone by and it's all a little hazy."

"It's one of the best bargains going. It's free, and you don't even have to worry about parking."

"I don't need extra inducements. It's always been a treat with you."

Vaguely dangerous ground. Let it go. He kissed her again, and moved his hand along her thigh. She reached for him. A little too soon; the reverberations of those death thoughts hadn't completely faded. She made a little noise in her throat. Hard to tell whether it was a throat clearing, a sigh, or a little laugh.

"Don't worry," he said. "I'll catch up."

"I have every confidence," she said. And then, "Ah, I think you're closing the distance already."

But then, just as things were starting to get serious, they both heard a noise from downstairs. They froze for a second, and then Zeke whispered, "Was that something?"

"Christ," said Molly.

Zeke groaned. The front door. He rolled to the side.

"If we're lucky, it's a burglar," Molly said, climbing out of bed. "I'll tell him to take whatever he wants and be right back."

"Maybe it's Owen."

"Nah. We both know who it is." She sounded very weary all of a sudden.

"Her timing is impeccable," Zeke muttered.

"It could have been worse. She could have come five minutes later."

Zeke groaned again. As Molly headed for the door, he said, "You want moral support?"

"Nah. Better not. She'll claim we're ganging up on her."

A few seconds later, he heard Molly from down the hall, her voice raised although not exactly shouting, saying, "Ashley, is that you? Where have you been? We have rules about school nights!"

He heard Ashley's voice answering. Too indistinct to make out the words, but the tone was agitated, the emotion characteristically veering toward the hysterical.

Then he heard Molly shout. A different sort of shout, surprised, alarmed. He could even make out the words, although they were wafting up from the ground floor. "Oh my God! Oh my God, Ashley! What happened?"

He sprang out of bed, grabbed his robe from the hook on the inside of the bathroom door, and started downstairs. This was turning into quite a night.

Fanny Stern wasn't so far gone that she didn't know who Molly was. She might be a little confused about the complicated history between her son and his wife—she wasn't alone in that—but she always knew Molly *was* her son's wife, and she always remembered her name.

She was a little less certain about Owen. She knew he was her grandson, and she never forgot she adored him. But lately she had begun assuming Molly was his mother; if you tried to correct her, or jog her memory by mentioning Angie, she got flustered, having obviously conflated Molly and Angie, and would react with defensive irritation. If you mentioned Angie's death, you could see a dim memory flicker behind Fanny's eyes and quickly sputter out.

"You've gotten so tall," Fanny was saying to Owen. They were sitting in a pleasant, well-lit alcove on the ground floor of the facility. Fanny was dressed rather stylishly; even transplanted to the East Bay, and even addled, she retained pride in her appearance, and displayed some of the flair she'd acquired as the former wife of an LA clothier: A cocoa-colored wool skirt, a cream-colored sweater. Earrings, a necklace. Expertly-applied make-up. She still had her hair colored.

"It happens, grandma," Owen said with a smile. He was incredibly patient with her. She had already mentioned his height three times in the last fifteen minutes.

"You're over six feet, aren't you?"

"Uh huh."

"Your father used to be tall."

"He's still the same height, grandma. Medium, I'd say. Not as tall as me."

"What are you studying in school?"

81

Owen glanced at Molly, a look of humorous helplessness in his eye. It wasn't merely that he'd answered this question several times already during this visit, and innumerable times in the past; it was also that the question was itself unanswerable. Did she mean what courses was he taking? What was his major? What postgraduate education did he intend to pursue? Of course, she meant none of those things, she didn't mean much of anything, she wasn't after information at all; she was just making conversation, phatic conversation, filling the void with amiable sounds. But even so, you had to answer. Every time.

An antic look entered Owen's eye, and as he leaned toward his grandmother, he said, with a perfectly straight face, "Animal husbandry. I'm studying animal husbandry. I want to become a large-animal veterinarian, like that guy on NPR."

Molly looked toward the floor to avoid laughing.

"That's wonderful," said Fanny. "You always liked animals."

"Especially large ones," said Owen. "The bigger the better."

Molly shot him a warning glance, to dissuade him from keeping on with this. She didn't begrudge him having a bit of fun—these visits could be deadly, Owen was admirably good-natured about them, and the joke wasn't malicious—but if Fanny ever realized she was being mocked, the hurt would cut deep. Only for about ten seconds, maybe, before she forgot about it, but who knew what residue might be left? Owen nodded back at Molly imperceptibly. He understood. This was a one-time caprice; Fanny wouldn't remember what he'd said, and he wouldn't push the joke further.

"Do you have a girlfriend?" his grandmother asked.

"No, grandma. I had one last year, but she went to New York for college and we decided to break up."

"That's very sensible."

"We thought so."

A muscle in Owen's jaw twitched. He'd never expressed much emotion about breaking up with Sara, simply presented it as matter-of-factly as he had done to Fanny just now, but from the start Zeke felt it hurt the boy far more than he would admit, and Molly was beginning to suspect Zeke had it right. He also thought, despite the absence of any evidence, that the break-up was Sara's idea and Sara's doing—she was primed and ready for the next stage of her life, and that stage emphatically didn't include hanging onto a high school romance—whereas Owen would have been willing to try to sustain a long-distance relationship. But Owen didn't talk about such matters, not to Molly certainly, and now not even to Zeke.

"Are you in college?" Fanny asked Owen.

"Yes." Evincing no sign of impatience. "I started this year. I'm a freshman. At Cal. You know, Berkeley. Where Molly teaches. I started this year."

"Your mom teaches college?"

"Not my mom. My mom died a long time ago. Molly here."

Fanny behaved as if she hadn't even heard the correction. "You're in college?"

"Uh huh." Again, no sigh, no eye-roll, his tone of voice uninflected.

"My goodness! College already! No wonder you're so tall! You must be at least six feet!"

"Yes, grandma, I am."

"What are you studying?"

After they left the facility about twenty minutes later, Molly proposed lunch. She felt she owed it to Owen, who was so accommodating about visiting Fanny, and so well-behaved during the visits. They stopped at an unpretentious store-front taqueria on Shattuck en route back into Berkeley. After they had ordered, Molly said, "Large-animal veterinarian, Owen?" She was smiling, but she also tried to introduce a slight suggestion of disapproval into her voice.

"I know." He looked only slightly sheepish. "But how many times can I say I haven't declared a major but I'm leaning toward anthropology? She can't follow a sentence with more than about five words in it, and she doesn't have a clue what anthropology is. And no matter what I tell her, she'll forget it in a minute."

"Well…just don't tell her you're gay, okay? *That* she'd remember."

"I won't. Not that I'm not tempted sometimes. The eighth or ninth time she asks if I have a girlfriend. But you're right, she might remember.

The last things to go will be who's gay and who's Jewish."

Molly laughed. "A residue of the Hollywood years. Those were both important considerations."

The waitress arrived with their drinks. A Diet Coke for Molly, a Corona for Owen. Fortunately—was it his height?—the waitress hadn't thought to card him. Owen, with his conscientious manners, murmured a thank you, and then, after the waitress moved on, said to Molly, "Can I ask you something? Why do *you* visit grandma? She's not your mother. Just some random old lady, basically."

Molly considered. "Well...first of all, she *isn't* just a random old lady to me. And you know, Zeke goes several times a week, he goes when he can. And he usually goes alone. It's painful for him, but he doesn't complain about it. Too much. By his standards." Owen smiled, and encouraged by the smile, Molly went on, "Your dad complains a lot, he's a chronic grouser. But in another way he's like you, he doesn't actually share his pain with people. He grumbles about Republicans and the weather and bad drivers and his digestion, but he usually keeps deep emotions under wraps. And seeing his mother this way...that's about as deep as it gets."

Owen nodded.

"But he had patients all day today, he couldn't get away, and he worries if too many days go by without some kind of visit. Even if she doesn't remember the visits themselves, she gets bored and anxious and depressed. So...I wasn't teaching today, it seemed like a nice thing to do. Nice for Zeke *and* for Fanny."

"But you didn't have to go," Owen said. "I would have gone by myself."

"Yes, I know." She looked at him, this sweet, troubled stepson of hers. "But I've known Fanny so long...I first met her when I was your age. Almost exactly. And in a way, in every way but legally, she's been my mother-in-law twice. And she was always nice to me. I always liked her, even though she was hard to get to know. Kept herself in reserve. So I guess I feel some sort of obligation. To her, I mean, not just to Zeke. And besides," she added with a smile, "you're so good about it, you shame me into it."

"Grandma seems to have forgotten my mom altogether."

"It's more she combines your mom and me in her mind, turning us into one person. Simpler for her, and she doesn't have to think about Angie dying."

"Or about you and dad breaking up."

Molly frowned. The kids were aware that she and Zeke had been together decades ago, but not much beyond that. "Well, maybe. I don't think that would bother her too much, really. Zeke and I were so young then, we were *expected* to break up. Sy and Fanny were probably relieved when it happened, not distressed."

"They didn't approve?"

"They'd been divorced a few years by then, they didn't react as a unit. I had a different relationship with each of them. But they both liked me okay. Until the break-up, then they didn't. I mean, they took Zeke's side, reasonably enough. But when we were together, they both liked me fine. Sy a little less than Fanny, maybe. They just weren't thrilled about the possibility we'd get married."

"Religion?"

"Maybe partly. They would never have admitted it. And it's not like they did better on that score with your mom. There was our age too. They must've felt we were too young, we'd met too early. Hadn't experienced enough life. Hadn't been exposed to enough people. They weren't wrong. It may be why things have worked out so well the second time around...we were mature enough to see...to see what we had going for us." She'd almost said, "to see how well-matched we were compared to all the other people out there," but realized Owen might take this as a slighting reference to his mother. She hurried on, "In addition, your grandfather had problems with me. They didn't rise to the level of dislike, but I made him uneasy."

Owen smiled. "I can't imagine. Why?"

"I wouldn't take his shit," Molly replied with an answering smile.

"Was he handing out a lot?"

"More than his share, I'd say. And he wasn't used to being challenged. Not by a woman. Certainly not by a young woman who looked like a hippy. Fanny deferred to him. His employees treated him like their boss. And Zeke just sort of absented himself. Emotionally, I mean. He didn't confront his dad no matter how outrageously the man tried to provoke him, he followed a Gandhian strategy. But I argued. Just didn't know better. And Sy didn't like it."

"He died way before I was born. Doesn't sound like I missed much."

"He had his strengths and weaknesses. He could be generous. He had a lot of force in him. But I didn't like the way he treated your dad. And he was full of shit in lots of ways. But I don't want to give the impression he was a bad man. He wasn't."

"A good man who was full of shit?"

"As are we all."

"Not you, Molly. And not dad."

She shook her head, not in contradiction, but in wonderment. Sometimes it hit her suddenly and unexpectedly how much she had come to love this boy. As if he were her own. And with all the *sturm und drang* around Ashley, all the difficult stuff they had to get through that she could banish from her mind only for brief intervals, it was comforting to realize things can get better. After a really explosive period with Owen, more than a year of feuding and slammed doors and tears and accusations and deeply, deliberately hurtful comparisons on his part, they had come to cherish each other, somehow. Such a sweet boy he was, too. He had Zeke's sweetness and then some. He might be too sweet for this mean-spirited world.

She reached across the table and took his hand. It startled him. Seconds later, he seemed relieved to have an excuse for withdrawing it, saying, "Ah, here come our tacos," as he swiveled toward the cute Mexican waitress approaching their table.

"A black eye?" Stan asked.

"Sort of purple and green," said Zeke, "if we're being precise."

They were puffing away on adjacent ellipticals at the downtown Y, sweating profusely. Like a couple of aging pigs, Zeke thought. Not much of an advertisement for exercise, although who knows what we'd look like if we *didn't* do this? I'd probably look like Stan, instead of the almost-trim fellow staring back at me from the mirror lining the wall in front of us. And Stan would look like…an even bigger version of Stan. Or maybe the Hindenburg impending over Lakehurst.

"D'you know what happened?"

"She won't say. Gave us some bullshit about bumping into something at a party."

"Maybe it's true."

"Stan, I'm a shrink. Sometimes when people lie, they want you to know it. Tiny smile, no eye-contact, no energy in the voice. She's *enjoying* the fact we don't believe her. 'Course, she also wants us to know what happened, but not until she's caused some tsouris."

"Are you worried?"

"Of course! Molly's frantic. Someone slugged her daughter, for God's sake."

"Maybe."

"Probably. Almost certainly."

"Think she's in physical jeopardy?"

"When a teenager comes home with a black eye, you have to take it seriously."

Stan leaned forward, grabbed the towel hanging from the front of his machine, and wiped his forehead. "These fucking things are always worse than you expect," he muttered. His breathing was labored, his face flushed.

"Are you referring to the elliptical, or to offspring?" Zeke asked.

"How long have we been doing this?" He glanced down at the timer. "Only seventeen minutes! Fuck me!"

"Take a breather," Zeke suggested. "You look whipped."

"Nah, Penman says this is okay. She prescribed it. I had my physical a couple of weeks ago, she recommended exercise, surprise surprise. You wouldn't know it to look at me, but my heart and lungs are fine. My prostate is apparently museum-quality. It's the rest of me that's fucked up."

"Remember gym class in the seventh grade? Speaking of being physical wrecks. What was that sadist's name? Okinawa?"

Stan managed a wheezy laugh. "Toragawa. I guess he was still pissed off about the war."

"Or having spent his childhood in an internment camp."

"Okay, you made a liberal feel guilty, congratulations, quite a feat. Anyhow, for whatever reason, he treated us out-of-shape Jews like dirt. Enjoyed doing it, too."

Stan had been regularly humiliated at gym class in junior high, unable to do much of anything demanded of him, and always the last to be picked for any team sport. Zeke hadn't been much good either, but never as hopeless as Stan. A small comfort back then.

"Remember the swats he used to give, with his whistle lanyard?" Zeke asked.

"Are you kidding? The mark they left on a kid's ass? The angry red line? You could see it in the showers for days. I lived in terror of those swats. Not the pain so much, but the possibility I'd cry. That's the sort of thing you can never live down. The girls would hear about it within minutes, through the pubescent grapevine." He picked up his towel and wiped his forehead again. "It's why I went up to Sacramento in '86 to work on the corporal punishment statute. Pro fucking bono. I knew how traumatizing it can be. From personal experience."

"You got swatted?"

"Hell no, I was a model citizen around Toragawa. He sometimes tried to goad us, remember? I wouldn't rise to the bait. Even the possibility was traumatic."

"I was the same," Zeke said. "Laughed along with all the other kids at the humiliation and the insults. Whether I was the target or somebody else."

"Usually it was me."

"That's true. He hated you."

"Fucking bastard."

"It was an interesting psychological phenomenon, the way we all joined in the sport. The literature calls it 'identification with the aggressor.' We're inclined that way as a species. We defer to alpha males. We side with bullies."

"Another reason to love humanity."

"Consider how the media covered Al Gore back in 2000. Classic example. Most of them probably voted for the guy, but that didn't stop them from hooting and whistling and catcalling and making stuff up about him."

There was a pause, and Stan suddenly gasped. Zeke looked over in alarm. His friend's face was vividly flushed, his face contorted in a grimace. A second later, his legs buckled, and he collapsed within the frame of the exercise machine, his arms hugging the central tower. It all happened very fast. Someone shouted. Zeke leapt off the machine he was on and leaned down over Stan, who seemed to be struggling for air. "Someone call an ambulance!" Zeke shouted.

"No," Stan managed to choke out. "I'm okay."

"Chest pain? Referred pain in your arm?"

"You're an MD all of a sudden?" Stan managed a crooked smile, although the question emerged with difficulty. "Fanny must be proud."

A small crowd was gathering around them. One man, bearded, in his forties, said in an authoritative voice, "I'm a doctor. Let me through." In his shorts and sweat-stained tee shirt, it seemed an unlikely claim, but Zeke stepped out of the way, and the man knelt down beside Stan.

"Get some water," the man instructed Zeke.

"Right."

A few minutes later, Stan was lying supine on an exercise mat in a darkened room across the corridor from the cardio room, focusing on slow, deep breathing. Zeke was seated on the floor beside him. "You should have pulled that stunt on Toragawa," Zeke finally said. "Would have taught the fucker a lesson. He might not have been afraid of *us*, but if he had to face your mother…" When Stan didn't answer, Zeke added, "Jesus, Stan, I thought we were headed to the ER for sure."

"Aw, I knew it wasn't serious," Stan said

"You're an MD all of a sudden?"

Stan laughed a brief phlegmy laugh. "Dehydration and low blood-sugar. The real doctor confirmed my diagnosis."

"Wait till you get the bill."

"There won't be a bill. I think he wanted to give me mouth-to-mouth."

"No one wants to give you mouth-to-mouth, Stan." And then, "How are you?"

"Better. Much better. Almost normal."

"That would be a novelty."

"Right."

"You gave me quite a scare."

"You scare easy."

"It's just, I'm not ready to bury you yet," Zeke said, trying to keep his tone light.

There was a little pause, and then Stan said, "Listen…there's something we should discuss… I don't know how to talk about it, but…"

It almost sounded like the start of a death-bed confession. Zeke felt an anticipatory prickling at the back of his neck. "What is it, Stan?"

"It's not that I think I need to apologize…this is my job, I can't apologize for that. And I really shouldn't be saying anything, it's a violation of confidentiality."

Zeke suddenly understood what this must be about. "Corin?"

"It's been weighing on me since Liam shot off his mouth at the poker game. I can't say anything, you understand that, right?"

"Just take it easy, okay? We can talk about it later."

"That's the point, though. We *can't*. I can't talk about it. But I'd hate for you to think I'm an asshole. It's just—"

"I know, Stan. I understand. It's okay."

Alarmingly but touchingly, Stan reached over and took hold of Zeke's hand. In fifty-one years of friendship, this had never happened before.

Molly paused in mid-sentence, looked out over the throng of students before her, and felt a little shiver of despair. How futile this was. Delivering a complicated argument verbally to several hundred students, most of whom hadn't done the reading and weren't paying attention…It was a ritual, like a mass celebrated in a dead language none of the communicants understood. We go through the motions because it's the way it's always been done, it's what's expected. How much better if I distributed my thoughts via e-mail; the few students who care could read them at their leisure. Instead, they get this *performance piece*, a waste of time and effort. Mine and theirs. Not that many of them are making much of an effort.

She looked up from the notes on the podium in front of her. She hadn't been consulting them—she didn't need to consult them—she had merely been looking down while considering what a pathetic charade this business was. "Modern readers and play-goers find Shakespeare's treatment of Kate and of Shylock problematic," she said. "*The Merchant of Venice* has been regarded as troublesome for centuries, at least among its liberal readers, and the advent of second-wave feminism caused many critics to re-examine *The Taming of the Shrew*, although, to be fair, there were people like George Bernard Shaw who already found it obnoxious more than a hundred years ago. Found it obnoxious for all the reasons we might find it obnoxious today, I mean. And even during Shakespeare's lifetime, John Fletcher wrote a play that was a refutation of its view of women. But in general, we're so far removed from the world in which such plays were conceived and performed, it's impossible to imagine ourselves into it. And the types they portray, the attitudes they embody—what a Jew is, what a woman is—these aren't merely unfashionable or politically incorrect nowadays, they're positively abhorrent."

Were they following this? Did they care? Did they experience any discomfort from the tension between Shakespeare's genius and his prejudices? Did it puzzle them, concern them, discomfit them? Students weren't engaged nowadays the way they'd been when she was a student; we were passionate about *everything*. It was the positive side of that era: The passion could start with drugs or rock and roll, but it could also attach itself to something worthy, something that could sustain your interest for the rest of your life.

Or you could be Liam, in which case a passion for rock and roll *did* sustain your interest for the rest of your life.

She went on, "But it's also important to say they illuminate a crucial aspect of Shakespeare's genius. We can never know what he really thought about these matters, or about almost any other; he is, along with all his other superlative qualities, the most personally elusive of artists, a complete cipher to us. To take one example, he lived in the midst of what we might call a religious Cold War, but we don't even know for sure which side he was on. And it's striking how he gives the most eloquent speeches in *Merchant* to Shylock, the despised Jew, and, at the end, endows him with so much humanity we may feel his pain more keenly than the emotions of any other character in the play. And he makes Kate, the shrew who needs taming, one of his liveliest and most attractive heroines, a prototype for the witty, headstrong women he created in his later plays, where they're treated with far more respect and affection. It complicates the picture, it's a testament to his almost superhuman capacity for human sympathy, which sometimes confutes his own dramatic intentions."

Hundreds of faces staring up at her. Respectfully, she'd have to say, if not attentively, and if not comprehendingly. Some were taking notes, some were just sitting there in bovine passivity. There was no point saying what she had recently come to believe: Even granted Shakespeare's superhuman capacity for human sympathy, and even granted that according to recent scholarship the Dark Lady of the sonnets might well have been a Jewess, the man was still a shit in the way that most men in those days were shits. One wanted Shakespeare to transcend all that, but he didn't. He couldn't. Fuck his human sympathy. He meant us to laugh at Shylock's anguish and find it fitting, even while evoking it with supreme artistry because he was incapable of doing otherwise; he wanted us to be amused by, and approve of, Kate's punishment at Petruchio's hands, to find methods the KGB would centuries later employ to break political prisoners amusing in themselves and appropriate measures for dealing with a recalcitrant wife. No amount of fancy-dancing could change that. Molly knew this as well as anyone; she'd fancy-danced for decades in order to be able to revere Shakespeare without reservation. She'd done—had had to do—her fanciest dancing back in college when she first studied Shakespeare in any depth, at the same time she was passionately devoting herself to the feminist movement. The only way to resolve the tension was to deny it.

She detected a certain restiveness among the students. While her mind was wandering, they had been waiting for her next sentence. Something within her just didn't want to go on with this today. Maybe it was the miserable business with Ashley. Must be. How can you help a victim when she won't even admit she's a victim? Did Ashley somehow think of herself as Kate, getting her just deserts? Ashley didn't know who Kate was.

Molly suddenly realized she'd have to rely on Zeke for this. He wasn't the girl's father, and he had his own difficulties with her, but he was a professional; maybe he could find a way to elicit the truth from her and help her see how destructive the situation was. It was unfair to enlist him, but fairness didn't matter, not in an extreme case like this, and not when her daughter was involved.

She looked down at her notes again. And sighed. The amplification system picked up the sigh, which was embarrassing. She saw that a few of the students were looking at one another. "See," she then said, "the thing is, even great artists aren't perfect human beings. And their imperfections sneak into their work, inevitably, and we can either dismiss the work because we disapprove of the people who created it, or we can marvel at the fact that so much genius, so much nobility, can co-exist with such meanness. We can marvel at how the impurities highlight the perfection. We mustn't let ourselves feel superior, because we're all the product of our times, even if we don't realize it, just as fish are said not to notice the water they swim in. Maybe someday, much later in our lives, when the world has turned a few times and the zeitgeist has shifted, we'll discover how many things we once took for granted and how many things we did in the full certainty we were justified, we now deeply regret. Shakespeare wouldn't write *The Merchant of Venice* if he were alive today. I believe that absolutely. But he did write it four centuries ago. That fact can teach us something about tolerance, and about history, and about the way society and individual consciousness interact. And no, none of this will be on the exam. It's just something to think about. We're going to end early today."

There was scattered applause as she gathered up her papers. There was usually scattered applause after her lectures, but it wasn't usually quite so scattered as this. Well, she'd been distracted. No point beating herself up. Her daughter had snuck out at night and come home with a black eye and wouldn't say what had happened; that kind of thing that can take your mind off the finer points of Elizabethan dramaturgy.

The students slowly filed out of the lecture hall. She waited at the lectern to see if anyone had a question. At first, no one approached, but after a couple of minutes, by which time the room had almost emptied, a man walked up to her rather hesitantly. An older man, too old to be an undergraduate, although sometimes older people came back to the university to complete a degree abandoned decades before. But it was mostly older women who did that, after their children had grown and left home, and often after they'd been widowed. This man didn't seem a likely candidate; he was in his upper fifties, craggy-featured, handsome in a weathered, rough-hewn sort of way, lean, wiry, dressed casually, almost like a student, in jeans and a blue-and-yellow striped soccer shirt.

"Yes?" she said. For some reason, she felt a little shudder of dread.

"Molly?" he said. And then he smiled. A smile of immense charm and amusement and good humor, the skin around his eyes crinkling, his eyes twinkling.

It was the smile she recognized. "Corin," she said. Her heart started racing.

Five

1972

When Molly joined a women's group, I was stunned. Not censorious or even disquieted, mind you, just flabbergasted. Only days before, or so it seemed, we'd been laughing about the whole phenomenon, about the artificiality of imposing intimacy by fiat and assuming solidarity by gender, and scoffing at...not feminism per se—the issue was too complicated for facile derision—but some of its more extreme manifestations. Germaine Greer's muddy thinking and Kate Millett's coarseness and Yoko Ono's self-regarding stridency. And suddenly, without a hint of mitigating irony, without even acknowledging anything had changed, she announced she was joining a group of women who, as she put it, planned to "meet to discuss their lives" every Friday night. At least she didn't refer to them as "my sisters." But even so, she was po-faced enough about the whole thing to leave me shaken. A few years later, when I saw the remake of *Invasion of the Body Snatchers*, it had a familiar ring.

It's not that I was totally out of sympathy. Not at the time, and like the rest of the world, I've come a long way since. Feminism may have been the biggest, most unsettling social change we boomers lived through—civil rights felt straightforward and uncontroversial by comparison, although bloodier—and I doubt there's a person who was sentient in the '70s who hasn't subjected himself to a sustained and drastic re-think about things he took for granted before. He and *she* took for granted, since, contrary to myth, the pre-feminist era wasn't made up of enlightened women and Cro-Magnon men; most of us, men and women alike, had inherited a similar set of assumptions we were all forced to re-assess.

But at the time, the media, in their inimitable way, were presenting a grotesque travesty of the various ideas that were bubbling up, and the spokeswomen they gravitated to were the most newsworthy, which meant the most outrageous. Often extreme, or downright nuts. So it was easy, at the beginning it was much too easy, to be skeptical. Molly was skeptical too. This was before a species of Leninism took over, and critical thinking on the subject came to be regarded as inherently sexist and reactionary, and every feminist theorist had to be defended against every doubter, regardless of how outré the theory and how reasonable the doubt. At this time, everybody I knew was skeptical, except maybe Stan, who mouthed a few feminist platitudes when he wasn't whacking off to *Playboy*. Okay, that's a cheap shot. And despite what many of my friends still profess to think, I don't believe masturbating to *Playboy* has political implications. But Stan's willingness to accommodate any putatively left-wing rhetoric because it bore a left-wing label wasn't an intellectual habit I admired.

Although there's another side to him too; he's never been totally in thrall to ideology. For example, one afternoon during this same summer, he was at the apartment and we were playing chess. At some point, he said something about how many men were left on the board. Molly was within earshot, and she reacted like a warhorse to the roar of musketry. "Men?" she shouted from the next room. "Of course they're men! So typical! God forbid chess pieces should be women!"

Stan looked up, squinted, and called back, "Listen, if we called them women, you'd say, "Typical! You pick them up and move them around like they have no will of their own. They're just there to serve you, they're nothing more than your helpless tools.' I mean, honestly, sometimes you feminists put us in a bind where we just can't win."

Which silenced her. Believe me, silencing Molly on this subject was no easy task in those days. Stan the future litigator was already emerging from the shadows.

But I'm letting myself get sidetracked again, aren't I? And of course there's a good psychological reason why I'm reluctant to get where I'm going. I'm not going to examine it, though. Shrinks can be as stubborn about such things as regular people.

Let's see…I was talking about Molly's joining a women's group. This was in the summer. She had just graduated with honors, Phi Beta Kappa, and was about to start graduate school in the fall. Her focus had recently shifted from Shakespeare to Virginia Woolf; in hindsight, that qualifies as a tell. And another straw in the wind, possibly, was the relentlessness with which she played Carol King's *Tapestry* and the Joy of Cooking's first album; both were fine LPs, but I came to hate them. Partly from sheer repetition, but I also began to feel as if Molly were hectoring me by proxy, as if every pleasure had to have a hidden message and a political dimension.

It hadn't been a great year for her, despite her academic successes; something had been eating her right from the start of the school year, even though she couldn't or wouldn't tell me what. She often seemed preoccupied or depressed or grumpy. It wasn't like her. But whenever I asked what was bothering her, she would tell me there was nothing, or, occasionally, that she wasn't sure, nothing she could explain.

Meanwhile, I was working as a clerk at the Textbook Exchange on Bancroft, near campus, in a rage about the war and about Nixon's inevitable re-election (most of my friends refused to regard it as inevitable, but I knew better, knew it from the moment the previous summer he announced he was going to China), and in a quiet simmering panic about what to do with the rest of my life. A sympathetic family doctor had lied and got me a 4-F, so at least I didn't have to worry about the draft. Many of my friends were in communication with the Canadian consulate in San Francisco, and others were trying to convince an array of shrinks they were either homosexual or bedevilled by one of several obscure but incapacitating mental illnesses (homosexuality was still officially a mental illness, so I should say "other mental illnesses"). I didn't have that worry, but I was worried about everything else. Like what to do with the rest of my life. I didn't have the equivalent of what religious people term "a calling." Just a set of interests and enthusiasms that didn't mesh, that refused to coalesce into a recognizable profession.

I'd talk to Stanley, who had already sweated his way through his first year at Boalt School of Law and coasted through his second and was about to start his third, and idly wonder if I should follow. Law school was what bright boys without a calling did. But Stan *did* have a calling, he loved the law and seemed to have a talent for it; like the yeshiva student he resembled, he was inclined to Talmudic-style reasoning even though he had no use for Talmud. He probably would have felt at home as a Jesuit too, studying, say, with Aquinas at the 13th century Sorbonne. He was on the law school journal and was getting all sorts of respectful attention from his professors and so on. If he'd just been another grind, I might have been able to sign up. But he'd found his metier, he burned with passionate commitment, his eyes caught fire when he discussed a case, even one whose political tendencies he abominated. That was an unintended rebuke to people like me, people who might go to law school for want of anything better to do. So I didn't apply. Instead, I wasted my time selling books to the committed people, people like Stan and Molly.

Molly and I were living on the ground floor of a funky Victorian gingerbread on Haste Street, between Milvia and what was still called Grove. It was a step up from our last two places, but just barely, and mainly from the outside. We were always strapped for cash; she had a scholarship and a smallish allowance from her parents, I had my measly bookstore salary. One very warm evening after I got home from the bookstore—things had been slow, fewer students bought textbooks in the summer, and it had been a long day, hot and boring—and after I showered and changed, I joined Molly in our kitchenette, where she was preparing a chef's salad. And without looking up or stopping what she was doing, she casually mentioned that she was cancelling our plan to see a movie Friday night; instead, she was joining a group of women who met on a weekly basis to discuss their lives.

Well, as I've indicated, I was nonplussed. "You're kidding," was how I responded. Not the most tactful of responses, but it slipped out of me.

It immediately put her on the defensive. "Don't start," she said.

"I haven't."

"You were about to."

"When did this happen?"

"When did what happen?"

She was being disingenuous, but it wasn't an ideal time to point that out. "That you got asked. That you decided to go."

"A couple of days ago."

"And you didn't tell me?"

"I don't have to tell you everything."

Which seemed more adversarial than the situation warranted. My good mood about being home from work, my animal enjoyment on a pleasant summer evening after having showered and changed, was fast evanescing. "Of course you don't. But this…I don't know, it seems like something you might mention."

"I wanted to think about it first."

"Uh huh."

"And besides, I knew you'd make fun."

"I'm not making fun."

"Yet."

She was holding a big knife, chopping roasted chicken breasts into chunks on a wooden chopping block. It wasn't an auspicious time to antagonize her. "I wasn't going to make fun."

"See that you don't," she said.

Boy, this was turning into a delightful summer idyll. I helped her prepare dinner after that, but we didn't speak again until we were seated at the small wooden table in our dining nook, the one with leaves we didn't have the space to open, when she broke the silence by saying, almost pleasantly, "This isn't a big deal, Zeke." She was making an effort, although the effort itself was patent, which undermined the effect a little. "Women have always found it comforting to talk to each other," she went on. "To compare notes and offer advice and support. Doing the washing by the river, or quilting in a big circle, or whatever. But the way urban life works, especially if we're at school or have jobs, those opportunities don't arise naturally. So we have to carve out a space where we can do the same thing. It's not a conspiracy."

"Right," I said. "Of course."

"It's not directed at you. Not you personally, and not men in general."

"No," I agreed. But I was thinking, even if it wasn't directed at me— only a genuine paranoid would dispute that part—it had the potential to re-orient our life in ways I might find unwelcome.

A threatening idea. Molly and I shared an intimacy that felt all-encompassing, and I don't think we were alone in that way among couples in our cohort. Was it dope that enabled the unfettered sharing of confidences? Or the vaunted "generation gap," which, because we felt alienated from our parents, urged us more tightly into each other's embrace? Politics? Music? I don't know the reason, but Molly and I had no secrets; in fact, as you've probably guessed based on what you've read so far, I rarely had a passing thought to which I didn't immediately give voice.

There was arguably something infantile about this, a cocooning against the hostile alien world. And there may have been a certain willed delusion to it too, faith in an affinity that might have been chimerical. But since the delusion was mutual and constantly reinforced, it did its job. We told each other everything, we reassured each other about everything, we depended on each other for everything. And now I could see the drawback to this arrangement: If one member of a co-dependency issues a declaration of independence, the other feels abandoned. And betrayed.

And given Molly's prevailing air of restlessness, I had to contemplate the possibility I was among the sources of her discontent, and that she expressed annoyance with me because she found me annoying.

So, for example, at a party the previous June, the night of her last final exam, the ultimate final exam of her undergraduate career, someone offered us mushrooms. Such things weren't common in our circle, but these were Molly's undergraduate friends, people we saw only occasionally, and tonight they were in a celebratory mood. I declined, saying I was content with jug wine, and Molly thereupon declined too, but an hour or two later, on the drive home, she rounded on me. "You just *had* to say no to the mushrooms, didn't you?" she demanded after we'd driven in silence for a minute or two. Her voice oozed scorn, scorn that would have been unimaginable the previous year. "You always say no to things, don't you?"

I answered mildly. "Psychedelics make me uneasy. I do say no to them. But I say yes to lots of other stuff."

"No you don't! The things you say yes to…it's always the same stuff, the same old boring comfortable stuff. You say no to everything that's exciting or new or novel. You say no to everything that makes you *uneasy*, as you put it. Which ought to be your nickname, by the way. *Un*easy. I mean, Christ, Zeke, take a few chances. You're like a sixty-year-old coot trapped in a twenty-three-year-old body."

Weirdly, she was echoing my father's accusations from that Christmas a few years earlier, the same accusations she had defended me from. It was so personal and so harsh I didn't have an answer. I was who I was, the same guy I'd always been. I wasn't about to become Errol Flynn. She was supposed to like me. I said, "You wanted to take mushrooms? I had no idea."

"I was curious. I've been curious ever since I read Aldous Huxley in high school. It seemed like a perfect opportunity. I've never tried anything but weed."

"I wasn't stopping you."

"Yes you were. I knew the look you'd give me if I said yes after you said no. And anyway, we should do stuff together. Especially adventurous stuff. Why should we be old when we're still young? You act like it's some sort of moral victory to get there early. This isn't just about mushrooms. I wanted to try them, yeah, and it seemed presumptuous to me, how you acted like you were declining for both of us. But that's secondary…" She shook her head. "I'm going straight from college to graduate school, and then I'll be on the job market and I'll get hired somewhere and I'll start teaching, and meanwhile, I'm living with the same guy I met at the start of my freshman year, and...Do you see? Everything's so cut-and-dried. So safe. So flat and sensible and uninflected. I can defend every decision we make, you know? Shouldn't we do something *in*defensible, just once? Just to prove we can? We're in a rut. Maybe sooner or later everybody gets in a rut, but what's the fucking rush?"

"If you wanted the mushrooms, you should have taken the mushrooms." I was being deliberately obtuse. I couldn't deal with the bigger picture.

"You're right," she said, with a tone of disgusted finality that made reconciliation or resolution—even further discussion—impossible. And I was as much to blame as she was. Feigned obtuseness doesn't advance a discussion.

That argument blew over eventually, as arguments do, but it left a residue, as arguments also do. And it wasn't unique; I was devoting a fair amount of energy that season to avoid noticing Molly's unease. And so, a month later, when she said she was joining a women's group, I tried to accept the news with a semblance of grace. I said, "Yeah, that should be interesting. I'll see if I can make other plans."

"I appreciate your not turning this into something it's not." Her tone was still a little prickly, but she was trying to ameliorate the earlier contentiousness.

"Wish I'd had a little more notice, though." I felt entitled to that one.

I phoned Stan after dinner and asked if he was free on Friday. He was. Of course. Stan was always free, unless he had a political meeting. And the next night we did something immature. Possibly spiteful on my part. We drove to San Francisco, had a burger at Clown Alley, and then went to a small porn theater off Broadway. My first time, and Stan's too, or so he claimed. Not with regard to Clown Alley, of course. As I say, this might have been a kind of protest, but it's just as likely the protest side of things was the excuse. I'd been curious about porn for a while. It was still exotic, and its legality still in question; internet ubiquity was decades away. Until recently, unless you were in Paris or a Mexican border town, it hadn't been easy to get your hands on. I almost said "easy to come by." The unconscious is always a loaded weapon.

Over dinner I complained to Stan (I almost wrote "bitched," but in context that's hardly an acceptable verb—this whole area is clearly fertile soil for my unconscious) about Molly's sudden change of plans and change of attitude. I did it with some hesitation; I wasn't sure of my position, and feared Stan might spritz me with ideological cant. He didn't, though. He said, "Lookit, the whole world's in flux these days, it's natural people want to consider their options. I mean, Jesus, in a couple of minutes we'll be watching people fucking onscreen. Think about that. It isn't something we could have done a couple of years ago, it was unthinkable. But it's out there and naturally we're curious. I can't even imagine. My palms get sweaty when I try. Not hairy, Zeke, sweaty." He flashed me his goofy sly-nerd grin. "Maybe it's a similar deal for Molly. She wants to try something people are talking about. Something that sounds interesting and might be relevant to her. Just relax about it. I mean, Molly and you…jeez, you guys are the envy of everyone I know."

Sometimes Stan surprised me.

We were both uncomfortable at the movie; experiencing lust in public was strange, and the fact there were men near us who were obviously masturbating in their seats was off-putting, to understate the case. Didn't really tempt us to reach for popcorn. Still, despite everything, those movies managed to creep directly into our limbic systems. When we drove back across the bridge afterward, I could still see the images behind my eyeballs, the flesh garishly pink, the sexual organs engorged, bulbous, disembodied.

And Stan must have been feeling something similar. When he dropped me off at my place, he said, "Must be nice to have a warm body to get home to." We both laughed at that. But the truth is, I really didn't know what I was going to find when I went through the front door. Probably not a pornographic fantasy.

What I did find was Molly and a pretty woman I didn't know, tall, with close-cropped bright red hair. They were in the living room, side by side on our maroon corduroy sofa, drinking wine. "Hi," Molly said as I entered. "This is Nita."

We said hello. I had the odd impression that ordinary good manners were somehow a charade. What did she know about me? What had they been talking about? I felt excluded, and some indefinable emanation coming off both of them reinforced the notion, made me feel like an interloper.

"Where have you been?" Molly went on. She sounded unnatural, too aware of Nita's presence.

"Out with Stan," I said, and quickly added, "I'm going to turn in. Don't want to inhibit your conversation."

If I thought they'd protest, I was mistaken. And if I thought they'd see any humor in my offer, I was wrong about that too. They said good-night with insulting alacrity. The initiative had come from me, but it felt like I was being dismissed.

Molly didn't come to bed for another couple of hours. I had already fallen asleep and was having a series of sharply vivid erotic dreams when she finally slipped into the bedroom. The dreams were sufficiently unsettling—they weren't the sort of languorous erotic dreams you luxuriate in, they were ugly and harsh with bad lighting and cheap film-lab color—so her arrival woke me right up. Nevertheless, harsh and unlovely or no, they had left me in something of a frenzy, and I reached for her.

"Uh uh," she said, gently enough. "Go back to sleep."

We were still making love more nights than not in those days. "Why not?"

"It's late. And my head's in a different sort of space."

"I'll do without your head tonight," I said.

It was a joke, but she refused to treat it as one. "Typical," she said, the distaste clear.

"I was kidding," I said. You always sound lame when you have to explain you were kidding. Lame and not credible.

"Maybe you think you were."

Christ, the Khmer Rouge took months to complete their re-education process. Molly seemed to have graduated to commissar in one evening. I quickly grasped sex wasn't on the agenda and began the necessary internal shifting of gears. I rolled over onto my back, put my hands behind my head, and asked, "How was it tonight?"

"Fine."

"That's all you're going to say?"

"I don't want to talk about it if you're going to sneer."

"I'm not sneering."

"You're not receptive either. You've got an attitude. I'm not in the mood to deal with it."

"That woman…Nita, was it? She's in the group?"

"Uh huh. And we got into a conversation at one point, kind of a sidebar, and we decided to keep it going after the group called it a night."

"She seemed nice." What else could I say? I had exchanged two sentences with the woman, but hell, I didn't want to have an attitude.

"She's a lesbian," Molly announced.

"Okay."

Molly seemed disappointed by my reaction, which I'd made a point of keeping muted. This was obviously an interesting bit of information in itself, and somewhat surprising since the woman wasn't overtly butch (our categories were less fluid in those days). And this very night, for the first time in my life, I'd seen two women having sex. Onscreen, yes, but vividly enough to make a lasting impression. Still, I kept my reaction muted. "If you want to make a joke," Molly said irritably, "just do it already and get it out of your system."

This was too much. "You have a real chip on your shoulder, you know that?"

There was a silent interval of maybe ten seconds. Then she rolled over to face me. "I do, don't I? I'm sorry, Easy. You're right. You haven't provoked any of this, really. But…you know. I'm dealing with a lot of new stuff all of a sudden."

"You and me both," I said.

"That's a fair comment too." She suddenly kissed me. On my nose. "Listen, it was interesting, okay? All our different lives, and most of us have never talked about what they feel like or what we're going through as women. What's the same for all of us and what's different. Lots of surprises in both departments. It's eye-opening. We make assumptions, we think people see the world like we do, and then...but...see, it mostly wasn't anti-men or anything like that. I mean, everybody has gripes, but that isn't what it was about. Or sexism and feminism and theoretical stuff. It's much more concrete. Personal."

"So I didn't get roughed up?"

"I wouldn't go that far," she said. And laughed for the first time all day, at least while I was there to witness it. "You got off fairly lightly." She was joking, but I still felt queasy. And then she said, "Listen, if you want to make love, it's all right."

She had never put it that way before. It wasn't enticing. Despite the jangly uneasy stirrings engendered by those movies—localized in my spinal column, it seemed, rather than my loins—I wasn't about to let myself become a recipient of sexual charity. That wasn't the way things were supposed to work, and it wasn't the way things had ever worked before. "Nah, forget it," I said.

"Really, it's okay," she said.

"Okay isn't good enough," I said, rolling over onto my side, my back to her.

From then on, Friday evenings were a deep hole in our week. No, in *my* week. Molly never saw them as a hole; *her* Friday nights were full. What bothered me wasn't so much that we weren't out together, it was the mysterious freemasonry from which I was excluded. She occasionally let drop a detail, and over time I learned the names of the women in the group, and began to form a rudimentary idea of what they were like. But what they talked about, what they actually said, how they spent those evenings, how they organized their discussions, all of that was terra incognita. Molly wouldn't say and within a couple of weeks I stopped asking. When it was her turn to host, I was peremptorily ordered out of the apartment and that was that. And she seemed unable even to refer to the group without a degree of solemnity I would have found laughable except I was required to emulate it or risk her wrath.

*　*　*

In mid-July, Stan decided to host a get-together at his apartment to watch the final night of the Democratic Convention. A potluck sort of deal. Molly and I brought guacamole and corn chips and a six-pack of Dos Equis.

Our circle of friends overlapped with Stan's to some degree, but there were two distinct groups we didn't know well, his law school buddies and his political cohort. These, not surprisingly, constituted the bulk of the other invitees. They weren't people I usually found congenial, and since Molly and I weren't getting along so well, and because it was clear to me McGovern was doomed, I wasn't looking forward to the evening. A political convention is a bummer when you know all the hoopla and ginned up enthusiasm are devoted to a lost cause.

We arrived at about six, and there were already maybe fifteen to twenty people jammed into the small living room, some on the solitary couch and the handful of chairs, most on the floor. They swooped down on our guacamole like locusts. From the look of things, ours weren't the first hors d'oeuvres to be attacked in this fashion; the remnants of several decimated cheeses and a bowl of what may once have been clam dip were still on the table. The TV was on, some anchorman attempting to inject drama into the proceedings, but the sound was down and nobody was watching. Instead, some bearded guy seated on the couch—beards were still the distinguishing mark of the dedicated political type, and most of the men in that living room sported facial hair—was explaining (and when I say "explaining," I do mean explaining; he spoke in the didactic, supercilious drone of a graduate student analyzing a question for not-very-bright freshmen) how McGovern was sure to win big, how all the voters who had sat out the previous five or six elections because no candidates had been radical enough to appeal to them would come streaming back into the process, flooding polling places across America to cast their ballots. "Workers and farmers and black people," he added, to clarify his position.

I didn't feel like arguing. For one thing, I'd shaved that morning, so I didn't have standing. In addition, his hectoring, dogmatic forensic style was enough to dissuade me all by itself. I knew what debating those types was like: You got spritzed with doctrine, unsupported assertion, and aspersions on your political and intellectual sophistication. A thankless exercise in non-engagement. But at just that point, another bearded fellow, seated on the floor, leaning back against the wall, a cup of red wine in his hand, rushed in where I wouldn't be caught dead treading. "That's bullshit, of course," he suggested. His manner of speaking was remarkably like the other guy's. Must have been the received style in that crowd. Still, I was almost ready to applaud his willingness to engage with Bearded Schmuck #1 until he went on, "Don't you see? McGovern's just another fascist. Part of the system, part of the problem. Did I say *part* of the problem? My mistake. He *is* the problem! Sure, he sounds marginally less crazy than Nixon. Who wouldn't, except maybe Hitler? But if you think he'd change anything fundamental... Jesus." He shook his head pityingly. "Don't you see? This whole campaign is a trick to fool the masses. McGovern gives American fascism—that's 'America' with a *k*—a cloak of legitimacy. That's why they're letting him run. To believe otherwise is naïve and, and *benighted*. The election is a sham. A fixed fight. Bread and circuses for the *lumpen*. Drama without substance. No matter who wins, the plutocrats stay in control. As always."

I felt Molly stirring beside me, a nervous flutter born of internal agitation. But such was the state of our relations at that time, and such were the divergent paths we'd lately been on, I couldn't be sure whether it resulted from annoyance with the views expressed or embrace of them. I looked at her. She was frowning, but that could have meant anything. Then she suddenly said, "Then why are you here?" She was addressing Bearded Schmuck #2. Perhaps only I could hear the apprehension in her voice; she didn't want a fight, she was a little intimidated in this company, but she couldn't let this go.

"What do you mean?" Bearded Schmuck #2 asked. He had a smug little smile on his face, just discernible under the facial overgrowth, and his tone was insufferably smug. He even shot a glance at the fellow sitting next to him, an amused "this should be rich" look that made me want to throttle him. But I stayed mum. This was Molly's fight, and gallantry on my part was no longer politically or personally acceptable.

The man's challenging tone had shaken her, though. Her voice wavered as she said, "I'm wondering why you bothered coming to see him nominated if it's a fascist charade. Some of us are here because we support him, and think he's offering a little hope, and want to hear what he says. And you're kind of spoiling the experience. What's the point of being here if you think it's a joke?"

He wasn't fazed. "It's amusing. Especially the way people take it seriously."

"Meaning the way the rest of us take it seriously?"

"Well, *some* of us," he said, the sneer audible as well as visible. "For most of us, it's mainly a matter of seeing how they stage-manage the con. You know, like parents who get into pretending Santa's coming. Nothing wrong with that, so long as they remember he doesn't exist. Only children believe in Santa Claus."

You could feel the tension in the room. All side conversations had ceased. The insult was deliberate, the manner bullying. And even now I can't say whether most of the people there were on his side or thought him an overbearing blowhard. Despite my misgivings, and fully aware Molly would resent it, I was about to say something in support of her, but somebody else spoke up first. A lean, muscular guy in his upper-twenties, wearing gray wide-wale cords and a blue work-shirt. A couple of inches over six feet. Handsome in a rough-hewn, craggy way. Ruddy, clean-shaven—*that* at least gave grounds for hope—thick sandy hair, a few strands of which fell over his forehead. He had a slight hint of an Irish lilt. The corners of his eyes crinkled when he smiled, which he was doing now, and which he appeared to do readily. "Well now," he began, "maybe it's possible to try to change the system while simultaneously making the best of a bad bargain."

He inclined his head toward Molly, a little sign of support, before turning back to Bearded Schmuck #2. "One activity needn't obviate the other, do you see? Go vote for McGovern, he's the better choice and there's no harm in it. And also keep working to destroy the whole rotten system."

You could feel the tension dissipate as he spoke. That seemed to be his purpose. Ease the tension, and, incidentally or not, get Molly off the hook.

Interestingly, Bearded Schmuck #2 seemed respectful of, maybe deferential to, this guy with a (possibly fake) Irish accent. He said, in a tone that was now interrogative rather than assertive, "But isn't it better if Nixon wins? To expose the system in all its rottenness rather than letting it show its most acceptable face?"

"Ah," the fellow with the brogue answered, "in theory, perhaps. Lenin might have said so. But in practice...well, for one thing, you needn't fear on that score. This other chap hasn't a prayer. I'm sorry to say it, since so many here harbor hopes, but sadly," he went on, turning to Bearded Schmuck #1, "your beloved workers and farmers and black people...well, the black people may be an exception, but your workers and farmers haven't achieved the political consciousness you wish to ascribe to them. They *like* Mr. Nixon. It's why we have so much educational work before us. They think him a splendid fellow. They hate *you* and they like *him*. Puzzling, isn't it?" And then he shrugged, and grinned an absurdly charming, disarming grin, and the whole room, including both Bearded Schmucks, laughed. As if the joke were on Nixon rather than a Bearded Schmuck.

It was at this point that Stan emerged from the kitchen, holding a chafing dish, his hands in absurd gingham mittens, oblivious to the little drama that had unfolded in his living room. "Lasagne!" he announced cheerfully. "Come and get it!"

A few minutes later, Molly and I were sitting on the floor in a corner, eating lasagne and salad off paper plates. Our eyes occasionally wandered over toward the TV screen, where the vice presidential balloting seemed to be taking forever. The sound was still low, though, so it was hard to tell what was happening. And then Stan glided up to us, holding his own plate of food.

"So," he said, as he awkwardly hunkered down on the floor beside us, trying not to spill anything, "is the smell of victory in the air? What do you think?"

"Depends who you talk to," I said. "Either it is, or it isn't, or it doesn't matter because the whole election is a vast fraud perpetrated on the American people."

"Those would be the choices, all right."

Molly said, "Who's the Irish guy? The one with the sandy hair."

Stan looked at Molly incredulously, and then at me. All I could do was shrug; I had no idea either.

"You don't know? Corin McCabe? You've at least heard the name, right?"

"Not really," Molly said. She was speaking for both of us.

"Jeez, he's been active in the movement since forever. Before most of us knew there *was* a movement. Organized some of the first teach-ins back in '64, '65. Liaison between the Yippies and the Weathermen in Chicago. Word is, he's been in Ireland the last couple of years, something with the IRA, no one knows exactly what. They say he got out one step ahead of the Tommies. There's supposed to be a price on his head. I don't know if that's true. Some things you don't ask."

"Is he wanted?" Molly asked.

"In the U.S., you mean? I'm not sure."

"You could be harboring a fugitive."

"Don't tell Interpol."

"Where's he from?" I asked.

"New Jersey, I think."

"That would explain the accent." Which won me disapproving looks from both Molly and Stan. Evidently, Corin McCabe was above irreverence. I could see how Stan might feel that way, even though it wasn't my favorite aspect of his character. But Molly? Jesus, she hadn't even heard of the guy until a minute ago.

About half an hour later, the speeches still hadn't begun, and I was in the kitchen helping Stan with the paper plates and dirty dishes, when Bearded Schmuck #2 came in. "Listen, man," he said to me without ceremony, and without offering to help with the clean-up, "sorry if I came on a little strong there with your old lady."

"Have you apologized to *her*?" I asked.

Stan was looking on, puzzled and discomfited. He had missed the earlier contretemps, but he could sense the ill-will.

"No. She seemed a little too emotional about this for a rational discussion."

"That's women for you," I said. He looked at me without answering, realizing he'd inadvertently said something politically incorrect and been busted for it.

"Fuck you," he finally said.

Another constructive exchange of views.

When I went back into the living room, there were still no acceptance speeches on the TV. But Corin was now in command of the living room floor. It took me a minute before I saw what was up: He was trying to get people involved in a plan to force their way into a local radio station, take it over, and broadcast anti-war statements until they were arrested. I listened for a bit, with growing incredulity; he had seemed almost reasonable before, but now he sounded as nutty as the bearded contingent. He seemed like the *king* of the bearded contingent, despite his smooth cheeks. And, in that company, consisting largely of graduate students and law students and junior faculty, it was strange to see him taken seriously. There was some debate back and forth, but about practical difficulties, not the wisdom of his plan. The general sentiment seemed to be, this was worth considering. Of course, a certain kind of social dynamic was partly responsible: Nobody wanted to appear cowardly or cautious, not in front of fellow radicals and especially not in front of a Movement personage. But it was appalling anyway. Can you really get people to do anything? Not just rabble, but people whose analytical skills are supposed to have been honed at one of the world's great universities?

Finally, although I'd resolved not to get sucked into any political arguments, I couldn't help myself. "Look," I said into one of the rare pauses Corin had left, "you said earlier we have a lot of educational work before us, right?"

"Exactly. This would be a start."

"But would it really? Let's say you're some guy who's conflicted about the war, okay? You're torn about Nixon too, you have some doubts, he's kind of a creep but he seems steadfast in ways Democrats don't. You're going through a process, in other words. Okay? You know there's something wrong with the war, but you don't like the other side either, and you're not comfortable with what's been happening with your kids and so on. You don't like crime, drugs are bad, and you don't think those issues are political, they're just problems, like potholes, and somebody should fix them. You're not nuts about black people either, they make you uncomfortable with all that anger and all those demands, even though you admit they've had a raw deal. And now you turn on your radio to listen to a ballgame, maybe you're in your car, maybe you're sitting at home with a beer, and instead of the game, you hear political rants from kids you don't know presuming to tell you what to think. And soon you discover they forced their way into the radio studio. Do you believe that's going to win you friends and allies? You think that will encourage an open mind, a serious re-think? It might be satisfying on some personal, petulant level, but I don't see how it's effective in terms of your goals."

A silence greeted this. This rant of my own. Impossible to interpret the silence. Nevertheless, I already regretted having spoken. I couldn't see why I'd bothered. Except it might have been satisfying on some personal, petulant level.

The smile Corin bestowed on me was friendly, warm, unantagonistic. "Ah," he said after a few seconds, "my friends, we have a *liberal* in our midst."

Almost everybody in the room laughed derisively. "Liberal" was a term of utter contempt in radical circles. Presaging what it would eventually become to the country at large, although for different reasons. His saying it immediately put me on the defensive, although I did consider myself a liberal, unfashionable as it might be. "That's not really an answer though, is it?" I pointed out. Pointlessly. But I went on, "It's sort of the opposite, in fact. Like when Agnew calls someone a Communist." I could feel my face burning. I didn't wait for Corin's response. I turned and left the room, going back into the kitchen.

Stan was still in there, scrubbing a pot at the sink. He looked up as I entered. "The speeches start yet?" he asked.

"Not at the convention." I was wondering what Molly thought about my little exchange. I hadn't caught her eye before leaving the room. I would have welcomed some support, but I also wanted to get out of the room as quickly as possible.

"They saving the world out there?" Stan asked. He could be ironic about his political passions, a saving grace.

"Destroying it in order to save it." I picked up a dish towel and began drying dishes in the drainer. To give myself something to do that would keep me here.

A minute or so later, Corin suddenly strode in, and without preliminaries said to me, "We need to talk." He came up very close. Stan turned off the running water, the better to hear. "Your name's Zeke, yes?" He sounded markedly less Irish now.

"Yes." I put the dish towel down. A rush of adrenaline: It suddenly occurred to me he might have come to call me out. Who knew what guys pretending to be Irish were capable of? If he wanted to fight, I supposed I'd have to accommodate him. It would be too humiliating not to, even though I'd never been in a physical fight in my life (excepting a couple of scuffles with Stan in the first and second grades). We'd go outside, he'd knock me down, and with luck, that would close the matter. With luck, I wouldn't lose any teeth or eyes or testicles or anything else I regarded as valuable.

"What I said to you before? I know it came off snotty. You raised a cogent point and I didn't have a ready answer, so I went for the facile dismissal. I apologize."

He put a hand on my shoulder. And at that moment, I understood why he was a personage in the Movement. His telling me this, and his putting his hand on my shoulder, felt like a benediction. Was this what they mean by charisma?

"Don't worry about it," I said. Trying to sound both casual and macho, but I felt like a teen-age girl, which was totally disconcerting.

Stan looked on in wonderment. The second apology offered to me in his kitchen in under half an hour. And this one from no less a figure than Corin McCabe. Corin McCabe apologizing to his childhood friend Easy Stern! Impossible!

Corin went on, "The answer to your question, by the way, is, before we can educate people, we have to get their attention. Sometimes that requires shock tactics. Sometimes it requires a demonstration of strength, sometimes recklessness. Sometimes we have to provoke the oppressor into overreacting, thereby revealing his true face. Sometimes we have to cow people into silence before we can talk to them. We have to use every technique available. We can't avoid ugly methods just because they're ugly."

"I don't agree," I said. "Not, at least, in this case."

"I'm aware of that," he said. "And I'm not saying your position is untenable. I just think it's wrong. An honest disagreement." He smiled his absurdly winning smile. "I'm still enough of a liberal myself to think that's okay."

He offered his hand. It would have been impossible not to shake it. Nor was I reluctant to. He was impossible not to like, and it was equally impossible not to want him to like you back. Besides, it gave me a mean little feeling of triumph to notice Stan looking on with manifest envy. Which only increased when Corin said, "I hope we can discuss this further, Zeke. I'd enjoy talking to you. I'll be in town for a while. It's safe for me here."

Before I could answer, there was a shout from the living room. The speeches were starting. I checked my watch. After 2 AM on the east coast. The McGovern campaign obviously wasn't merely doomed, it was jinxed.

The next Friday night, Molly came home from her women's group at about midnight, as usual, but in higher spirits than usual. All I'd done that evening was eat a take-out pizza-on-french-bread from Giovanni's and read a book, and when she came in I was lying on top of the bed watching Dick Cavett.

"Hi," I said. "How was it tonight?" I always asked, even though I never got an informative answer.

"It was good," she said. "Really good. We got into some very heavy stuff." That was about as far as she ever went. Farther. She usually avoided adverbs.

"Like what?" I knew there was no point, but asking seemed obligatory.

"Personal stuff. About one of us. I can't talk about it, but it was intense. And then we had this really interesting conversation, totally unexpected, but Nita said her girlfriend hates the group, feels threatened by it, veers wildly between asking lots of questions and closing off completely when the subject comes up. So that was a big surprise to the straight women. Like, we figured lesbians would be okay about it even if guys have insecurities. But it turns out it's not a gender thing, gay women feel mystified and threatened and left out too. They wonder why they're excluded, what's going on, what's being said." She was in high spirits as she told me this, talking fast, her eyes bright.

I got up and turned off the TV. We didn't have a remote. "What do you conclude from that?"

"That's what was interesting. It turned into a kind of...I don't know how to characterize it, but it became almost confessional, where we all admitted that maybe we'd been enjoying the mystification a little too much, that maybe there's been a certain level of malice in the way we've been conducting the group and keeping our lovers in the dark. Something punitive. See, all the guys hate the group, Zeke, not just you. Some say so and some don't, but apparently they're all a little freaked. And not just the guys, as we learned tonight. Even Nita's girlfriend, Rose. Everyone feels weird that the main person in their life is talking about intimate things with a group of people they don't know from Adam. Who are probably hostile or disparaging, or at least inclined to take the member's side if a dispute is being rehashed. Not that it's necessarily like that, it mostly isn't, but the truth hardly matters, does it? I mean, it might be like that or not, but we all let you *think* it's like that. And enjoy letting you think so. Which led to a big discussion about anger and the politics of exclusion and what not. It was eye-opening."

"Okay," I said cautiously. The whole subject was still a minefield, and

116

I wasn't going to venture out into it without more encouragement.

By now I was back on the bed. Molly had kicked off her shoes and climbed on beside me, sitting on her knees, smiling more affectionately than she'd done in a while. "So I'm not the only woman in the group saying 'I'm sorry' to her significant other tonight. But I'm one of them. It was shitty and I know it and I apologize."

"Yeah?"

"Relax, Easy," she said, laughing. "This isn't a trap." She leaned down and kissed me.

Well, I wasn't immune to a display of affection. I kissed her back.

"And," she continued after she'd come up for air, "to make amends, we want to give a party. For boyfriends and girlfriends, although there's only one of those. A couple of the women even plan to bring their moms. And Joanie, I'm sure I've mentioned her, her boyfriend has a house with a big backyard, so we'll do it there. Pot-luck barbecue. Next Friday. We're all excited."

I wasn't especially excited myself—and deciding to apologize via committee seemed slightly ludicrous—but one had to appreciate the gesture. And if I'm being honest, I can't deny I'd developed some curiosity about these people; just putting faces to names would be interesting. In addition, such is human nature, I'd begun, without being aware of it, to think of them as sitting in judgment of me, and therefore—again, almost completely unconsciously—to attribute to them a stern, rather unforgiving sort of wisdom. This is a phenomenon I later studied with far more rigor and eventually made the subject of my doctoral dissertation; it's a variation of the Stockholm Syndrome. It may even explain certain aspects of religion, although I consigned that point to a footnote, since I didn't want to risk offending anyone on my thesis committee. To whom I of course attributed all sorts of unforgiving wisdom.

"Is it clothing optional?" I said.

She frowned. "You have to promise to behave, Zeke. Seriously."

Which invited more irreverence, but that was an invitation I knew I'd accept at my peril. So I restricted myself to a humble, chastened nod.

As I say, I had imbued these mysterious, faceless women with a mantle of authority, so it was almost disconcerting to meet them in the flesh and see how ordinary they were. I don't mean this pejoratively; I only mean that, had we met under less fraught circumstances, they would have seemed exactly like people I might have met under normal circumstances. The only things distinguishing them were circumstantial: They were known to Molly and not to me, they were unknown to me by design, and they conceivably knew a lot about me when I knew almost nothing about them. And I didn't know what they knew.

It was a warm late-summer night, and we were gathered on the lawn in the fragrant backyard of a guy who, I learned, worked in the offices of Mason-McDuffie, a property-management firm. Possibly alone among the people there that night, he drew a real salary, so he could afford to rent an almost grown-up sort of house. There were vegetarians amongst us, so plenty of vegetables were on the hibachi—peppers and mushrooms and onions and zucchini and eggplant—along with, thank God, burgers and sausages for the despised carnivores. And endless jugs of Almaden wine. Almaden weaned a whole generation of Californians off Coke. It was affordable without being altogether vomitous. I'd probably find it vomitous today, but in those days it seemed tolerable, and a step away from Coke and toward adulthood.

Things were awkward at first. I knew no one, and felt like an exhibit in a diorama. With a label: MOLLY'S BOYFRIEND—YOU KNOW HIS ISSUES. Everyone was friendly—no one pointed a finger at anyone else and proclaimed, "So *you're* the guy who jerks off when you think she's asleep!" or "So *you're* the guy who pees with the toilet seat down!"— so the mass humiliation imagined in my most fantastical moods didn't materialize. Which in turn led to a feeling of relief that at times resembled elation.

When I encountered Nita, for example, standing off to the side with her girlfriend, a cute, slight, short young woman of twenty or so wearing a man's blue work shirt and jeans (but looking appealingly gamine all the same), I said hello a little hesitantly. I wasn't sure she would even recognize me, or, if she did, whether her greeting would be cool and perfunctory. She hadn't been the soul of warmth the evening we'd met over a month earlier. (Of course, speaking of exhibitions in a diorama, she was decidedly another, bearing her own label: TOKEN DYKE WITH LOVER. But I was too self-absorbed to notice.) She gave me an unexpectedly friendly smile, addressed me by name, introduced me to Rose, and said, "This is weird, isn't it?"

"For you too?"

"God yes."

At which point Rose spoke up, in a small, sweet, high-pitched voice. "You want to know *how* weird? By comparison, meeting Nita's parents was a piece of cake." Got a laugh out of me.

Later, I was sitting on the grass by myself—Molly was helping out in the kitchen—a paper plate with a burger on it in my hand, a plastic cup of Mountain Burgundy on the ground beside me, when a guy about my age approached. He had a paper plate in his hand too, with a couple of sausages and some potato salad on it, along with a bright yellow puddle of French's mustard. In his other hand, he carried a whole big jug of the same brew. Moustachioed, blond, compactly-built, shaggy page-boy hair. Big sideburns. It was a look back then. Hasn't aged well. What has?

"Mind if I sit down?" he asked, with the vaguest wisp of a southern drawl.

"Not a bit. Welcome the company."

He extended his right hand, the one holding the jug of red wine, down toward me as a sort of symbolic offer to shake. "I'm Liam," he said.

I extended my tumbler up toward him. "Zeke."

He bumped the glass jug against the plastic tumbler, as if we were toasting. Then he sat down beside me and said, "Who dragged *you* here?"

"My girlfriend. Molly Hilliard."

"Don't know her. 'Course, I don't know anybody. Except *my* girl-friend. If her. Candice?"

I shook my head. "I don't know anybody either," I said. "I met one of the other women once, but only for a second. We said hello and then I was sent packing."

"This whole thing is peculiar, isn't it? Like…I'm afraid to say my name to anyone. Can't not, but I feel kind of…leery. In case…in case it *rings a bell.*"

"I doubt there's any danger with a guy. I have no idea what awful stuff's been said about you. These women take their vows of confidentiality very seriously."

"You think?"

His tone of amused skepticism, couched in that southern lilt, took me aback. "Molly doesn't tell me anything. Not even topic headlines. Do you mean…what was your girlfriend's name again?"

"Candy."

"And she tells you stuff?"

"Sometimes."

"Shit."

"What was your name again?" My face must have fallen, because he laughed. "Just kidding. Your name's Zeke and I don't have any dirt on you. When Candy tells me stuff, it's mostly 'cause it reinforces her side of an argument. Not hot gossip, more like, 'Everybody in the group says I'm right.' Invoking the nameless, numberless hordes as supporting witnesses. The way that fucker Nixon does. The silent majority. Except there's nothing silent about Candy's majority. But tell me, what are you hiding?" He grinned again, and it was friendly, conspiratorial. "Small dick? Premature ejaculator? Violent drunk?"

"So you *do* know."

"Like there's something wrong with any of that."

"Women can be so narrow-minded."

He snorted. Then, after re-filling my tumbler and taking an impressively huge swig directly out of the jug, he said, "I always liked women. Now they're starting to get on my nerves."

To show him the nervousness needn't be gender-specific, I told him about Nita and Rose, which interested and amused him in about equal measure. Then he asked what I did. So I had to ask him the same question, and he told me he wrote about rock music for a few local magazines: *Earth, Night Times,* the *Berkeley Barb, Rolling Stone.* Was I meant to be impressed? Well, I was, sort of. At least by *Rolling Stone*, which had already risen above its competitors and acquired some cachet. The John Lennon interview, the Bob Dylan interview, the relatively sophisticated graphics; it wasn't just fans saying "Groovy" and pretending that constituted criticism. Liam seemed genuinely casual about it, though, not remotely boastful, and without that nauseating see-how-hip-I-am attitude. "It's not a career, really," he said. "Doesn't pay squat, doesn't lead anywhere. I'm like completely floundering. Thinking about journalism school, although that's just a way to kill a couple of years, postponing a decision. Not that there's anything wrong with that."

"You're not beavering away on a novel?"

He colored, caught. "Of course I am. You learned that from your girlfriend?" He shut his eyes for a second, then opened them, showing laugh lines at the corners. "Nah, you figured it out, didn't you? It's that obvious. Unfortunately, it's total crap."

"About a rock band?"

He blushed deeper. "Look, it's totally adolescent, okay? I don't want to talk about it."

"No, wait, I'm on a roll here: The formation of a band among a group of high school friends, the rivalries within the group, their girlfriends, their arguments about who's the leader, local fame, jealousy, they find a manager, they get a contract, they make a record, the manager says they have to fire one of the guys in the band, and then their song shoots to number one. Am I close?"

"Fuck you!" he exploded. He was laughing, but he sounded truly indignant at the same time. I must have hit the bull's eye. "I said I don't want to talk about it! Jesus!"

What I thought at that moment was, It's going to be a best-seller. Someone has to write that book, nobody's done it yet, and this guy has Golden Boy written all over him. But I was wrong. When I finally read it, over a year later, when Liam entrusted me with a copy of the manuscript, I discovered he had no false modesty, it *was* adolescent and it *was* total crap. It was ultimately published as a paperback, with a lurid cover that made it look sexier than it actually was (there were only three sex scenes in the book, and they were all disappointingly bland), and as far as I know Liam never wrote another piece of fiction. But while I was definitely on the wrong track about the best-seller business, he was just as wrong about the "not a career" thing. Who would have thought back then it was possible to become a personage by writing about rock music as if it were a serious cultural endeavor? Probably not even Liam. He just got lucky following his bliss.

And get lucky he certainly did. And take popular culture seriously he certainly did as well. We didn't get into the subject much that evening, but in the coming weeks I learned his passion for popular music was almost limitless, his knowledge encyclopedic, his theories about its social implications grandiose and, to my mind, deeply wrong-headed. It wasn't just rock music, either, although that was his most compelling obsession. But he was almost as au courant about Hollywood movies and network television—especially from the '50s, that despised decade—and sports, and gossip magazines, and old comic books (not just the superhero ones, either; he devoted a chapter in one of his essay collections to those icky romance comics aimed at teenage girls, the ones with the dialogue balloons over the heads of two kissing lovers that say things like, "Oh, my dearest darling!"). And *Mad Magazine.* He thought it all mattered. He devoted his career to making the case that it did, that Superman unwinding in his Fortress of Solitude was as important and as enduring a figure as Achilles brooding in his tent. That Doris Day fending off Rock Hudson, or Tony Randall lusting after Jayne Mansfield, or Annette Funicello frugging on the beach with Frankie Avalon, was as vital and as profound as *The Seventh Seal* or *La Strada.* Unconvincingly to my mind, but thousands of readers and some respectable academic critics disagreed. But that came later. After we'd spent a few minutes on his novel, Molly emerged from the house and joined him and me on the lawn. I could tell she was pleased to see me talking to somebody, not sitting by myself feeling paranoid and forming harsh silent judgments. When I introduced her to Liam, she said, "Oh, Candy's boyfriend!" which made him roll his eyes.

She caught it. But there was something so likable about Liam, she didn't take offense. "What?" she asked. "What is it?"

"Nothing. Except…well, you tell me. What do you think? As advertised?"

"I don't know yet," she answered. "Do I?"

"Depends what you've heard."

"Only good things," she assured him.

It had obvious flirtatious tendencies, this exchange, but it didn't make me uncomfortable. Liam's considerable appeal was invariably flirtatious, I could already see that. But it didn't seem purposeful, just playful.

A little later, a skinny, very tall, slightly ungainly, not especially pretty girl approached us. Liam and Molly both greeted her, and Liam introduced us. This was Candy, his girlfriend. She surprised me; I expected someone more attractive. My cynical observation back then—and I haven't found reason to revise it—is that good-looking people sleep with good-looking people. Or rich people. Candy wasn't especially good-looking, and gave no sign of being rich. But really, none of this mattered, it was just a casual observation. I was on the lookout for attitude—by which I mean hostile, unwelcoming attitude—and since she gave no sign of that, I decided I liked her. I'd already taken to Liam. I was a pushover that night.

A little later, while Liam and I were at the picnic table that was serving as a buffet table, helping ourselves to fruit salad, I surreptitiously indicated Nita and Rose to him. They were standing some distance away, heads together, and it looked as if they were talking heatedly. Occasional vehement gestures. "Those are the ones I was telling you about, over there by the tree," I said quietly. "The lesbians. Don't be too obvious. The redhead's the one in the group. The little one's our sister-in-exile."

He looked. "They make a cute couple," he said, with such muted inflection I couldn't tell what sort of humor, if any, he intended. We weren't required to be solemn about lesbians yet, but crude dyke jokes would clearly have been out of place.

A little later, when I was talking to Molly and the guy with the job at Mason-MacDuffie (and the girlfriend who used his home to entertain a group he was barred from attending), I noticed that Liam had joined Rose and Nita at the other end of the lawn, and was pouring them wine and saying something that made them both laugh. About a half-hour after that—it was past dusk by this time, and the light pouring out of the windows at the back of the house was casting long shadows across the lawn—I saw him with Candy and Nita, and not long after that I saw him pouring Rose another glass of wine, and the two of them laughing uproariously. And I thought, "My my, this fellow's sure cultivating the lesbians tonight."

The barbecue went till past eleven, a sign that all had gone unexpectedly well. As we were driving home, Molly said, "There, that wasn't so fearsome, was it?"

"No," I agreed, "everyone seemed nice. And perfectly normal. It was almost disappointing."

"But in a good way, right?" Molly prompted, with a little laugh.

"Oh yes, if only everything could be so disappointing."

"And you and that guy Liam seemed to hit it off."

"I liked him."

"He's not a segregationist or anything, is he?"

Back then, a southern accent was all it took to arouse suspicions. "I didn't get that impression, no."

She touched my right hand, resting on the steering wheel. "I appreciate you made an effort tonight, Zeke. Didn't just sit back and glower."

I glanced over at her. "Why, thank you."

"Maybe we ought to do something with Liam and Candy sometime."

"I'm game."

"He seems like a good guy. Candy's nuts about him."

"He..." I wanted to say he struck me as too good-looking for her, but that seemed ill-advised, so I said instead, "He's an attractive fellow, isn't he?"

"Quite dashing, no question about it. Candy's worried about being able to hold on to him. But he tells her he loves her and doesn't want anyone else."

"It's a mysterious thing, love is," I said. I had to choose my words with care; I was afraid mentioning I found a woman unattractive would be regarded as evidence of contemptible crudity. The same would be true if I admitted finding her attractive, of course. To acknowledge physical appeal at all, even its existence in the abstract, had somehow become politically unacceptable.

God, the horseshit we had to put up with.

As it turned out, Molly and I never did get together with Liam and Candy. They broke up before the summer ended. And Molly's women's group, which was occupying so much of her energy and attention that same summer, didn't survive to autumn either. It disbanded abruptly, with shocking suddenness, amidst a swirl of rage and recrimination and screaming feuds. Cries of betrayal. Irreparable injuries. Startling sexual shenanigans. All of it fascinating stuff, unquestionably, but all of it soon to be the least of my concerns.

Six

NOW

Zeke's first impulse was to use his office. He felt at home there, and it was arranged with the specific purpose of encouraging clients to relax and open up. An autumnal color scheme, soft furniture, blandly soothing art on the walls, area rugs to absorb reverberation. An additional advantage, it was the only place on the planet where Zeke was more accustomed to listen than talk. But it would have been a mistake. For one thing, Ashley would regard it as *his*, and therefore alien. And, of course, it was an official, certified, unapologetic, tax-deductible psychotherapist's office; she would resent the notion that she required anything like therapy, even in the form of an ostensibly casual chat with her stepfather. She was scornful about psychology anyway (although that had more to do with wanting to wound Zeke than any evolved position on the issue). In addition, using his office would make the whole transaction feel too focused, too purposeful. Under those perceived circumstances, she would raise her personal drawbridge and flood her personal moat and position her personal archers at every window-slit in every turret. Ashley wasn't an easy girl to have a casual chat with at the best of times, but he knew he'd better try to engineer one if he hoped for anything useful to come of it.

So instead, he offered to drive her to San Francisco Monday evening. She had a regularly-scheduled dinner with her father every Monday— every Monday when he didn't choose to cancel at the last minute—and transportation was always an issue. Olivia used to go too, and Olivia drove, but she'd been boycotting recently, angry at some perceived dereliction on Dennis' part; it was an untypical display of spite from the older daughter, almost a reversal of roles, with Ashley compliant and Olivia stubbornly rebellious. She'd been sticking to her guns for over a month now. It bothered Molly, and it might have been having some sort of impact on Dennis, but Zeke refused to get dragged into *that* dispute. Dennis never offered to come to Berkeley—he apparently felt ninety minutes a week for the offspring of his first marriage was sacrifice enough—and since Ashley disliked BART, especially at night, Zeke was confident she'd accept him as chauffeur. Which she did without argument. She must have realized he intended to ask about her bruise. On some level, she'd probably been waiting for him to make an overture.

"You okay about taking BART home?" he asked her as he eased the Prius out of the garage.

"You're not going to wait for me outside the restaurant?" And then she added, "Wearing a dark jacket and a little cap?" just to make clear she was kidding.

"That wasn't my intention, no," he said with a smile. "But you'll be half a block from the Embarcadero station. I'm sure Dennis'll walk you to it. Give Olivia a call when your train's near North Berkeley and she'll pick you up."

"Man, you just can't find good help nowadays," she said. And then she added, "Or good fathers." No way *that* statement was innocuous, but since it was aimed at Dennis rather than him, Zeke didn't rise to the bait.

Dennis Baker. Father of his step-daughters. His husband-in-law. A tricky relationship at best. The man did something in the high-tech world, Zeke could never figure out exactly what, he either owned a company or occupied some powerful position in a company, and seemed to be doing quite well for himself, thank you very much. Not, perhaps, by the extravagant standards of Silicon Valley, but according to any sensible human yardstick. Zeke figured his wealth must be in eight figures. Enough so that Zeke was glad Molly wasn't an avaricious type, one who might cast an occasional wistful glance backward. But no, when she spoke about Dennis at all, it was in a tone lying somewhere between indifference and mild disrespect. Stan would claim Molly was a different person from the Molly who married Dennis, and therefore felt no connection to either the man or even the woman in that marriage.

For his part, Zeke's dealings with Molly's ex were at least correct, maybe even cordial. There had been no overlap between them, so neither had reason to feel territorial proprieties had been violated. Dennis was always affable the rare times their paths crossed. He'd declined the invitation to Zeke and Molly's wedding, pleading a scheduling conflict, but no one really expected him to accept. The invitation was a courtesy, issued at Zeke's insistence, to set an example for the girls. Dennis sent them a generous gift, a handsomely-framed Matisse drawing, to demonstrate the absence of hard feelings.

For a while, Zeke even thought he might like the guy. Dennis had been trained as an engineer at Stanford, but his considerable intelligence wasn't narrowly focused; he was interested in the world, he had social skills, even a sense of humor. There had been some unexpected kidding around between them at a couple of junctures, and the spontaneous laughter that ensued had felt genuine and comradely. Not bad for a Republican, was Zeke's assessment at the time.

When Molly confessed to Zeke that her first husband was a Republican, Zeke's incredulity was unfeigned, as, to all appearances, was Molly's embarrassment. "But he's one of the good ones," she added, a little defensively. "Pro-choice and okay with gay marriage and so on. He just likes their tax policies." When Zeke just stared at her, she added, "Also, did I mention he's an asshole?"

The only, but ultimately decisive, problem Zeke had with Dennis was that he was a negligent father; over time, witnessing slight after oblivious slight, Zeke soured on him, concluding he was a self-indulgent prick. In a way, it made life easier, Dennis' neglectful behavior; the girls were less confused by conflicting sources of authority, and there were fewer logistical complications when planning travel and holiday celebrations. But it was still unconscionable, and Zeke knew as a matter of fact both girls felt deeply hurt by, and resentful of, their father. He'd started a second family a couple of years ago, with a very pretty and much younger second wife, and his devotion to his new baby daughter was so extravagant it sometimes made Olivia and Ashley laugh out loud, but with fury and astonishment, not mirth.

Now, out of the corner of his eye, Zeke saw Ashley examining her eye in the mirror on the reverse of the passenger-side sun visor. He suspected he was meant to see it. She was giving him an assist. "How's it look?" he asked.

"You tell me."

"Fading."

"Yeah, I think it's mostly gone."

"Good. I wouldn't want Dennis to suspect me of anything."

"He won't notice. He never notices anything. And he trusts you."

"Nobody trusts anybody when their daughter has a black eye." He added, "Or their step-daughter."

"Dad's different. Where Livy and I are concerned, he'd rather trust than verify. It's easier."

"Well, it's tough with a second family—" Zeke began.

"Nah," Ashley interrupted, "he was like that before Megan was born. Before he married Kate, even. You don't have to defend him, Zeke. He's a selfish jerk."

"Yes, he is," Zeke was surprised to hear himself saying. Was he agreeing to win her trust, or because what she said was true and she deserved to have it validated? He felt her eyes on him. She was more surprised than he was. He and Molly had spent a lot of time defending Dennis over the years. It was meant to spare the girls' feelings, but at some point it may have begun to have the opposite effect, denying them the evidence of their own experience.

129

"It isn't that he doesn't love you," Zeke went on. "But he's one of those people…I'm not defending him, Ash, honestly, but he's…it's hard for him to think about what isn't in front of him. It may be selfishness, as you say, or it may just be a failure of imagination."

"It's selfishness," Ashley said flatly. "If there's something he wants—a car, or a painting, or a woman—it doesn't matter if it's in front of him or not. He'll remember. He'll do whatever it takes to get it."

Zeke nodded. She was obviously right. Dennis was careless when his appetites weren't engaged, attentive when they were. It was as simple as that.

"Did you just nod?" she asked. She was sharp today.

Busted, he couldn't help laughing. "I did, yeah. You're right. I wish you weren't, but you are."

"Shitheads should be castrated before they reproduce," she said.

"That might be a little draconian." He waited a few seconds, and abruptly decided not to wait any further. "Okay, Ash, you ready to talk?"

She sighed dramatically, and turned to look out the window on her side. "Oh brother," she said. "I should've known. You had an ulterior motive all along."

"Cut the crap," he answered, but good-humoredly enough so she wouldn't take umbrage. "We've been tiptoeing around it for a couple of days now."

"Look, okay, I'll tell you about it, but you have to promise not to tell mom."

A clear non-starter. "You know I can't do that."

"But—"

"If I agree, we'll both know I'm lying. Of course I have to tell Molly."

After a long pause, she said, "Yeah, okay. But some of this might press some of her buttons. Will you at least…God, I don't even know how to say it…"

"You want me to explain it to her in the least awful way I can?"

She actually laughed. "I guess that's what I'm asking, yeah."

"I'll do my best, Ash. That's all I can promise. Buttons are buttons."

"See, the thing is…God, this is embarrassing. The thing is, I sort of had it coming." She laughed again. Or so Zeke thought, until he looked over and saw she was crying.

Molly had to admit Corin was looking good. Whatever he'd been through, presumably a lot, he'd aged with rough-hewn grace. It didn't necessarily come as a surprise: He had the kind of looks that could sustain a lot of wear and tear. Craggy, crinkly, strong-featured, he could absorb punishment and emerge looking virile, wised-up, toughened. Like Clint Eastwood, say, or John Wayne. And like them, he'd kept himself lean, he'd stayed wiry, he still moved with cat-like grace.

They were sitting in a coffee house on Bancroft, across from campus. Corin poured the entire contents of a small paper packet of brown sugar into his coffee and stirred. The sugar seemed anomalous. Sissified. Did John Wayne empty a full sachet of sugar into his coffee? Or was she looking for something to disapprove of? That would have been Zeke's interpretation. The thought of Zeke gave her an unpleasant jolt, as if she were doing something wrong, something treacherous, rather than simply acceding to an old friend's invitation to get coffee. Yeah, right. She took a sip of her latte. A latte was *really* sissified, but hell, she was a girl, it was okay for her to be sissified. It had taken her a long time to accept that.

"You looked good up there," he said. The Irish lilt in his voice was still in place, maybe even more pronounced, or at least more convincing, than in the past. "In that big lecture room, I mean. You looked like you belonged."

"I do belong. It's what I do. It's what I've done my whole adult life."

"I wasn't suggesting otherwise," he said. "But some people, they try to exude authority and they can't pull it off, it just diminishes them. Whereas it fits you like an old pair of Levis."

"Well—" She was never good at accepting compliments, and accepting compliments from Corin occupied its own uniquely difficult niche.

But he rode right over whatever she might have managed to stammer. "Besides, it wasn't only your authority. Forgive me for putting it like this, but you've aged so beautifully. You look wondrous, girl. I would have known you instantly."

Best not even to acknowledge this. She could sense the color rising in her cheeks, and cursed herself for it. "It's been a long time," she said. "Am I allowed to ask what you've been up to all these years?"

"Depends. Are you prepared to become an accessory?" He grinned, a sudden, incandescent grin, to signal this wasn't serious. "No, the thing is…God, it would take hours to tell you everything. Days. I've been all the hell over. Was afraid to stay anywhere too long. North Africa for a while. The Middle East, Palestine and that. Knocked around Europe a bit. Lately Dublin's been home base, insofar as I have one. With plenty of side-trips. My lamentable instinct for turmoil."

"How have you managed?"

"Living off the land, I'm tempted to say. Maybe that's too grandiose. It hasn't been pure resourcefulness. There are people who help fellas like me."

It was hard to maintain eye-contact. She peered into the muddy depths of her latte and asked, "And…has all this been…I don't know… fulfilling in some way?"

"Oh, Mols…no. No. Christ. It's mostly just been exhausting. Especially when it finally dawned on me I've wasted my time. Wasted my life. We're given a finite span on the planet, and I've pissed away far too much of mine."

He was staring at her. She could feel it. She forced herself to look up at him, an effort of will. Perhaps she was seeking some sign of falsity. But the expression on his face was set, serious. His sky-blue eyes looked troubled, almost haunted. With Corin, though, it was always hard to disentangle blarney from truth.

Almost as if he could read her mind, still looking her squarely in the eye, he said, "I've been full of shit for so much of my life." No drama or apparent self-pity. "Radicalism is a young man's game not only because it takes energy, but because you need to be callow. Or a bit stupid." A sad smile; he wasn't expecting contradiction. "You know the old drug-dealer saying? 'Don't get high on your own supply?' We activists need the same lesson. I let myself get high on my own doctrinal crap."

"You don't believe it anymore?"

"Oh Jesus, I don't know *what* I believe. I'm like a fucking whisky priest with night-sweats. I suppose I still—to be pompous—believe in justice. Although hearing myself utter the word is enough to make me gag. But nevertheless, justice seems worth fighting for. I still think the world's fucked up and capitalism's bollocks. But I have no answers. I'm not sure there *are* answers. Maybe we just have to muddle through and cultivate our garden and try to be decent to each other, one small act of kindness at a time." He caught himself. "God, listen to me! I sound like a liberal. After all these years."

"You sound more like a conservative, actually."

"I used to deny there was a meaningful difference."

"So…" It wasn't merely that the next question that occurred to her was almost impossible to pose. It was also that she wasn't sure she wanted to delve into anything so deeply with him. But having started, it was impossible to stop. "So when you look back…when you consider…I mean…" She gave up helplessly, looking pained.

He grinned at her again. "Molly Hilliard at a loss for words! Unthinkable!"

"I'm only fluent about English literature," she said, laughing self-consciously.

"You were always fluent about everything, Molly. Quite the intimidating lass you were. Forced a fella to scramble, just to try to keep abreast."

She stared down at her latte again and didn't respond. This was exactly the sort of conversational byway she wanted to avoid.

"You were going to ask about regrets, I think?" he prompted after a few moments.

"Something along those lines."

He nodded. "Yeah. Well. Nothing but. Every waking moment. My conscience is like a Dali painting. On bad nights, Hieronymus Bosch. But…there's nowhere to go with those feelings. Do you see what I mean? It's unseemly even to talk about them, isn't it? Just another luxury I don't have the right to grant myself. Since there are no reparations I can make, no way of changing anything. Unless—not that this would be adequate—unless I volunteer in some African AIDS clinic. Which I may do yet." He hesitated, and then he smiled a melancholy smile, but there seemed to Molly to be at least a hint of self-mockery in it. "I'm still re-assessing."

"Sounds like you've been doing quite a bit of re-assessing."

"It's been a long process. Long, ongoing, and probably, at the end of the day, another form of futile self-indulgence."

"Was there a moment when it started?"

"When the scales fell from my eyes, like? No. No. And it's not as if the nonsense stopped after...after what happened here. There was further mischief in various venues. Much. All for a noble cause, needless to say." He rolled his eyes. "But then....I don't know, years went by, things quieted down, and it began to dawn on me that the world had moved on and everything I once believed was either completely wrong or had ceased to matter. As if I'd been a member of a cult where we'd been saying the end of the world was nigh, and then the world didn't come to an end, and for a while we just revised our predictions, but it became progressively clear it wasn't going to, we'd got it entirely wrong. And after that, I had no defenses at all. As if I was in Jonestown and it started dawning on me Jim Jones was a fucking lunatic. Except it was worse, because to a modest degree I *was* Jim Jones."

She had no immediate answer. It was too immense. Also too immense to be dissimulated. Probably. With Corin, you couldn't be 100% sure. As a con man, he had always been his own first, most gullible victim. That's why he was so persuasive.

The silence lingered. Almost anything either of them said would have been inadequate. Finally, Corin said, "I understand you're with Zeke."

It was evident he was offering this as a simple way out of the dead-end in which they found themselves, but Molly stiffened. "I don't want to talk about that," she said. And then, "Where'd you hear that? Who have you been talking to?" And before he could answer, she went on, "We were apart for over twenty years. Completely out of touch. We're together now. It's a different lifetime."

"And you're married," he said. "I heard it from Stan."

"You've been talking to Stan?"

"Yeah, we've been in touch. He's going to help me. With my...situation."

"Your legal situation?"

"That's the hope."

"Does he think—"

He didn't let her finish the question. "I'm not supposed to discuss it, Mols. Shouldn't have said anything. It's much too early to tell. The whole thing might fall apart. Whatever happens, he assures me it won't be a cakewalk. But I'm not looking for a cakewalk. Just closure." Another sad smile. "Still...serving a long stretch...maybe I have it coming, but at my age, a long stretch is a life sentence. And it wouldn't bring anyone back, or teach me anything I don't already know."

Despite your passion for justice, is what she thought to herself, ginning up a rancor she wasn't really feeling. It almost made her uneasy, that she felt so little. Not on her own behalf; she couldn't and didn't regard herself as an injured party. But there was so much to deplore about Corin, however hard he might be to dislike.

He took a sip of coffee. "I'll tell you one thing that's changed about this town since the old days. The coffee. The coffee got good. When did that happen?"

She smiled. "While you were here, actually. You just weren't paying attention. And not just coffee. There was a foodie revolution."

"So at least *one* revolution succeeded." He paused. "It's surprising, something so bourgeois happening in the radical capital of the United States."

"The radicals grew up. Some of us."

"I didn't realize maturity excludes idealism." He quickly added, "Not that I'm complaining. The food in Dublin...there are a couple of wannabe bistros and that, but no one gives a shit about creature comforts, not in fucking Ireland. We wouldn't know pleasure if we stumbled over it. Except for fags and Guinness and sex. And I've given up fags. The Dail banned 'em in public places, I've quit in private."

"Never thought that could happen."

"Doctor's orders." He shrugged. "Oh, there's heroin now too."

Her eyes widened. "You do that?"

He looked startled. "No, no. Drugs were never my thing. Even in the day. Maybe a little pot, to be sociable. And those two acid trips we took together, so I wouldn't lose your respect. But otherwise...I thought drugs dissipated revolutionary energy, that's the sort of prat I was. Even when I made a good decision, it was for naff reasons. Dublin's got a heroin epidemic, but not my crowd. We're a bunch of old fogies, nattering on about socialism over our pints, bitching about modern youth."

"Did you ever get married? Have kids?"

"No to the first, probably not to the second."

"Is it dangerous for you here?"

"More than elsewhere?" He shrugged. "Stan thinks not. The case is cold, so's the trail. Nobody's looking...It's been forever since I felt hot breath on my neck. I mean in a bad way." A sudden grin, and then, when it wasn't returned, he quickly went on, "That's why Stan thinks we might be able to strike some sort of bargain."

"When I first heard about...that whole business, I thought it might be a frame-up."

"I wish." He sighed. "They already didn't like me, true. I was in their sights. But I provided the ammunition they needed."

"It just didn't seem in character. I knew something was coming, maybe even something bad, but nothing like that."

"It wasn't meant to happen the way it did. Things got out of hand. But no excuses. I knew the risks. When you plan a thing like that, you're not assembling a chapter of Mensa, you don't sift through piles of applications for the ideal candidates. You push ahead with what you've got. Which often means cretins and hotheads."

"Did you pull a trigger?" Even as she spoke, she realized how presumptuous this was. Not just presumptuous; its bluntness channeled an anger she otherwise wasn't aware of feeling. But her emotions were unclear to her right now. Seeing Corin was a shock; it would take a while to untangle all the things she felt.

"I'm not supposed to talk about it," he said. "Stan's orders. I've already said more than I should. Because I'm a big mouth by nature. And because…" He struggled for a moment, visibly, to figure out how to finish the sentence, and then didn't. "Anyway. Yes, I did. Pull a trigger. Not at first. When all hell broke loose." When she didn't respond, he added, "Not that it matters, but mine weren't the lethal bullets. Frankly, I was too panicked to aim. So I hit a wall, a desk, and a cardboard display of favorable mortgage rates. It makes no difference legally, and it doesn't make much morally, but it's a very small, very cold comfort." He bit his lower lip and looked out the window at the people walking up and down Bancroft.

"Something bad was due to happen," Molly said. "I didn't know it would be *so* bad, that was a shock, but you were bent on getting yourself into trouble. To prove you weren't like those grad students you hung with, all that big talk and wankery."

"You knew that then?"

"It wasn't hard to see. You despised them. Even while dazzling them."

"No, that I'd end up doing something."

"Yes."

"Is that why you—?"

"Only partly. I can't even say whether that side of your personality was more attractive or repellent to me. I mean, obviously it was both. And the balance shifted over time. Because of other things. But we're not going to discuss this, okay?"

He reached across the table and took her hand. It startled her, even offended her, slightly. Her impulse was to pull her hand away, but she was afraid that would seem too rude, too definitive. "Can I see you again?" he asked.

"I don't think so," she said, and withdrew her hand. Firmly. Not disguising the gesture. Why should his sensibilities be the ones that were spared? "I don't think it would be a good idea."

He nodded, apparently accepting it. But then he went on, "There's so much I'd like to ask you. And tell you. That's the thing. It feels like we have unfinished business. Maybe another coffee sometime, that's all I'm asking."

"I don't know, Corin."

He smiled at her. "I'm making progress," he said.

Stan had agreed to host the Bay Area launch party for Liam's latest book, *White Bucks*. It wasn't the first time; he'd done two others. He had the house for it and enjoyed the hoopla. Carla wouldn't let him use caterers, a point of simultaneous consternation and pride to him. Given the sort of guest list Liam and his publishers drew up, replete with San Francisco's monied boho and its well-connected, Stan was aware the canapés ought to be nouvelle and flashy, with things like raw fish and duck carpaccio and little bits of kiwi lurking where they didn't belong. Not chopped liver and egg salad and stuffed derma, not even lox, not unless it was re-dubbed smoked salmon. According to Stan, Carla either failed or refused to understand this. "I can do it better than any caterer," she'd insist.

"That isn't the issue, honey," he would say. "Of course you can. But you're a haimisher cook and this isn't a haimisher crowd. It's Liam's people. Francis Coppola might be coming. Michael Chabon. Jerry and Anne Brown, just maybe. Your food is great, everyone acknowledges that, but it isn't the right *kind* of food."

"If they want my house, they can eat my food," Carla would say. "If they don't want my food, they can have their party someplace else."

When it reached this point, Stan told Zeke, and it always did sooner or later, he stopped arguing. Her tone declared the issue non-negotiable. But as Zeke knew from past experience, at the end of the night, after the last person on Liam's stellar guest list said goodnight, it was Stan who would point out there wasn't a scrap left, they'd annihilated Carla's offerings like a ravening mob of starved shtetl dwellers.

Zeke was finding some amusement in these reflections as he hurriedly dressed. After dropping Ashley off in San Francisco, he'd rushed home to prepare for the party. Molly had gone on ahead of him, to provide Liam some personal support as things got underway. Liam was a nervous wreck at these things, often even felt tempted to take a calming drink. Before sobriety, he used to get very drunk at launch parties and sometimes made an unpleasant scene before the evening was over.

Zeke now stood in his boxers and socks in the doorway of his closet, trying to decide what to wear. Unlike most Berkeley events, this one required a jacket and tie. Once upon a time, in high school and briefly in college, he'd been a bit of a dude, probably because of his ready access to Sy's stockrooms. That was a long time ago.

But he felt an obscure desire to look good tonight. One of the things he liked about Berkeley was how irrelevant personal vanity, or at least personal adornment, was. He dressed casually when he saw his clients, in khakis or cords or jeans, and usually dressed similarly when he and Molly went out to dinner with friends. Tonight, though, he found himself examining the paltry contents of his closet with serious attention. He didn't want Liam's crowd to judge him as just another college town schlump. Why? That was a question for another time.

Picking a jacket wasn't a problem. Last Christmas, Molly had bought him a Brioni blazer that was just the ticket for an event like this. Cashmere. Must have set her back a pretty penny. He'd been waiting ever since for an occasion worthy of the garment. Its pattern, a yellowish tan and azure blue windowpane, was a little louder than anything he would have picked out for himself, but when he tried it on, it looked damned snappy. But dress pants remained a challenge. Dress pants were always a challenge. Not just selecting a pair that matched the jacket, but worse, the trauma attendant upon zipping up the fly and buttoning the waist. Would there be uncomfortable tightness, a rebuke for having put on weight? These were always an anxious few moments, and the outcome could wreck his mood for the evening.

He grabbed a hanger with a pair of navy gabardine pants and held them up against the jacket. Looked fine, although he wished Molly was around for a consult. But there was blue in the jacket, it was probably okay. He got the pants off the hanger, stepped into them, pulled them up, and, holding his breath, closed them. Triumph! They might even require a belt. Praise Jesus!

Tie and shirt, no prob. He had a natty Armani combo from the Christmas before last—blue shirt, blue-and-taupe striped tie—that went well with the jacket. Molly had already told him so. The ensemble had her official endorsement.

Shoes on. These Bruno Maglis I never wear. O.J. Simpson might have regarded them as "ugly-ass," but damn it, they're just the ticket.

And I'm outta here.

Finding a parking space close to Stan's house on Grizzly Peak proved impossible. So many cars lined the street on Stan's block, the party must already be in full swing. In the end, he had to walk almost half a mile from where he left his car. There wasn't much illumination up here, and there was no sidewalk; it was a nervous six-minute trek from car to house. He could hear the noise from the party almost as soon as he started walking. When he reached Stan's house, he entered to find a mob-scene. Le tout Bay Area. There was Willy Brown, suave and elegant, holding court in the living room. Dick Blum, sans Dianne, discussing something unimaginable with Boz Scaggs. Michael Tilson Thomas, Dave Eggers, and Francis Ford Coppola formed another tight little cluster near the fireplace. Man! Liam traveled in exalted circles when he wasn't slumming with his old pals.

The beauty of being a Berkeleyite, though, was that it was hard to tell when you were slumming and when you weren't. Everybody did such different things, and had such different values and aspirations, you were rarely in direct competition with anybody else, and so could never be sure how your status rated. Social life was egalitarian because the pecking order was so hard to determine. Oh, if you were in the physics department, say, you knew which of your colleagues had a Nobel. But in general, a democratizing aesthetic prevailed. Tom Wolfe would be totally at sea here.

Zeke set off to find Molly, but before he succeeded, he bumped into a flushed and happy Liam, a glass of sparkling water in his hand. "Zeke!" he said. "I was starting to worry." If he had suffered pre-party nerves, he was past them now. His manner was excited and happy, with no sign of anxiety. He was wearing chinos and an open-neck shirt, making Zeke worry he was over-dressed.

140

"Had to take Ashley to the city," Zeke answered. And then, surveying the room, he added, "You got quite a turn-out."

"Yeah. Must've been a slow night across the bay. Everybody said yes."

"They're fans."

"Hardly. I doubt any of them'll read the book."

"*I* will."

"Yeah?"

"I always read your books, Liam."

"But you think they're crap."

"Well, don't ask for the moon." And then, "What's this one about?"

Liam hesitated, knowing he was likely to be joshed. But then he plunged in. "Those white, sort of proto-rock or quasi-rock type singers from the fifties. Not Elvis, of course. Or the Everly Brothers, or Buddy Holly. I've already written about those guys, the ones with hillbilly authenticity. This is about the *really* white ones. The commercial ones. Pat Boone. Rick Nelson. Jimmy Clanton, remember him? Bobby Rydell. Fabian. Frankie Avalon. That breed."

"It's a reassessment? Explaining why they're actually better than we think? Loaded with significance from a cultural-historical perspective?"

Liam refused to look abashed, and he never took umbrage. But he did grant Zeke a lopsided smile, just to signal he didn't take himself or his life's work too seriously. "Sort of. I mean, I make distinctions among them, of course. Some were better than others. But it's analysis rather than appreciation. What it meant in the context of the post-war period, what it said about popular culture and sex and race relations and so on."

"See? Your books *are* crap."

Liam laughed and put an arm around Zeke's shoulders. "Ah, Easy," he said, "it's old friends who keep a guy humble."

"But don't judge by me," Zeke said. He was worried he might have gone too far. It was so much fun to tease Liam, and for this group of old friends, joshing was such an accustomed modality, he sometimes let himself forget Liam wrote these books because he cared about this stuff. Had devoted his life to it. And possessed a *Jeopardy*-worthy store of knowledge. "I'm sure there are lots of folks who consider your books provocative and illuminating."

"First of all, fuck you. And second, get yourself a drink. And while you're at it, elevate your cholesterol count. Carla's handiwork is in the kitchen."

"Have you seen Molly?"

"She was in the kitchen a couple of minutes ago. With Melanie. Avoiding the chopped liver while singing its praises to Carla."

"That's my girl. Tact's her middle name. I bet Melanie avoided it too."

"Circled it warily. Listen, I gotta mix, Zeke. I'm the guest of honor."

"Go. Go."

He watched Liam head into the living room, making a beeline for Willy Brown. Networking. Liam nurtured his networks, with movers and shakers and with old friends. More power to him. He hadn't abandoned the latter when he'd been embraced by the former. Zeke smiled affectionately, and then turned, heading toward the kitchen. There was a worse mob scene in there; as at the poker game, the food was laid out on the central island, but tonight a bar with a white table cloth on it and a white-jacketed bartender behind it had also been set up against one wall. No immediate sign of Molly. Zeke got himself a scotch-rocks, and then braced himself for the gauntlet that was the buffet. But before he delivered or endured even a single body block, somebody said, "Hey, Zeke, nice threads," and he turned to find Stan.

Stan was wearing a gray pin-striped suit and bright red tie. Must be what he wore to court. Except for his wild Medusa head of gray hair, he almost looked respectable. "You too." Then, casting a glance toward the mob milling around the food, Zeke added, "Quite a bash, Stan. You'll be in Leah Garchik tomorrow."

Stan smiled, a wacky gleam in his eye. "Not too shabby, eh? We've got two former mayors, and the governor might be coming…Pretty good for 'a prominent left-wing lawyer,' as the *Chron* still insists on calling me."

"How'd you manage it?"

"Liam."

"That was my next question. How does *he* manage it?"

"He's carved out a unique identity for himself."

"But his books are bullshit."

"No one reads his books. They read Leah Garchik."

Zeke surveyed the room again. It had filled up even further in the last few minutes. "I hope his publisher is paying for all this," he said after a moment.

"I stopped hoping for that two books ago. Please don't tell Liam. He'd try to pay me back, I'd never hear the end of it." Suddenly, a slightly uncomfortable look appeared on Stan's face. He lowered his voice to say, "Listen, this probably isn't worth mentioning, but…a certain person asked if he could come tonight."

Zeke's body understood before he did. Sweat sprang into his armpits almost instantaneously, his pulse accelerated. "Corin."

Stan nodded. "He-who-must-not-be-named."

Zeke felt a tremor of irritation, complicating the unwelcome agitation he was already experiencing. "Jesus, Stan. I'm not a child." Anything to preserve face.

"It isn't to spare your feelings. I assume you can handle hearing his name. It's for legal reasons. For everyone's protection."

This was news; previously, Zeke had only picked up hints. "He's here?"

"You really want to know any of this?"

"Might as well. We've come this far."

"Okay. He's staying here now. For the time being. I'm putting him up. Which you must forget immediately, as soon as this conversation is over."

"Carla must be thrilled."

Stan made a twisty-mouthed face. "Overjoyed. She feels like the yenta Harriet Tubman." This got a reluctant laugh out of Zeke. "It's supposed to be brief. Till his situation clarifies, or he finds a place. Anyway, about tonight's party, I told him, under no circumstances. Now please, I haven't told you any of this."

"Okay. Got it. Thanks for…you know, not letting me know."

"I put it on Ed Lee and Jerry and so on. Said it would be uncomfortable for them. He said he understood. I'm sure he won't make a surprise appearance. Now go get yourself some food, for Christ's sake. It's not gonna be there for long."

Zeke nodded, and insinuated himself into the crowd around the central island. Despite the multiplicity of unpleasant sensations he was feeling, he was suddenly also aware he was famished. Parties like this were troublesome places when you were hungry; you could wolf down several meals' worth of canapés and not feel you'd eaten at all. Still, once he'd forced his way through, the best he could manage were a couple of Saltines with chopped liver before he let himself be elbowed aside.

He wondered if he should tell Molly about Corin. What would her feelings be? And where was she, anyway?

That's when he saw her waving to him. She was in the family room adjoining the kitchen, standing with Melanie, largely hidden behind the mass of people who had also congregated there. Deliberately lying low, probably. Molly and Melanie were both shy in big crowds, especially crowds full of luminaries. He saluted his wife with his drink and then made his way toward her. It was slow going, seeing as how he didn't want to spill any scotch. Macallan was not something to be spilled lightly.

"Howdy," he said when he finally reached them. He gave Molly a kiss on the cheek, and then gave Melanie one as well. Was it his imagination, or did Molly receive his kiss somewhat passively? She didn't meet his eye, barely inclined her head in his direction, and perhaps most surprising, didn't mention his jacket.

"You two look swell," he said. And it was true; both of them had taken advantage of this rare occasion for dress-up; Molly was in a sleek navy-blue chalk-striped Armani suit, fetchingly tapered at the waist, and Melanie wore a black cocktail number that flattered the body she had kept so trim over the years. Zeke suddenly had an odd memory, from the eighth grade, of Stan taunting Melanie for no reason Zeke could recall, calling her "Captain Kidd with the sunken chest." An uncharacteristic expression of gratuitous cruelty. Well, hormones do odd things to thirteen-year-old boys; all that balked lust needs an outlet, and social aggression is one of the more readily available alternatives. That small bosom of Melanie's didn't seem like such a drawback now; she had the kind of body that sustained itself elegantly over the long haul. "You really dolled yourselves up," Zeke added.

"Just in case some rock stars show up," Melanie said. "This could be our last chance to make the groupie scene."

"Were any invited? Besides Boz Scaggs? I spotted him in the living room."

"You're joking, right? *Were any invited?* To my husband's party? Take a guess." She made a face. "These events are a chance for Liam to meet his heroes. The entire membership of the Rock and Roll Hall of Fame is on the invite list. Even dead people. He's secretly hoping Elvis'll show up. Like Elijah at a seder."

At which Zeke thought to himself, This is a moment that would be unlikely to occur anywhere in time or space except 21st century California. Miraculous, really. A woman whose parents came from some village in China is invoking for the benefit of a man whose grandparents came from a shtetl in Ukraine a poor white singer from Tupelo, Mississippi, at the same time knowledgably alluding to a millennia-old ritual whose origins lay in a narrow strip of land in Asia Minor. And we don't think twice about things like this. It's just part of the air we breathe.

"Be sure to have a bottle of pills and two under-age girls in panties handy, just in case," Zeke said. He felt Molly's eyes on him. A quick glance told him she wasn't smiling. She had something on her mind beyond idle banter about Liam. In fact, it was surprising she had let this byplay go on so long without interruption. He turned to her, and said with a nod, "Hi, Molly. How was your day?"

She hesitated, while attempting to keep her expression bland. There was too much going on for her to be able to answer easily. She was worried about Ashley, first and foremost. But then there was that meeting with Corin…did she have an obligation to tell Zeke? Or would it be a greater kindness not to?

He thought he understood her silence. He said, "I know you're wondering. Well, Ashley and I had our talk. We got somewhere."

Molly glanced at Melanie, mouthed an "Excuse us," and took Zeke's arm to steer him to a relatively secluded spot. Melanie didn't mind; she knew they had a problem with Ashley. But they'd barely gone a step when they heard some sort of noise from the living room. A shushing noise, the unmistakable sound of coming-to-attention. And they noticed that most of the people in the kitchen were starting to head in the direction of the living room. The speeches were evidently about to start.

"Shit," Molly said under her breath, and, still holding Zeke's arm, she led him out of the kitchen, following the crowd. It was an obligation, the reason they were there. There were too many people jammed into the house for her and Zeke to get closer to the action than the entrance foyer, but they were able to look through the archway into the living room and see what was happening.

It was mercifully quick. Boz Scaggs drawled a sentence or two of appreciation, calling Liam "one of the fraternity of rockers, even though he doesn't play." Then Ed Lee said a few words, although it was unclear whether he knew who Liam was, beyond a vague awareness he was a local guy who wrote books. Tonight's party might just be another stop on a crowded evening's itinerary. Liam's editor went next, delivering a toast, a rather succinct paean to Liam's oeuvre, referring to him as "a noted chronicler of his generation's popular culture." Which was true as far as it went, Zeke reflected, but seemed like rather muted praise. Liam himself then said a few self-deprecating sentences, quoting George Steiner to the effect that "the critic walks in the shadow of the eunuch." After that, he launched into one of his patented encomia to the life-enhancing properties of rock and roll, a speech he could presumably deliver in his sleep. But on this occasion he tailored it to fit his new book, claiming that rock music, as it made its way into the suburbs in the mid-1950s, liberated white youth from the shackles of an oppressive, conformist, sexless existence. Which was by now both a cliché (originally retailed, if Zeke's memory was functioning properly, by Eldridge Cleaver) and a dubious proposition, but hey, this was Liam's stock in trade. A few minutes of such palaver and he stopped, and everybody applauded, as if he'd been praising world peace or brotherhood or progress in the battle against hunger, and then the ceremonial part of the evening was over.

As the guests, with unseemly haste, started flooding back into the kitchen for food and drink, Molly, still holding Zeke's arm, stood braced against the tide, and said, "Okay, Easy, tell me."

"Let's get out of here," Zeke said. "Somewhere quiet, where we can talk."

"If you want. But at least short-hand it now. It's been worrying me all day."

"Is that why you look so preoccupied?" Zeke was aware he had been noticing, subliminally, something abstracted in her manner since he had first seen her tonight. Something self-absorbed, almost furtive.

"Do I?" A shadow crossed her face for a moment. "That must be it."

"Anyway. Well. You won't like this. You know Shawn? That kid she's sort of been hanging around with?"

"Just the name. Black kid, right?"

"Right."

"Oh God. He hit her?"

"Yes."

"Oh God." And then she blurted, "Jesus, why does it have to be a black kid?"

"Is that relevant?"

She gave him an unfriendly look. "Please, Easy, don't you dare make this a liberal guilt thing. If he's black, it's more complicated. For all sorts of reasons that are perfectly real even if it's hard to talk about them."

Zeke was about to answer, but Carla, in some multi-colored tent-like schmata, suddenly bore down on them. "Into the kitchen, you two!" she brayed. "There's food! Quick, before it disappears!"

She was such an overpowering force, they allowed themselves to be herded into the crowded kitchen. But once there, while standing near the bar with its white-jacketed bartender, they waited for Carla to turn her attention elsewhere, at which point, without saying a word, even to each other, they headed back toward the front door. It was their good luck to encounter Stan rather than Carla in the foyer.

"Going?" he asked mildly.

"Yeah," said Zeke. "It's a school night. Give our regards to Liam again, okay? Tell him we're in awe of his productivity."

Stan smiled, and said, "We're giving away copies of the book. There are stacks of them in the living room."

"I'll go to Pegasus tomorrow and buy one. It's the least a friend can do."

"Very noble," said Stan.

"Tell Liam. I'd hate for the gesture to be wasted."

A few minutes later, Zeke and Molly were seated at a table at Britt-Marie, each with a glass of wine. It was a comfortable place to talk, a neighborhood bistro without airs, where they were greeted by their first names and treated with casual cordiality, and with informal, unemphatic attentiveness. If you had to be out in public at all, it wasn't a bad setting in which to discuss a family crisis.

Molly let Zeke take the initiative. No way he would play coy, not after their exchange at Stan and Carla's. She waited patiently. He stayed silent on the subject until they had ordered, and even after, until the waitress brought them each their glass of wine. Then, after taking a first sip, he said, "The thing we need to decide is, what should we do? I think you need to talk to Ashley, but—"

"Before we decide what to do about it," Molly interrupted, "I really need to know what 'it' is."

But Zeke had a full head of steam, and went on as if Molly hadn't spoken: "Because the girl has some cockamamie ideas, God knows where they come from, it's like she grew up in a 1950s trailer park. I think I've managed to talk her out—"

Molly interrupted with, "Zeke, please, can you back up a little?"

The waitress arrived with the salad they were going to share. When they first started eating here, she'd been a cute little ingénue. Now she was a cute middle-aged woman. Molly noticed, not without a tiny hint of satisfaction, that her delicate figure had filled out over the years, and her face had acquired flesh and wrinkles and a certain weary expression around the eyes. But she remained pretty all the same, and had the same non-threateningly flirtatious manner that always pleased Zeke without causing Molly distress. That she was still waiting tables at Britt-Marie was peculiar, though. Hard to know whether to find it reassuring or deeply depressing.

After she withdrew, Molly met Zeke's eye, just to signal him he wasn't off the hook. He sighed before saying, "All right. But before anything else, you ought to know, Ashley asked me to explain this as tactfully as possible."

"Go on," Molly said warily.

Zeke began forking some salad onto Molly's plate, but as an evasive tactic it was hopeless, so he resumed, "The thing is, Shawn kind of thought of Ashley as his girlfriend. It wasn't completely delusional. *She* kind of thought that too."

"But what can that possibly mean? They're fourteen years old."

"Well, exactly. I think that might have been Ashley's notion as well. She was his girlfriend, she wasn't his girlfriend, they sat together in study hall, they never went out together, it's all pretty vague. Anyway, there was a party…" He hesitated. "See, they're just starting to experiment. At least, I hope they're just starting. I believe they're just starting. And she was at some party and Shawn was there—it's not like they went to it together or anything—but anyway, she was dancing with some other boy, and then they started making out."

Molly looked stricken. It seemed an excessive reaction to Zeke. He had half-expected her to be amused. Instead, she turned ashen.

"Just hormones, I guess," he went on. Forking some salad onto his own plate, he continued, "You know, they're slow dancing, the lights are out, bodies touching, one thing leads to another…"

"In front of everybody?"

"Exactly, that's the problem. For Shawn, I mean. He must have felt humiliated. Not only was she making out with someone else, but in front of all their friends. He'd probably been bragging she was his girlfriend. I'm guessing, but it's plausible. You know, at that age, just *having* a girlfriend is kind of an achievement. And then, suddenly, this. In public, as you say. So he kind of lost it, I guess."

"Right there and then?"

"After the party. He was waiting outside. He'd had an hour or two to brood."

"Are you taking his side?" she asked sharply.

Zeke was nonplussed. "I'm not taking his side, Molly, no. I'm trying to contextualize it. For Ashley, not Shawn. She's the one we're concerned about." Jeez, this was going worse than he had expected. "See, she thinks it's her fault. She blames herself, and pretty much exonerates Shawn. I tried to tell her that, even though she provoked the boy in a hurtful way, a very insensitive way she should never repeat, still, hitting isn't an acceptable response, and no one should put up with it. It isn't a simple message, though. Especially for an adolescent. There's plenty of blame to go around, but she has to understand that even if she did something wrong, Shawn was totally out of line. But I think she needs to hear all this from her mom."

Molly pushed her plate away. "God," she said. "What a mess."

"We probably need to have a word with Shawn's parents, and that might be uncomfortable, I don't know who they are or what they're like. As far as Ashley's concerned…well, I think she's learned a couple of lessons. She gets that she needs to think about other people's feelings. She saw that right away, on her own, before I spoke to her. To her credit. And I think, or I hope, she realizes she never, under any circumstances, should tolerate physical abuse. At least, I tried to impress that on her. But the message would be reinforced if she heard it from you too."

"Yes, I see."

"Is something else bothering you?"

There was a pause so long as to seem interminable. Molly was wrestling with herself, torn by the conflicting pulls of kindness, candor, consideration, and cowardice. She finally looked down at the table and said, "No, no. I'm sure you're right. I'll talk to Ashley tomorrow."

Seven

1972

C orin phoned me a couple of weeks after the night at Stan's. I didn't expect to hear from him, hadn't given him a thought, but he called on a Friday night, when Molly was at her woman's group (in what would prove to be its penultimate convening, although nobody suspected that yet). In retrospect, I have to admit he handled things artfully. After a few pleasantries, he said, "I've been thinking about our conversation at Stan's. I rarely talk to anyone with your point of view. They don't usually interest me enough to go on talking to them. Or," he added with a little chuckle, "to go on listening to them, at any rate. Any interest in lunch or coffee?"

Was this designed to flatter? At the time, I took it at face-value. Hell, I fancied myself an interesting fellow. And he seemed amiable enough, more original, certainly more charming, than most other specimens of his genus (consider the two bearded schmucks as Exhibits A and B). That Stan was so impressed with him probably contributed some luster as well. I'd never heard of Corin McCabe, but he evidently enjoyed some prestige in certain circles, and that probably influenced me too, shameful as it is to admit.

We decided to meet for lunch the following Monday, at The Terrace, the cafeteria on campus, a few steps from the bookstore where I worked. No inconvenience involved. We claimed a table outdoors, on the eponymous terrace—it was a lovely summer day, hot but not stifling, smelling, as summer did to me at that age, like freedom (ironically enough, considering I had to get back to work in an hour)—and we chatted over our food (I took a tomato stuffed with tuna salad, he had eggs and bacon and toast, explaining he'd gotten off to a late start that morning). Nothing dramatic occurred. He made himself pleasant. No doubt by design, but I had no reason to be suspicious, and he was very accomplished at being pleasant. When, after several minutes of boiler-plate political chat, I told him, in as friendly and even humorous a manner as I could, that politics wasn't a topic I found inexhaustibly fascinating, he laughed good-naturedly—apologetically—and said, "Yes, of course. That's part of what interests me about you. You aren't narrowly focused. Unlike most of the people I meet, and to be honest, unlike *me*. I sometimes wonder, what am I missing? All this running around, fomenting God knows what...Is that all there is?"

I imagine he'd thought all this through, planned the gambit in advance. Corin always had a strategy, he approached every situation as a soluble problem in transactional dynamics. And he had skills, his instincts were political in the traditional as well as the radical sense. "That's the question, isn't it?" I answered, following him down the garden path. "We're young, the world seems like Eden. No? There's some sort of renaissance going on, and a technological revolution as well. And it's ours for the plucking. We're in the right place at the right time. Politics is only a small part of it. If you let it become the totality, I think you're missing out."

Non-political types can be insufferably pompous too. But although, even at the time, I was inwardly writhing just to hear myself opine, wondering how he had inveigled me into sounding like that (and loath to admit I did indeed sometimes sound like that without any inveigling), he gushed admiration. "Yes, that's it! I'm afraid I'm missing out. You're a chap who seems to have his priorities straight."

"But I don't *have* priorities. Molly gets on my case about it all the time. I sit around eating lotuses. Jeez, all my friends are *into* something. I have this new friend, Liam, he's fanatical about pop music. It's his religion, he worships at the shrine of Back Beat. Sometimes I think he's on to something and sometimes it's more like his head's up his ass, but either way, he's obsessed. And Stan. He's political, sure, but that's nothing compared to his feelings for the law. Sometime, as an experiment, ask him about a dissent by Oliver Wendell Holmes, something like that. It'll be midnight before he shuts up. *Those* are people with priorities. I'm just drifting."

"But in a way that's my point. See, I'm beginning to feel...not because I've lost faith, but...I don't know if Stan told you..." He lowered his voice. "I was in Ireland for a couple of years. Got involved in some things. It was exciting, the cause is noble, I'm not sorry. But sometimes..." He opened his fists. "What have I got to show for it? As I say, no regrets, I'm proud I made a contribution, modest though it was, but I also feel, speaking selfishly, time was wasted. I didn't expand, I let myself be used as an instrument by forces greater than myself. I'd like to branch out a bit."

So I said, as I now realize I was meant to, "Well, if you ever want a break from political palaver, you're welcome to join me and my friends. We might bore you silly...But it could be a change of pace, at least."

"Yeah?" Warm smile. "I'd like that." His eggs and bacon and toast were already consumed, his plate was clean, and the ashtray in front of him held three cigarette butts. He'd handled every aspect of this encounter with laudable efficiency.

A few days later I came home from work to find Molly in a state of enraged agitation. At first, as she banged around the apartment, cursing, I couldn't figure out what was bothering her, but assumed it must be me. Some level of anger was directed at me a lot in those days. Since my first impulse was to keep my distance, it was a while before I learned what the matter was. She finally calmed down enough to come to the bedroom, where I was lying on top of the bed, trying to read, trying to ignore the tumult. I looked up at her, no doubt a little apprehensively, as she stood in the doorway, hesitating at the threshold.

"I'm sorry if I yelled."

"'If?'" I closed the book on my index finger, holding the place, unsure whether this would be a brief, pro forma exchange or an actual conversation.

"*That* I yelled. At you. This has nothing to do with you."

"That's a relief."

"I'm sure it must be."

"Well, but less than you might think."

She made a face, torn between amusement and ongoing anger. "See, about an hour ago, I got a call from Joanie. You know, the woman in my group—"

"I remember." The woman whose boyfriend worked at Mason MacDuffie, the one who had hosted the barbecue. How could I forget?

"And..." And then, after a brief hesitation—probably resulting from a feeling that the story in some way compromised the moral high ground feminists felt they occupied in those days simply by virtue of their beliefs and their gender, a notion with which the rest of us were expected to concur unquestioningly, a notion Molly defended with humorless, tight-jawed, Mme. Defarge-like zeal—but anyway, after hesitating a moment, after preparing herself for the possibility of my derision (as if I would dare!), she came into the bedroom, sat down on the bed, and told me what she had just learned. A jaw-dropping revelation. My new friend Liam, Candy's boyfriend, had been sleeping with Rose, Nita's cute, diminutive, but (or so at least I thought) somewhat androgynous girl-friend. It started about a week after the party. As soon as Molly told me this, I remembered the attentiveness Liam had shown both lesbians that night. It amused me at the time, but never in a million years did I think he had any prospect of a conquest. It was enough to make my head spin. And to wonder how he managed it—how he effected the transition from party chat to intimacy, and in how many discrete stages—although I certainly wasn't going to express that particular curiosity to Molly.

She went on to describe the dismay and chagrin with which the news was greeted this afternoon as its members learned of it (although I couldn't help noticing a certain excitement on Molly's part as she told me the story, a certain gleam in her eye, that didn't resemble dismay or indignation, but frankly looked more like titillation). Two group members betrayed by their partners, and those partners doing the betraying with one another, crossing sexual-orientation lines in the process. Wow!

There was going to be a special meeting of the group that very night to discuss what should happen next. It would probably run late. This was something that, like those visions of Joanna, could keep you up past the dawn.

I let her tell the story without interruption. Even though she had only rudimentary information at this point, it was still a gripping yarn, and I was content to listen. In addition, I was afraid to offer any commentary, or even ask too many questions; she was treating me as a confidant, probably because of the pleasure she was taking in telling the story and the interest I was taking in it. The classic narrative transaction. But that could change on a dime if she thought she perceived anything on my part resembling disrespect. And at this period in our lives, her antennae often twitched even when there was no stimulus to set them in motion. I sometimes got the impression my very existence was an irritant.

It was frustrating how little information she possessed, though. Liam had been sleeping with little Rose for several weeks. Rose believed she might be in love with him. Nita had just found out—Molly didn't know how—and was as shocked as she was heartbroken; another woman would be one thing, and painful enough, but a man! It wasn't just betrayal, it felt like repudiation. And she'd never had a moment's suspicion. Rose never expressed any interest in men. Quite the reverse, in fact.

The group was going to assemble this evening to hash things out. As far as news went, that was it for the time being. I wished I had more confidence in Molly's curiosity, I could only hope she would return from the meeting having asked all my questions and received a rich fund of additional information, but I doubted it, and in any case, I doubted she would share all she gleaned. She was so discreet about the group, it was surprising she'd shared even this much. I guess the story was just too explosive to contain. But I wanted her to be as nosey as I. There were questions I didn't dare utter, since they would sound prurient to Molly, and she'd be offended, and that would put me right back in the path of her wrath.

"Who's getting the brunt of this?" I ventured to ask. "Are they—are you—angrier at Rose or Liam?" It seemed like an innocuous enough question.

Fortunately, she found the it intriguing. "I don't think anyone's figured that out yet. We feel betrayed. But by whom? Who's the worse traitor? Is treachery the operative concept? Are we all victims, or only Nita and Candy? There's a lot of anger, but we're all confused about out how to direct it."

"I have a hunch that by the time the night's over, you'll have decided."

She frowned. "I don't know, Easy. We don't always come to a consensus. Candy and Nita are hurting, and part of what'll happen tonight will be the rest of us offering comfort and sympathy. This isn't a tribunal, it's more like a support group. I'm sure there'll be lots of tears."

"Kind of shakes your faith in lesbianism, doesn't it?"

There was a long, ominous pause. And then, thank God, Molly laughed.

A week or so later I invited Corin to join Liam, Stan, and me at an Irish pub on College Avenue, just over the Oakland line. I figured the venue would appeal to him.

It was a complicated evening to contemplate. This only occurred to me after I had issued the invitation: My inviting Corin might ruffle Stan's feathers, since Stan knew him first. Would he think I was poaching on his territory? After Corin agreed to meet up with us, I suddenly thought, Whoops, maybe I'd better ask Stan if he minds. Without admitting I'd already done it. A risky strategy, since if he objected, the invitation would be hard to rescind. But it wasn't likely he'd mind much. And doing it this way was more respectful than informing him after the fact. Which was exactly what I was doing, but with luck, he'd never find out.

I hope this is clear.

It was complicated with regard to Liam too. Not because of the Rose business (except for Molly, if I chose, that is, to tell her). But he was a new friend, I didn't know him well, and he barely knew Stan at all. He wasn't one of our set of guys yet, and he and Stan hadn't established a mode of dealing with each other. Nor was it clear they would; you'd be hard-pressed to find two people more dissimilar than Stan and Liam (even now, decades later, I'm mystified we're all friends). So even without Corin—and Corin was potentially an impossibly volatile agent—I was queasy.

When I got to the pub that night, a little early, on purpose, since I couldn't help feeling like the host, Liam was already there, sitting at a table in a corner with a double scotch in front of him. Neat. He was a purist in those days; he considered water a pollutant. From his demeanor, I got the impression this wasn't necessarily his first drink of the evening.

The pub wasn't especially inviting. A big, warehouse-like space, with no effort having been expended to make it cozier. Rough wood floors, sticky in places. Rickety, mismatched tables and chairs. Bare walls painted some dark color (I later discovered it was green). A jangly, reverberant acoustic. Not dim enough to be atmospheric, not bright enough to let you to see clearly. A pervasive smell of stale cigarette smoke and stale beer, and—maybe—piss. Stale beer by another name.

My hope was that Liam and Corin would be impressed by the place's authenticity. Authenticity had a lot of prestige in those days. Even the faux authenticity of an ersatz Irish pub in Oakland, California.

Liam saw me before I saw him. He stood up and waved me over. "Hey," he called, and when I crossed the room to his table, he gripped my shoulder with one hand, shook my hand with the other, and said, "What are you having?"

"Just a pint of something."

"Sit down. I'll get it."

He walked over to the bar. From the way he dealt with the authentic Irish bartender—just the body language, I couldn't hear them—I got the impression they'd already forged some sort of bond. He came back a minute later with a pint of draught Guinness, the white head slopping over the rim of a thick glass mug, and another double scotch for himself. Without meaning anything by it, I must have glanced toward the half-full glass on the table, because he said, with a trace of self-consciousness, "To save me another trip. I'll get to it eventually."

It would have been graceless to tell him I disliked Guinness. We clinked glasses. He said, "Cheers." We took a drink. He glanced around the pub. A large majority of the tables were unoccupied. "I like this place," he said as he wiped a little whisky from his droopy moustache with an index finger. "Good choice, Zeke."

I checked his face for irony but saw none. No accounting for taste. I pushed on. It would be inexcusable to let the moment go to waste. We might not be alone again for some time. I said, "It seems you've wreaked a little havoc."

He gave me a tight smile in response. Tight but not humorless. "I could pretend I don't know what you mean."

"Any point?"

"Sure. Make you work a bit harder. But yeah, I have. Wasn't my intention."

"I'm not blaming you, Liam."

"You're not?"

"Hell no." The truth wasn't quite so simple. Of course I blamed him; he had been irresponsible and incontestably selfish. But I also—at least in those days, and to a certain extent still—was puzzled by issues of sexual morality, rarely felt certain enough of my ground to go in for hardcore, unequivocal condemnation. And, if I'm being honest, there was also simple envy. I still regarded Molly as the center of my life, still relied on her for emotional sustenance, but as I've indicated, we hadn't been getting along for some time now. As a concomitant, we weren't having sex nearly as often as before. And leaving all that to the side, I was young and lusty and I'd been faithful to the same person for over four years. A few times, in the face of temptation, real or apparent, there had been an inward struggle; there certainly were moments when I wondered

158

what I was missing. I'd been with only four women my life. It wasn't necessary to be Casanova to wonder about, and to regret, the experiences I hadn't had. So given all that, I didn't feel I had any right to sanctimony. I still don't. Which I think my clients appreciate.

I wasn't going to get into all of that with Liam. I just asked, "But what the fuck were you thinking?"

"Just…aw look, I just wanted to ball Rosie, okay? That was about as evolved a plan as I could manage. I'd had a lot of wine, so I wasn't thinking clearly, certainly not about anything so intricate as consequences, and…there's something about her…that stray-cat quality, you know? The wiry body. The off-kilter cuteness. The butch hair-do, all of it. Got to me. I wanted my hands over her."

"But several days went by, right? It didn't happen there and then, with the wine in your veins and Rose in your sights…"

"Well, that's true." He rolled his eyes. "I guess where pussy's involved, I'm kind of a jerk."

"And also…" Aw hell, I thought, go for it. "I mean…she's a *lesbian*."

"Well, that was the working hypothesis, anyway."

"So was it like a challenge, or did you—?" I stopped in mid-question, having registered what he said a fraction of a second after he'd said it. "Wait a minute. 'Working hypothesis?' Did you suspect she wasn't? Is that what you're saying?"

He leaned back in his chair, his ass slid forward along the seat, his shoulders hunched slightly, all at once he was slouching. His posture was sending a clear signal: "Go easy," it proclaimed, "I'm not defending myself." But his tone of voice was normal as he said, "Look, I'll answer. But you have to agree not to use it against me. It's not enough to Mirandize me, either. I don't need a warning, I need a guarantee. I don't want to discover I've blundered into a trap."

"Relax. I'm just looking for enlightenment. And, frankly, entertainment."

He took a long pull from his glass of whisky. He hadn't reached the other one yet, but he was closing in. And the effects were starting to show. "Okay," he said, "you want enlightenment, you've come to the right place." He gestured with a large, grandiose motion of his arms, guru-like. To let me know he wasn't serious. But I already knew he wasn't serious.

He straightened up, ran a hand through his blond bangs, and said, "Seriously, maybe this won't clear up anything, but here's what I think. For one, lesbianism can be a fluid category at this age. It isn't necessarily a commitment yet. Especially now, when being a dyke has such *prestige.* 'I support my sisters so much, I even eat their pussies.' Like it's a statement instead of an appetite. And also…" He hesitated. "Look, you can hate me for this, it's something gentlemen aren't supposed to talk about, but for whatever reason, girls like me. Always have. I check myself in the mirror and I don't get it, but there it is. Stop looking at me like that."

"I'm not looking at you any way in particular."

"Yes you are. Like I'm some braggart asshole. You asked, man."

"I did. And I appreciate your answering. I don't think there's any mystery about it. You're a good-looking guy."

"I'm not a braggart asshole."

He was starting to get truculent, in that way drunk people sometimes do, inventing contention to justify their aggressive impulses. I quickly said, "I agree. You're neither of those. Anything else?"

He took a breath and chose to be mollified. "Well, I'd just say, when I was talking to Nita and Rosie that night…look, you can tell when something's happening between you and a woman, right? It's not some occult phenomenon, it's palpable. Might be subliminal, but it's palpable. A look in her eye, a lilt to her voice, the way she orients her body? Pheromones?" He shrugged. "Whatever. You know it's happening, even if you don't know *how* you know. And it was happening with Rose. I don't know if *she* knew it—who knows what girls know?—but it was there."

"So where do things stand now?"

This last question didn't make him happy. "Oh God, I don't have a clue. It's a mess. I guess Candy and I are kaput. Which wasn't the plan, but Jesus, I mean, *I* wouldn't take me back. Who'd want to stay involved with a total fuck-up? And Rose and Nita…they're probably finished too. This was just a catastrophe on my part. A train-wreck. A fifty car

160

pile-up. All I was after was a harmless escapade." He sighed. "Well, at least it was a damned fine escapade. That girl…it was like my dick was her first Barbie Doll, if you see what I'm saying."

"For what it's worth…"

"Go on."

"Look, this is empty speculation on my part. Like I told you, Molly never breathes a word about the group. But what occurs to me…at least with regard to Nita and Rose…not to take anything away from you…"

"For Christ's sakes, Zeke, will you just say it?" He was laughing, but the exasperation was real.

"I have a feeling maybe Rose was already looking for an escape hatch. From Nita. Maybe from the whole lesbian thing. And you happened along. I'm not suggesting she didn't like you—"

"She likes me a little too much, frankly."

"Maybe not, is what I'm saying. Even if she thinks so now. After the smoke clears…I just have an inkling Rose and Nita's relationship may have already run its natural course. Its *un*natural course. And as for you and Candy, well, maybe you were looking for an exit strategy too."

He considered. "It kind of fits." He gave me a hard look. You're pretty shrewd about people, aren't you?"

"If I am, I wish there was some way to put it to practical use." This was an ongoing source of worry, my lack of any career path, any concrete ambition.

That's when Stan entered the bar. Standing uncertainly in the doorway, blinking behind his wire-frames, apparently wondering how he'd found his way into such a dive, and whether it was too late to flee. I felt a huge wave of affection, seeing him there, disoriented, apprehensive, trying to work up the guts to take a decisive step over the threshold. I put him out of his misery, standing up and waving him over.

When he got closer to the table, I saw he had shaved off his beard (it was so scraggly, you couldn't really see it or note its absence from a distance). "Good lord," I said, "what happened to your face?" I hadn't seen that moon-face bare since high school; he looked years younger, and, a dermatological correlative, there were a few dots of acne on his chin.

At my words, his hand automatically went to his cheek. "Yeah. I finally figured..." He gave me his lopsided grin, more obviously lopsided now without the foliage. "I figured, if it hadn't fully grown in after five years of patient cultivation, it probably never would."

Which got a nice laugh from Liam. A good augury for the evening. I laughed too, but I had an uneasy intimation he'd shaved mainly because Corin went smooth-cheeked. I hoped that wasn't the case, I'm not sure why. There must have been something about Corin that struck me as hazardous to Stan's well-being.

Which is what you call irony.

"You look good," I said. He didn't, but he seemed to need reassurance. Exposing your face after so many years is a big step. "Definite improvement."

"Next order of business: Getting my foreskin restored."

"Microsurgery," said Liam. To my surprise, this got a big laugh from Stan.

So, unexpectedly, the three of us got off on the right foot. Corin arrived about a half-hour later, making a grand entrance, somehow attracting attention simply by striding across the room to our table; he had dramatic flair that can't be learned, and maybe, to be fair, can't be quelled, either. As he seated himself, dispensing loud greetings and warm handshakes (and an unwelcome wet kiss on my cheek), he evinced no regret about being late.

Despite my initial queasiness, the evening proved lively. It wasn't easy, but it wasn't dull. The quantity of drink we consumed helped. Stan and I restricted ourselves to beer—lots of it, though—and Corin ordered an Irish whisky the moment he arrived. And a second one soon after. And so on. He couldn't keep up with Liam, but he tried; alpha male that he was, he'd identified Liam as the alcoholic competition from the get-go, and wouldn't cede the field without a battle.

There was a brief silence after the hellos had been exchanged and the introductions made. Corin lit up a Pall Mall. We all looked at each other uneasily. I thought, Oh Jesus, what happens now?

It was Stan (along with the alcohol) who gave the evening its propulsion. After a bit of desultory chat—weather and sports, those Y-chromosome fall-backs—Stan began to describe a case he was researching. He found law so interesting it was inconceivable to him he couldn't convey its fascination to anybody within range of his voice. And after a little bit of back-and-forth on the facts, Corin said something dismissive about the very concept of legality, called it "a bourgeois category," and contrasted what he called "court-legal" with "street-legal." And then he invoked deconstruction—Corin may not have been a deep thinker, but he was a dependable early adapter whenever newly fashionable concepts and buzz-words appeared—and suggested it should be applied to law and history and sociology as well as literature, and assured us that if we analyzed the western tradition of legal scholarship, including rabbinical and Jesuitical, and especially British common law, through the illuminating lens of semiotics, we couldn't avoid recognizing an "encoded system of oppression," a set of rules designed to shield those with power and property from those without. Landlords from tenants. Peers from peasants. Capital from labor. The game was rigged, the rules a fraud, fairness a chimera.

There was something spiteful about this argument. Not the argument itself, but Corin's propounding it there in the pub. He probably believed it, but that's not the point. He knew—he had to know—how much respect Stan had for him, respect almost amounting to awe, and he also must have had some inkling of Stan's devotion to his legal studies. He was mischievously putting Stan in a position where he felt forced to choose, at least for the immediate purposes of the conversation. You could call it a tease, but like so many teases, it was a power-play first and foremost.

I'm proud to say Corin underestimated his man. After hearing him out for a good long ten minutes—and Corin, a practiced rabble-rouser, spoke well, in eloquent, well-shaped periods—Stan, revealing a hint of agitation, said, "There's obviously some truth to all that. We know who writes the laws. Who gets elected to Congress. And you've no doubt read Charles Beard on the Constitution." (He probably hadn't, but he didn't demur.) "We all know the Anatole France quote about—I'm paraphrasing—the law in its majestic even-handedness forbidding the millionaire as well as the beggar from sleeping under a bridge. So in one way what you say is inarguable." Just when I thought he had surrendered without offering resistance, he went on, "But it's also trivial. I mean, yes, of course, those with power use their power to safeguard their power. But the law isn't restricted to that. It also establishes rules and methods whereby those intentions can be confuted. The king's laws can be used against the crown. That's a *good* thing. And it provides for some uniformity of expectation and outcome, which on the whole is also a good thing. It makes the arbitrary exercise of power more difficult."

"Oh?" said Corin, poised to pounce. "Like the way black defendants and white defendants in criminal cases are treated uniformly?"

Stan wasn't fazed. "Like all human institutions, the system's imperfect. But it's evolving, and generally in the direction of fairness. It was lawyers who decided Brown v. Board of Education. Who gave us Miranda and Gideon. And…well, the thing you just mentioned, the lack of sentencing uniformity, that's a great basis for an appeal. The system gives you tools that can refine the way justice is rendered."

Corin rolled his eyes. I don't think he'd expected this level of contradiction. "You can be blasé about its imperfections, but if you were on the receiving end, it wouldn't be so easy to shrug your shoulders and say, 'C'est la vie.'"

"Well, okay, so what would you put in its place? What perfect institution would you substitute for the imperfect one we have?"

"I don't have to answer that. My position doesn't logically require me to propose an alternative."

"Not in the abstract. But since, as we know, you advocate violent revolution, this isn't a purely abstract argument. Before you spill all that blood and disrupt everyone's life and destroy root and branch what we already have, I think it's incumbent on you to tell us your plans."

"So you aren't a radical anymore, is that it?"

This ad hominem thrust was an indication, I thought at the time, that Stan had been scoring points. But Stan chose to take it at face value, and answered as if he'd been confronted with a serious argument. "I don't believe radicalism is incompatible with a consistent, reliable, independent legal system. In fact, it's when you dispense with that that things get ugly. Being a revolutionary doesn't absolve you of the obligation to pursue justice. Having decent intentions doesn't mean you can dispense with decent praxis. So I ask again: What's your alternative?"

"Well, okay…They're at least trying new ways of doing things in places like China and Zaire and Vietnam and Cambodia—"

Stan was appalled enough to interrupt. "China! Zaire! You're offering me, what? People's tribunals? That's your preferred way to dispense justice and arbitrate disputes? Sorry, no sale. Those are nothing more than sanctioned reigns of terror. If that's radicalism, I want no part of it. There's a lot wrong with this country, but we do need a codified legal system, one that at least aspires to consistency and fairness. With independent judges and clearly-established rules of evidence and procedure. To advocate violent revolution with only vague assurances of good intentions, which in any case you're in no position to offer, is nuts. This romantic notion of people's justice, which in practice is mob rule and kangaroo courts…it's fucking insane. It's reckless and historically obtuse and…and criminally irresponsible."

They went at it like this for a while, as Liam and I looked on silently. But if my account makes it sound acrimonious, then I'm giving the wrong impression. They were impassioned, and they raised their voices and occasionally even pounded the table, but the antagonism didn't feel personal, it felt high-minded and serious.

On the other hand, I had a clear indication later that Stan had gotten under Corin's skin. He never said anything abusive while they were arguing—other than asserting at one point that Stan was "a captive of bourgeois modes of thought," which I don't think was meant as praise—but still, he was unused to being contradicted like this, certainly by someone he didn't consider an equal, and he was no doubt unused to encountering arguments for which his facile rebuttals weren't sufficient. But other than the occasional eye-roll or sidelong glance in my direction—could he possibly believe, after our dispute in Stan's apartment, I was on his side, or did he think his personality was so compelling my own convictions wouldn't matter?—other than that, he remained reasonably affable. That the whole thing bothered him more than he let on became apparent to me soon enough, though.

A little after 1:00, when we were finally ready to call it a night, Corin asked me if I would give him a lift to where he was crashing.

"Too much to drink?" I asked. I was far from sober myself, but I'd been drinking beer, whereas he'd been knocking back Midleton.

"Nah. I don't have a car. I hitched here. Too late to hitch back."

So I said, "Sure. Where are you staying?"

"With some friends in the city."

Bastard. The old bait-and-switch. Now it was too late to say no. And it got worse; he was staying, it turned out, in an apartment in Hunter's Point, the most crime-ridden ghetto in San Francisco. I think he was pleased to let me know in this indirect way that his hosts were black. And that he felt comfortable in Hunter's Point after dark (this was a period when black anger was, you might say, all the rage, when accepting accusations of racism and being called a honky were part of the price you paid for your liberalism). He doubtless intended this as a challenge to me, a throwing down of a gauntlet. Well, I was more upset about a long drive at one AM than the complexion of the neighborhood he was staying in, but I definitely wasn't pleased.

After we said good night to Liam and Stan, as Corin and I walked down College Avenue, dark and deserted at this hour, toward my car, he suddenly snarled, "What about that Stan? Fancies himself a radical, but down-deep he's just another liberal apologist. What a load of shite." Remembering in the nick of time to put a little Irish on the ball.

"Well, Corin, as you know, I'm a liberal apologist myself."

He shook his head. I guess he was so unused to being ideologically outnumbered, he had misjudged. Then, without uttering another word, he abruptly stopped, kneeled down, and picked up a rock that happened to be lying in the gutter by his foot. Bigger than a golf ball, smaller than a baseball. I'm not sure how he even managed to spot it in the dark. Puzzled, I stopped beside him. He looked at the rock, he tossed it in the air a couple of times. And then, still saying nothing, with no warning, he suddenly hurled it, with all his might, at the window of the shop we were standing in front of. The window shattered noisily, a huge crash, and then shards of glass came raining down in front of us like a hailstorm. A burglar alarm went off almost instantaneously, loud, jarring, and insistent.

It was all so sudden, so unexpected, I was immobilized for a moment. It felt as if the night had somehow split in two. Then I collected my wits—more or less—and shouted, "Jesus, Corin! What the fuck?"

He had already torn off down the street, and now yelled over his shoulder, "Run!" I really had no choice, with the alarm blaring into the night, and a couple of lights going on in apartments above the shop front, other than to run after him, just get the hell out of there as fast as I could. My heart was racing, my mind was reeling. And I was fairly drunk—too drunk to drive, if the truth be told, but we weren't always sensible about things like that—and I thought, Shit, the bastard's gone and done it, we're going to spend the night in jail. And then, ridiculously, How will I explain this to my mother? I pulled abreast of him and pointed to the side street where I'd parked. We made the turn and kept running till we reached my car, about half-way up the block. The sound of police sirens could be heard in the distance.

"Jesus, Corin," I said again. It was all I could say. I was panting for breath. Less perhaps from the exertion than the adrenaline flooding my system.

"It's cool," he said. Whatever that might mean. He was doubled over, panting harder than I; his tobacco habit.

"What do we do now?"

"We get in the car and drive."

"What if they stop us? There won't be many cars on the road at this hour."

He stared at me. A look came over his face, evident even in the darkness, a mixture of scorn and pity. I was apparently letting him down as a brother-in-arms. "So?" he finally said, with a maddening, supercilious show of patience. His breathing was returning to normal. A quick recovery. "We're driving home. We don't know anything about anything. Not that they *will* stop us. No probable cause."

"Oh yes, probable cause," I said. "Part of that bourgeois legal system you despise." I knew I was risking his wrath saying this, and so, before he could organize a response, I added, "Unless they decide our age and the crappy old VW bug I'm driving are enough to constitute probable cause by themselves. Which is possible, especially if we're the only vehicle on the road. The only game in town. And the problem is, if they do stop us, I can't pass a sobriety test."

"We'll be fine. Nobody'll stop us. Get in the car. The worst thing we can do is stick around here yabbering. Brush your clothes off in case any glass got on you."

At least the excitement had cleared my head some. But I made a point of driving cautiously anyway. Heading south, I stayed off primary roads till I was near the freeway, and kept the car below the speed limit, checking the speedometer almost as often as I peered through the windshield.

A few seconds after we started, Corin said, "For God's sake, man, move it!"

I knew better than to listen. "I'm not going to attract their attention," I said. "I refuse to give them an excuse."

He shook his head in exasperation but didn't answer. I continued driving very slowly and cautiously. After a half mile or so, I hung a right and headed back toward College Avenue. After another couple of blocks, near the freeway onramp, I hit a red light. I stopped, of course. Sure enough, an Oakland black-and-white pulled abreast of me on my left. I looked over; couldn't help myself. The cop in the passenger seat looked at me hard. I nodded at him. He didn't nod back, just continued staring. Aw shit. I wasn't sure of the best tack at this point, but I turned and faced forward. I didn't want him to feel I was challenging him.

I heard Corin say the word "Pigs." He was staring toward the cop car, evidently still in the mood for trouble. I turned to face him. "Please don't do that."

"Whatsamatter? You scared?" He didn't sound remotely Irish now; he sounded like an all-American jerk.

"Let me put it this way. I'm scared of *them*, yes. But I'm not scared of *you*. If you say it again, I'll take you apart." God knows where that came from, but it sounded convincing to me. Even though he was taller, bigger, and tougher than I.

It must have sounded the same to Corin—my earnestness, if not the substance of the threat—because he said, "Okay, okay. Don't sweat it."

The light changed. The cop car and I played a little Alphonse-et-Gaston game, but I finally edged forward and crossed the intersection first. Neither Corin nor I said anything further until, a block or two on, I turned onto the freeway on-ramp and headed toward the Bay Bridge. The police car didn't follow. At that point, I said, "Now, what was that window shit about?" I figured I already knew; frustration with how the conversation with Stan had gone. But I wanted to hear his version.

"It wasn't about anything," he answered, sullen and dismissive. "Just a random act of rebellion. A protest against private property."

"Doesn't Lenin condemn such things?"

"Who cares?"

"I thought he was a figure of reverence."

"The dude's been dead fifty years."

"Well, yes, there's that."

We were silent again for a couple of minutes, until we were approaching the tollgates. Then he started to speak, and at first, I assumed he was going to offer to cover the half-dollar toll as a thank-you for the lift. But no, that wasn't it. He said, "Anyway, thanks for broadening my horizons with a non-political evening."

I laughed. Genuinely. His flat, affectless line-reading made it funny. Or funnier. "You can't predict how these things'll go advance," I said. "Mind you, you're the one who got the politics rolling."

"Me? It was Stan."

"Nope. You. The reactionary legal system. Remember?"

"Oh yes," he conceded, "that's right. Damn. It's a bad habit of mine, launching into those harangues." He sounded a good deal more relaxed all of a sudden, and his charm was on display again. He said, "And it was an okay time in its way, and I liked that Liam fella. And Stan's all right, even if...whatever. But can't we just...you know, grab a bite, catch

169

a movie, hear some music. You bring your old lady, I could bring this chick I screw around with. Act like normal people."

"Sure. But bear in mind normal people don't go around smashing windows."

I was late for work the next morning—I must have turned off the alarm clock in my sleep, and didn't wake up for real until nine—by which time Molly was already gone. To campus, I assumed; she'd been spending a lot of time in the English Department that summer, talking to professors, meeting other people in the program, preparing herself for graduate school.

Before I left the apartment, I quickly leafed through the *San Francisco Chronicle*. Not for news—you don't read the *Chron* for news—but to see if there was any mention of a broken window on College Avenue the night before. There wasn't. Isolated acts of vandalism don't rate, and Berkeley hadn't had a riot worthy of the name for a while. The last serious unrest had been People's Park, during my sophomore year, that first glorious year with Molly. It was a big deal, with daily demonstrations, a curfew, Ed Meese's county Tactical Unit in full riot gear marching up Telegraph Avenue in attack formation, and National Guardsmen, with their fixed bayonets, stationed at every major downtown street corner (one of them once flashed me a covert "V" sign, which made my day). Berkeley felt like an occupied city. Like Prague. It was exciting and scary and memorable, a milestone in Berkeley history. One person was killed, an innocent man perched on a roof watching the spectacle below. Another was blinded by buckshot. There were billowing clouds of tear-gas, some laid down by helicopters hovering above campus, and there were beatings and mass arrests. It felt like—I realize it wasn't, I'm just saying it felt like—a wild, romantic brush with guerrilla warfare. *For Whom the Bell Tolls.* And I experienced that whole mad spring through the prism of new love; People's Park and my affair with Molly were inextricable, then and ever after. To be young at such a time was very heaven.

Corin would have been like a pig in shit if he'd been here at the time. But he was elsewhere. I'm not saying he wasn't a pig in shit, though.

Hell, I'm digressing, aren't I? There's a novelty.

Okay, we're back. Summer of '72. When I got home from work that afternoon, I told Molly about Corin and the window. "I thought we'd be busted for sure. Thought you'd have to come bail us out of the Oakland hoosegow in the dead of night. Or worse, the next morning. I was already contemplating endless hours with no bed and an open toilet."

She was looking at me wide-eyed. I added, "The whole thing was so childish. No, worse. Infantile."

"I guess that's one way of looking at it," she said.

"You don't agree?"

"I wasn't there, Easy."

"As a reaction to Stan, especially. To being bested in a political argument."

"If that's what it was."

"It seemed like it to me."

"Yeah, well…" She hesitated. "Sometimes the reasonableness of people like Stan, his earnestness and logic and respectability…even when he's right…*especially* when he's right…" She shrugged again, this time in self-deprecation. It was rare for her to struggle for words. "Maybe Corin feels that scoring points, wielding dogma, yammering away about Stalin-this or Trotsky-that or Mao-something-or-other is a waste of breath. Maybe he feels a sensible, enlightened, respectable ivory-tower intellectual will never be more than some guy wanking in his ivory tower."

"You're saying Stan's a wanker?"

"Maybe we're all wankers."

"Except Corin?" The idea struck me as absurd. In those days I was incapable of seeing Corin's behavior as anything but self-indulgent acting-out, of regarding his self-presentation as anything beyond self-conscious preening.

"Well, or he's a different *kind* of wanker. I have a sense his approach to politics—his approach to everything—is sort of…I guess you'd call it existential."

"I wouldn't, no."

She ignored that. "I'm just speculating here, based on nothing. But it's as if he views politics as an *adventure*, an exploration, rather than a bunch of policies and programs. So, sure, throwing a rock through some random store window is, like you say, childish. But it's also…it's also…I guess I don't know what it is. It's *different*. Something about it feels romantic. In the literary sense. Like those loony nineteenth-century Germans, say, or early Wordsworth. Elevating feelings and experience—and sensation, the sensation of existence—above intellect."

"You sure see a lot of nobility in some drunk guy smashing a window."

"And all you see is vandalism. Maybe you're missing something."

She was in a feisty mood. But then, Molly was feisty. She was in a feisty mood the night we met. You didn't push her around; that was part of her appeal. She wouldn't be bullied and she refused to be patronized. She'd come to that aspect of feminism long before the ism itself was in fashion; it was an outgrowth of her Wyoming girlhood, a rugged self-reliance and self-assurance. She wasn't intimidated by a horse, so she certainly wasn't going to let herself be intimidated by a horse's ass. "In that case," I said, "you'll like this. He suggested we get together. Not just him and me. You too. He mentioned you specifically."

"He did?"

"Well, not by name. He referred to you as my 'old lady.'" She didn't react; on some level I'd hoped it might provoke her, since something in her manner was bothering me. Now, "old lady" was common parlance back then, awful as it always sounded to me, and wasn't considered derogatory. Still, if it had been Liam who'd said it, she might have taken offense; for some reason, some people are given a Get Out of Jail Free card. I went on, "You and me, him and some woman he sees. Or 'screws around with,' as he delicately put it. A foursome. From what you're saying, maybe that appeals to you. Until tonight, I thought it probably wouldn't."

"Either way. I don't have strong feelings about it."

That could have been that. I took her professed indifference at face-value, and was far from eager to see Corin again myself. Not that my feelings about him were simple, or simply negative. I could still perceive his charm and magnetism; he had a politician's gift of making you feel you were more interesting than anyone else he knew. But against that, there was his bullying manner with Stan. Hideous. It wasn't at all clear to me why I'd been spared. And there was that window, of course. Calling his shenanigans existential gave him license for all sorts of mischief; I didn't feel he deserved the license and I didn't want to deal with the mischief.

So it seemed likely he was out of my life. Our paths had crossed a couple of times and probably wouldn't again. He'd seemed inexplicably eager to explore a friendship, we'd given it a shot, but it was like one of those first dates where there's no chemistry. These things happen. No hard feelings.

But then, a couple of days later, he wandered into the book store. Mid-afternoon. He didn't immediately come looking for me; in fact, I chanced upon him, browsing in the politics section. We mostly sold textbooks, not trade books, but he was rummaging through the shelves with every appearance of interest when I noticed him. "Corin!" I said. "I didn't see you come in."

"Right," he said. "The thing of it is, I was…you might say I was gathering up my courage before…before accosting you. And then you fortuitously came to the rescue by accosting me." His Irish lilt was back. With a vengeance. "You see, I rang your house earlier. Molly said I'd find you here."

"Uh huh." The blarney was already giving me a headache.

He noticed. "Patience," he said, "this isn't easy. I'm attempting to apologize, you see. Not my customary line. Seems indulgent after damage has been done. But seeing as how I was an utter cunt the other night…" He paused. "I could say I was so drunk I don't recall everything, which is true but no excuse. A fella has no call being a cunt, drunk or sober. If drinking makes him one, that's his lookout. Besides, I do remember the window—" He shut his eyes. His mortification looked genuine. "My bad luck, I haven't managed to forget that bit. I can't offer explanation or justification, no matter what I may have claimed at the time. It was just whisky and undiluted cuntery. I'm deeply sorry. And thoroughly embarrassed."

He offered his hand. Of course, I shook it. The apology was handsome, the smile worth a million dollars, and my mistrust had always been less than total. "At least we made a successful getaway," I said.

"True."

"And brought the capitalist system to its knees."

He granted me a crooked smile. "Yes, someday there'll be statues of us in the public square. So, is our foursome on? I mentioned it to Molly when I phoned, she seemed amenable. This Saturday? I'll mind my intake, that's a promise."

Trapped. But tellingly. I didn't *feel* trapped, didn't feel the jaws spring shut.

We arranged to meet in the city. Corin suggested a place in Chinatown, which didn't appeal—especially to Molly, who judged Chinese food by the glop she'd been fed in some rinky-dink pit in Cheyenne, never challenging her prejudices in a more authentic venue—and I countered with a few other options, and we finally settled on a Swedish place on Geary called Einer's. It offered cheese fondue, a dish enjoying a small vogue at the time. I suppose any European-style restaurant felt it could plausibly hop on the fondue bandwagon, no Alpine decor required. Einer's added sesame seeds to theirs, providing it with an aspirational Swedish accent.

Molly and I dressed up a bit. By our standards. Molly wore a cotton dress, thin fabric, all pastels, a hippy-style garment if ever there was one. I warned her she'd be cold—summer nights are raw in San Francisco— but she was determined. No bra under it, which added considerably to its allure (and made the chilly night that much more hazardous). I had on one of my few pair of not-jeans and a gaudy floral shirt and a leather blazer. Sounds quaint now, and with my Zapata moustache and sideburns I'm sure I resembled an especially unsavory small town used-car salesman, but it was the best I could do. I was no longer raiding Sy's stockroom.

As we drove across the bridge, Molly said, "Who's he bringing?"

"No idea. Someone he screws around with."

"A phrase shimmering with ambiguity."

"Is it? I interpreted it to mean they have sexual intercourse, but perhaps that was coarse of me. Anyway, we'll see soon enough."

Einer's wasn't much more than a storefront, not remotely fancy, with Swedish tschotchkes scattered about, sepia photographs and candles and wooden folk carvings. When we entered, it was Molly who noticed Corin at a corner table, waving to us. As we approached, I stole a glance at his date, seated across from him. Dark hair, full lips. Impressively stacked, enough so that I made a mental note not to be caught staring at her chest, to avoid being accused of objectifying body parts on the drive home. We all greeted each other. Corin didn't stand as he said hello. He introduced his date as Sylvia. Molly sat next to Corin, I to Sylvia.

"I've promised Sylvia, no politics," he announced when we were settled.

"Good luck with that," she said.

She said it lightly, but Corin frowned. He stubbed out his cigarette and said, "I'm serious. Let's see if we can get through dinner without a political argument."

"Molly thinks your politics are existential," I offered.

He turned to Molly with a smile; the idea pleased him. "Do you really? I like that. Much more dashing than Marxist. But what does it mean?"

"I think we're better off not talking about it, like you said." She looked away.

"Fair enough." And then, "It's a sort of literary idea, no? That fits. I mean, you study English."

"Where'd you hear that?" I asked.

"Oh...uh...it must have been Stan." He turned back to Molly. "Do you have an area of concentration? Any particular writer or period or anything?"

Molly looked stricken by the question, as if a battery of floodlights had been trained on her. She answered in a nervous, breathy rush. "My thesis was on Virginia Woolf, but I don't know if I'm going to stick with her. Feminist authors still interest me, but she's become a cliché, everyone's doing her, so I'm toying with one of the proto-feminists instead, Mary Shelley maybe. It might be fun to treat *Frankenstein* seriously. But...who knows? I'm just starting graduate school, it's probably best to leave myself some wriggle room."

"Always," he said. "But it'll be fiction? Not poetry?"

"Fiction, yeah. I think so."

"You don't like poetry?"

"I *read* poetry," she said.

"Do you ever write it?"

"Oh no. No. I don't write anything. Just academic papers."

"Don't you think you should?" Corin said. He certainly was intent on keeping the interrogation going. "Even if you aren't good at it, which I very much doubt, mightn't it give you insight into how it's made? And help your critical writing?"

Molly frowned. "You know, I've thought about that, and I think the answer is no. The way a clueless amateur would go about it is too different from the way a real writer works. It would be like playing 'Chopsticks' at the piano and thinking, Now I know what it's like to be Horowitz. Do you see what I mean? Any insights it gives you would be illusory."

Corin smiled appreciatively, flashing his dimpled grin, eyes sparkling. "I take your point," he said. "Elegantly put. Although you're hardly a clueless amateur. But okay, how about this? Don't you think we ought to read poetry precisely because our lives are consumed by prose? As a sort of antidote, if nothing else?"

Molly frowned again, this time in puzzlement. "I'm not sure I understand."

Meanwhile, Sylvia and I were sitting silently like a set of salt and pepper shakers.

"I read a lot of poetry," Corin said. "More than anything. And not only because I love it, although that's the main reason. But also...it's hard to explain, but as a way to balance myself. Counterpoise a little yin against my yang, which always threatens to predominate." He nodded to me, the first indication in some minutes he remembered I was there. "I read a lot of political stuff, yes. But Zeke here must think I'm so constantly immersed in Marcuse and Fanon and the like that I have no time for anything else."

"I hadn't really given it much thought," I said. It would be nice to think the adverb "drily" characterized my tone.

"It's true," Sylvia piped up. She was probably starting to feel a little left out of things as well. Corin had barely glanced at her since we'd arrived. "He's always got some poetry paperback shoved into his pocket."

"Yeats, Joyce, Louis MacNiece. Those would be my current faves."

"Uh huh," Molly said. Politely, but non-committally. Perhaps she'd had enough of being in the hot seat. And there wasn't anywhere interesting this conversation could go: At best, a litany of names of favored poets might follow, and Molly detested those catalogue conversations. I'd heard her ridicule them: "It's this vapid way of establishing affinity with somebody else, affinity and cultural bona fides. It's like cows mooing while they're grazing side-by-side, to let the other cows know fellow-creatures are nearby." (As I've said, Molly, despite her angelic demeanor, could be a tough cookie. People who didn't know her well had no idea.) And she wasn't by inclination effusive about her literary enthusiasms; she considered them private, a part of her life not to be discussed outside the academic cloister, certainly nothing to be displayed or paraded. Like a divinity student reluctant to sully her faith by talking too freely to the laity about her love of God.

"Corin writes poetry," said Sylvia.

He actually blushed. "We don't need to talk about that." For some reason, having this piece of information revealed unsettled him. He picked up his menu. "Have you eaten here before? What's good?"

"It's really very sensitive," Sylvia went on. "You'd be surprised."

"And we should get a bottle of wine, shouldn't we? Where's our waitress?"

I laughed. I couldn't help it. His discomfort was patent, and, because it was unfeigned, unexpectedly appealing, and I laughed out loud, partly in sympathy, partly simple amusement. Corin relented and laughed too, an easy, contagious chuckle, and then Molly did as well. Sylvia contented herself with a small, puzzled smile.

"A tender subject for me," Corin said. "At least in this company. Poetry is just a hobby. Or therapy. Which is even worse. God, can we change the subject? I feel like a complete berk."

"I don't know why you're shy about it," said Sylvia. She addressed Molly: "A lot of poets do other things, don't they? I mean, they have real jobs?"

"Some of them," Molly said. "A lot of them teach. It's hard to make a living writing poetry."

"Exactly!"

Corin tried again. "But they're immersed in it in a way I'm not, Syl. That's the point. Literature is Molly's life's work. My little efforts wouldn't interest her."

"But his stuff is good," Sylvia said to Molly. "Seriously. It's very poetic." She suddenly, self-consciously, laughed at herself. "'His poetry is poetic.' That was dumb, wasn't it? I meant to say it's soulful. You know, about nature and stuff. Not Che Guevara and the workers' struggle or stuff like that."

Corin sighed. There was a long pause, permitting the poetry conversation to die a natural death, and we rallied and talked inconsequentially about other things. In response to my queries, Sylvia told us what she did—she was a part-time student at San Francisco State, majoring in psychology, and also worked in a clothing shop in the Haight, selling batik tee-shirts and tie-dyed skirts and leather sandals and other already-dated gear, mostly to gawking tourists hoping for a fleeting glimpse of hippies in their natural habitat—and then I discussed my confusion about what to do with my life, and Molly talked about Wyoming and the extreme culture-shock when she first arrived in Berkeley, and Corin, in his colorful but guarded way, talked about Ireland. We ordered. Everything was normal, if on the dull side of normal, until someone—I think it must have been Sylvia—mentioned what had just happened the previous week in Munich.

It didn't initially seem she was opening any floodgates. The massacre of those Israeli athletes was so horrible and gratuitous it felt like it had more in common with, say, the Manson murders than an event whose political dimension mattered. Nor did it seem a promising area for table talk. I mean, what was there to say that wasn't obvious? But out of politeness, and a desire to encourage Sylvia, who had been so quiet all evening, I offered some conventional statement about how awful it was.

Bad call.

"*Awful?*" Corin said. His face flushed again, but not from embarrassment this time. "It was harsh I'll grant you, maybe even brutal. But driven by desperation. Which means by necessity. A dramatic way to get attention for an oppressed people who have no other access to world opinion. A blow against a fascist state."

"It was cold-blooded murder," I said.

"I don't accept the word 'murder.' Killing, yes, of course. An armed struggle by definition involves killing."

"And I don't regard Israel as a fascist state."

"You wouldn't." He pretty much spat that one out.

A moment of silence; Molly, sitting across from me, stiffened, and I weighed whether to rise to the bait Corin had just dangled. And decided against. Why play his game? "Look, no matter what you suppose, I have plenty of problems with how Israel treats Palestinians. But the word 'fascist' is so extreme and disproportionate, it makes a mockery of any serious discussion. And defending a brutal massacre at the Olympics… these were non-combatants. Engaged in a peaceful pursuit."

"In a struggle like this, no one's a non-combatant. No one has the luxury of defining themselves that way. Certainly not citizens of an oppressor state."

"I can't believe you're defending what those people did." I really couldn't; up to now, no one I knew had tried, not even the most radical of my friends. "Some things are so barbaric, the cause they're ostensibly supporting is irrelevant."

"Oh? Do you apply that principle to the ANC? The Viet Cong? Sinn Fein?"

"Of course."

"Well, first of all, I don't believe you. I think, whether or not you admit it to yourself, you have a double-standard. And second, if you *are* telling the truth, you're an even worse fool than I thought."

Let no one say Corin's forensic style was mannerly or gentle. This was the moment I thought I might have to ask him to step outside. Not my kind of gesture, but some provocations don't leave you any choice. It's their purpose. I went through a small internal check: Was I restrained by fear or common sense? Hard to say.

I was curious how Molly was reacting, but I wasn't going to take my eyes off Corin. Meeting his gaze seemed crucial. "You talk about a double standard?" I said. "You, who defend Cuba, and Vietnam, and the Cultural Revolution of your beloved Mao?" Before he could answer— his answer didn't interest me—I cut him off with, "Okay, never mind that. And leave morality aside for a minute. Just think practically. Do you believe this helps the cause? Because it doesn't. It'll produce a wave of revulsion that'll set the Palestinians back a decade. As it should."

"Like when the Stern Gang blew up the King David Hotel?"

Hmm. I hated to admit it, but that blow landed. So I said, "Killing innocent people in cold blood can't be the answer. It just can't. There has to be a peaceful solution to all this. A homeland for the Palestinians, recognition for Israel. I don't believe massacring innocent young athletes makes that eventuality more likely."

His color deepened, his voice rose menacingly. "You want to know why people like me despise liberals like you, Zeke? Because you say things like that. You just want everyone to be nice, as if that's a strategy for solving the world's problems." And then, in a pathetic, sing-song whine, he said, "Oh, why can't we all be sweet to each other?" And while my gorge was rising, he snarled, "Well now, see here, everyone *can't* get along, we *can't* all be sweet. Interests are sometimes in conflict, goals are irreconcilable, and lots of people take kindness as a sign of weakness. Cops and robbers aren't meant to get along. Greens and Orangemen. Spades and the Klan. Some differences can't be split. It's time you woke up. Eldridge Cleaver says, 'If you're not part of the solution you're part of the problem.' When it comes to the Middle East, you bleeding-heart Jews are part of the problem, don't kid yourself. You *are* the problem. You stole Palestinian land and established an apartheid state. Bad as South

Africa. Maybe worse. Based on religion as well as race, and by people who should know better. But you've consigned the indigenous people to camps that only good taste and a captive press prevent the world from calling concentration camps. No peace can result from that. No justice, no peace. And there won't be either until you Jews stop acting like Nazis. So no one's going to be sweet to anyone else. Okay?"

This rant wasn't only offensive, it was meant to be offensive. I stole a glance at Molly and saw she was looking down at her plate, biting her lip, agitated by what I took to be distress and what I hoped was also outrage. As for me, I was feeling that inner roiling that comes directly from the limbic system, the kind of turmoil that tells you you've been challenged on a very primal level. This was an instinct I trusted; I wouldn't be reacting this way unless the reaction was intentionally provoked. No matter what words Corin uttered, this wasn't about his words, wasn't about what it purported to be about. And I want to stress again, I hadn't been raised as one of those Zionist romantics, I hadn't swooned over *Exodus*, not the book or the movie or the Ernest Gold tune, and my feelings about Israel, at least in the years since the Six Day War, were deeply ambivalent. But Corin wasn't engaging me on the level of ideas. He couldn't have cared less about ideas. He was kicking sand in my face.

He was diagonally across the table from me, eyes slit, exhaling cigarette smoke and glowering. I had the impression he was seconds away from uttering something really unforgivable, like "jewboy" or "kike." So much malice, so much spite, such a goulash of fair argument and sophistry, and so much goddamn *testosterone* were being deployed in my direction I could barely sort through my reactions. I suddenly was on my feet. It alarmed him; he realized he'd misjudged the situation, or my timidity. He said, "Calm down. We're just talking." It was a retreat, and we both knew it. We stared at each other for what seemed like an eternity.

Sylvia broke the silence. "Corin has very strong feelings about this issue."

To which Molly replied, "Yuh think?" An astonishing response. I'd never heard her be sarcastic before, certainly not toward anybody less intelligent and less sophisticated than herself. To this day I sometimes wonder whether it was provoked by Corin's rudeness or Sylvia's lovely bosom.

This exchange gave me a chance to sit down without feeling I was yielding. I took a deep breath, and then heard myself addressing Corin as if our disagreement was simply that, a principled disagreement. I tried to sound temperate, reasonable. "We Jews, to use your locution—and let me say, Corin, parenthetically, I find it quite offensive—we Jews aren't responsible for Israel's policies. Any more than you radicals are responsible for, say, Libya or Syria. Countries you seem more inclined to defend than I do Israel, incidentally. You probably wouldn't defend them at all if their people weren't dark-skinned."

"I wouldn't defend them if they hadn't been the playthings of greedy European powers," Corin stated. "That does alter the moral calculus slightly, yes."

"Jews have also been the playthings of European powers," I said.

"And now they're the cat's paw of the Europeans. They *are* the Europeans."

"And being surrounded by enemies who have declared their intention to destroy them, that doesn't earn them a measure of leniency?" How had he managed it? I'd been maneuvered into a position where I was defending Israel. When I argued with my father, I sounded more like Corin.

"Not when you're a colonial power yourself."

"Okay, we're going to drop this now," Molly suddenly announced. Sternly, although her voice stayed low. Commandingly, brooking no opposition. She'd had enough. Her lips were compressed, her eyes hard. She wasn't looking at either Corin or me; her glance stayed fixed on her wine glass. No one said anything, but I was thinking, Hey, are you blaming us equally? But I didn't give it voice, and she went on, her tone still steely, "We know where everyone stands. No minds are going to be changed. It's boring."

"Yes, okay," said Corin. "You're right. I'm sorry if I got a bit heated there. I probably said things I shouldn't have."

"I don't just object to your *saying* them," I answered. "I object to your *thinking* them."

"That's enough," Molly said, her voice rising.

"Maybe we should talk about Corin's poetry," Sylvia said. Her first attempt at humor all night, and it couldn't have been more opportune. What followed was more a matter of relief than amusement, but we laughed uproariously. After that, and with a mighty effort, we managed to get through the rest of dinner with a strained semblance of cordiality. But the evening obviously never really recovered. It didn't end as quickly as I'd been expecting and hoping, though: After we were outside the restaurant, Corin had the nerve to ask for a lift home.

"Hunter's Point again?"

"No, I'm crashing with Sylvia."

"It's not far," Sylvia said. "Fourth Avenue, the other side of Clement."

"Okay." I had been looking forward to being quit of them, but five or so more minutes promised to be just about tolerable, at least with a definite end in view. We drove in silence until we were a block or so from Sylvia's apartment, when Corin said to Molly, "Listen, if you'd like to read some of my poems, I'd be honored."

I was nonplussed. But Molly said, "Sure," as graciously as if she'd graduated from some young ladies' finishing academy in Boston.

After we dropped them off, we were too shell-shocked to speak for a while. Or maybe it was just I who was shell-shocked, but anyway, neither of us said anything until we neared the Bay Bridge, when Molly broke the silence by saying, her voice thick with distaste, "Well, that was fun."

"Oh yeah, I never wanted it to end." And then, "I was beginning to doubt it ever would." And then, "You're really going to read his poems?"

"Jesus," she said with a little laugh. "I'm sure he'll never send them. But what could I say? He backed me into a corner."

"He does that."

"Yes."

This next bit was tricky, but I felt I had to say it. "I would have appreciated a little support back there, Molly. He was really being a jerk.

Worse than a jerk."

"I thought about it. But I figured, if I added my voice to the throng, it would just raise the volume. I wanted it to stop."

"But—"

"And I didn't think you needed help. You were doing all right on your own."

"That isn't the point. He was saying hateful things."

"I didn't see a need to adjudicate. You were both getting heated. I wanted to douse the flames, not pour oil on them."

A minute or two of silence. I was stewing, thinking, Where's your loyalty? It had been bothering me all evening, her apparent plague-on-both-your-houses disapproval. I was trying to find a way to express this without opening a whole new set of hostilities. I finally contented myself with saying, "I don't like him. At *all*. For a while I thought I might, despite lots of misgivings, but I've had it with him."

"Yeah?"

"You don't agree?"

"In a way. But he's different. An original."

"An original shithead."

"You have to wonder, though: Is he like that just because he's out of control, or is there a measure of courage in it?"

"The courage to be a shithead?"

"To take risks. Being a shithead is one of the risks he's willing to take."

"You give him too much credit."

"You may give him too little. The way you argue with him…it's like you're missing the point."

"*I'm* missing the point?"

"The point of his world view."

"How am I doing that? By insisting on logic and facts and coherence?"

"Mmm. By insisting on linearity. On traditional modes of thought. By being so literal and, and kind of, I don't know, grown-up and humorless about everything."

"Yeah, I guess I overlooked the humor in the Munich massacre."

184

And then, to mitigate the harshness of this—but disinclined to retract it—I said, "The thing is, if you believe in violent revolution, and are willing, at least in theory, to kill people and upend the lives of millions of others, and undo a couple of centuries of tradition, maybe you have an obligation to think things through before the atrocities get under way." I didn't realize it at the time, but I was echoing what Stan said in the pub.

"Well, it's not as if thinking things through has worked so well in the past. For all I know, Robespierre thought things through. Lenin definitely did. Or believed he did. Maybe it's wiser to accept in advance the need to improvise rather than think everything can be neatly planned. Life doesn't always go according to expectations. And besides, you talk about Corin as if his fantasies might come true, and as if that imposes some sort of responsibility on him. We both know there's no way."

"But *he* thinks they will."

"Does he? Perhaps. But even still, we know better. They're pipe-dreams. So all I'm saying is, his pipe-dreams are more interesting and more, more idiosyncratic, and, and *ardent*, than, say, the dogmatic drivel Stan's friends put out."

"And the anti-Semitism? That didn't bother you?"

"I don't think...look, you're maybe being a little too sensitive. He didn't say anything anti-Semitic. Anti-Zionism isn't the same thing as anti-Semitism."

Which made me think she wasn't being sensitive enough. I said, "But he went beyond anti-Zionism. Or at least edged right up to the line."

"He likes to be provocative."

"Right. And anyway, his poetry is poetic."

She laughed at that, and said, "She was awfully sweet, though." As if she had already mentioned Sylvia's intellectual shortcomings—a thing she would never dream of doing—and were only afterward offering mitigation.

"She seemed sweet enough."

"Completely crazy about him, of course."

"Is she?"

"Totally," she said. "In his thrall. Whereas I think he's getting tired of her."

"I agree with you. I'm not even sure they're a couple. Or ever were, I mean."

"Really?"

"Even if he *is* crashing at her apartment." Maybe I just didn't want to grant him that privilege, resented his access to those breasts. "He barely acknowledged her tonight," I went on. "Except when he got annoyed."

About a week later, I accepted Liam's invitation to watch a baseball game at his apartment. Yankees vs. Red Sox. Not my sort of night, really, for all sorts of reasons: I wasn't much of a baseball fan under the best of circumstances, and anyway, as an LA boy just coming to consciousness when the Dodgers moved west, I only cared about that one team insofar as I cared about any. But I wanted to nurture this new friendship, so I decided to accept. Besides, staying home with Molly was no longer so enticing a prospect. Things had been fraught over the entire summer, and they'd become even worse during the last few days.

I walked to Liam's straight from work, with only a quick stop en route at the hilariously misnamed Garden Spot, a bleak little convenience store near campus, to pick up a couple of six-packs. When I'd told Molly my plans, she'd grunted in a way that could only be interpreted as disapproving, and I didn't relish going home and having to defend Liam, let alone my growing affection for him, as the tax due for showering and changing clothes. Better to skip the whole business, even after a hot summer day. Her feelings about his behavior with Rose weren't the sort that could be assuaged, and rehearsing it was bound to exacerbate the ill feeling in the air.

I hadn't been to his place before. He rented a sort of in-law cottage in the rear of some professor's old shingle house south of campus, on Russell Street. When he let me in, I saw it was a pigsty. Not a big surprise, and not, in that day and age, all that disturbing to me. Guys' places, guys of my age at least, usually were pigsties. Whether that was the Y chromosome unchained or the way we were brought up I won't venture to speculate. My place would have been a pigsty too, except I shared it with Molly; her fastidiousness was contagious.

Anyway, what I first noticed, besides the state of the living room, with its dust and grime and dirty clothes casually strewn about, were several empty beer cans on the coffee table and a fat, glowing, perfectly-rolled joint in an ashtray. The marijuana smell hit me immediately. That Platonic ideal of a joint wasn't the first that had been rolled and lit in that room this afternoon. As I handed the six-packs over to Liam, I said, "You got a head start on me." I had to shout. Paul Butterfield was on the stereo, at full volume.

"I've got a head start on the rest of the planet," he said. Even shouting, he sounded spacey, but then, he usually sounded spacey. Never inarticulate, mind, quite the reverse in fact, but disengaged. As if other things were clamoring for his attention while he was conversing and he had to filter them out in order to focus on you.

The TV was on, the volume turned down. The music was so loud the floor seemed to reverberate, thudding with bass and percussion. I was beginning to regret coming. We sat on his soiled, lumpy sofa, I opened a can of beer, took a gingerly hit off the joint he proffered, and glanced toward the TV. The game hadn't begun yet.

"When the game starts, can we have the sound on?" I asked.

"You need commentary?"

"I'd prefer it."

"The game is happening right before your eyes, Zeke."

"I must understand the fine points less well than you. I find it helpful."

"Okay, that's cool." Easy-going. With the stoner's gliding absence of agenda.

"You prefer a blues accompaniment?"

"To just about everything," he said. He took a big hit off the joint— the large tip glowing ominously—and handed it back to me.

I took another hit, thinking to myself, Oh boy, this is going to be quite a night. I passed the joint back, and then, after holding the smoke in my lungs until I couldn't, exhaled and said, "You're really a fan? It doesn't fit. I mean, baseball's so...unhip."

He was already toking during my question, so I had to wait for several seconds before he said, "Nah," elongating the syllable as he released a dragon-lung's worth of smoke. And then he went on, "It's only square if you don't understand it. Baseball is...it's..." He lost his train of thought for a second. Then he remembered, and resumed, "It's like, you know, Grandma Moses. Or the blues. Or the Corvette. Or, I don't know, barbecued meat. Quintessentially American." His tone shifted as he launched into a long riff, a foretaste, although neither of us knew it, of the books he would write one day. "Not in a boring political way, but as an expression of cultural identity, which is often diametrically antithetical to the political. The fundamental nature of American culture is subversive and oppositional even when it thinks it's conservative. Jeez, I mean, take the fucking Confederacy, it was a racist, evil, feudal entity, I'm not defending it even though my forebears wore the gray, but it had some weird kind of rebellious integrity anyhow, a thumb in the eye of authority, a get-off-my-back, don't-tread-on-me kind of fuck-you. That's why rednecks put the stars and bars on their trucks, the racism is secondary, although I don't deny it's part of the package. But baseball, in its gentle way, has some of that spirit. Along with a yokel-comes-to-the-big-city feeling. And a give-me-your-tired-and-poor too, with Italians and Jews and blacks and Dominicans and Puerto Ricans lined up on the bench as the years went by. Where else would a Sandy Koufax meet a Filipe Alou? Baseball's the real melting pot, not the bullshit one you read about in civics class. A spontaneous, organic expression of our national selfhood. No accident it's the national pastime."

The dope was already kicking in. I must have been staring at him in amazement. It wouldn't surprise me to learn that my jaw was hanging slackly open. "What?" he said.

"It's just, it's incredible, you spew this stuff even when you're like totally drunk on beer and stoned out of your skull."

He laughed cheerfully. "And tripping. I dropped some acid a while ago."

"You did?" I felt a premonitory shudder.

"It's cool. Small hit. Modest buzz. No problem."

He seemed no weirder than usual, so I let myself relax, and said, "That's even more amazing. You can sing those arias while tripping."

"Oh , better than ever. Frees me up." And then, with a shrug, as if it explained everything, he added, "It's what I think about."

"I thought you thought about rock and roll."

"I think about every emanation of the zeitgeist. 'Specially when I'm loaded."

Little did I realize this sort of crap would end up being his life's work. I had no idea it *could* be a life's work. The arrant nonsense he spouts has never let up, and it's rarely struck me as anything other than arrant nonsense, not even when I was 22 and inclined to give arrant nonsense the benefit of the doubt. Every once in a while he's managed to say something dazzling, but that's beside the point. I've always found his cock-eyed, cockamamie zeal entertaining, and even—though I'm reluctant to concede this—stimulating. It's stimulating to consider the ways a fine mind can erect elaborate, self-sustaining structures out of thin air.

"Do you actually...*follow* the game as it's being played, though? In real time? Pitch by pitch, play by play?"

"Uh huh."

"You don't just groove on the visual patterns while listening to the blues?"

"Fuck no, man. I know my shit. You want stats? I can quote stats. I've got this stuff down cold."

"I would never have figured."

"That's 'cause you didn't grow up in Atlanta, you don't remember the Braves coming to town, and you didn't have my daddy. It's what we did, him and me, when we did the father-son thing. What we had in common. Went to games, talked strategy, threw a ball around in the backyard before dinner."

"Did you play? In Little League or whatever?"

"In school. Shortstop. Till I discovered dope. That kinda reoriented me. It fucked up my coordination. I had to choose. Chose dope. Never looked back." He flashed a goofy grin. "Let's order a pizza. Or two. The game's gonna start soon."

A considerate host, he turned off the stereo, turned up the sound on the TV, phoned LaVal's, rolled another couple of jays, and we hunkered down on the sofa and watched the game. An odd few hours. We got quite drunk and very stoned, and Liam really did sit silently in front of the tube and watch the game. He never shushed me if I spoke to him, but I rarely had reason to, and he almost never initiated conversation beyond, "Be a pal and pass me a beer." The quietest I'd ever seen him.

And it was pretty boring. The dope didn't enhance the experience. If anything, it made me more conscious of the stasis that's such a fundamental part of baseball, stasis periodically punctuated by brief flurries of activity. But it was a relief not to be interacting, given the effect marijuana has on me, and it was intermittently interesting simply to watch the game in Liam's company. Anything that could engage him to the point where he didn't speak or allow his attention to wander, no matter the quantity and variety of intoxicants he'd consumed, was worthy of note. I spent almost as much time surreptitiously eyeing him as watching the tube.

The game ended close to nine o'clock. I hadn't been this blotto in a long time. God knows how many beers I'd drunk, or how many joints we'd shared. The pizza didn't help, either. Simply standing up was a heroic achievement.

"Can you make it home?" he asked. He was tripping on acid, but he was worried about me. I must have looked as unsteady as I felt.

"Think so. I'm on foot, I don't have to drive. That would be beyond me."

"You'll still be operating heavy machinery," he said.

We both laughed at that. My body did feel unwieldy and recalcitrant.

"The air will do me good." In truth, I was feeling claustrophobic, and the air in his bungalow was so saturated with marijuana smoke I felt starved for oxygen.

"You can stay here if you need to. No problem."

Not an enticing prospect. "Nah, thanks, but I need to clear my head. Will *you* be okay?"

"Oh yeah, yeah. I'm already coming in for a soft landing."

He was popping another beer when I left.

The walk home, a good two miles, was an odd combination of delightful and weird. It was nice to be outside: The sky was cloudless, the air was sweet-smelling, and the moon was big and bright and silvery. It felt fine to be moving again after all that immobility on Liam's ratty sofa. The neighborhoods I walked through weren't the best, but I never felt any jeopardy. Still, my mind was in a bit of tumult. All the usual dope effects, presumably kept at bay by the soporific, tranquilizing rituals of baseball, came rushing in on me. About Molly, and the problems we were having. About my life, and what to do with it. About parents, friends, the world situation. I couldn't find anything to feel good about, no point of reassurance or comfort.

When I reached home, it was still shy of ten. I let myself in, shouted a hello. There was no answer. All the lights were out, which was puzzling. It was surely too early for Molly to have gone to bed. I turned on the lights in the living room. Nothing seemed out of order. I was beginning to get a bad feeling, but I put it down to the marijuana, told myself not to be silly.

I went into the bedroom and turned on the lights. At first, with a small internal lurch, I thought there had been a burglary. Several of the bureau drawers were open. And then I noticed that the closet door was ajar. I went to take a look, and saw with a shock that it was largely empty: All of Molly's stuff—the bulk of the closet's contents—was gone. I checked out the opened drawers next. Empty. But a quick look told me the drawers that remained closed were the ones that contained my stuff. When I opened them, I saw they were full. This was no robbery.

My stomach did something unpleasant. I felt the first stirrings of panic. Back into the living room. I was starting to hyperventilate. Only then did I notice something had changed in that room as well: Some of the LPs were gone from the shelves, and more than half the books. Into the bathroom. Molly's hairbrush, toothbrush, and assorted toiletries were gone. Plus the Head Shampoo we both used.

I staggered back into the bedroom, in a daze, far too agitated to think straight or sit still. I noticed a 3x5 card on the bed. On the pillow on my side. So I wouldn't miss it as I settled in for a good night's rest, presumably. The white card hadn't been immediately noticeable, lying on top of a white pillow slip. Tremulously, knowing this would be bad—but not *how* bad—I picked it up. Written in Molly's small handwriting, in ballpoint pen, less neatly than her usual careful script, were the words, "Zeke, I'm leaving. This isn't working for me anymore. I don't know where I'm going yet. I've only taken what I think is mine. I'll contact you later so we can divide the rest of our stuff, etc. I'm sorry if I've hurt you. I'll always love you, but it's over. Molly." There was a postscript, appended in pencil: "You're going to find out sooner or later anyway, so I might as well tell you I've gone with Corin."

I sat down on the bed. The next few hours are a complete blur to me, even now.

Eight

NOW

W hat struck Molly with a little shock—it was hard to say if the shock was predominantly pleasant or unpleasant—was how sexy Ashley looked. Of course, this development hadn't happened overnight, not literally. The girl had had her first period almost six months before, so it wasn't as if there were no warnings. But still…it was odd how you suddenly noticed these things. When had her body started to look like that? She wasn't especially busty yet—perhaps, given the genes she'd inherited from her mother, she never would be—but she definitely was shapelier. Shapelier than she'd looked yesterday, as far as Molly could recall. And she *had* a bust now. Plus, her whole frame had elongated, legs and torso both, and her hips had taken on definition. She occupied a woman's space on the planet, not a girl's. There must exist societies— *National Geographic* probably still featured several in every issue—where she would be regarded as nubile, literally nubile, marriageable.

Molly had read, probably in a woman's magazine perused while sitting in some doctor's or dentist's anteroom, that this current generation of girls were experiencing puberty earlier than their mothers had.

What could cause such a change, and in a single generation? Surely not diet. Molly and her cohort had grown up well cared for and well nourished; if the '50s had been about anything, that reviled decade had been about plenty. Whatever the reason, the scientific evidence was apparently indisputable. Nevertheless, to Molly's mind, the basic physical facts were secondary. There was something beyond the physical, or at any rate the physiological, about Ashley that Molly was noticing today. About Ashley and these other girls Ashley's age who had flocked to the Mill Valley Banana Republic on this lovely Saturday morning. Something in their demeanor, some special sort of erotic alertness. As if sex were in the air these children breathed and the water they drank.

And the clothes they wore, of course.

Molly was waiting, seated on a tan leather bench, uncomfortable, no back support, and Ashley was in a changing room. It surprised Molly that Ashley had opted for this store in Mill Valley, the chain's mother ship, over the one in San Francisco—these classic mother-daughter shopping excursions were traditionally big-city affairs, and in any case the San Francisco Banana was bigger and better-stocked—but Molly didn't mind, was even relieved. Easier parking, smaller crowds, less tumult. Mill Valley, for all its self-conscious tweeness, was an authentically charming town; Saturday in downtown San Francisco was pure stress test. She was in any case happy to defer to Ashley, in hopes it would ease that chip off the girl's shoulder a few degrees.

Ashley emerged from the changing area in low-slung jeans cut tight in the pelvis, looser in the leg, with a skimpy pale green sweater bottoming well above her midriff. Yowza. Her navel was revealed in all its innie glory, holding a silver ring Molly hadn't known existed. Well, better than a tongue stud, if you were looking for cold comfort. But the whole gestalt...Jesus. If Nabokov wrote *Lolita* today, Humbert might be a salesman at a mall clothing store. The ripe fruit was dropping off the tree.

But the girl looked fabulous, no denying that. Her face blended Dennis' bland WASP handsomeness with Molly's pert prettiness, and the combination was better than the sum of its far from negligible parts.

She might even be beautiful; it was hard for a mother to judge. And her body…well, the word "jail-bait" came inescapably to mind. There she stood, a fully sexualized ninth-grader. It was unnerving. And the onset of puberty wasn't, per se, the crucial thing. Hell, *we* didn't look like that even by fourteen or fifteen or sixteen. Or twenty-five.

No, Molly thought, at bottom—ha ha—this isn't about physical maturation. It's attitude. When she herself first started looking like that, or at least when her body started adopting those kinds of contours, it had been a source of embarrassment; the whole world was now privy to her most secret physiological workings, and she found it mortifying. A personal violation. As if strangers on the street were following her into the bathroom every day. Whereas Ashley and the other girls frolicking through the shop seemed to be exulting in it. Flaunting it. Italicizing it. Theatricalizing it.

She must have been frowning. Ashley was regarding her quizzically. "You don't like them?"

She smiled, touched that Ashley cared (although the concern may largely have been Molly's control of the purse). "No, no…It's just startling to me, that's all. You look so…luscious. So sexy." Ashley grinned, spontaneously and happily. Molly went on, "You have a *body*. It just hit me." Any minute now, she thought, I'm going to launch into a chorus of "Gigi." Feeling a spasm of protective tenderness toward her daughter— such feelings were increasingly rare—she said, "But do *you* like them? You do, don't you? Well, why not? The fit's perfect. Let's get them."

Less than an hour later, they were ordering lunch at the nearby Cantina. Mothers and daughters have been doing this for generations, Molly was thinking. The thought was reassuring. It suggested today's problems were part of a parade stretching toward the horizon, and that issues looming ominous and insurmountable would pass into irrelevance or somehow work themselves out satisfactorily.

Ashley ordered fish tacos and an iced tea; Molly opted for a vegetarian tostada, and then allowed herself a glass of white wine. The next hour might prove challenging. And she deserved a reward for resisting the siren song of a margarita.

After the waitress moved off, Molly said, "When I was your age, we weren't allowed to wear jeans to school. We had to wear skirts or dresses."

Ashley considered Molly's childhood to have taken place in some dim, distant historical epoch. Despite elite private schooling, she had only a vague sense of any era before her own, except, at best, as an academic abstraction, a jumbled pageant of colorful costumes and wars and stilted speeches and beheadings, with Franklin Roosevelt, say, all but rubbing shoulders with Henry VIII; it wasn't that she was ignorant of the appropriate dates, but she still seemed, as a practical matter, to divide time between *now* and *not-now*.

"What would happen if you didn't?" she asked, polite but unenthralled.

"I don't recall anybody disobeying. They'd probably have been sent home."

"And nobody complained?"

"It never occurred to us to. It's just the way things were."

"I can't imagine putting up with that."

"You would have, though."

"I think we might have rebelled."

"You think that because you were never in that situation."

"I don't know, mom. We're pretty rebellious."

"*We* were rebellious, Ash. We were famous for it. Racial segregation, the war in Vietnam, drug laws…you name it, we rebelled against it. Sometimes we were right and sometimes we were insanely wrong, but protest was our default response. Still, even with that, there's so much you never even think to resist. Things that feel as natural as breathing. Like…I don't know, like crossing on green, waiting on red. It isn't a natural law, but it might as well be. Or the music you listen to. You think it's great, you can't imagine listening to anything else, but that's because it's what's been handed to you. If you lived at another time, you'd be listening to something else and feeling the same way about it."

"You were lucky. You had the Beatles."

That much history she knew.

"And it wasn't just jeans, by the way. Girls could be sent home if their skirts were too short. Mini-skirts were just becoming fashionable, so some of the girls kind of pushed the limits. How short could they get away with?"

The waitress arrived with their drinks. Ashley put a spoonful of sugar into her iced tea, stirred it, and took a sip. Molly forced herself to hold off on the wine until her food arrived, contenting herself—really anything but contenting herself—with a sip of water instead. One sip of wine would lead to another, and she didn't want to have drained her glass by the time the food arrived. Then she would be tempted to order a second. One glass was already pushing it.

Ashley was spooning more sugar into her iced tea. While doing so, she asked, "Did *you* ever get sent home?"

Molly smiled. "Well…not for a short skirt."

Ashley visibly perked up. Her interest was piqued. "For something else?"

"Once, yeah. For organizing an anti-war rally. The principal wouldn't give us permission, he thought the whole business was Communist propaganda, but I went ahead anyway. So he sent me home for the day. For being the instigator. Which I was. But… it's not like I was a trouble-maker. The opposite. I was a goody-goody. Straight-A student, class presi-dent, pretty much teacher's pet. This was my first-ever act of defiance. So he was confused, there was no familiar category to put me in, he didn't have a clue what to do. And I wasn't the only one. It was like…have you seen that movie about pod people? It was like that. We looked the same, but we'd changed. And it was happening all over. All these demure, obedient, pious girls and boys were up in arms about everything, ques-tioning all the stuff they'd been taught to accept unconditionally. Their families weren't prepared for it. Their communities weren't prepared for it. Nobody knew what hit them."

"Were grandma and grandpa mad?"

"The time I was sent home? More puzzled than mad. They thought I was wrong, but they were proud of me, too. In a funny way. You know, the thing about grandpa…he was a mean old coot a lot of the time, and

I doubt he had an unorthodox or interesting idea his whole life, but he admired guts. He thought I showed guts."

"What if you'd been sent home for a mini-skirt?"

Molly laughed. "Good question. I have no idea."

"You'd never do such a thing?" Ashley was laughing along with Molly. She got a kick out of picturing her mother as a priggish teenager.

"I sneered at mini-skirts. They were a sign of girly frivolity. I liked jeans, but only because I liked to ride horses, and because they were comfortable. I wasn't interested in looking sexy back then."

"Unlike now, huh?"

"You saying your mom isn't sexy?"

Ashley made a disgusted face, but the effect was intended humorously, and she added "Ewww!" with the clear purpose of getting a laugh out of Molly. Then she said, "But my friends…not that I want to hear it, mind you, but when we talk about parents, everyone says you're a babe."

"A MILF?"

It was instantaneous: Ashley blushed scarlet. "You know about MILFs?"

"I teach kids who aren't a whole lot older than you, Ash."

"And they tell you about MILFs? Oh my God, is that what happens in college?" And then, "That must mean they think *you're* one! Ewww!"

"That's gross too?"

"Well, sure. The fact they'd like to…you know…"

Molly gave in and took a sip of wine. You can hold out only so long. "Sorry if it distresses you," she said, "but students do get crushes on me sometimes." She said it seriously, forsaking the bantering tone. She saw an opening. "It's not uncommon. Like patients falling for Zeke. Shrinks even have a name for that, they call it 'transference.' Freud said it was supposed to happen, it *had* to happen for therapy to work. But it isn't restricted to therapy. You often see it when one side has power and authority and the other is in a supplicant or submissive position."

"Do they tell you?"

"Students who get crushes?"

"Uh huh."

"Well, sometimes, but they don't have to. You can tell. They show up at office hours and ask about things you know they aren't interested in. They look at you in a sort of puppy-dog way. They try to maneuver conversations onto personal topics. They flirt a little, usually ineptly." She was smiling in spite of herself. "Although sometimes they manage to get a little groove working."

"So what do you do? Or maybe I don't want to know."

"Don't be ridiculous, Ashley. Honestly." She shook her head. "If they don't say anything, I ignore it. There's no need to acknowledge it."

"And if they do say something?"

"Well…" She paused to collect herself—this was the moment she'd been hoping for, and she didn't want to blow it—but just then, damn it, the waitress arrived with their orders. With the various side plates, the beans and rice and tortillas and guacamole and salsa, it took time. Additional time wasn't necessarily unwelcome by itself, but she didn't want to lose the thread.

When the waitress moved on, Molly noticed that Ashley's fish tacos looked awfully tasty and briefly regretted her own choice. Well, too late to worry about that. Forking up a bit of lettuce and red bell pepper, she said, "See, the thing is, when somebody likes you, even if you don't feel the same, it puts an obligation on you. It may not seem fair, you may not have invited it, but still, you have a responsibility."

Ashley was looking at her attentively. Good.

"Not a responsibility to like them back. Or give them what they want. I'm not suggesting anything of that nature."

"You mean, like, *put out?*"

Molly laughed. "'Putting out,' as you put it, is just one example. Kind of an extreme example, I dearly hope. But this isn't a sex talk, Ash. It's about everything in the world. You don't have to do something that makes you uncomfortable just to be nice, or because someone expects it. *Ever.* Make your own choices according to your instincts, don't let yourself be pressured or manipulated into anything that feels wrong. But the point I'm trying to make, and believe me, I've learned it the hard way, is, you need to be sensitive to other people's feelings. Especially people who care about you. Be as kind as the situation permits. We all have spiteful impulses, but that doesn't make it okay to give in to them. The only unforgivable sin, I think, is to be meaner than you need to be."

Ashley nodded. She'd been listening seriously. "So let's say a guy comes to your office and says he really likes you. Or—" making a face, "however they put it."

Molly smiled. "Well, right off I say I'm married. Usually, that's enough. They probably know it already, I wear a ring, but my saying it tells them the door's closed. And I say our pedagogical relationship makes any other kind impossible. I'm careful not to say it in a way that suggests regret. Nothing wistful. Just matter-of-fact. But I *don't* say, Listen, get real, you're a fumbling, gawky post-adolescent who wouldn't have appealed to me even when *I* was a fumbling, gawky post-adolescent."

Ashley laughed. "Sounds like you'd like to."

"It's tempting sometimes. Guys can be obnoxious. Preening, acting like they're doing you a favor. But...what's to be gained? Other than momentary satisfaction, what's to be gained? And the thing about guys— not just gawky post-adolescent guys, *all* guys—they're more fragile than we are. We're fragile too, but men...under that I'm-tough exterior, which probably makes things worse, having to keep that up, but underneath it they're a mass of insecurities. So you might have a hankering to take them down a peg, but you need to be careful, because you can do harm." She frowned. "Real harm. Irreparable harm. It isn't worth it."

"What if they won't take no for an answer?"

"You do what you have to do. All I'm saying is, keep things proportional."

"So, like, a knee in the balls is a last resort?"

Molly almost choked on her wine. Ashley had been so difficult lately, it was easy to forget she could also be quick and droll. A second daughter, an accident, conceived late in Molly's first marriage when it was already unraveling, Ashley had been difficult from the start. From conception, virtually. Molly had regarded the pregnancy as, at best, a very mixed blessing, especially when contemplating her likely future life as a single mother. And she hadn't been wrong about the problems, even with Zeke unexpectedly entering the picture. Some problems were just getting underway. Still, it sometimes seemed worth it, seemed more than worth it. Ashley was a pain in the ass in about a thousand ways, but she was also a remarkable child, a lively, tumultuous counterpoise to the placid Olivia.

Molly said, "The thing about men is, if you say or do the wrong thing at the wrong time, it's pretty much the same as a knee in the balls."

There was a long pause. Ashley was frowning all of a sudden. "Hey. Are we talking about Shawn?"

Molly put her wine glass down. She looked at Ashley levelly. "Yeah, we are. But not *just* about Shawn."

Zeke had a cancellation. The best kind, coming at the last minute, or at any rate with less than 24 hour's notice. That's how doctors, lawyers, shrinks, and hair-dressers define the last minute. It meant he had the hour free and could still charge. A gift. Especially for a shrink, since the missed hour and the obligation to pay for it were rich sources of material, excellent entry-points for examining resistance and transference issues. Everybody wins, thought Zeke, even if only one of us knows it.

It was 11:00, too early for lunch, but he was restless. Lately, he'd been feeling restless a lot. If only he were in therapy, he might be able to get to the bottom of it. It was a beautiful morning, and his next client wasn't due till noon. Maybe he'd go for a walk and grab a cup of coffee at Peet's. Without succumbing to the temptation of pastry, although coffee without pastry was close to pointless.

He took the side exit, the one provided for clients who were shy about being observed leaving his office. Why? Well, you can examine these things too closely. He had to leave one way or the other, and either route could be accorded psychological significance. Sometimes a cigar is just a cigar, and sometimes you go through the first door you see.

Once out on the street, he jay-walked across The Alameda and pointed himself toward Solano Avenue. In that first stretch of Solano, past the Israeli cafe and the Iranian jeweler and the realtor who had been there forever and the high-tech, punked-out salon with its purple-and-green-haired, multiply-pierced, extravagantly tattooed, sexy-but-schmutzig stylists, and Noah's Bagels, and Cactus Cantina, down near the Turkish restaurant, there was a familiar hazard, if one could call it that, and it never failed to induce a moral queasiness in Zeke. There were two panhandlers who had staked out territory less than fifty feet from one another; by an odd coincidence, both were rail-thin black men with scraggly beards, both in their late thirties or early-forties, both bearing hallmarks of sustained substance abuse. The quandary for Zeke was that, despite their similarities, similarities a census might have judged so defining as to render them virtual clones, they were in fact very different characters. One, with his bravura and glib repartee, his willingness to accost strangers and his good-humored refusal to be ignored or rebuffed, was an obnoxious, intrusive pest, polluting an otherwise charming stretch of small-town, small-scale commercial street. The other, with his dreamy, haunted look, and his reticent, distracted manner, and his air of pained, constrained silence (he never came out and asked you for a contribution, although he might permit himself a small gesture with the Styrofoam cup in his hand, while risking, at what seemed immense personal cost, momentary eye-contact), was a person you spontaneously felt moved to help, without solicitation or prodding.

But, Zeke often asked himself, weren't these largely aesthetic judgments? And if so, did they play any defensible role in deciding how to allocate one's generosity? No doubt the fund-raising efforts of animal-rights groups were more successful when they featured cute baby seals instead of, say, an itchy little snail darter, but was cuteness a legitimate way to determine need? And if it wasn't, why should a simpatico personality be different? Was withholding a buck a fitting punishment for unattractive self-presentation? Had panhandling become another reality show where every put-upon pedestrian could regard himself as Donald Trump?

The whole transaction was demeaning to everybody, Zeke thought. Them and me both. And, of course, entertaining such a notion is a luxury I can afford and they can't. As often happened, he found himself slipping each man a five-dollar bill as he passed. And resenting it.

He entered Pegasus Books, one of the few bookstores remaining in Berkeley. A shonda for a college town, so few bookstores. And was surprised to find Liam, hunched over the "Staff Recommendations" table at the front of the store, assiduously signing copies of *White Bucks* with his treasured Mont Blanc pen.

Zeke sneaked up behind him. "Bribe the staff?" he said.

Liam looked up with a start. And grinned his pleasure at encountering Zeke. "Best three dollars I ever spent. This should be good for, and this is just a guesstimate of course, but should be good for moving an extra, oh, zero copies."

"Gotta start somewhere."

Whereupon Zeke hoisted a copy from the pile. "From zero to one in under a minute."

"You're gonna buy it? Really?"

"I always buy your books. I thought you knew that."

"I'm touched."

"But I'd appreciate your making the inscription a little more personal than—" He opened the book to the title page, and read aloud, "'Best wishes, Liam Hunter.'"

"Fair enough. Hand it over." He took the book out of Zeke's hands, opened it, and started writing. "You plan on reading it?" he asked.

"Don't push your luck," Zeke said.

Liam snorted, amused as always by Zeke's show of disrespect. He handed the book back. "Thanks," Zeke said, opening it. Liam had drawn a little carat before the word "Best," and had written the word "Very" above it. Zeke laughed out loud. "Almost embarrassingly effusive," he said.

"You want more, read the damned thing."

"This is going to require a rigorous cost-benefit analysis."

"Fuck you."

"How's it selling?" Zeke asked. "Any numbers yet?"

"Not from the publishers. Much too early for them to start lying to me. But I doubt it's doing much business."

"Needs to build."

"Needs to but won't. It's basically over for me. I barely get reviewed anymore. Sometimes I'm consigned to those 'Books in Brief' columns, those round-ups of books that don't merit reviews all by themselves. That sucks, I can tell you. 'Hunter offers another microscopic analysis of pop culture.' Which isn't wrong, it just isn't adequate. They could engage with my ideas, but that takes work. It's easier to pigeonhole me, portray me as doing my tired old thing rather than seeing if I have anything to say. When I die, the obits will call me a national treasure and there'll be no one who has a clue what I've written. And meanwhile...You know the...the sort of...cachet that used to attach to my willingness to write seriously, eruditely, with all the scholarly appurtenances, the citations and footnotes and so on, about total crap? The novelty of that, when I started doing it in *Rolling Stone* and *Crawdaddy*...that's gone. I made a little noise at the start, got invited on a few of the higher class talk shows, etc. An interesting weirdo. And out-of-context quotes were sometimes used as blurbs. But I never had the kind of following that keeps coming back. So now it's just...maybe a few aging bolshie profs who assign me to their media studies classes. To give the kids something novel and counter-cultural, or to prove how hip they are."

There was a pause after this tirade, and then Zeke said, "You're depressed."

"Is that a professional diagnosis?"

"A friend's observation."

"I'm not depressed, just realistic. If I was depressed, I wouldn't be visiting every fucking book store in the Bay Area to sign these suckers. I wouldn't be going on Michael Krasny tomorrow, wishing he was Terry Gross. And listen, I bitch and moan, but it's a living, man. I earn back my advances. I'm lucky to be doing what I like doing."

"Okay."

They had moved toward the cash register. When Zeke presented the book and a credit card to the cashier, Liam suddenly announced, with no perceptible change in tone, "I saw Corin the other day."

Zeke couldn't tell whether Liam had been saving up this information until what he regarded as the right moment, or whether he was really offering it as casually and artlessly as it sounded. It's sometimes hard to remember other people don't live inside your head, they don't participate in your experiences. Zeke made an effort not to give anything away as he replied, "Oh? How was that?" Not losing one's cool was apparently an ineradicable remnant of the boomers' code.

"It was interesting. We met for coffee, shot the shit. I get the impression he wants to re-connect with his old life. He's been unanchored for a long time now. On the lam. It seems to have gotten to him, finally."

"How'd he strike you?" Still keeping his emotions carefully reined in.

"Different. Really different, Zeke. Chastened, is how I'd put it. Rueful. You still get glimpses of the old Corin, but he seems like a changed person."

Zeke permitted himself, "Gotta be an improvement."

Liam responded with a thin smile. While Zeke was signing the credit card slip, Liam said, "Aw, you should let that go, it's a lifetime ago." And then he added, "He's looking for a place to stay. You know he's been crashing with Stan, right?"

"Stan mentioned it the other night."

"Well, I don't know what happened, but apparently he's been evicted."

Zeke's eyebrows went up. "Really?"

"Yep. Stan told him to find other lodgings."

"That doesn't sound like Stan at all. Especially where Corin's concerned."

"Nooo…but it does sound like Carla." That got a grudging laugh from Zeke. "Don't you think?"

"I can picture her putting her foot down. To Stan, I mean. And making him deliver the bad news to Corin. Corin and Carla…it's like King Kong vs. Godzilla."

Which got a laugh from Liam, who said, "Plus, she's home all day while Stan's at the office. So she's the one who has to deal with the guy."

"No buffer zone."

"Things must've been getting tense. He asked after you, by the way."

"Stan?"

"Corin. He's hoping to see you. He seems eager to talk."

"An eagerness I can't say I share."

"It was all such a long time ago, Easy."

"I'm not saying it keeps me up nights."

"Aren't you curious?"

"Not so much." Zeke accepted the receipt and the book proffered by the cashier. After thanking her, he turned to Liam. "Come next door, get some coffee?"

"Can't. Miles to go before I sleep. I've got Moe's, Book Smith, Mrs. Dalloway, B and N, Jack London Square, every fucking East Bay bookstore still standing. By the time I get home, writer's cramp'll be so bad Melanie'll have to spoon-feed me dinner. A procedure I happen to enjoy, fortunately."

Zeke forced a smile at this, but after they parted, and Liam had headed across the street toward Andronico's, in whose lot he was no doubt illegally parked, and Zeke had started the few steps toward Peet's, he knew his earlier good mood had evaporated, and also knew things would be getting worse over the afternoon. A few seconds later, when the obnoxious panhandler approached him for the second time that morning, and seemed, with his usual frenetic familiarity, disinclined to take no for an answer, Zeke growled, "Will you please fuck off?" It worked. The man had no snappy come-back. He gave Zeke a wounded look, surprised and hurt, but he retreated without another word.

Owen patted the sad-looking donkey's brow, just the way he'd done as a child. "Hi there, Isaac," he said. "How's life treating you? Pretty well, I bet."

Zeke watched him, marveling. When Owen was little, they visited this little farm in Tilden Park several times a week after pre-school. But they hadn't been back in more than ten years. Owen had gradually lost interest, or had become interested in other things, video games and music and friends and God knows what. Zeke occasionally tried to interest him in paying a visit, especially after Angie died and he thought the two of them might find it comforting, but Owen always politely declined, or suggested they do it some other time in the indefinite future. But now, returning after so many years, Owen seemed transfixed.

"It hasn't changed much," Zeke observed.

"Isaac's gotten older," Owen said. "He seems slower."

"He was never what you'd call speedy."

Owen glanced up at his father. "Didn't you find it boring, coming here all the time?"

"Well...I liked spending time with you. It was fun watching you have fun."

Owen nodded. The answer didn't appear to resonate with him, but he accepted it. "It's dinkier than I remembered."

"The dinkiness is part of its charm." And then, recalling a long-forgotten incident, Zeke said, "You got attacked by the goat once. Do you remember?"

"I do! The little one. The kid. Not the big goat."

"That's right. Thank goodness for that. Just little bumps, no real horns. Still, you were traumatized. For about three minutes."

"I thought we were buddies. I felt betrayed."

They smiled at each other, sharing the memory, recalling the little boy's tears of consternation. Zeke suddenly put his arm around Owen's shoulders—no easy matter, given the difference in their heights—and pulled him close. Owen laughed, and said, "Who're you hugging, dad? Me at five or me now?"

It was a shrewd question, but on some fundamental level off the mark. Even though Owen now stood over six feet tall, and even with his lean frame and scratchy, unshaven face and baritone voice, Zeke loved the boy with an undiminished intensity that was almost painful. "Both," he said. "But I accept there's a difference."

"Let's check out the Nature Center, see if the Komodo Dragon's still there."

"Sure," Zeke readily agreed.

They began the stroll down the shallow knoll to the low-slung structure housing the Nature Center. Zeke asked, "What led you to suggest this little outing?"

"I don't know. Seemed like a nice idea."

"Feeling bad about something?"

Owen abruptly stopped walking and, smiling a small, skeptical smile, turned to face his father. "Are you theraping me, dad?"

It was an old family routine: When Zeke expressed concern about someone's emotional state, he was accused of "theraping," of employing his armory of professional techniques and methods. And the accusation, whether justified or not, playful or not, put him on the defensive; it implied he viewed family issues from a detached or elevated vantage point. This was a notion he rejected categorically.

"No, no. Or, that is, I don't think so." A mistake to protest too much. "It's just, you've seemed a little...down lately, that's all. 'Down' isn't a diagnostic category, okay? Just a paternal observation."

"Yeah. Well—" Owen resumed walking. Zeke scrambled to catch up, and walked abreast of Owen, keeping mum, waiting patiently. He *was* theraping, of course. It would be silly not to use what he knew when dealing with people he cared about. Over the years, working with clients, he'd found that prompting too eagerly or at the wrong time could backfire. People retreat. They bridle at being interrogated; they need to find their own pathway to saying what they have to say. This was something most shrinks know instinctively, nothing arcane about it, and they no doubt hold it in common with priests, cops, and high school principals. People want to confess. You don't pressure them, you give them room.

"Maybe it's being away at school," Owen said. "Even if I'm not really away. Like Thomas Wolfe says, you can't go home again. Even when you do go home."

Zeke didn't say anything. Clients often proffer more or less plausible explanations for things before they work their way through to what's really on their minds. You have to let them process.

"And by the way," Owen said, "I know he isn't the same Tom Wolfe who wrote *I Am Charlotte Simmons*." A little dig; Zeke could be pedantic about such things. Owen waited for Zeke to acknowledge the comment, which he did with an amused grunt. Then, "And sometimes...lately I've been thinking about mom."

"Have you?" Zeke wasn't entirely convinced, but this was more interesting, less generic. A little encouragement might be in order.

"When things happen, you know? Milestones and stuff."

"Like...what? Going away to school?"

"Yeah. And..." Owen looked at his hands. "I sometimes think about how much mom has missed. How much has happened since she died. I know this is nuts, but I even feel like she's missed out on Molly and Olivia and Ashley. I realize they wouldn't be in our lives if mom were alive. Or if they were, she'd be plenty pissed." He gave Zeke a small smile. "But..." He hesitated, and then said, "It's just so unfair. To her and to us."

Zeke put a hand on Owen's shoulder. "It is. It totally stinks. It bothered her terribly, you know. That she wouldn't see you grow up."

"She told you that?"

"Uh huh."

"You talked about that stuff?"

"Once it was clear there was no hope...you know what Dr. Johnson said?" Uh oh, he thought, here I go again. But he plowed on, "About how knowing you're about to hang concentrates the mind wonderfully? Well, that was the situation. Angie and I had the kinds of conversation most people never have. We talked about everything. There was no reason to hold back."

"How was that?"

Another telltale sign of resistance, bouncing questions back at the questioner. But this was also a legitimate source of curiosity. And there was so much Owen didn't know, could never know. "In the '60s we would have said it was 'heavy.' It was a big thing. Awful. It's hard for me to think about, even now. But it was also...I'm glad we had that time. We were never closer than the weeks before she died. And so we maybe felt a little more ready for the inevitable when it came. No regrets about all the things we should have said but didn't."

"Wow."

There were tears in Owen's eyes. Zeke felt tears spring into his own, or at least their warm, moist precursor. He tried to speak, and his throat felt furry. He coughed, tried again, coughed again. And then regained a measure of control. Not looking directly into Owen's eyes helped. "Anyway," he said.

There was a wooden bench in front of the Ecology Center. Owen plopped onto it. Zeke sat down next to him.

"Sometimes," said Owen, "I can't tell whether I'm remembering mom or remembering remembering her. That bothers me. Things getting hazy like that."

"Did something happen recently?" Zeke asked. He sensed the time was right. "I don't mean about Angie, necessarily. Just...anything?"

"Not really. And...I mean compared to...it's really pretty trivial. Just, I got an e-mail from Sara a couple of days ago." Sara had been his high school girlfriend. Three intense years together. They'd agreed to break up at the end of the previous summer, before she went east for college, recognizing, sensibly enough, that a long-distance relationship would be unmanageable. Nevertheless, the maturity of the decision notwithstanding, Zeke suspected it had largely been foisted on Owen. Although he'd put a brave face on it, assuring Zeke and Molly the decision was mutual, Zeke suspected the boy had been presented with a *fait accompli*, and had decided to voice agreement because any other reaction would have been futile. His agreement was supererogatory, face-saving. Once Sara broached the idea, the deal was done.

"Uh huh." Zeke could guess the rest, but waited for Owen to continue.

"It wasn't anything unexpected. You could say it's the whole point."

"She's gotten involved with somebody?"

"Yeah." Owen was looking down at his hands again, clasped in his lap. "Starting to, anyway. It was obviously going to happen."

"It still hurts when it does."

"And the tone of her e-mail...I guess it doesn't matter, it would hurt the same no matter what, but...jeez, dad, it was so matter-of-fact. Worse.

Cheerful. Nothing regretful or ambivalent in it, not even for...for the sake of good manners. It's like she honestly expected me to be happy for her. As if we had no history. And she asked me if I was seeing anyone, and it sounded like she hoped I was. Which made it seem not only like things are over between us, but like they'd never happened at all."

"No one knows how to handle these things well," Zeke suggested. "Someone once said that good sportsmanship is just being a good liar. The same is true for how people act around their exes. There's no natural way to behave with someone you once were intimate with and no longer are, so we just try to act gracious, at *best* we try to act gracious, and we often fail. Think of Molly and Dennis. You've seen them together. All very civilized, they're both decent people, but you can feel the tension. They used to be one way, and now...It's awkward for them to remember how they used to be, but it feels fake to be some way else. So try not to judge Sara too harshly about her e-mail. She's probably as confused as you how to handle this. I understand that's not the main thing, but don't assume she feels as casual as she sounds."

Owen nodded. "I can't honestly say I was hoping she'd change her mind. Not when I was thinking rationally. If she decided to break up when we were still together, what could possibly induce her to change her mind when we're thousands of miles apart? Unless she was feeling really lonely, maybe, but a girl like Sara, it wasn't likely she'd be lonely for long." He looked so miserable, Zeke wished he could literally shoulder his son's misery, take it on himself. He'd have done it gladly. "See, the thing is, I was...it's probably trivial, but, see, I was the first guy she'd ever been with. The only guy. So there was something special about it. That's what I thought, anyway. Something that belonged to her and me. Even broken up, it was something we still had with each other and no one else. And we told each other stuff. Things we'd never told another person. We told each other everything. And now there's this other guy, and he's there and I'm not, and they're going through whatever she and I went through, they're doing whatever we used to do, they're sharing *their* secrets, and I can't help but think—" His voice trailed off. "It keeps me awake at night. I feel so awful, dad."

Zeke put a hand on his son's shoulder. "Insomnia? Does it wake you up in the middle of the night, or do you have a hard time getting to sleep in the first place?"

"Hard time getting to sleep, mostly. Does it make any difference?"

"It can. How's your appetite?"

"I don't have any."

"I kind of envy that," Zeke said. "Feeling listless?"

"I guess."

"Dating?"

"Not really. I've been out a few times, but…see, when I'm with a girl, I just feel worse. Makes me want to go home and be by myself. I think of all the ways she isn't Sara." He made a face. "I'm listless *and* lustless."

Zeke moved his hand from Owen's near shoulder across his back and over the farther one, gripping it, pulling the boy closer to him. Owen offered no resistance. After a few seconds, Zeke said, "You're depressed."

"No kidding."

Zeke smiled, gave Owen a gentle, affectionate shake. "For what it's worth…and I know this doesn't provide much comfort when you're in the thick of it, but for what it's worth, virtually everybody in the world goes through this at some point. More than once, more often than not. It's brutal, especially if you're sensitive enough to really know and care about the other person. But it's part of being human. Without it, we'd have far fewer Shakespeare sonnets. Very few novels. No country music at all. Which you might regard as a mixed blessing."

Owen managed a smile. Watching him out of the corner of his eye, Zeke thought, I'd take a bullet for this boy, but there's no way I can spare him this anguish. No more than I can relieve him of the need to draw breath.

"Although," he heard himself adding, "thirty years as a therapist, I've acquired some appreciation for country music. It gets at some pretty real, pretty raw emotion." And cursed himself for having said it. He could easily imagine Molly admonishing him, telling him this was neither the time nor the place for such an observation.

212

Owen said, "I feel like a jerk, mentioning Sara right after we talked about mom." Gently getting Zeke back on track. Owen was too polite to say so, even when hurting, but a disquisition on the virtues of country music wasn't useful at the moment. "It's so minor by comparison," he went on, sensitively assuming responsibility for being insufficiently sensitive.

"Listen." Getting the message. Making full-on eye contact with his son. "Close to 100% of my clients come to me because of heartbreak. They have other problems too, and part of my job is to unearth those other problems, but they mostly don't come because of those. They come because they've been dumped. Or think they're about to be. Or wonder whether to dump someone else. Or they're cheating on their partner or being cheated on. Some have life-threatening eating disorders, or suffer from depression including suicidal ideation, or have a whole range of incapacitating phobias, but the reason they feel so miserable, the reason they seek help, is because something's wrong with their love life. You have absolutely no reason to feel bad about feeling bad. Even if there's war and terrorism and mass starvation and global warming. One set of miseries doesn't make another set of miseries hurt any less. The longer I'm in this business, the more I realize that for most people, love matters as much as or more than anything. The song writers have it right, the economists and political scientists have it wrong."

"Okay."

"And another thing is, you do get over it. Sometimes it happens quickly, sometimes not, but it happens. You have to get through it, there's no shortcut I know of. But you'll be stronger when you emerge on the other side, and you *will* emerge on the other side. And maybe wonder what the fuss was about. Oh, and something else. Part of what hurts is vanity. You think you occupy a unique role in another person's life, and then you discover someone else can occupy it too. Maybe lots of someone elses. The space exists independent of your having filled it. It's a blow to the ego."

"Yeah, I'm aware of that, dad."

"No, but listen, the thing to remember is, that *isn't* something to

213

apologize for. People are always trying to make us feel guilty about natural emotions, but saying it's vanity isn't saying it has no validity, or it's unworthy, or it's trivial. It's *important* to feel you're crucially important to someone else. It's deeply hurtful to discover you aren't. There's nothing illegitimate about that pain. Okay?"

"Okay. Thanks, dad."

"Shall we go look at the Komodo Dragon?"

Owen paused, and then said, "Nah, that's okay. We can skip it."

Zeke found this, in an odd way, the most touching moment of the afternoon.

Olivia was at her desk, trying to concentrate on writing a paper for history class about the annexation of the Philippines, but she was being inundated with IMs, windows popping up all over her computer screen. Her friends Lara and Nick, the two best-looking kids in her class, had just broken up—Lara's choice, or so the official story went, though Olivia suspected there was more to it that that—and their whole circle of friends was buzzing with gossip and speculation and opinions. Olivia wasn't especially engaged by any of this; she had a sense that much of the excitement was self-generated and vapid, almost as pointless as taking seriously, say, the celebrity romances chronicled in *US* magazine. All these high school narratives of friendships formed and ruptured, of romances dizzyingly initiated and heartbreakingly terminated, struck Olivia as false, an artificial injection of drama into their ordinary lives, prefabricated to fit a predetermined mold rather than an unfolding of spontaneous emotion. It wasn't simply vicarious, all this excitement, although it certainly was that; there was also something vaguely hysterical about it.

On the other hand, she knew better than to express this opinion. The crowd she ran with was considered a desirable crowd, *the* desirable crowd, and her membership in it felt both implausible and perhaps tenuous. She was liked well enough, but she was also considered too serious, too studious, to fit in. She was a provisional member, so to speak, almost a mascot. The girl whose company everyone enjoyed despite all the good reasons not to. Mascots aren't supposed to question basic assumptions, they're there on sufferance. So Olivia read the IMs as they came in, flashing onscreen and obscuring her essay, and she occasionally made a brief response, just to signal she was present and paying attention. But she was also trying, in the midst of all the cyber-palaver, to focus on President McKinley's foreign policy. Which struck her as almost as silly as her friends' adolescent soap opera.

She was determined, when she eventually dated someone seriously, that it wouldn't primarily be about social prestige, but rather about something personal. It didn't have to be true love or anything as exalted as that, but it at least should be about itself, not other people's reactions to it.

And the sooner the better, she added to herself. She was ready. More than ready. Not that guys weren't interested now—she knew she was attractive, it was the main reason they permitted her on the A-list, or at any rate the A-list auxilary—but there was no point being with a guy who bored her silly. Even if some friends urged her to do precisely that.

The doorbell rang, jolting her. Maybe it was only the raucous *arooga* of the electrical chime when she wasn't expecting it, but she felt her pulse kick into a higher gear. Or maybe it was because she was alone in the house.

She saved the document on her computer screen, jumped up and left her room. Heading downstairs toward the entrance foyer, she could see through the thick-slatted blinds covering the front door the shape of someone standing on the porch. A man. Tall. When she reached the door, she was careful to attach the chain before opening it a crack. "Yes?" she said, peering outward.

The man facing her was probably about her dad's age. It was hard to be sure; his skin was in worse shape, tanned and creased and leathery. But he was handsome, maybe handsomer than her dad, his face more interesting, with laughing eyes and a high-voltage smile. Thick, sandy hair. There was something friendly about him, something reassuring; she relaxed.

"Hi there," he said. "Is Zeke around?"

Although the guy seemed safe, Olivia knew better than to answer that one. "Is he expecting you?" she asked carefully. Zeke had warned her and Ashley more than once that one of his patients—clients, he called them—who was disturbed in some way might get ideas about him or became fixated on him. It hadn't happened yet, or at least had never gotten worrisomely out of hand; once, a couple of years ago, there had been a series of phone calls with silence at the other end when you answered, enough of them so Zeke had the phone number changed and kept the new one unlisted. Even at the height of that little crisis, Zeke was soothing, assuring the kids he was only concerned about the nuisance, not physical danger. But he'd also taken care to explain that some of his clients had emotional problems, there was a chance one might someday assume a personal relationship that didn't exist or want more from Zeke than he was professionally permitted to give. So the girls should be cautious about giving out information, even innocuous information, to anyone they didn't know. In addition to never talking to strangers anyway, blah blah blah.

But this guy didn't look disturbed, and didn't look dangerous. After a youth and adolescence in the Bay Area, Olivia had seen enough street people—drug burn-outs and schizos discharged from institutions that could no longer afford to keep them—to have a notion of what crazy people looked like. They looked crazy, or at least disorganized on a very basic level, and they behaved differently from people without mental illness, laughing at nothing, or carrying on conversations with invisible interlocutors. This man standing on the porch was nothing like that. He had a nice warm smile, and a comfortable, comforting demeanor. And an aura…it was hard to pinpoint, but you could tell he was cool in a way that most of Molly and Zeke's friends weren't. "No," he said, "he isn't expecting me." His voice was smooth and mellifluous, with a hint of an accent. "I'm an old friend. Of his and Molly's. I'm in Berkeley for a visit. Thought I'd drop by and say hello. Kind of surprise them."

Olivia hesitated. Then she said, "What's your name?"

"You're reluctant to let me in," the man said. "I understand."

"I'm not supposed to," she confirmed apologetically. And then, although she realized this wasn't information she should divulge, added,

216

"There's no one else in the house." It was just, he wasn't the sort of person you felt good about saying no to.

"Very wise policy," he said. "I'd like to wait for them, though. At least for a few minutes. And it's awfully hot out here." He shifted his weight, tamped at his forehead with the sleeve of his shirt. There were sweat stains at his arm pits, she noticed. "I could…would it help if I proved I really do know them? For example, Molly's maiden name was Hilliard. How's that?"

"That's still her name," Olivia said.

"Oh. Oh dear. Well…Could I maybe just have a glass of water, then?"

"I guess so," she said. "Sure. Hold on, I'll be right back." She shut the door, went to the kitchen for the water, went back to the front door, and re-opened it without removing the chain. When she passed the glass of water through the narrow crack permitted by the chain, the guy laughed. But his laughter seemed friendly, if slightly mocking at the same time, and she found herself laughing along with him. He nodded his thanks, took the water, and drank from it. He wiped his brow again. "Does it always get this hot in spring? I don't remember its being like this."

"It happens," she said. And was relieved to hear the sound of Molly's car alarm being activated, a distinctive double-chirp. "That's my mom now," she said.

Molly and Ashley appeared on the stairs moments later, a big bag from Banana Republic in Ashley's hand. Olivia, from behind the door, could see them ascending, could see first their heads and then their bodies come into view as they got closer. And she could see her mother's reaction when she finally became aware of the man standing on the porch. Something unpleasant happened to her face, and she froze for a brief second before continuing the rest of the way up the stairs.

"Hi, Mols," the man said.

Molly didn't answer until she finished the climb. Then she said, "A surprise." Not much inflection. It was obvious to Olivia she was displeased, although it might not have been apparent to anyone who didn't know her well. Then Molly noticed her elder daughter watching

217

from behind the door. After a second or two, she smiled a tight smile, and said, "Olivia wouldn't let you in?"

"Quite rightly."

"Yes. Quite rightly."

The man said, "She seems a lovely girl, Mols. Very poised, very attractive. There's a serenity about her." Then he glanced at Ashley. "And this one must be yours as well. She looks like you. Your mouth, your eyes. I can safely say *both* your girls are lovely. You must be very proud."

"Yes," Molly said, "I am. They are. Thank you." She sighed before continuing. "Girls, this is Corin McCabe. A friend from a long time ago."

Ashley muttered a hello, barely making eye contact, either uncomfortable with the situation or simply bored. Or maybe she needed to pee. Olivia, vaguely aware something seemed off-balance about the whole exchange, nevertheless said with a polite smile, "Very nice to meet you. I'm sorry I didn't let you in before."

Molly turned toward Olivia. "Honey, you were right to be careful."

"He told me he knew you and Zeke. But I just—"

"You absolutely did the right thing. But you can open the door now."

Olivia colored, uttered an abashed, "Oh, sorry!" and unlatched the chain. She knew beyond question something odd was going on. Impossible to guess what, but she was picking up lots of agitation. She'd never seen her mother so tightly withheld. Molly didn't seem angry at the guy, exactly, but he definitely wasn't welcome.

Olivia opened the door wide and stepped back. Ashley dashed through and up the stairs. Molly and Corin entered after, and they and Olivia stood in the entrance foyer for a silent moment. "Lovely house," Corin finally said.

Molly caught Olivia's eye. Nothing further was necessary. "Uh, I was doing homework when Mr. McCabe rang the doorbell. Would it be okay if I—?"

Molly said, "That's fine, honey. Get back to it."

She waited until Olivia was half-way up the stairs before she turned back to Corin. "Do you want to sit down for a minute?" she said.

"'For a minute?'" he echoed, with a satirical smile.

She did not return the smile. "For a minute."

"We really ought to let it breathe," Stan was saying.

At some point in his early forties, it dawned on Stan that he'd become quite rich and that he was clueless about spending money. He lived frugally, had never considered doing otherwise. He'd always been generous about charitable donations, but now he figured the time had come to acquire an expensive hobby and spend some money on himself. Having no long-term passions to indulge, he rummaged around for an enthusiasm—avoiding anything that violated his political or moral values, or risked life and limb—and finally concluded wine was just the ticket.

"Do you even like the stuff?" Zeke had asked him at the time.

"Sure," Stan said. And then amended his answer: "It's okay. But I can barely tell red from white. I'm hoping I'll like it better if I know something about it."

Which he systematically set about accomplishing, with the Talmudic rigor he brought to all intellectual challenges. And soon became an intolerable bore on the subject, pontificating over every sip, using the most precious nouns and pretentious adjectives in the oenophile's lexicon, endlessly comparing varietals and storage methods and fermentation techniques. At restaurants, he often engaged sommeliers in interminable colloquies before ordering. It was Liam, still drinking in those days, who finally set him straight: "Listen, buddy, if you can talk about booze and bore *me*, that pretty much clinches it, you're a bore. Period. So give it a fucking rest, willya?"

He probably would have given it a fucking rest eventually anyway; Liam just hastened the process. But he kept assembling his cellar, laying down bottles that wouldn't be worth uncorking for decades, attending auctions, spending untold thousands of dollars—maybe untold tens of thousands of dollars, maybe even more, it wasn't something one asked—on his new hobby. Carla didn't approve, but since the hobby didn't involve other women, and since Stan's actual intake was moderate, she restricted her opposition to a passive, almost Gandhian tactic: She refused to drink any of the stuff herself. She preferred seltzer, she insisted.

Which worked out well for Zeke. Stan didn't like drinking alone. Now that Liam had taken the pledge, Zeke was the main beneficiary of Stan's beneficence. Lucky timing: Some of the wine Stan had bought when his collecting binge started was reaching full maturity.

It was a very warm spring afternoon today, and on balance, as they sat out on Stan's deck, Zeke was in the mood for a gin-and-tonic rather than a claret, no matter how splendid. The sunlight was pouring through the treetops at that distinctive late-afternoon slant, dappling the deck, the air was redolent with eucalyptus, the wide expanse of bay visible from this height was glinting spectacularly; but it had been a morning of troubled clients and an afternoon with a troubled son, and in addition, Zeke was feeling like a troubled man himself. The totality cried out for a very stiff snort of something distilled. But hell, don't want to seem churlish.

"It's probably semi-aerated by now," Stan was saying. "It'll keep opening up for a while, but let's go for it."

"What are we drinking?"

"Lynch Bages '86. It's youngish, but…I got a case, so this is an experiment to see how ready it is or isn't." He poured a glass for Zeke and one for himself, then hoisted his, swirled it, smelled it, and watched the legs as they slithered downward.

Zeke went ahead and took a small sip. He had no big immediate reaction. The wine was complex, that much he could tell. It had an earthy undertaste, as if you could still dimly discern the soil in which the vines had grown. "So, what should I think?" he asked Stan. "You have license to opine."

Stan still had wine in his mouth. He swished it around a bit, then swallowed. There was a thoughtful look on his face. "First sips can be misleading. Especially so soon after uncorking. My guess is, it may need a few more years before it's at the top of its game." He swirled it around the glass again, then took another swallow. "On the other hand, it's pretty fucking good."

"It is," Zeke agreed.

They both leaned back in their wooden deck chairs. The setting, the view, the beautiful spring afternoon, the wine...they merited respectful attention. Stan's deck, occupying a landscaped terrace behind and somewhat to the side of the house itself, was spacious, tree-lined to the rear, and afforded an unimpeded view of the bay. It was hard to imagine anything pleasanter.

"Life is good," Stan said.

Zeke sighed.

"Or isn't it?" Stan had caught the sigh.

"Yes, yes," Zeke answered quickly. "Life is very good. But today was hard. It's going to take a few sips before I unwind." Stan was looking at him steadily, waiting for more, knowing there was more. Zeke said, "I scheduled some clients today, which can ruin any Saturday. The endless whining! I mean, it's one thing when *I* whine, that's a racial prerogative, but other people? Give me a break!"

"Isn't that what they pay you for?"

"Exactly. They wouldn't pay if it wasn't a chore. And I saw Owen a while ago, and he's going through some shit. I want to help, but there's nothing I can do."

"Girl trouble?"

"Yeah."

"He'll be okay, Zeke. He's a wonderful kid. Bright as hell. And good-looking, that's just dumb luck, he got Angie's face. He'll be fine." Stan had always felt like a sort of unofficial godfather to Owen; his affection for the boy ran deep. Owen's attitude toward Stan was more complicated, salted with a healthy pinch of irony and, sometimes, downright incredulity. Once, when he was in high school, he'd said to Zeke, "Dad, can you explain how you got such a geeky best friend? I mean, you're almost cool"—a grudging concession that pleased Zeke enormously—"but Stan's like a poster boy for dorkhood." Zeke had defended Stan, although it took some doing, and also delivered a sententious and arguably hypocritical lecture on the negligibility of coolness as an attribute, while trying at the same time to stifle his own amusement;

of course, he'd frequently posed some variation of the same question to himself over the years. Still, for all of Owen's professed puzzlement, it was obvious to anyone who saw him and Stan together that their affection was abiding and reciprocal. Zeke was sure it was Stan to whom his son would turn in a crisis if he or Molly weren't available.

"Of course," Zeke agreed now. "It's just…sometimes knowing things will get better doesn't help. Not short term, not while you're hurting. Between then and now falls a vast shadow, and that's all you can focus on. And…" Dangerous ground lay ahead. "There's more. Problems of my own." Stan waited. Zeke finally blurted, "Corin. Fucking Corin. It's like he's lurking everywhere, poised to spring. Everyone seems to have seen him but me and Molly, and it's starting to freak me out."

There was a long—a curiously long—pause. Stan took a sip of wine before asking, "You haven't seen him?"

"Uh uh."

"But you want to?"

"Hell no. But it's starting to feel like a horror movie. He's out there, you know? Around some corner, down some alley, behind some door. And just when I least expect it, boom! It would be a relief to get it over with."

"He wants to see you."

"Yeah, he apparently told Liam the same thing."

"He's trying to make amends. Not just to you. To everybody. To the world. He's changed a lot, Easy."

"So what?"

Stan made a face. "You haven't forgiven him?"

"Forgiveness isn't the issue. What happened, happened. I'm not on a moral high horse. I just don't want to have anything to do with him."

"That doesn't sound terribly forgiving to me."

It was at this moment that Carla appeared in the doorway leading from the house. She stood there for a moment, weighing her options, and then took a step onto the deck. She was wearing a loose fitting pink velour warm-up suit and a pair of Adidas. Her ginger hair was up, and tied. She was sweating heavily.

Zeke couldn't decide whether her arrival was a relief or an unwelcome interruption. He offered a hello, and Stan said, "You were working out?"

"No," she said, "I was at a ladies' luncheon for Mrs. Obama."

Stan had installed gym equipment in his basement a few years before, even though he still used the Berkeley Y more often than not. "I need witnesses," was his explanation, "I need admiration and approval." But Carla preferred privacy. She had recently put herself on a health kick; though still hefty, she had lost some weight. Considering what came out of her kitchen, that wasn't a minor accomplishment.

She took a couple of steps further onto the deck. "Mind if I join you for a minute before I get in the shower? I need to stop sweating."

TMI. But that was Carla. She strode toward them, pulled up a wicker chair, and said to Stan, "How's your expensive wine?"

"Not quite mature," Stan said.

"Funny how that works."

"It's actually pretty fabulous," Zeke said.

"You want something to eat maybe?"

"No, no thanks, Carla. Too close to dinner."

"There's plenty. I've got a fridge full of leftovers."

"I never doubted it."

"Suit yourself." After settling herself in her chair—the wicker offered a creaking protest—she said, "So what are you two talking about? Sex and sports?"

Stan smiled, charmed. Hard as it was to credit, he was authentically uxorious. Zeke found himself bewildered: *Sex and sports?* Carla and Stan had been together over twenty years; in that time, it was doubtful she'd *ever* heard him and Zeke discuss either sex or sports. Did she think they waited until she was out of earshot?

"We were talking about Corin," Stan told her.

"Ugh," she said, and made a face.

Carla arrived on the scene too late to have known Corin in the old days. It wasn't clear how he'd earned her enmity, but it was a recent development.

"I asked him to leave the other day," Stan explained to Zeke.

"Liam mentioned that."

"I hated to do it, but Carla and I felt it had to be done."

"Did he take it okay?" Zeke asked.

"Well, he was decent about it. Said he understood, said he appreciated all we'd done for him. But I could see the fear in his eyes. He looked desperate."

"He gave him money," Carla said. Her voice was hard, scornful.

Zeke looked to Stan. "Yeah," Stan confirmed, "I wrote him a check." Flatly, without much inflection. Evidently, he and Carla had hammered this one out already, and—had this ever happened before?—she'd lost the argument. Or perhaps she found out too late. Either way, it plainly still rankled. "He's broke," Stan went on. It wasn't clear whether this was directed at Carla or Zeke. "Stuck. Had nowhere to go. If I was going to throw him out, it seemed right to help him buy a little time."

"Conscience money," Carla said.

"If you like."

"For not letting him live in our house indefinitely."

"I didn't feel good about it, okay? I did it, but I didn't feel good about it."

"You'd done enough. *We'd* done enough. We did plenty."

"I didn't see this as an instance of I-gave-at-the-office." An unfamiliar bit of bristling on Stan's part.

"Five thousand dollars," Carla said, directing her words to Zeke. "And he'd already been staying here for almost a month. Meals, laundry. Sleeping late, coming in at all hours. Borrowing our car, which was so nuts it still makes me shiver. We didn't owe him *bupkis*." This last sentence was aimed at Stanley again.

"It's not a question of owing," Stan said. "I wasn't discharging a debt."

"And that's not even mentioning the lawyering." Carla had lost the argument, but she wasn't about to let it go. "How many free hours did he get from you?"

"However many, I wasn't much help."

This got Zeke's attention. "No progress?" he asked.

"Stone wall."

"You were negotiating? With the Feds?"

"I wouldn't call it negotiating. Just feeling them out. Very, very cautiously. Not tipping my hand, just posing hypotheticals. I thought we had a fair chance. A lot of time has passed. No particular heat. It wasn't a huge story nationally. I figured they might be happy to close the books. They seemed amenable at first."

"And then—?"

"The door suddenly slammed shut. I'm guessing they took it upstairs and someone higher up, probably with a political portfolio, nixed it. One of the victims was a cop, so that always makes things complicated. Anyway, they suddenly weren't interested. Or rather, they were a little *too* interested, but not in making a deal."

"You explained this to Corin?"

"A little less bluntly than I've explained it to you. I told him my results had been disappointing so far and I wasn't optimistic."

Carla almost yelled: "It was madness for him to stay here after that! It was bad before, but afterwards it was insane! We were harboring a fugitive! A murderer! And this *schmegegy* here is hinting to the Feds he knows the guy's whereabouts!"

"Corin is not a murderer," Stan said.

"Pardon me, Mr. Clarence Darrow, but you're forgetting the law. Two people were killed in the commission of a felony. If he's convicted, he's a murderer. First degree. With special circumstances. It could be a capital case."

"No it couldn't," said Stan. "There was a moratorium on the death penalty when the crime occurred. It can't be applied."

"Oh, that's comforting," Carla said. She swiveled to face Zeke. "That makes it okay to hint the guy's our houseguest."

"I did nothing of the kind," Stan said mildly. "In fact, I suggested he was abroad, thinking about coming home."

"Like they wouldn't suspect."

"I was careful."

"You could be disbarred! Worse! You could go to jail as an accessory!"

"Attorney-client privilege," Stan said.

"Doesn't apply. You're an officer of the court."

Stan took a very big swig of wine, the kind no oenophile would countenance. "Well, it's over now," he said after swallowing. "I told him to go and he did."

Carla shook her head, unmollified.

"Is he in jeopardy?" Zeke asked.

"What if he'd crashed our car?" Carla suddenly exploded. "Or just run a stop sign! We'd *all* be in jeopardy!"

"But that didn't happen," Stan said. He turned back to Zeke. "What I was about to say," he went on, and shot a sidelong glance at Carla, an unusual show of annoyance at the interruption, before turning to Zeke once again. "I was going to say, they haven't been actively looking for him in ages. It's an old, cold case. They might even assume he's dead by now. And despite what Carla thinks, I didn't mention his name, or provide enough information for them to guess who I was asking about. They're not going to blow the dust off his file or gear up a manhunt. He'll be safe if he stays out of trouble. But his situation is tough, no question. Getting a new passport, social security, a driver's license, Medicare, all that...he can't do it legit. He's underground and he has to stay underground."

"Six feet underground is where he should be," Carla said.

This was so harsh, Zeke couldn't resist following up, even though he recognized troubled waters when they were roiling right in front of him. "What is it you dislike so much?"

"Don't ask," she said.

Zeke found himself looking to Stan, who shrugged, clearly discomfited. Everything about his body language suggested embarrassment.

"He's trouble," said Carla. "That's all I'll say. A mischief-maker. I know the type. Charming and good-looking and thoroughly bad news. Unreliable. Not happy unless they're stirring things up, creating chaos, then waltzing away from the mess. Guys like that used to be my weakness." A glance at Stan. "I got over it."

Did the glance at her husband signify the loving suggestion that knowing him had cured her, or, on the contrary, that, unlike herself, Stan had failed to overcome a similar weakness and was still susceptible to Corin's roguish charms? An ambiguity never to be resolved. Zeke could, with his fund of therapeutic experience, imagine a version of Carla's amatory history that made her account accurate, or in any event true to how she'd experienced it. Her life pre-Stan must have been replete with men who took her to bed at the end of a sodden evening and then took off in the cold clear light of dawn. She would have attributed such behavior to unreliability, but it surely felt different to the men in question, pure coyote self-preservation as they rued their unruly urges and hurriedly pulled on their clothes, assuring her they'd call but knowing they never would. Zeke could easily picture such scenes, but they were no joy to contemplate. This was the sort of clear-eyed knowledge of human conduct that could carry a therapist, easily, frictionlessly, to the brink of despair. You needn't be a monster to behave monstrously. All that's required is the normal allotment of human weakness, the ordinary susceptibility to the crosscurrents of desire and distaste.

"Did something happen?" he asked.

"Nothing happened," said Stan.

"Depends what you mean by 'happen,'" Carla said.

"Nothing happened," Stan repeated. "Carla thinks Corin's a bad influence."

"I can speak for myself, Stanley," Carla said. She permitted herself a smile as she said, "I think Corin's a bad influence. I'm sorry, honey, he is."

"Just let's drop it, okay?"

He might as well not have spoken at all. She went on, "Keeps Stan up late, asks him what happened to his ideals, wonders how he let himself get trapped in such a bourgeois, sterile existence—that's a reference to *me*, by the way—expresses crocodile sympathy about how hard it must be for him, having sold out and all. Gets him riled up and angry and dissatisfied and self-disgusted."

Stan had colored. "It's not like that."

"I know you, Stanley. I know what goes on inside that *kopf* of yours. You listen to him, you impute some sort of cockamamie authenticity to him, and it has an effect. You dismiss it at first, but it seeps in. You start to look around and wonder where you went wrong, how you lost your way, when the truth is, you've done nothing but right, you've built a wonderful life. Ethical as well as successful. *That's* the thing he can't forgive."

"Fine." Stan was not enjoying this conversation.

She faced Zeke again. "He's *tsouris*, Zeke. I know he's an old friend of yours, so forgive me, but the guy's a human mortar shell. I can feel it. He's going through some kind of mid-life crisis right now—wait, do shrinks sneer at the idea of a mid-life crisis? I can't remember."

"Not at all. Except it's a misnomer, they can happen any time."

"Well, anyway, he's going through *some*thing, is the point. He's back here out of some crazy need. I didn't know him before, I'm not even clear how long he's been away, so this isn't based on, on…I can just tell. The way he talks about the old days. Like it was a Garden of Eden he got banished from. He wants it back. Everything's soured on him and he wants back what he lost. To laze around campus like it's his natural habitat. To bullshit with Stan about socialism and anarchy till three in the morning, and always be in the right, always be the one to tell Stan why he's mistaken. To hang out with Liam, two mad Irishmen arguing about music and poetry—they got together the other day, you know—"

"Liam told me."

"And he saw Molly last week, and he's been trying to get hold of you too." She missed Stan's warning frown, missed the little head-shake, although Zeke caught both, and tried not to react. He could feel himself coloring, and was mortified, not for the first time, at the inadequacy of his defenses. Meanwhile, unwittingly providing diversionary fire, Carla bulled on, "He wants to re-connect with all of you, the old crowd and the old life, and it's going to turn into a destructive mess. It's bound to. He wants a version of you all that doesn't exist anymore, and for good reason. The world's a different place, and none of you are twenty years old. But he thinks *he* is. Which is what happens when you put your life on hold."

"That's enough!" Stan said suddenly, harshly, slamming his wine glass down on the table. The wine sloshed over the rim. "Stop talking!"

It was startling enough to make the other two jump; Zeke had never heard Stan raise his voice to Carla, and judging by the look on her face, it was a novelty to her as well.

"I was just—"

"Don't explain. *Just fucking stop.*"

She subsided immediately. Maybe their relationship was more complex than Zeke realized. Maybe Stan wielded more power within it than was visible to the naked eye. Well, anyway. It was time for Zeke to extricate himself as gracefully as the situation allowed. Past time. It was pointless to pretend nothing untoward had happened. Not with Stan yelling and banging his wine glass, and Carla looking hurt and intimidated, and he himself presumably still flushing a deep shade of crimson. "This whole subject is fraught for all of us," Zeke said. "I'm going to move along." No one protested. It was time for a time-out. He stood. "Sorry not to have inflicted more damage on the wine, however," he said.

Stan had been looking down at his hands. Now he looked up, smiling wearily. "No worries. I'll take it from here."

Zeke headed back into the house. When he reached the kitchen, he realized Carla was behind him. "You don't have to see me out, Carla," he said.

"That's all right." As they walked toward the front door, she said, sotto voce, "It's a sore subject for Stan, you see." She was apparently unaware that Stan wasn't the only one upset by Corin. Good thing, too. "Throwing Corin out of the house was hard for him. He didn't want to. I insisted."

"I got that impression."

"See, this is a really touchy area for Stan. Corin was very disrespectful. To Stan, but to me too. Stan prefers not to see it. He finds ways not to notice, or to rationalize it away. It was a misunderstanding, it was a joke, I'm too sensitive, all that shit. And he's out of the house all day, so he doesn't see everything."

It was difficult for Zeke to focus on Carla's troubles. He had troubles of his own. But now he found he was getting a little curious in spite of himself. "So are you saying something *did* happen?"

"Well, I don't know if I'd put it that way exactly. He was…presumptuous, I guess you could say. Or like I said before, disrespectful."

He finally thought he grasped what Carla was hinting at. Usually he was quicker than this. "Are you suggesting Corin…hit on you?"

She blushed, and hesitated. Then she said, "Nothing so overt, Zeke. But…he was making me very uncomfortable. There was something in his manner, the way…the way he…occupied space, almost. *My* space. Something insinuating, something kind of…some hint of trespass. It felt wrong, you know? Almost menacing? Maybe you have to be a woman to understand."

Or delusional, Zeke thought, but checked himself. Who knew? Carla might be a pain, but she was no dummy, and people's instincts in this regard were often sound. Unless vanity or sheer lunacy interfered. Maybe she'd picked up something real. For many men, Zeke had come to realize over the years, sexual appetite is less sensual than territorial. It was inconceivable to Zeke that Corin found Carla attractive— although that too might just be his own blind spot, who knows?—but it was certainly possible some stray colonizing impulse had been at play. Corin might easily find Stan's success, his affluence and standing in the world, galling. And Corin always needed to work his will, to establish his primacy, to assert his alpha status.

Which brought Zeke full circle back to his own situation. No surprise; he was going to get there willy-nilly, sooner rather than later.

"He saw Molly last week," Carla had said, oblivious to what she was imparting. Stan had vainly tried to shush her. Presumably right now, this very moment, as Zeke walked along Grizzly Peak to his car, Stan was telling her why he'd done so, explaining how indiscreet she'd been. Perhaps he was also suggesting in future she consider keeping her big fat mouth shut.

"I was going to tell you."

"Were you?"

"Of course, Zeke. Jesus."

"Then why didn't you?"

Molly stopped what she was doing—chopping vegetables for the wok—and turned to face him. She made sure to put the heavy chopping knife down on the board first. This wasn't a conversation that would benefit from having a lethal weapon in your hand. "The time was never right. It's not like I'm unaware how delicate this is. For you more than me, but it's loaded for us both. I didn't want to mention it when the girls were around, or we were dealing with something else, or there wasn't enough time to discuss it fully, or the mood was icky for some other reason. And one or more of those seemed to be happening at just about every moment. You know what our lives are like. There's always something. And besides," she added, "I was scared."

Zeke was puttering around in a cupboard, assembling crockery.

"Easy, please, look at me."

He reluctantly stopped his search and turned to face her. "Listen," she said. "He's not after me. He came by this afternoon to see *you*, for goodness sake. He's been staying with Stan, he's seen Liam, he wants to see everyone he used to know."

"And did he make your little heart go pit-a-pat?"

"That's unworthy of you, Easy."

"Is it? Stan would call your answer non-responsive."

"He shocked me, okay? It was an ambush. He came up to me right after class. I wasn't prepared. It was an unpleasant surprise, something I was forced to cope with. To confront. My heart may have been beating faster, but trust me, it was *not* going pit-a-pat."

"You should have told me."

"Of course I should have. I kept hoping for the right moment. I should have realized there wasn't going to be one."

Something in Zeke's manner changed, however subtly, some contentious quality softened. "So how was it?" he asked. "How did you find him?"

Perhaps it was inevitable that curiosity would vie with suspicion, but it was also Molly's impression he was starting, tentatively, not to doubt her.

"He was…I don't know, Easy. He was *sad*. Not just unhappy. Reduced. Diminished."

"That must have been a disappointment."

Zeke had some pugnacity left in him. "It wasn't anything," she said. She approached him, put her hands on his shoulders, forced him to meet her eyes. "It's not just that it was a long time ago, although it was. A very long time ago. So long ago it's like it happened to someone else." Zeke blinked; was he alone in not believing he'd become a different person over the years? Pure delusion. We don't shed our skins like reptiles. Meanwhile, she was continuing, "But even back in the day…it was never about *him*. Not really. It was an act of desperation. And a mistake, like most acts of desperation. I knew it was a mistake even while making it. He happened to be there. In the right place at the right time."

"I think there was more to it than that," Zeke said. His arms remained limply at his sides, but he wasn't pulling away from her.

She pressed against him, wrapped her arms around him. "Of course. It was a confusing time for me, just awful, so of course there was more to it than any account I can offer four decades later. But I wasn't in love with him, never thought I was. Not for a second. Not for a millisecond."

"I guess that makes it all right, then."

"You know I'm not saying that. I can't begin to count the ways it wasn't all right. Not a day goes by when I don't feel…not just sorry, sorry's easy, but mortified. You know, that awful, hot, squirmy feeling of shame?"

"Almost like it didn't happen to someone else?"

She granted him a thin "touché" smile, and said, "Trust me, the shame's all mine. The events may seem distant, but some of the emotions…I can't distance myself from those. You mustn't think I'm cavalier about it. The only comfort I can take is that, by a miracle, you and I are together now. And I'm able to appreciate it. And that Olivia and Ashley and Owen wouldn't be in our lives if I hadn't fucked up."

"So everything worked out for the best."

"Stop being a hard-ass, Easy. You know perfectly well what I'm saying."

He laughed at that, a low chuckle. He always liked it when she busted him. His arms went around her waist. "The thing still hurts," he said. "Hurts bad."

"I know. I do know that."

"And…mistake or no mistake, it still…I mean, it hurts when…oh shit, Molly, no matter what else, you can't say it wasn't exciting for you. It must have been. You can't say you didn't find him attractive, that that wasn't part of it. He *is* attractive. I'm sure there must've been nights when…" He sighed and didn't finish the sentence. Instead, he said, "He wasn't *just* in the right place at the right time. You wouldn't have run off with just anybody. You wouldn't have run off with…well, Stan, say."

She was hunting for an answer to that one when Ashley suddenly stuck her head into the kitchen. Seeing them embracing, she mumbled a startled, embarrassed, "Oh, sorry!" and started to withdraw. Molly and Zeke called her back. When she came back in, still looking discomfited, Zeke said, "Don't worry, Ash, you weren't interrupting anything major. Just a tender marital moment."

"Gross!" She made a beeline for the cupboard. It was her night to set the table, and, unusually, she hadn't needed a reminder.

Zeke turned back to Molly. "I forgot to ask you how he's looking."

That got Ashley's attention. She swiveled away from the cupboard to face them. "That old friend of yours, you mean? He's *gorgeous!*"

Nine

1972

I fucked Melanie the night of Nixon's re-election. Please keep this information under your hat.

It happened on an especially bad night in a very bad season. Molly had run off with Corin a few months before, and by November, far from having recovered, I was sinking deeper into despond every passing day. I woke up each morning to a fog of fresh pain, I struggled to get through the day, functioning like an automaton—going to work took reserves of strength I wasn't sure I possessed, and simple tasks like shopping for groceries loomed immense and daunting and barely worth the trouble— and my social impulses were moribund as well. I wanted to crawl into a cave, lick my wounds, and not emerge till my personal winter ended. Assuming it ever would. It was hard to deal with shop assistants and bank tellers and waiters, forget acquaintances. A few of the people in my life, Liam and Stan especially, made Zeke-reclamation a pet project, and wouldn't let me disappear totally into my own misery; they proved themselves great friends, loyal and forbearing, even if at the time I found their attentions wearisome and unwelcome. And an affront, since I knew they both occasionally saw Corin and Molly. I didn't blame them for this, except I did.

My sexual instincts at that time were almost as dead as my social. This was, in a small and meaningless way, ironic: Even when things with Molly had been at their best, I'd occasionally find myself chafing in a monogamous relationship. I was, after all, in the full, lusty vigor of my 20s, my experience was limited, and this was the early '70s, after the pill but before HIV, when rampant promiscuity was coming into fashion. Friends who'd led relatively restrained sexual lives throughout their college years—from absence of opportunity rather than preference, but regardless—were out having adventures, going to bars, meeting like-minded people at parties, having one-night stands as if it were the most natural thing in the world. Casual, careless, recreational, all but anonymous sex, with a variety of partners and without emotional significance or personal consequence, seemed to be the new norm. Even Stan got lucky occasionally. Stan! He'd now had more lifetime sex partners than I. A violation of the natural order!

And as if that weren't enough, Liam was in my world, Liam, who regarded a day without a new conquest as a day lost. The way he conducted his life dangled fantastic possibilities before one's eyes. It's not that I wanted that sort of sex life—necessarily—but in my days of devoted monogamy, I had to wonder what I was missing. If I'd been any less contented with Molly, I would have been very discontented indeed. I felt like a diabetic in a candy store.

And now, through no decision of my own, there were no constraints on me. But life being the practical joker it often is, I was too depressed to take advantage. As an additional irony, depression seemed to flatter me somehow, add to my allure, endow me with a brooding Byronic melancholy. Me, safe and sane Zeke, the least Byronic personality imaginable. Nevertheless, one way or another, I sensed an interest from women where previously there had been none.

There had been a couple of chance encounters that fall, brief, perfunctory couplings with women I met at some party or other to which some well-meaning friend dragged me. But my participation was passive and acquiescent rather than eager, and the experience left me feeling empty and forlorn. Quite a let-down, given all those years of curiosity; *post coitum omne animal triste* indeed. I was starting to wonder if sex itself hadn't been oversold, if the urgency of the drive was incommensurate with the pleasures sex itself, sex without Molly, had to offer.

And now it was election night, a night that suited my black mood to a tee, a night whose depressing outcome wasn't in the slightest doubt, and who should I bump into but my lifelong acquaintance Melanie Lee?

We'd both attended UC Berkeley, but we weren't friends as under-graduates. Not enemies either, we just moved in different circles. I'd occasionally see her on campus, or bump into her at a movie or a restau-rant—sometimes she was with a posse of good-looking girls, sometimes with a guy (always handsome, invariably Anglo)—and we'd say hello. But that was pretty much the extent of it.

I took her presence for granted, accepted it as an unremarkable given. Which is in itself remarkable. This, after all, was a girl I'd met soon after my sixth birthday. We'd never been close, we'd progressed along parallel rather than overlapping tracks, but still, we'd known each other our entire sentient lives. Our scholastic careers had mirrored one another precisely, from Melrose Avenue Elementary to Bancroft Junior High to Fairfax High to UC Berkeley. We knew the same people, we'd taken many of the same advanced classes in high school, we'd repeat-edly served together in student government over the years (and had worked together on the yearbook editorial staff when we were seniors), we'd been to many of the same parties, we'd dated each other's friends, we'd been in each other's homes. And yet, when we chanced to see each other at college, maybe a couple of times a year, it felt commonplace, no big whoop. We'd exchange perfunctory greetings and feel nothing out of the ordinary had occurred. I'd been seeing her all my life, and now, in another place and under other circumstances, I still bumped into her occasionally. It's only now that I wonder at it. Or maybe I first wondered at it election night, 1972.

Our paths started diverging even before college. When the post-Beatnik counter-culture of the '60s began to make itself felt, I was one of the few kids who was at least intrigued. I had my obligatory fling with marijuana in high school (by college I disliked the stuff), I was listening to Bob Dylan before he went electric, along with Phil Ochs and the Velvet Underground and the unlamented Fugs and so on; I read Norman Mailer and Thomas Pynchon and Kurt Vonnegut; I thought Andy Warhol and John Cage might be onto something. I went to a midnight screening of Kenneth Anger's *Inauguration of the Pleasure Dome* at USC one Saturday night and pretended to find it provocative, although in fact I'd been hoping for nudity and was bored almost beyond endurance. I opposed the war in Vietnam when doves were routinely derided as "kooks" and "peaceniks" with their heads in the clouds and no grasp of global reality. These aren't boasts, understand; much of this was nothing but adolescent posturing, the assumption of an identity I thought might work in my favor, adding pizzazz to my unglamourous self. There weren't many ways a timid guy like me could seem daring. But when this road was briefly beckoning, Melanie was on the other side of the street. She was pretty and slick and well-turned-out, a "sosh" at Fairfax, one of the cool, good-looking girls who hung out with other cool, good-looking girls, who in turn hung out with cool, good-looking boys, the set who ate together at the lunchroom tables tacitly reserved for them, and partied together on weekends, and in general constituted a high school elite. A kind of secret society: Their secret was the cabalistic knowledge of what it's like to be beautiful. You could see it conferred something beyond the obvious: To be blessed that way is to feel blessed. They had their own diversions and enthusiasms, and exploring the new underground culture didn't qualify. If only because of its scruffiness. They had so much invested in clothes and grooming, in maintaining their aura of jaded imperturbability, it never occurred to them they'd be scurrying to hop on the bandwagon within a year or two.

Now, this was Fairfax High, a superb school academically, among the best public schools in the country, so the cool group didn't consist exclusively of idiots, and it was possible to be as bright as Melanie, a straight-A student with SAT scores above 1500, and still be welcomed into their ranks. But the group ethos had limits: Intellectual seriousness was too po-faced, too pimply and solitary and earnest, to be acceptable. The soshes privileged a different style of preening.

And this chasm between Melanie and me, firmly-established by high school graduation, in a year when culture and politics seemed to determine everything about one's place in the scheme of things, this same chasm separated us in college. I don't believe Melanie was in a sorority—the Greek clubs were so out of favor during that period they had to rent out rooms to non-members—but she and her friends were the kind of girls who would have pledged in any other epoch. Attractive, affluent, vaguely disdainful. Being Asian was no impediment to acceptance by the late '60s; in fact, it might have qualified as a desirable attribute. Even in those pre-Benetton days, boasting a minority member gave any group a spicy soupçon of multicultural chic. Besides, in California, Asian girls were notorious guy-magnets. And Melanie's friends had mostly been white anyway. Given Fairfax's ethnic make-up, she grew up going to friends' seders every spring and, in seventh grade, attending bar and bat mitvahs; she probably knew as many Yiddish words as I did. In later, more militant times, she would have been dismissed by her own racial group as "a banana." But it was the world she grew up in, and these were the people she grew up with.

After college graduation, I didn't see her at all for a year or two. Not that I gave the matter any thought; I probably assumed, if I bothered to assume anything, that she'd moved back to LA to begin her adult life. This supposition, it turned out, was wrong; like me, she'd chosen to stay in Berkeley. There was no obvious reason we hadn't bumped into each other, we just hadn't. But hers wasn't an absence that signified. She'd barely been a presence.

And then, on this doomed election night in the worst autumn of my life, Stan and I went to Spenger's for a late dinner. Spenger's still exists, under different management and with a rather different ambience, but at the time it was a family-owned, old-timey fish-shack-plus-bar in an almost barren section of town, an area in the flats near the water that's been lavishly re-developed in the intervening years, but at the time boasted abandoned railroad tracks and an abandoned railroad station and a seedy bar and a gay bath house and that was about it. Spenger's itself consisted of a long labyrinth of rooms decked out in old nautical timbers, with a nautical motif to what passed for interior decor, the whole scene funky and rough, the entire interior redolent of the sea and beer and untold tons of ripe seafood. It had a clientele whose ilk you otherwise wouldn't know were to be found in the area at all, fishermen and weekend sailors and working stiffs and their women folk, many of the men boasting tattoos on bulging forearms, the women predominantly buxom and brazen, with big, bottle-blond hair. Service was fast and rude, and the fish was usually fresh and presented without frills. Fries, tartar sauce, a wedge of lemon, maybe a sprig of parsley for appearances. Served for breakfast, lunch, and dinner. You were as likely to find people drinking boilermakers at breakfast as at dinner. But before the foodie revolution expanded our range of choices and altered our expectations and elevated our standards, Spenger's was an A list venue. And the bar area boasted a lively, noisy scene. There was occasional violence in the parking lot at closing time, but if you had half a brain you avoided the parking lot at closing time.

Why we picked Spenger's I can't recall. In one way, it was a perverse choice: There wasn't another restaurant in town as likely to boast a majority of Nixon voters among its patrons, and so, as the evening followed its inevitable course, we could expect vociferous, celebratory applause to add insult to injury. Maybe we just needed to be within hailing distance of a television set so as to monitor the catastrophe as it rolled over us. You always think not knowing is worse than knowing until you know. The Spenger's bar had several TVs, generally tuned to sporting events. Not on election night, though; the World Series was over (and, one small redeeming grace, our home team had won) and the only hot contest left was the presidential election.

The place was jammed when we arrived. It was always jammed. They didn't take reservations. You left your name at the entrance and waited in the bar to be called. Sometimes it took hours, even though Spenger's was reputed to have the fastest turn-around of any restaurant in the United States.

Stan fought his way to the bar to get the first round of drinks. A beer for him, a Manhattan for me, to fortify myself against what was to come. I found a couple of empty seats at a table in the bar area. There were some people at the table already, but other than nodding when I pointed interrogatively to the two seats, they paid me no mind. It was clear our parties would be maintained as discrete social entities for the duration. This was a night for wariness.

When Stan sat down, he and I quietly toasted George McGovern—in the manner of mourners toasting the deceased at an Irish wake—before taking our first sips. Then he said, "So seriously, you think there's any chance at all?"

"None."

"Like maybe turn-out could—?"

"Uh uh."

"Or—?"

"You're just going to make things worse for yourself, Stan."

"The Watergate break-in thingie?"

"A big zero. We're done for. That sweaty cocksucker's going to win big."

"Shit."

"So drink up, laddie. I'll get us another round."

"You haven't finished your first."

"Liam's taught me to stockpile. Save my seat, I won't be long."

As I said, it was very crowded, and threading my way through the bodies, taking care not to spill someone else's drink, was a challenge. I got close to the bar, and was wondering how to get the bartender's attention—and to reckon my position in the non-existent queue—when I heard a woman's voice yelling, "Zeke!"

One thing about being named Zeke: When someone yells "Zeke!" you can be pretty sure they're yelling at you.

I turned around and there was Melanie, seated at a nearby table—a long, crowded table—waving to me. It had been close to two years since I'd last seen her. She was dressed in a dark business suit, she looked put-together and composed. As always, but more so. Grown-up and serious.

Every hair in place. Make-up expertly applied. Altogether a slick and attractive presentation. I approached her table.

"Hey, Mel. Visiting?"

She looked puzzled. "Visiting?"

So after a bit of Abbott-and-Costello, we established that she'd never left. She introduced me to the other people at her table, a mixed group, men and women, ranging in age from early twenties to...to who knows? Much older than that. All were white except for Melanie and one black woman, and all were, like Melanie, in business attire. Some sort of election-night office party, I figured.

"I'm here with Stan," I told her.

"Stan?"

"Pilnik."

"Stan Pilnik! I haven't seen him since high school."

"He's been in Berkeley since freshman year."

"I had no idea." The university was so big, this wasn't inconceivable. "You guys are still friends?"

"Yep."

"That's so sweet."

"I suppose." I was starting to pick up vibes from the table: Not hostile, but impatient, restive, as if I were preventing their evening from getting started. Maybe if I'd been in a business suit it would have been different, but in jeans and flannel shirt, I was an interloper. I quickly assured Melanie it was good to see her, and headed back to the bar for our drinks.

When I told Stan about the encounter, he wasn't impressed.

"You don't think it's amazing?" I said.

"Not especially."

"That she's here tonight?"

"She has to be someplace."

"But we've known her since first grade."

"Barely. She never had much time for me. She was just some random girl."

"You insulted her once."

"No I didn't. Why would I bother?"

241

"Beats me, but you did. Made a disparaging reference to the size of her tits." I laughed at the memory in spite of myself. It was so stupid and gratuitous—as only thirteen year old boys can be—that I suddenly found it endearing. "In eighth grade."

He suddenly colored. He remembered. "Oh yeah."

"What was that about?"

"You're asking after all these years?"

"Uh huh."

"I don't have a clue."

"Yes you do. I can see it your eyes. What was it?"

"Nothing."

"Stan."

"You and your fucking x-ray vision! I was thirteen years old, okay?"

"Right."

"And like I said, she never had much time for me."

"Oh wait! I get it! You liked her!"

Stan colored again. "Fuck you."

"How come you never told me? You had a crush on Melanie Lee!"

"Grow up."

He was right; my reaction was adolescent, or even pre-adolescent, as if I were about to launch into a chant about Stan and Melanie, sitting in a tree. But the information came as a surprise. He'd never given so much as a hint. I usually knew these things. I usually knew them before I was told.

"How long did that last?"

"Did *what* last? There was nothing *to* last."

"That you carried a torch for her?"

"Oh, please. Maybe a week. I was thirteen and horny, she was pretty and smart and kind of exotic, she probably borrowed my eraser or something and I let myself daydream for a couple of days. She wasn't interested. Like everybody else. I quickly pulled myself together and moved on to greener failures."

I've always suspected he was lying that night. The way he colored, his vehemence, the way he responded to her later.

242

But we didn't waste any further breath on Melanie. We watched TV now and then—no comfort there—we drank steadily, we occasionally checked with the maitresse d', only to be told it would be "a while" till our table was ready. Sometimes she varied it, saying "a few minutes." Those few minutes were starting to add up.

At a certain point, hunger, plus despair at what was unfolding on the television screens, got the better of us, and we decided to skip the dining room and settle for bar food. Some fresh-shucked oysters, some cold cooked shrimp, some fish dip with Ritz crackers. By then, we were so hungry it looked like a feast. The overflowing pitcher of beer we'd bought helped. It was near eleven and the networks had called the election for Nixon long before. There had been sporadic clapping at other tables throughout the evening, and one sustained but rather scattered ovation when McGovern conceded, but the reactions were generally subdued.

Then, as we slurped our oysters, Melanie suddenly and surprisingly materialized at our table. "Hey guys," she said.

We both said hello. I cast a surreptitious eye on Stan; he didn't seem strongly affected by this unexpected apparition. She went on, "My God, Stan, I haven't seen you in ages. You're looking the same, more or less. I'd have recognized you." Her tone was friendly, but her manner was odd, nervy and tentative.

"No, well…" Stan had no ready answer. He hadn't seen her in ages either. "And you look…like an adult."

"Can I sit down?" Again, something about her seemed slightly tremulous.

"'Course," I said. I was surprised. She'd sought us out. I couldn't remember the last time that had happened. Sixth grade?

"Let me get you a glass," Stan said. Always a gentleman. Before she could demur, he'd jumped up and gone to the bar.

She took a seat. "I hope this isn't too pushy."

"Far from it. We're getting a bit sick of each other's company, is my distinct impression."

"That's my problem too. The whole office is here. Including my boyfriend."

"That's the crowd at your table?"

"Right."

"What sort of office?"

"I'm a realtor." She sounded almost apologetic; no coolness quotient in real estate, certainly no feminist cachet. But still…it was a real grown-up job, maybe even a career. With grown-up money; California was experiencing a real estate boom. It explained the business clothing and the heterogeneity of her group. People working in the same office. A mixed bag by definition.

"And you and your boyfriend do this together?"

"That's how we met." She rolled her eyes. "What can I say?"

"Hey, I'm not judging." I didn't ask which one he was. No individual at the table had registered. But I figured he must be one of the younger guys at the table, and, knowing Melanie, probably the best looking. "So tonight's an office outing?"

"Our boss's suggestion. Spur-of-the-moment. Declining wasn't an option. But he's buying, it's a pretty congenial group, so what the heck. Except…like I said, it's been awful."

"I don't think you did say that."

"I'm saying it now. It has. Horrible. I couldn't take anymore."

Stan had come back with a glass for Melanie and a fresh pitcher of beer for the table. As he poured her a glass, I was asking her, "Why's it been so bad?"

"We're a real estate office in Albany. You can probably guess the rest."

"Republicans?" guessed Stan. He could be quick.

"Eight to three," she confirmed. "That's how our office breaks down. So even though the boss didn't say so, this was obviously supposed to be a victory celebration." She slackened her jaw and extended her tongue, a comic representation of extreme nausea. "I've been quietly steaming all night. And then not so quietly. It isn't that I mind losing. I mean, of course I do, but I'm not stupid, I knew we were going to lose. It's the disgusting triumphalism. And the so-called jokes. 'At least your man's gonna carry Hanoi.' Shit like that. As if they're *right*. Fuckers!"

I had never heard her swear before. She'd been aggressively prim in high school. "When did you become a Democrat?" I asked. "You were for Nixon in '60."

She gave me an interesting look, as if re-appraising me. "That's some memory you've got, Easy." I didn't tell her political affiliation is something I remember about almost everyone, a salient element of their personality. She was flattered, and there was no reason to disabuse her. "My mom and dad were Republicans, so I was too. A lot of upwardly mobile Chinese were. Then, in '64, Goldwater scared them, so they jumped ship and supported Johnson. So I did too. Being a Republican at Fairfax was no picnic anyway. They switched back again in '68—they always liked Nixon, don't ask me why—but I just couldn't. And the last few years have been sort of radicalizing for me. Living in Berkeley and all."

"It's good to have you aboard," I said. And then, "I'm guessing the black woman at your table is one of the other two Democrats."

"That's awfully stereotyped thinking on your part."

"I'm wrong?"

"Well, no." She smiled prettily. She'd always been exquisitely pretty. "I'm just saying it's stereotyped thinking on your part."

I didn't bother defending myself. She was just teasing, and besides, we had a little groove working. "And your boyfriend's the third?"

She rolled her eyes. "Hardly. There's an older guy, Ben, nice old rabbinical type, he's the third. Not David. That's part of what made it so horrible. The others I could take. But David! The teasing. All night long. Hostility disguised as teasing. And so supercilious, as if my politics are like, I don't know, some girlish deficit, like not understanding how a car engine works. Do you have any idea how nasty it is to be patronized by someone who isn't as smart as you? Probably not. Only women have to put up with that kind of crap."

"You're smarter than your boyfriend?"

She didn't answer directly. She probably regretted having said it. "I suppose he thought he was being cute. A serious misjudgment. I needed to get away."

"What'd you say?"

"I told my boss I had to say hello to an old friend, and I told David to go fuck himself. Quietly." She knocked back the remainder of the beer in her glass.

"This going to be okay?" I asked.

An indifferent shrug. "We'll muddle through. For a while." She reached for the pitcher and poured herself another beer. "We'll be mad at each other for a while, then we'll make up. We fight a lot. This relationship isn't built to last."

Stan said, "How can that be? The guy isn't smart enough for you, he's too dumb to know it, his politics are abhorrent, he's a sore winner, he disguises his hostility with aggressive teasing, and you fight all the time. Where's the problem?"

"You left out he's a realtor," she said, laughing.

"I didn't want to give offense."

"Oh, did I mention the sex is lousy?"

At which point, David himself appeared. A good-looking guy (genus: WASP) in his upper twenties, red-blond hair short and neatly parted (this was an era when hair was a declaration of principle), with a frown on his square-jawed face. He was wearing a navy blue blazer and grayish plaid slacks. A white shirt, a blue and red rep tie. Grotesquely wide, but that was the fashion, it wasn't his fault. Ditto his ungainly sideburns. I had them too, but at least I had the Ashkenaz 'fro to match. He stood watching us for a moment, forcing a very forced smile. I don't believe he heard what she'd just said—he reached our table too late, at least I hope he did—but he couldn't have missed the hilarity, which was ongoing when he arrived, and from which he had to have felt excluded.

He finally nodded to Stan and me—unsure, I think, whether to regard us as enemies or not, and so granting us provisional but minimal courtesy—and then turned to Melanie. "We're getting ready to go," he said.

"Tell everyone good night for me," she said, and polished off her glass of beer in one impressive chug.

He reacted with concern as well as annoyance. "Melanie," he said.

"I don't feel like leaving yet," she announced flatly.

He looked from Melanie to Stan to me and back to Melanie, thwarted, puzzled about what was happening and how to react. And no doubt about how ridiculous he was being made to look. Finally, he said, "Can I talk to you alone for a minute?"

"Uh uh." She was pouring herself another glass of beer.

"Haven't you had enough to drink?"

"Uh uh."

The frown was back on his face, the forced smile no longer enforceable. "You're telling me you intend to stay with these two characters?" he demanded.

"Hey!" said Stanley. "I'm not a character."

Melanie laughed. Stan looked over at her with pleased surprise; he hadn't meant to be funny, but she found it funny, and now they were allies. So he laughed too. I didn't; I was starting to feel queasy about this transaction. Not because I'm a saint, and not because I found anything about David to like. His calling Stan and me "characters" was gratuitous, calculatedly rude. But still, I'd recently been humiliated by the woman I loved, and in a sufficiently public manner—all my friends knew the particulars—that I'd felt belittled as well as injured. I knew what that feels like; I was still experiencing it afresh, keenly, every waking moment. Several times a day, in the midst of doing something unrelated and unremarkable, I'd find myself almost literally paralyzed with grief and mortification, unable to function, unable to concentrate. So I hesitated about colluding with Melanie to inflict anything similar on anyone else, regardless of where fault lay or where my loyalties belonged.

"Shut up," David now said to Stan.

That complicated the picture a little.

"Look," I said, "cool down, okay?"

"Butt the fuck out."

He wasn't making it easy to be a good Samaritan, but I still hoped to smooth things over. My impulse was to invite him to sit down and have a beer, but it wasn't my invitation to proffer, not with Melanie there. Despite that restriction, I gave it one more try: "You might want to reassess the situation. Stan and I are old high school chums of Melanie's and we haven't seen her in a long time. You don't have a beef with us and we don't have one with you. There isn't any call to be obnoxious."

He flashed me a look of pure, withering contempt. The contempt of a blond WASP in a suit for two younger swarthies in scruffy clothing. In his own mind, his superiority was patent; everything in his manner proclaimed it. He didn't deign to answer me. Instead he addressed Melanie. "Enough of this bullshit, Mel. It's time to go." He used that peculiarly masculine tone combining menace with wheedling entreaty. The menace sounding the dominant note, of course.

Under the table, Melanie put a hand on my upper thigh. That introduced a new bit of complexity into the proceedings, although it wasn't visible to anyone else. "No," she said, "I thought I'd made myself clear. I'm staying. Good night, David."

"Because I made a couple of jokes?"

"Whatever."

"I really think you'd better come with me." He was dialing up the menace a perceptible tad.

"Nope."

He put his hands on the table and leaned in. "Maybe you didn't hear me."

It was liberating, his insistence on being a complete asshole. It gave me the freedom to scrap my remaining scruples. I was drunk enough, provoked enough, and—this isn't something I'm proud of—emboldened enough by that hand on my thigh, to rise to the bait. "Melanie's given you her answer, pal," I said. I almost ruined the effect by giggling, barely checking myself in time. It's just, I had never in my life called anyone "pal" before, not, at least, in that Warner Brothers tough-guy way.

He looked at me, shifted his weight toward me. Suddenly there was blood in the air. You absolutely, positively could feel it. We primates are wired to feel it.

"You telling me what to do?" he demanded.

It was the wrong time to push me, the wrong night in the wrong season. I had too much rage in me to feel much in the way of fear. I stood up, dislodging Melanie's hand. Keeping my voice low, I said, "If you want to turn this into something between you and me, be my guest. There's no reason to, but I'm willing."

Another primate moment. The tables around us grew quiet. Adrenaline travels. He stared at me, assessing my willingness to see this through, gauging my implausible capacity for mayhem. He might even have been considering the relative value of his blazer vs. my flannel shirt. It was like a poker game: What cards are you holding? When do you stop raising? Which of you is bluffing?

He was the one to blink. I'd had an instinct he would be. He flushed, said, "Eat shit," and turned on his heel and withdrew.

"Not exactly Noel Coward," I said as I resumed my seat. My heart was thumping, but my voice stayed steady. They were both looking at me, Stan with something resembling wonderment, since he'd never seen me do anything remotely like this, and Melanie—and I apologize for putting it this way, but the adverb's precise—inscrutably. I made a point of not reaching for my beer right away.

"My hero," Melanie finally said. Her hand was back on my thigh.

Stan's face was registering a sequence of emotional changes, ending in displeasure. His brief moment of solidarity with Melanie was over, he could see that. He could probably also see that she and I were going to go home together.

"So tell me," I asked, "does he sell a lot of houses?"

Even Stan laughed at that. But he'd had enough. We went through the charade of figuring out who was leaving with whom, although it was obvious enough. Melanie had a car, I had come in Stan's. The logistics were blessedly simple, requiring little pretense.

After Stan said goodnight, grumpily, Melanie asked, "Is he okay?"

"I think so. He hasn't had a great night, but he'll be fine. What about you?"

"In relation to Dave? Yeah. We'll straighten it out." And then she said, "He's nicer than you think, by the way."

I shrugged. Dave's personal qualities didn't interest me just then.

A few minutes later, we were in the big parking lot across the road from the restaurant. The one that could be dangerous at night. She was driving a Porsche. A gift from her parents, or was business booming? I didn't ask. After she unlocked the passenger side door—no remotes back then—we melted together in a wet sexy kiss. It lasted a while. When we separated, I was as aroused as I'd felt in months. "This is about six years overdue," she murmured.

A surprise. I said, "We never came especially close, did we?"

"It was always there in the background."

"I guess it was." Huh.

"We kissed at Marla's party once, remember? Tenth grade? Tongues were involved. I expected you to follow-up, but it never happened."

"You were way out of my league, Melanie." Now that she mentioned it, I did remember; one sustained kiss I'd interpreted as an act of charity on her part.

"Nah. All the girls thought you had potential."

That was news. Too late to do me any good. And "had potential" is a pretty tepid testimonial. But at that moment, the issue was moot. I kissed her again, and then we both got into the car, and we started kissing in earnest, right there in the front seat. In a few minutes, her hand was on me, and mine was under her blouse—no bra, this was the '70s, and as Stan had pointed out almost ten years earlier, she didn't need one—and she whispered, "Let's take this someplace else, don't you think?"

"Sure. Drive fast."

She laughed at that. And was smart enough to disregard the advice. We were both pretty loaded. She followed my directions to my apartment on Haste, driving slowly and carefully. That was the last slow or careful thing that happened that night. As soon as we got through my front door, we were all over each other. We barely made it to the bedroom; I have no memory of our clothes coming off.

Well. It was a night of genuine lustful extravagance. I can't say what was driving Melanie: Anger at David no doubt, plus, perhaps, the balked lust that can bedevil a routine relationship, and maybe simple curiosity about an old schoolmate. For me, there were more reasons than I can count, some of them having to do with Melanie, and more, I'm afraid, with my situation. Whatever. It was pre-HIV, pre- even the herpes scare, she was on the pill, so we had no negotiating to do, no precautions to take, no misgivings to slow us down.

We were, I suppose, more companionable than romantic. But that didn't diminish the heat. We were at it all night, and the way things worked, if either one of us expressed curiosity or eagerness about anything we'd fantasized about or wondered about, the other went along for the ride. (Melanie had a longer and more adventurous list than I; that was enlightening all by itself, not to mention challenging). Maybe I'm not making the night sound very passionate, but in its own way it was. We laughed a lot, we reminisced a little, comparing notes on our shared past, but we also came repeatedly, with that unwavering, unapologetic focus on physical sensation that carries its own harsh passion. She was far more ardent, more frankly curious, and a lot more insistent, than her social presentation hinted. We were still going strong at five AM, without a second's sleep, when she happened to glance at the clock and announced with a startled gasp that she needed to go home and get ready for work.

There was a little awkwardness before she left. I was in a robe, she was back in her skirt and now-rumpled blouse, her charcoal jacket hanging over her arm, her straight black hair as disheveled as it was capable of looking, and we were standing by the front door. It had been an amazing night, but she needed to make something clear: "Listen, Easy, this was… well, you know. You were there."

"Uh huh." Suddenly wary.

"And I'm not sorry. I can't imagine ever being sorry about this."

"Good."

"The memory'll warm me on lonely nights. But I am seeing David, and—"

Her voice dribbled away to silence. I wasn't sure whether to be disappointed or relieved. This was the first time I'd enjoyed myself in bed since Molly left—since longer than that—and for that alone the experience was something to cherish. But I wasn't looking for a new girlfriend. I wasn't remotely ready for it. Which isn't to suggest I didn't feel a passing rue; what had just happened opened unimagined vistas. Never to be glimpsed again? "Just to be clear. You're saying no repeats?"

She smiled hesitantly. "To be honest, I didn't mean anything so cate-
gorical. But something along those lines. For the time being. I guess
so."

Mitigation may not have been required, but either way, the uncertain
look on her face provided some. I said, "It's okay, Mel. I think people
usually wait for their tenth high school reunions before doing this, but
I'm delighted we jumped the gun."

She smiled. Then she said, "David probably called about eight
hundred times last night. I'm going to need a good story."

"We drove somewhere. You cried on my shoulder till all hours. I was a
brick about it. I took his side. I said the fight was just about politics, you
need to get over it if you care about him."

"Very good. He's dumb enough to buy it." She frowned. "But...shit,
he'll want make-up sex, and I'm too sore. I need to put him off for a
couple of days."

"You'll think of something. Does he track your cycle?"

"No he doesn't. You're good at this. Have you had a lot of experience?"

"None."

"'Course, I'll have to come up with an explanation when I *do* get my
period."

"I'm a little out of my depth here."

"Right, right. I can handle it. I can handle *him*. I've got his balls in
my purse." She gave me a kiss on the cheek, much different from the
greedy, urgent, traveling kisses we'd been exchanging all night. "Thanks
for everything, Easy. Especially the fucking. I feel better about life. I
almost feel okay about Nixon."

There *weren't* any repeats. Not because her thing with David lasted
long. A few months, maybe. He accepted her cover story, even phoned
me the next day to apologize. Amazing. Everything in his voice and
manner told me he was doing it at Melanie's insistence; she was obviously a steamroller when she chose to be. But it turned out to be an office
romance with a short half-life, as she'd intimated. Over the next few
years, there were times when something could have happened between

us. Our timing was always off, though. When I was free and potentially interested she was involved and vice versa. But some echo of that night remained in the air between us for the longest time. We didn't lose touch again, we started seeing each other pretty regularly, and it was years before I could be in her company without thinking, if only fleetingly, of the spectacular sex we'd shared. I have to believe she experienced something similar. But it went unmentioned.

Except once. This was soon after I'd introduced Melanie to Liam, in the early '80s. I had no ulterior motive, no desire to play Cupid, but the spark between them was immediate and incendiary, and, despite Liam's rambunctious past, I think Melanie made up her mind right away that she wanted him and could manage him. One afternoon a week or so later, she phoned my office. I was with a client, but she left a message, and I called her back as soon as I could. "What's up, Mel?"

"Oh, hi, Easy. Look, I need to ask you a favor. It's kind of personal."

"Shoot."

"It's…if Liam ever asks you if we ever got it on, say no, okay?"

"Why? That was a long time ago. It had nothing to do with him."

"I know. But…well, for one thing, he asked me and I denied it, so I don't want to be caught in a lie. But this is for you too. You know guys. You're a shrink. And a guy. I don't want him to start brooding about it, and brooding about you. It doesn't matter whether he has any reason to. Liam's a brooder."

"I don't think he's the jealous type." I was thinking that, considering the kind of sex life he'd led, jealousy was a luxury he couldn't afford. But since I didn't know what Melanie knew about Liam's wicked past, I kept that thought to myself.

"Guys are guys," she said. "Something like this could poison things between him and me. Not right away, but over time. And we may have a future, so I need to think about the long haul. And it could mess things up between him and you. I know it's silly, you're old friends and what happened is ancient history and we've both forgotten all about it. But Liam has a dark side, especially if he's been drinking, and I wouldn't put it past him to look at you one night and think, This fucker's been in my woman's pussy. And things would never be the same. Why risk it? Trust my instincts, okay? Lie for me. It probably won't come up, but if it does, back me up."

"If that's what you want."

"Thanks."

"It was quite a night, though, wasn't it?" Forbidden territory, as I've indicated. We hadn't mentioned it in a decade.

Her voice softened. "It certainly was," she said.

This was an awful time. It may be unacceptable to say so, but it was harder to get through than Angie's death. I don't mean it was a worse tragedy—it obviously wasn't—but that I coped less well. I had weaker defenses in those days, I was younger and less calloused. And there was no real warning, no preparation. I was completely blindsided. And it was personal. Not a simple (though horrible) twist of fate, but a deliberate, emasculating betrayal. Also, I didn't have many responsibilities yet, no son to care for, no patients to see. Those were a terrible burden when I lost my wife, but at the same time they forced me to move beyond my own misery. Reporting for work at the Textbook Exchange wasn't in the same league.

It was such a nightmare after Molly left, I find it painful to describe even now. The simple heartsickness, coming to consciousness every morning with a jabbing sense of anguish. If anything interesting or good or even bad occurred, my first impulse was, as it had been for years, to tell Molly. Followed immediately by a lurching reminder that that wasn't an option. Waking up alone, navigating the day alone, coming home to an empty apartment, eating dinner alone, going to bed alone. I'd never lived alone before. And I'd never felt so alone. I was always alone now, even when I was with people.

And there was a feeling of diminishment. My persona seemed to contract in on itself. Being in a couple does something for you, especially at that age, gives you an aura of solidity and puissance. We were at the center of our circle of friends. Even separately, we enjoyed the prestige that being in a couple bestowed. But now I was just another lone wolf, a lost soul amongst all the other lost souls, and more lost than most. I was a negligible social presence in those days.

And there was the deep shame of being cuckolded. We can tell ourselves any rational or sensible thing we like, but it doesn't alter the feeling of having been judged as a man and found wanting. That reaction, silly as it might be, is encoded in our DNA; I've heard countless variations of it, in fifty-minute segments.

The thing is, sex is so *intimate*. I don't mean just in the obvious sense; I'm trying to convey some of the explosive, excruciating impact the very concept of intimacy had for me back then whenever I thought about (and it was impossible for me to stop) Molly permitting Corin access to her most intensely private physiological processes, rawest sensations, most personal textures and secretions and smells. Whenever I recalled the sounds she made prior to and during orgasm, and realized that Corin was now privy to that and I no longer was. And whenever I thought about the fact of orgasm itself, how dark and veiled it is, almost occult, a cabalistic mystery to which only other initiates are admitted. And the impulse to confess secrets that often—maybe invariably—follows. Letting someone else be a witness to and a participant in these things, especially for a person as private and modest as Molly, was no casual gesture. It was enormous. It had enormous ramifications. I had once believed it was reserved for me alone, but now I had to acknowledge it was transferrable.

In my misery, I played and replayed all my dealings with Corin, and went back and forth between scorn and a very grudging respect. I despised him, but I could see his appeal. I could see why Molly might prefer him, even if I also felt her being with him sullied her as well as injured me. I figured she must want to be with him, and be willing to hurt me so cavalierly in the process, for all those Stanley Kowalski reasons beside which everything else pales into insignificance.

And in her mind I too must have paled into insignificance. I thought about her constantly, but I couldn't escape the fact she probably wasn't thinking about me much at all. There's very little better calculated to make you feel worthless. She might, very occasionally, vouchsafe me a backward glance of pity or contempt, regret or amusement; but fundamentally, I no longer counted, barely registered.

These thoughts permeated every aspect of my existence. For months and months in the most intense way imaginable, and for a couple of years thereafter with gradually diminishing force. I slowly put my life back in order, I eventually reconstructed a workable identity. But I had to start from scratch. And I never recovered completely. There's scar tissue.

I saw Molly twice more that year, and then she completely disappeared from my life. The first time was in October. She'd been gone a little over a month. She phoned one evening. I was alone in the apartment, trying to read, when the phone rang. Just hearing her voice on the other end of the line wasn't only distressing, it was literally nauseating. I felt my pulse accelerate, and then felt the dinner I'd eaten start to rebel against the impermissible insult of being digested.

She sounded awkward, hesitant, but I listened in vain for a hint of remorse or contrition. She wanted to get her stuff. Could she come by tomorrow evening for it?

What could I say? It was her stuff. It was just taking up room in my apartment and reminding me of her absence. I would open a drawer and her sweet smell would waft up and send me into a tailspin. I may not have felt inclined to do her any favors, but there was no way to refuse. Besides, I ached to see her. I knew it could only do me harm, but I ached to see her all the same.

When I got home from work the next day, I showered, neatened up the apartment (cursing myself for caring), and got Molly's clothes out of the closets and bureau and piled them on the bed (I had selected and boxed her books and LPs some weeks previously, a melancholy wallow I almost relished; every book and record contained a memory, it was like re-reading old love letters). There wasn't much. Some skirts, a couple of dresses, and some blouses had been hanging in the closet. There were a few sweaters and some tee shirts in bureau drawers. That was about it. She'd been considerate enough not to leave any underclothing.

She arrived promptly, but I was startled by the doorbell anyway. I'd been on edge all evening. I opened the door and there she was, looking pretty much the same as the last time I'd seen her. Bell-bottoms and a white cotton blouse hanging loose outside her jeans. Hair straight, as always. But shorter, a new look. Trivial changes like that felt symbolic, and delivered a fresh, painful wound: Life moves on, decisions get made, alterations take place, and where once we would have consulted about them, they were no longer my affair. I was nothing to her beyond the jettisoned debris of a former existence. And I found myself thinking, Two months ago we walked around naked in front of each other, and now she's standing at my front door like a stranger. With a new haircut.

She had two suitcases at her side, presumably empty. My heart almost exploded as I admitted her. Her voice was tremulous when she said, "Hi, Zeke."

I nodded in reply; I couldn't quite locate my own voice.

"Are you okay?"

"Yes," I managed to say, squawking slightly. The rest came out more or less normal: "This isn't exactly easy, but I'm okay. How about you?"

She shrugged. Helplessly, not dismissively. "It isn't easy for me either." And then a short nervous giggle escaped her, and she added, "It's awful."

"But you're doing all right otherwise?"

"I suppose."

Which was, I guess, a tactful answer. But it sent me into further paroxysms of misery. I knew enough to know what the early stages of an affair are like: Joyous, thrilling, adventurous, sexy. She didn't have to say it. She could downplay it out of tact. No matter. There was nothing but horror there.

"I put your things on the bed."

Ever the gentleman, I hoisted her two empty suitcases and led her to the bedroom as if she didn't know the way. I can't say if she looked the place over en route, since she was behind me, but when we got to the bedroom she hadn't turned into a pillar of salt.

She promptly opened the suitcases and started packing. I stood there, an interloper in my own bedroom. This was worse than I'd expected—

being in the bedroom made it especially difficult—and I never doubted it would be bad.

So much was clamoring for expression, so much fury, outrage, pain. But I didn't give voice to any of it. What would be the point? Surrendering the last shreds of my dignity so that, at best, she might offer a soupçon of pity?

"I'll wait in the living room," I said after a couple of minutes.

"I'm almost done."

So I had to stand there while she kneeled down and closed and latched the bags. I made a move to pick them up, and she said, "It's okay, they're not heavy."

As we walked down the corridor toward the living room, I said, "What about the books and LPs? Those *are* heavy."

She frowned, and said with evident reluctance, "He's outside, in the car…"

"'He?'"

The faintest trace of a twisted smile. She knew I was being punishing, although it wasn't clear, even to me, which of us was being punished. "Corin. Corin's outside in the car. Of course, I told him to wait."

"Of course."

"He offered to come in."

"I'm sure." I fleetingly wondered—not for the first time, but with more immediacy now—how I would act if we were face-to-face. I said, "He would have enjoyed it, I imagine."

She ignored that. "I told him it wasn't necessary. I told him to stay outside. But what I was thinking is, if you could carry the boxes to the foyer, he can come in afterward and take everything to the car."

"Very ingenious. Worthy of Feydeau."

The apartment was in a converted Victorian house, so the foyer was neutral territory, common to the four apartments in the building.

Like an automaton, and for the moment almost emotionless, although I knew the pain would arrive soon and be almost unendurable, I opened the front door to the apartment, let Molly carry the two suitcases out, and then, one by one, heaved the four heavy cardboard boxes to the foyer. When I was there, it took an exercise of self-discipline not to peer through the windows that gave onto the street; I didn't want my glance to fall on Molly's car, no doubt parked under the street lamp directly in front of the house, with Corin's triumphant silhouette visible inside it.

Once I got the last of the boxes out—I wrenched my back on the third one, but the pain was so irrelevant to the situation I tried to camouflage it—there was a brief, profoundly awkward moment of silence, while Molly and I stood facing each other. Then, with her voice for the first time sounding completely natural, without the artifice of trying and failing to sound natural, she said, "I'm so sorry, Zeke. Really. I can't tell you how sorry I am." It seemed as if she might be on the verge of crying. But maybe that's what I wanted to believe.

"Whatever," I said.

There was so much more to say and nothing more to say. Even a habitual bigmouth like me knew which tack to take. I silently swiveled away from her, hesitated for one further second, and then hastened through the open door into my ground-floor apartment, taking care not to slam the door behind me. I spent the next couple of hours sitting in the dark sobbing. I didn't know I had that many tears in me.

During this period, during the worst of it, a few friends tried to be helpful, even though someone else's heartbreak always seems slightly... not ridiculous, but abstract, ephemeral, self-indulgent. Not like a serious illness, more like a cold. One of those unpleasant things that, in some form or another, everyone goes through and gets over. If you harp on it too much, there's a suggestion of something weak about you, neurasthenic, indulgent, emotionally incompetent. So I tried not to talk about it, and also tried not to *not* talk about it too obviously. I didn't aim for garlicky *c'est-la-vie* insouciance—that would have been beyond me, and in any case too blatant, not my style—but more a battle-scarred, mordant weariness. The scary part is, I carried it off. Maybe because people would rather not know, especially when there isn't any practical help they can offer. And often even when there is.

It was also how I stayed abreast of Molly and Corin. If I appeared too wounded, friends would make a point of keeping mum about them, to spare my feelings, and spare themselves my ruining the evening by moping. But I was ravenous for information, even while recognizing it would make me miserable.

Stan saw them regularly. Not frequently, but a few evenings a month, say. There were times when I regarded this as a betrayal, when I felt Stan should be more sensitive to my feelings and more outraged by their perfidy. But if he'd been more sensitive, he wouldn't have been Stan. And I'd tried hard not to reveal the extent to which I was hurting, so I couldn't really blame him for letting my ruse succeed. And anyway, he'd been friends with Corin for a while; it would have been high-handed and even solipsistic of me to expect him to drop Corin on my behalf. And regardless of any unvoiced misgivings I might have had, I never doubted where Stan's loyalties lay. He might look up to Corin, he might enjoy a little reflected glory by claiming him as a friend, but if push ever came to shove, Stan was my guy.

What was I able to glean from him during those months? They were living in the city. Corin had got a job. In a bookstore! The son of a bitch sure was following in my footsteps, wasn't he? He was a little evasive with Stan about what he was up to politically, which Stan found both intriguing and worrisome. He told Stan he had fallen in with "some serious people," whatever that might mean. Astonishingly—and to me distressingly, although it was no longer any of my business—Molly had decided not to go to graduate school after all, had abandoned the PhD program at Cal before she'd even begun. She also had a job, some implausible position as a salesgirl at one of the tourist places in Ghirardelli Square.

It was all too strange. As if, overnight, Molly had become a different person, someone I wouldn't know, would barely recognize. Could it have happened so fast? It was additional grounds for despair. We had been everything to each other, and now, in the blink of an eye, we were utter strangers.

Liam and I cemented our friendship that autumn. Fairly early on, he turned up at my apartment one night, a warm Indian summer night, and announced he was taking me for a drink. I demurred, but he was so insistent it was finally easier to give in than keep resisting. We drove to some unprepossessing dive on San Pablo, almost completely deserted. After fetching us two Irish whiskies—doubles—he told me he'd just made his first-ever sale to a glossy, a piece on the Bay Area rock scene for what would prove to be the short-lived *Playboy* spin-off *Oui*. And he'd been well paid, he said, so drinks were on him. Then he raised his glass in toast, looked me in the eye, and said, "Now see here, I can tell you're hurting, I know the signs. You're handling it like a brick—what your people call a *mensch*—but I'm not fooled."

"I won't argue."

"So this is your night. You can say anything you want and it won't count, no shame, no loss of face, once it's over it never happened. Whine, cry, snivel, rail at the fates, I'll just listen and nod. Everybody gets one of those, and this is yours."

It was a handsome gesture, in its way the most generous anybody offered in those bad months, and I was touched. But it's not easy to grieve on command—even if my profession sometimes expects precisely that—so I said, "Tell you what. Let's just talk, and if something maudlin comes up, I won't hold back."

"Any way you care to handle it," he said.

I took a sip of whisky and considered my options. "Have you seen them?" I finally asked.

"Corin and Molly?" I hated the way he made it sound like one word, a unit. The way people used to say "Easy and Molly." "A couple of times. We're not close. He can be hard to take. I don't love being hectored."

Music to my ears. But I pressed on. "How do they seem?"

He was thoughtful for a second. "I'm not sure you'll like this."

"I'm sure I won't. What? They can't keep their hands off each other?"

"That isn't what I was getting at." Which wasn't a denial. He went on, "What I was going to say is, I think she may be good for him. She pulls him back, you know? He's so used to running roughshod over people, but he can't run roughshod over her. She's too smart, and she doesn't take his crap."

261

"She challenges him?"

"Exactly."

"Directly?"

"As directly as it gets. She tells him he's a jerk."

"In front of people?"

"Yep. And forces him to back down a lot of the time."

In a way, this was almost as hurtful as if he'd said she was fellating him in public. Because it reminded me of her bluntness, her candor, her toughness. She had apparently transferred those amazing qualities intact right over to Corin. Did he recognize it as a blessing?

"How does he handle it?" I asked.

"He hates it, he loves it. Who knows? Sometimes he glares at her, sometimes he beams like a proud papa. You've probably heard enough on this subject."

"Yeah, okay."

"You ready for another?" He was referring to our drinks.

"I can be."

So we drank and talked. Mostly about other things. I didn't cry or whine or snivel or rail against the fates, not overtly, but I occasionally acknowledged how much I hurt, and asked more questions without feeling I had to feign indifference: Had she changed? Did he know why she'd dropped out of school? (He did, more or less; they were broke, and besides, she was no longer sure studying English literature in a fucked-up world made sense, maybe it was just bourgeois self-indulgence.) Were they going to get married? Did he know who they hung out with? It was a bit of a wallow, this conversation, but it was also comforting to have someone there to listen and to answer my questions, someone who accepted it all without censoriousness or condescension, who seemed honestly concerned, and who didn't waste time offering facile reassurance.

And then there was an interesting moment, toward the end of the evening. We were both quite drunk, and even I had grown bored with my own misery, so I said to him, "This stuff you write. Tell me about it. Is it bullshit, or is there anything to it?" He laughed, he must have thought I was joshing him, so I pressed on, "Seriously. What do you bring to the table? What's the value added?"

"It's mostly bullshit."

"Come on, Liam."

"You're serious? You really want to know?"

I nodded. He gestured to an upright piano in a corner of the room. Other than one old lush in a stained tweed jacket slumped at the bar, the place was empty. "Come on. Nobody'll mind."

We walked—more accurately, staggered—to the piano. Liam sat down on the bench, I pulled over a wooden chair. Liam caught the eye of the bartender and pointed at the piano to signify, "Is this okay?" The bartender shrugged. That was all the permission he going to get, but it was all he needed.

He touched the keys, not depressing them far enough to make a sound. "Since you asked, the value added is..." He paused, seemed to be going through a brief internal tussle. His reluctance to talk about this part of his life was real. But then he said, "Are you familiar with the exchange between Clarence Darrow and William Jennings Bryan during the Monkey Trial? When Bryan was on the witness stand?"

"Uh uh."

"Darrow was quizzing Bryan about contradictions in the Bible, and he was scoring points, and Bryan finally said, 'I don't think about what I don't think about!' And Darrow said, 'Well, do you think about what you *do* think about?' That's what I bring to the table: I think about what I think about."

"Can you give me an example?"

"That's why we're here, Easy." He looked down at the piano keys. "Forget rock for a minute, let's talk about...you know 'Night and Day?' Cole Porter?"

"I mean, I've heard it. Sure."

"You know the introduction?"

"I don't think so."

"'Like the beat, beat, beat of the tomtom?'" he prompted.

"Nope."

"Well, that's how it starts."

"Okay."

"But the point is…What's the song basically about? 'Night and day, you are the one.' It's about obsession. 'Only you, beneath the moon and under the sun.' See? About this one constant among all the shifting phenomena of life."

"Go on." Liam was warming to his theme, he was past his initial reluctance. And he was drunk, which made him expansive, fluent. I was already enjoying this.

"And the lyric keeps reinforcing the idea of obsession. Does it obsessively, you might say. 'This longing for you follows wherever I go.' And the introduction begins by listing things that give you no peace: Beating tomtoms, a ticking clock, dripping raindrops…You with me?"

"Sure."

"And then it ends, the introduction ends, with the words, 'you, you, you,' tying those other images together. That's the obsession. *You.* But here's the thing that makes the song so perfect. I mean, aside from the fact that it's beautiful, this pud-pulling exegesis be damned." He hit a B flat with his index finger. "Pay close attention to this note, okay?" He played the note over and over. "That's the entire first eight measures. Just that one note, not changing at all, in a relentless, implacable sort of rhythm. 'Like the beat, beat, beat of the tomtom,' etc. Then, after eight measures, it does change, slightly, it creeps up a half-step, to the adjacent note, and then goes up an additional half-step, there are four measures shared by those two new notes, always maintaining the same steady rhythm, and then it comes back down to the first note, same rhythm, for the remainder of the introduction."

"I see where you're going with this," I said.

"Wait, don't jump ahead, there's more. Listen to the accompaniment. Listen to the first note of the accompaniment." He played the B flat with his right index finger, and struck an E natural in the bass with his left. "Totally unrelated note, right? That interval…it's called a tritone, and it's so strange, so awkward, in the Middle Ages it was called 'the devil in music.' But that's just the first note. Listen to what happens as it goes along." He started to play the introduction from the beginning, using both hands. "The right hand, the melody, keeps repeating that same note over and over, like I said. But the bass keeps moving all over the place, playing all these other notes that have no demonstrable connection to the melody note. As if this one clear, obsessive thought is standing firm against all these foreign ideas that try to impinge on it or subvert it or distract it. It all eventually resolves, of course, these foreign notes are always sort of circling around notes that make harmonic sense, and after all its wanderings the left hand finally reaches a chord that leads naturally into the song itself, but…Do you see what I'm getting at? It's the objective correlative in song. The music *enacts* the lyric, both in melody and harmony. The introduction encapsulates everything the song is about. The melody, that one-note melody, *is* an obsession, an obsession with B flat, and it refuses to waver despite all the things that are shifting around it and beneath it, and it finally pulls everything else into its orbit."

He looked at me sheepishly, self-conscious about having shown himself to be so earnest about anything. "I could go on," he said. "I'm drunk enough. About how the song proper begins on that same note, that B flat, even though it isn't the tonic. How it keeps recurring in the main tune with different harmonies. How unstable most of the accompanying chords are, all the way through. But you get the point."

I'd been staring at him while he had been explaining all this. And it must have started making him uneasy, because he suddenly said, "What?"

"Liam!" I said.

"What?"

"It's just…that was fucking dazzling!" Of course, he'd picked the perfect example to wow me. If I knew about anything in those days, if any subject was going to resonate with me, it was romantic obsession. But still, I was blown away. I'd had no idea he was capable of anything like that.

He was discomfited by my admiration. "It's not such a big deal. The thing is…Aw shit, Easy, there's nothing especially complicated or mysterious about it. You just have to pay attention. You just have to think about what you think about. Most people don't bother. When I experience stuff, I notice the stuff I experience and I want to share it. You know what that's like. You play an LP for friends, something you're ape-shit about, and they say, 'Very nice,' or, 'That's pretty,' and you suspect they haven't noticed one-tenth of what's there, they're incapable of noticing *any*thing except what's on the surface, and there's no way to ask, it gets people's back up. You can't lecture them, it's rude, nobody wants to be lectured to even if it's worth hearing. But it's different in print. So what I bring to the table is, I'm the guy who takes pop culture seriously, who pays attention and points shit out."

"Does it always repay the scrutiny?"

"Mostly not. Most of it is disposable commercial crap. But commercial crap can tell you something interesting too. And sometimes there's more there...When that happens, even the wasted effort seems worth it. Like finding a perfect diamond everyone else has overlooked."

When we left the bar that night, I knew I was going to keep razzing him about what he wrote. It was too much fun to stop, and it seemed to tickle him too. But from then on, I'd always wonder, at least a tiny bit, if he might actually be on to something.

I bumped into Corin only once, purely by accident. Or at least I think it was by accident. I was approaching Stan's apartment on Arch Street, going up the cement path to the flight of stairs that led to the front door of his apartment house, and came face-to-face with Corin, heading the other way. Alone, thank God. But that was small comfort at the time; you can imagine how it felt. I don't know if I would have tried to hide if there had been any chance—I'd like to think not, but I'm honestly unsure—but it wasn't an option. He was lighting a cigarette as we approached each other, so I had a few seconds to prepare before he became aware of me. I made a point of not smiling when our eyes met. Which is harder than you might think when you unexpectedly encounter someone you know, even when you hate him. Some reactions are reflexive.

"Zeke," he said, when we were in that imprecise region we instinctively experience as shared social space. I'd have to characterize his manner as warm; he gave me that winning smile and extended his hand. "How you getting on, mate?" His voice was caring, compassionate, with even more Irish in it than usual. I stared at him and didn't take his hand. After a second, he transferred his cigarette to it, a pretty smooth improvisation to cover the awkwardness, and went on, "I realize this feels a little weird, but I'm glad we bumped into each other. We need to talk."

"No we don't."

I was acutely conscious of occupying the inferior position. In the alpha male-off, he'd won and I'd lost (I hadn't realized we were competing until the contest was over, but that didn't affect the results). No, it was worse than that. He had won resoundingly, leaving me pummeled and unmanned. There was nothing I could do about it, except one thing: I could refuse to act the beta male in his presence, I could refuse to placate and propitiate and pretend everything was okay and I didn't mind. A small thing, an all but meaningless thing, but it was all I had.

"Aw now, don't be that way," he said.

"I don't intend to be any way at all. Excuse me." The path was narrow. I couldn't get past him unless I pushed him aside or he let me by.

"It wasn't personal, Zeke."

"That's a comfort."

"Oh, come now." His tone was almost wheedling. I was too agitated then and there to find the fact interesting, but later I found it very interesting. He apparently wasn't as comfortable with his alpha status as I might have assumed. He needed to win me over, to secure or coerce my acquiescence. "All's fair, you know."

"May I get by, please?"

"And it's not like…it wasn't the Sabine women, for Christ's sake."

That was his strongest argument. He'd been sneaky, but he hadn't carried Molly off against her will. Nothing would have happened if she hadn't wanted it. My beef wasn't with Corin, or not with Corin alone. Would I have felt better if Molly had thrown herself at him and he'd declined out of respect for our friendship? I might have felt better about *him*, but it's unlikely I would have felt better.

And I wouldn't have felt much better about him.

I didn't have a snappy come-back. And didn't feel he merited one. I just pushed past him and continued on to Stan's place. With severely diminished enthusiasm, be it said. I felt like Churchill at Potsdam, unexpectedly relegated to the status of onlooker, paying a sociable but pointless call on Harry Truman.

My father died in mid-December. 1972 was a hell of a year.

It was a heart attack. He didn't have a history of coronary disease, and he always seemed healthy and vigorous. Worked twelve-hour days, played tennis and golf, had a robust social life. But it happens that way sometimes. He died alone, in bed. Maybe in his sleep. I hope so. He was only 54.

I flew to LA for the funeral and to help my mother, although not much help was needed. They'd been living apart for four years, and legally divorced for over two. She wasn't responsible for anything she didn't choose to take responsibility for.

But there were a few things that needed to be done, and someone had to do them. Dad had been living on his own in one of those high-rises on Wilshire, not too far from his Beverly Drive store, and somebody had to go through it and empty it out. That fell to me. There was a sort of girlfriend in the picture—I had met her a few times on previous visits to LA, and had gone to awkward dinners with the two of them once or twice—but the relationship seemed fairly casual. Cathy wasn't the eye-candy trophy I had prepared myself for, but rather a divorced mother of two college-age kids, in her forties, attractive enough but no love-bomb. She owned a fine-fabrics shop on the Strip, across the street from dad's West Hollywood store. They weren't living together, and as far as I knew, hadn't discussed marriage, so the practical arrangements after his death weren't her problem, and she didn't try to horn in. I took a few personal items as keepsakes, offered my mother whatever else might be of value—she declined almost all of it, except a big television and a leather chair—and we donated the rest to Goodwill.

He left Cathy $25,000. When I told her, it was evident she'd expected nothing, and seemed touched. I got $50,000, which was welcome, although, given the size of his estate, not exactly bounteous. The rest, surprisingly, went to my mother. Including the two stores. She'd already been treated generously in the divorce settlement, so this was a lot more than she expected. I guess there weren't any other obvious beneficiaries, and maybe he still felt a sense of obligation. He knew I wouldn't want the stores. Even without career plans, I had no interest in or aptitude for business. He'd tried to involve me in their operation when I was in college, but it quickly became clear I was just going through the motions.

The memorial service was unobjectionable. My mother asked me to speak, and I did, but I didn't have much to say. Platitudes. We'd had an okay relationship through the years, but it could be edgy, and grew increasingly distant after I left home. His drinking and my growing resistance to his domineering style doubtless took a toll. There was probably more to it than that, though, on both sides.

It was interesting, however, to listen to his former employees, some of whom offered brief eulogies. They really liked him. He must have been a good boss. There were stories of small kindnesses, acts of generosity, moments of warmth and wit and solidarity. A couple of the pretty girls who spoke may have had crushes on him.

My mother and I hosted a party after the service. Not really sitting shiva, since we didn't observe any of the religious customs, just a get-together of his friends. It might have seemed odd for my mother to be involved, but their lives had been intertwined from the time he'd got out of the service until a few years before he died, and they'd stayed in touch after the divorce, and his friends had mostly been her friends, and she had a large-enough house, and she was the mother of his child, and hell, somebody had to do it. We made sure to invite Cathy, who stayed for about an hour—a sensitive calculation of what was appropriate, I think—and then slipped away without fanfare.

My mother was dry-eyed and steady during it all. Not bitter, but far from grief-stricken. If she had any deep feelings about the marriage, the divorce, or the death, she chose not to share them with me. Nor did she ask me what had happened with Molly. She expressed the requisite sympathy at our rupture and left it at that. We propped each other up during that difficult season, but we didn't confide.

The closest we came was my last night in LA, when she took me to Scandia for dinner. A sentimental nod to old times, arguably, or maybe just conveniently near to her house. It was hard not to recall the night almost exactly five years before when my parents had taken Molly and me to dinner there. A lot had changed. During the meal, I dared to mention that while I hadn't felt exactly estranged from Sy during the last few years, our relations had felt strained. With a frankness unusual for her, my mother said, "He sometimes talked about that. Even after the divorce, when we'd see each other. It was a relatively safe topic. He just couldn't figure you out, Zeke. He didn't know how to talk to you, or what to talk to you about. I don't think he was disappointed, just puzzled. Puzzled and maybe slightly defensive. The way you look at people…it made him nervous. It makes a lot of people nervous. I think he had the feeling you just…see too much. It threatened his sense of control. Sy didn't like not being in charge." Hardly a blinding revelation, but it would have to do.

I was terribly conscious of Molly's absence, of course. It was Molly I needed to talk to. About the grief I was feeling and the grief I *wasn't* feeling. About my complicated relationship with Sy. I needed her to tell me he was a bastard to me, and I needed her to tell me he wasn't such a bad guy. I needed her to be willing to come to LA, even though she hated it, because she sensed my confusion. I needed her to talk to my mother, since the two of them got along and I was clueless about what to say. I needed to be listened to and held.

It's something I used to feel guilty about, that my greatest grief at the time of my father's death wasn't for him, it was for Molly. But I'm reconciled to it now. All those emotions were intertwined, the hierarchy of loss was illusory. Therapy helped. It ended up changing my personal direction in all sorts of ways. As, ultimately, did my father's bequest. One impelled me into graduate school, the other enabled it.

I stayed in LA for a bit over a week. I could have stayed through Christmas, but in various subtle ways my mother let me know it was unnecessary, maybe even unwelcome. She no doubt had plans of her own. My father's death interrupted what had long since been her ordinary life. Which included holiday plans. So I headed home to face the most depressing Christmas season ever. Which, as any clinical psychologist can tell you, sets the bar high. Holidays are boom times for us.

Thanksgiving had already been brutal, a foretaste of the yuletide to come. In each of the preceding four years, Molly, Stan, and I had gone up to a little townlet in Marin County, not far from Point Reyes Station, for Thanksgiving Day. One of Stan's political acquaintances, a musician-cum-activist who answered to the name of Buzzer, lived up there with a group of about ten other people, most of them also musicians, in an isolated old wooden house in a lovely wooded area near a shallow creek. An idyllic setting that always put me in mind of the cover photo for the Crosby, Stills, Nash, and Young album *Déjà Vu*, the one awash in ersatz sepia rusticity. It was essentially a hippy commune, although they were all too self-consciously cool to call it that except when speaking ironically. I might have been skeptical about the philosophy behind their ménage, but there was no denying what we used to call the good vibes. On every other day of the year the place might well have been a boiling cauldron of personal acrimony, but I can vouch for the fact that on Thanksgiving it stood as a glowing advertisement for peace, love, and rock and roll. There was always lots of music, lots of dope (it was one of the rare settings where I'd succumb to the group ethos and take a few cautious tokes), lots of laughter, lots of dogs and little kids running wild underfoot, with all the adults crowded into the kitchen in the afternoon, pitching in. We always stayed the night—it would have been suicidal to do otherwise—sleeping in bedrolls on the living room floor, and then driving back to Berkeley the next day, sated and happy. Those Thanksgivings were my only remaining connection to '60s wackiness, a treasured vestige. And they celebrated such an old, established national holiday, they provided a comforting sense of the continuities of American life despite all the obvious discontinuities.

But this fateful year, sometime in mid-November, I asked Stan whether the Marin event was on the agenda. He said, "Of course. Can't imagine Thanksgiving without it." And then (how typical of Stan to consider this an afterthought), he added, "I don't suppose this'll make any difference, but Corin and Molly'll be there."

I felt my heart sink. All I said was, "I didn't realize Buzzer knew Corin."

"By reputation. He's excited about meeting him. And of course he knows Molly. He asked me to invite them, and they said yes. But hey, Buzzer likes you too, Zeke. You're still on the list. We can drive up together. It'll be fun."

"Sure," I said. "And in the meantime, hell's gonna start freezing over."

Stan seemed taken aback. "You don't wanna go?"

"Bingo."

"Because of Molly and Corin? That would bother you?"

"Yes, Stan. It would bother me."

"But that stuff happened months ago."

There was no point trying to explain. Stan was free of malice, of course, but he could be an emotional idiot, and I felt betrayed. He should have had the simple grace to consult me before inviting those two. It reminded me all over again how marginalized I'd become.

So instead, I corraled Liam, and we went for burgers at the place then called Fat Albert's on what was then called Grove Street (a subsequent lawsuit forced the restaurant to rename itself Fatapple's, and the street long ago became Martin Luther King Jr. Way). This was the first and, at least to date, sole non-fowl Thanksgiving dinner of my life, consumed in an otherwise vacant burger joint. Pretty fucking depressing. Liam ginned up some high spirits, probably with chemical assistance, but they didn't prove contagious. After we'd eaten, he suggested we hit a few singles bars and try to get laid. "To have something to be thankful for," was his all-American argument. It struck me as unlikely the pickings could be anything but slim on a night like this, and anyway, slim or fat, I wasn't tempted. My interest in anything like that was months away. I wished him Godspeed and went home to bed.

And then, almost exactly a month later, 1972 still had one final insult in store. The day after I got back from LA, two days before Christmas, the phone rang. It was Molly. "I heard about your father," she said. "From Stan. I'm so sorry, Zeke."

Everything went topsy-turvy: Heart, stomach, lungs. I sat down on the bed, trying to regulate my breathing. "Okay," I managed to say, "thanks for calling."

"No, listen…" Her voice sounded unnatural too. "This doesn't seem adequate. Can I come by? I'd like to talk."

"It's not a good time," I said. I don't know why. It was no worse a time than any other. I just wasn't prepared.

"What about tomorrow? Can we maybe have dinner?"

"Tomorrow's Christmas Eve."

"Oh, right. Well, if you have plans…"

"Don't you?"

There was a pause. Then she said, "Corin's out of town till Christmas Day, and I'm going to Wyoming on the 27th , I'll be there through the New Year. So if you're free tomorrow, that actually works for me."

Sitting on the bed, everything roiling, I did some rapid processing: Maybe it would be endurable, I was so numb I could barely feel anything anyway, and besides, I had nothing planned for Christmas Eve and we'd spent every Christmas Eve together for the last five years, and…and I don't know what else. I blurted out a yes, but insisted we meet in the East Bay. I couldn't see driving back over the bridge after a meal guaranteed to be full of *sturm und drang* plus, as a direct consequence, a lot of drink. Let little Jezebel cope with transportation.

We met early, at 6:30, at Chez Panisse, which wasn't famous yet, just a newish local hang-out. Amazing we got a table; they must have had a last-minute cancellation. The 6:30 time slot didn't bother me, and I figured Molly might prefer to be driving home early, before carousing drunks started hurtling homeward in droves. I can't recall why I chose such a high-class, festive venue; I wasn't feeling festive. Maybe it was the first place I phoned that had a table. Or maybe the $50,000 check I'd just deposited made me feel flush for the first time in my life, and I felt I deserved a good dinner after what I'd been through and was about to subject myself to.

I took enormous pains getting ready, choosing from my limited wardrobe with care, shaving with special attention. I even put on a tie, a wide, brightly-hued number that was fashionable then and hideous in any other era. It was pointless, going to these lengths. Just a way of keeping myself distracted, or deluding myself into feeling I had some control over some aspect of the evening. It was raining, which felt right. When I got to the restaurant, they told me my dinner companion had already arrived, and was seated upstairs. The hostess led me up to our table, and I steeled myself as we climbed the short, steep flight of stairs. I had been steeling myself for 24 hours. There was no effective way to steel myself.

Molly was seated in the middle of the crowded room. She saw me almost immediately, waving in my direction while I was still ascending the stairs. "Merry Christmas," she said as I pulled up a chair. She was wearing a big loose sweater, gold colored, and chocolate-brown wool slacks with a herring-bone pattern. Hard to tell if she'd taken extra pains. She always looked lovely.

"Hi," I said. I was short of breath, and it wasn't because of the stairs.

"It's great to see you, Zeke. I've missed you." And then, as I seated myself, she said, "Don't I get a kiss?"

"Uh uh." It's ugly to report this, but the truth is, I was thinking with intense revulsion of her lips around Corin McCabe's cock. I didn't want to go near it.

Her smile froze and turned downward. The waitress, pretending not to notice this exchange, poured me a complimentary glass of champagne, topped off Molly's glass, gave us menus—the meal was prix fixe, the menu's purpose solely informational—and withdrew. I held up my glass. "Cheers."

She was still smarting from the rebuff. She raised her glass, but only as far as her mouth, and after taking a small sip, said, "I was sorry to hear about your dad."

"I thought you disliked him."

She blinked. I don't know what she expected, but not this, not a candor to equal her own. The evening was already refusing to go according to plan. "I did. It's true. But I'm still sorry he died. Anyway, any negative feelings I had were mostly because of how he treated you."

I nodded. I knew that was the case.

She added, "I don't think he was too nuts about me either."

"Nah. He liked you fine. It's just he couldn't win you over, that's all. He wasn't used to being balked. A pretty young girl with a sweet demeanor…he assumed he could charm or bully you into submission, no sweat. He interpreted your refusal to be entranced as mulishness. I could have warned him, but that need of his to dominate wasn't something we acknowledged, so there was no way to tell him he didn't stand a chance. Not that I had an inkling of what you were really capable of."

There it was, another shot across her bows. She recoiled and didn't answer. What did she expect? That we'd be buddies?

"Where's Corin at?" I asked into the silence.

"I don't know," she said, her voice small.

"You don't know?"

"Out of town somewhere. He had a meeting."

"But you don't know where?"

"Uh uh."

"Or you can't say?"

"No, I don't know. It's better that way."

The waitress came back to take our drink orders. I went for the house red, a local Zinfandel. I didn't care, wouldn't have cared even in less fraught circumstances, and assumed it wouldn't be their house wine if it was lousy.

"So," I asked, "how're things?"

She just about smiled. "That's an awfully big question."

"Well, okay, I'll narrow it down for you. How's the sex?"

For the second time that night, her smile dissolved into a frown. "Zeke," she said, her tone almost coaxing, as gentle a rebuke as possible.

But the rage, which had been stealing up on me since I'd ascended the stairs to this dining room, wasn't so easily banked. "I'm curious."

She bit her lip.

"Come on," I said. "Up to expectations? That must have had something to do with all this."

"So much less than you think, it's ridiculous even to talk about."

"Not to me."

"The only way it had anything to do with anything…God, do we really…? I didn't think tonight was going to be like this."

"Funny how that worked out."

"I mostly wanted to express my condolences."

"For my father or for what you did?

She blinked. "This doesn't seem like you at all."

"It's nice how we can still surprise each other now and then."

She sighed, she drained the remainder of her champagne in a gulp. "All right, Zeke," she said. "I'm going to answer, but only because, the way I handled things, I guess I owe you whatever explanations you ask for. This is way out of bounds, but if you insist, maybe I've forfeited the right to say no." She took a deep breath. "For the past year or so I was going nuts. Everything was predetermined. My life—however many years I have—was feeling like one of those mazes they run rats through. I was in a panic. I'm 22 years old, and it seemed like there were no surprises or adventures left. When I first came here, it was a big scary change, but I was ready, I was eager, I was over the moon. I chose Berkeley because it was the place that scared me most. But after a while I started to feel like I might as well have stayed home. Freshman year was great, but afterwards…we settled down, you and I, and eventually I started to feel we'd just *settled*. So if you want to know if sex entered the picture, the answer is, sure. You were only the second guy I'd ever slept with. We'd been together four years. That was one of about a thousand ways I was afraid I hadn't lived enough."

"And so—?"

She rode over me. "Even that fiasco of a women's group. You were right to find it threatening. Not in the way you thought, I didn't turn into a man-hater or a termagant. But I mean…Lesbians, that crazy cunt-bandit Liam, women talking about their vibrators and all the guys they'd fucked. Getting competitive about the sluttiness they pretended to regret. I felt like a fucking nun. I'd have to have been dead not to wonder what I'd been missing. It wasn't about you, Easy. It was never about dissatisfaction with you. It was about me. Me and the wide world."

"So how's the sex?"

She sighed. It would be too strong to call her emotion disgust, but my bone-headedness annoyed her. Which didn't bother me. I was past caring how she felt.

The waitress arrived with the wine. As she removed the cork, I said to Molly, "Enjoy the respite, I won't forget," which made her laugh, amazingly enough. The waitress handed me the cork and poured a little wine into my glass, and I went through the charade of looking at it and smelling it and tasting it and giving it my approval. She poured us two glasses, and then left us.

"Cheers," I said for the second time, raising my glass.

"Merry Christmas."

After we sipped, I said, "Gonna make me ask again?"

"He's different from you. Is that what you're after? It's different. He's greedy. At first it was a novelty, all that unruly appetite, there was something forceful about it, it was exciting. Then it wasn't. Gobble gobble. A Mac attack. It had nothing to do with me. I started to feel like a bystander. Or prey. And now...well, never mind. It doesn't matter. I didn't go with him because I thought the sex would be hotter. What an idea. That wasn't it at all."

"You just thought it would be different."

"Be careful what you wish for," she said quietly.

"Still, you chose him."

"Maybe what I chose was not making a choice. He's such a disorderly creature, you can't be sure what the future holds for him. You're not committing to anything. That appealed to me. I needed it. Or thought I did."

"Plus, he's a handsome devil."

"So are you, Easy. It wasn't about that."

"Then it must have been his poetry."

"Oh God," she said. "He really did get me to read it the next day, after that awful dinner. Just like him, not knowing to quit when he's ahead."

"Doesn't appear to have done him much damage in the long run."

"We haven't reached the long run."

"The poems were bad?"

"Dire."

We seemed to have moved away from sex. How had that happened? Well, even in my agitation, I could see I had already pushed that line past any acceptable limit. And also that her answers could have been worse. So, while wishing I could have them all in writing, to parse and deconstruct at my pained leisure, I let the subject lapse. "Liam said you dropped out of grad school."

She grasped at that like a lifeline tossed overboard. "Before I even started."

"He suggested your reasons were political."

She rolled her eyes. "What a crock."

"He had that wrong? He said you no longer believed English literature was relevant to the world situation."

"Christ." This reaction was reassuring; if Molly had said those words, she would have borne no resemblance whatsoever to the woman I thought I knew. "He must've got that from Corin. It's the kind of crap Corin would retail."

"Yes it is."

"You thought I'd become Trilby? Look, I may live with the guy, but that doesn't mean I buy the bullshit." She snorted, if so ladylike a noise can be called a snort. More a delicate sniffle of derision. "I needed to get off the train, that's all."

"Like with me."

"Like with everything. I'd been hurtling down those tracks so long, I had to find out what it's like not to be going anywhere. And I—we— we're broke, so getting a job was kind of pressing."

"If a trifle bourgeois."

"What's the bohemian alternative? I wasn't tempted to audition for Alex De Renzy. That would have been fine with Corin, but not me."

Alex De Renzy was a local porn film director. Had they actually discussed the possibility? Even posing the question took me into nightmare territory. I shied away. "Liam says you're working at Ghirardelli Square."

"Mmm. I never thought I'd say this, but I may never eat chocolate again."

"Well, what else can a Phi Beta Kappa do?"

"'Twenty years of schooling and they put you on the day shift,'" she said. Our generation quoted Bob Dylan the way the ancients quoted Homer.

The waitress arrived with our salads. I didn't let it break my stride. "Did he mention I ran into him?"

"Who?"

"Your young man."

"Corin?" She registered my choice of words—a little moue—but her eyes widened in surprise at the same time. "You saw Corin?"

"That was a pleasure."

"For all concerned."

"He wanted to be friends."

"I'm guessing you weren't buying."

"Full marks."

"No wonder he didn't tell me. I only hear about his triumphs."

"Of course. You're his biggest."

"I'm not sure he sees it that way." She put a fork in her salad, then laid it down. "For what it's worth." Then, "You never wanted to be his friend, did you?"

"I wish I could give you an uncomplicated no. I always had reservations. There was a lot to dislike. But things are simpler now. I can just hate him."

"It wasn't all his fault," she said after a pause, reaching for her wine glass.

"Oh, I blame you much more than him."

The glass froze on its way to her mouth, but then she completed the motion and took a sip. Only afterward did she say, "I guess I deserve that."

"You guess?" The rage was welling up inside me again. "Like there are two sides to the question?"

She regarded her salad, but made no move toward it. "If it's any comfort, we're not going to make it. Corin and me. The whole thing was a big mistake."

"Gee, that's rough."

"Not just how I handled it. That was totally awful, I cringe whenever I think about it. I was feeling desperate, but that's no excuse, only cowards think desperation excuses anything." She met my eye. "Saying 'I'm sorry' is so inadequate I won't even try, but honestly, Zeke, I'm sorrier than you'll ever know. But that's not even the mistake I'm talking about. I'm talking about…everything."

"I guess the moral is, think twice before you do irreparable damage."

She was still looking at me, but her eyes seemed to be focused on something else, some interior vision. "The damage is irreparable?"

"Are you joking?"

"I was wondering."

"You don't have the right to wonder about that." I was so angry all of a sudden I heard a hissing in my head. But I was aware enough of my surroundings not to raise my voice.

"Because you can never trust me again?"

"There's that, sure. But that's only a tiny part of it. Why? Does it matter?"

"It could. What else?"

"Because…" My anger, without much warning, was now joined by a nearly overwhelming grief, and I felt a catch in my throat and was afraid I might start sobbing if I didn't shut up. But being me, I kept going. "Because you were willing to let yourself be sullied by that pig of a human being, that's one thing. And because of what you were willing to do to me, the position you put me in when it suited you. Why would I forgive that? How can I accept it? The well is polluted. You can't unpollute it with an apology, or by sniveling about things not turning out the way you hoped. Serves you fucking right. I don't give a rat's ass."

There was a long silence. Then she said, in a tiny, strained voice, as she gently urged her salad plate away, "I'm not very hungry." And then she started to cry. No sound; tears sprang into her eyes and in a matter of seconds were streaming down her face.

I fought the impulse toward tenderness this triggered.

She stood up abruptly and, without a word, half-stumbled, half-ran to the bathroom. I signaled for the check. Didn't we want our dinner? Was something amiss? Would we perhaps prefer something not on the menu? The serving people were very concerned and considerate, and they finally refused to charge us, even though it was Christmas Eve and our simply having the table was worth plenty.

I put down some money and got out of there before Molly reappeared. I never wanted to see her again. It made me feel too bad in too many different ways. Too much rage, too much pain, too much misdirected longing. Her remorse, however real, however deeply felt, signified nothing.

But I left a large tip. It was Christmas.

Ten

NOW

At least it wasn't *Our Town*. But Zeke had resisted anyway. "Do we *have* to go?" he'd asked Molly, knowing it was hopeless but giving it one desperate stab. "It's not like either of the girls is in it."

Molly was amused. She found Zeke's tetchiness endearing. She knew how short-lived it usually was, and she understood it was usually a substitute for doing something; when he intended to do something, he mostly didn't bother griping, he just went ahead and did it. "We don't *have* to, no," she said. "But we should. As you know perfectly well. The girls' friends are in it, their friends' parents will be there. It's a gesture of support for the CPS community."

"Support for the CPS community? Jesus Christ, we're paying them a goddamn fortune. We've sent them three kids! Isn't that enough support?"

Molly didn't bother reminding Zeke that Dennis paid the girls' tuition. He was just venting. She said, "It's a couple of hours out of your life, Easy."

"A couple of hours here, a couple of hours there...they add up. How many of these things have we gone to? Plays and Suzuki concerts and dance recitals and karate tournaments and soccer games? And there are still four more years to get through. Not counting college. By the time Ashley graduates..." He rolled his eyes. "Our lives have fewer hours left all the time, we can't be cavalier about a couple here and there. They're precious. Like rare gems in a dwindling collection."

As if he hadn't ranted at all, Molly said, "It means a lot to Olivia, especially. I don't know why, but she made a point of saying she hoped we'd go."

Zeke groaned, which was his way of giving in.

And on the night it wasn't so bad, Molly didn't think. *Born Yesterday* was a clever choice on the part of the school's drama teacher, relatively fresh, entertaining, not outrageously beyond the abilities of his student actors—although, for anyone who'd seen the movie, the memory of Judy Holliday was impossible to expunge, an unfair burden placed on the pretty, shapely girl playing Billie.

It wasn't easy to tell how Zeke was reacting, though. During the first act, he squirmed a bit, although that might have been discomfort rather than boredom. The seats in the CPS auditorium were cramped, and his back might have been acting up. His back often acted up. Of course, it mostly acted up when he was bored.

At the intermission, when the house lights came on, Molly turned to him with a smile and said, "So?"

"Very enjoyable," he said. But with Olivia and Ashley there, plus who knew whose parents within earshot, he was pretty much obliged to say something positive. "Enjoyable" wasn't a word he normally used when he experienced enjoyment.

"I think it's very good," Molly said, bestowing a smile on Olivia. Could Olivia have a crush on one of the cast members? That was Molly's suspicion. She seemed more passionately invested in this production than usual.

After the play ended, and they'd congratulated cast and director and greeted an assortment of parents, and after Olivia had let them know she wouldn't be coming home with them, but would be attending the cast party instead, as they were driving home, Ashley piped up from the rear, "Okay, Easy, what'd you really think?"

Zeke had to laugh. Her intonation was uncannily like Molly's. Hard to tell whether it was deliberate imitation or unconscious mimicry. "It was fine," he said.

"Jesus," said Molly. "She wants more from you than a bland adjective."

"I get that," said Zeke, "but I never know how to assess these things. What yardstick are we supposed to apply?"

Ashley offered up an exaggerated yawning sound from the backseat. Molly laughed. Zeke seemed to be considering whether to take offense, but then laughed too. "Look," he said, "it's obviously not professional level. And the kids aren't grown-ups, so they can't really embody their parts convincingly. So is the criterion, is it better than most high school productions? I'm sure it is, but I don't go to other high school productions, I can't make that comparison. Or are you asking if I had a good time? Sure. It's a good play, and I haven't seen the movie in a while, and it's fun to see your kids' friends acting and everything—"

"Oh, for the love of God!" This was Molly protesting. There was amusement and affection in her voice, but the exasperation wasn't feigned.

"I can't win!" he protested right back. "I say it was fine and you jump on me for not saying enough, so I try to explain why it's hard for me to say more and you jump on me for...for I don't even know what."

"For being a pedantic poop," said Molly. "For taking yourself and your opinions too seriously. For not realizing you can just say you had fun and then single out one or two things you liked. It isn't differential calculus."

"Yeah," said Ashley. "What she said."

"Okay, fair enough," said Zeke. "I had fun. I wasn't bored, I laughed in spots. The guy who played Paul was especially good."

"Olivia will be pleased to hear that," said Ashley, confirming Molly's hypothesis.

"But...am I permitted to voice a criticism?"

"You're going to anyway," said Molly.

"I'm perfectly content to keep it to myself."

"What is it?" Ashley asked. "Now you have to."

"The kid who played Brock?"

"Donnie Harris."

"There was something odd about him."

A protracted silence followed. Long enough to inform Molly and Zeke that Ashley was withholding. If she had nothing to say, she would have said something. After a few more seconds, Molly broke the silence by saying, "Now that you mention it, there *was* something a little off about him. His timing, maybe. His pacing."

Another long silence. Long enough for Zeke to come to a conclusion. "He was high," he announced.

More silence from the back seat. Molly said, "Ash?"

"Why are you asking me? I'm not in his class. I'm not in the play."

"You're saying you don't know?"

"Something along those lines."

The carefully-hedged answer made Zeke smile, although he trusted it wasn't visible to Ashley, seated directly behind him. "Come on," he said, "we're not going to rat him out." Zeke had established a rule some years before, when his son first started middle school: Owen could tell them anything about any other kid, and, unless it involved immediate physical jeopardy, confidentiality was guaranteed. Molly approved of the rule, and when the time came, extended it to cover Olivia and Ashley. Zeke and Molly both felt it was more important to know what was going on in their kids' ambit, and to encourage candor and trust, than to police their friends.

The policy worked well. They probably had a better sense of what was going on among their kids' cohort than most parents: Who was drinking excessively, who was messing with drugs, who might have food issues, who was having sex either with a steady or promiscuously, who was downloading or unleashing mischief on the internet. Knowing the names wasn't so important, although there were some interesting surprises. The vital thing was learning what misbehavior had currency, which in turn told you what needed to be discussed and what warning signs to watch for. So far—Zeke surreptitiously tapped the wooden dashboard as he thought this—all three kids seemed to have dodged the worst of what was out there. And it was his impression they appreciated the chance to discuss troublesome issues without triggering World War Three. The arrangement benefited everybody.

"Well, okay," said Ashley. "If you promise. The thing is, I heard he was thinking of dropping acid before the show."

Zeke was astonished. "He took acid?"

"Some kids at CPS take acid." Impatiently, as if he were absurdly naive.

"I realize that," Zeke said. She was missing the point; he was aware LSD had made a modest comeback among her crowd. "Although I sincerely hope you avoid it. It can be dangerous stuff. But the reason I'm surprised is…*before going onstage*? That's nuts!"

"Maybe he didn't. I just heard he was thinking about it. To steady his nerves."

"*To steady his nerves?*" Molly and Zeke echoed this one together, with almost identical-sounding incredulity.

"That's what someone said."

Zeke said, "I can see how psychotic symptoms might *distract* you from stage fright, but…you'd have to be psychotic just to consider doing something so crazy."

"Acid makes you psychotic?"

"It sort of mimics some of the symptoms."

"Did you ever take it?" Ashley didn't sound snotty and challenging when she asked, just curious. Funny it hadn't come up before. She'd often asked about pot.

After a pause, Zeke admitted that no, he never had.

"Mom?"

A longer pause. Then Molly said, "Twice," in a very quiet voice. She felt Zeke's eyes on her; it was news to him too. She said, "It was one of those what-the-hell periods in my life. You know the kind. There's something you know is a dumb idea, but you're under a lot of pressure, or you're in such a bad mood you just don't care. We all have moments like that, and they're the ones we have to be on guard against. That's when we make mistakes we regret for the rest of our life."

"Have you regretted it for the rest of your life?"

Molly wasn't expecting the question. "Oh…I don't know." This didn't sound firm enough. "I suppose. In a way. I don't think it did permanent harm. But there's always that risk. And…" It was harder to answer with Zeke sitting there, silent, but, or so it seemed to Molly, keenly attentive. Otherwise she might have tried to explain it took place in an almost entirely regrettable part of her life.

"What was it like?"

"Not much fun. The not-fun parts were much more not-fun than the fun parts were fun. Some of it was awful. I hope you're smart enough never to try it."

"You didn't do it with Zeke?"

"Uh uh."

They were pulling into the garage. "You never tried it again?"

"Wasn't tempted. Would have gone out of my way to avoid it."

"What about you, Zeke? Were you ever tempted?"

"No."

"Didn't you ever wonder what you were missing?"

"Sure," he said. "Just like I've wondered about combat and prison and childbirth. Not to mention the Spanish Inquisition and eating Spam for breakfast. But I can die content not knowing."

When they were climbing the stairs to the house moments later, Ashley kept it up. "Didn't you guys smoke a lot of pot?" They had been over this ground before, more than once, but Ashley appeared to find the repetition entertaining, like a frequently-requested bedtime story.

"Not a lot," said Molly. She glanced up at Zeke, half-way up the stairs, well ahead of them. He didn't want to make a big deal out of it, but he was uncomfortable with the conversation and eager to put some distance between it and himself.

"But wasn't pot a big deal in the '60s? Especially here?"

"A lot of things were a big deal then. Not all of them as silly as getting high."

"Yeah, okay, peace and love and so on, I get all that. But drugs were part of it too. I don't understand why you didn't do more weed if it was all the rage."

Up above them, Zeke was already opening the front door. "I might have smoked more back then under different circumstances. Maybe. The first time I ever got high was with Zeke."

"It was?" Even in the dark, Ashley's widened eyes were visible. She hadn't known this part.

"The night we met."

"Wow. And you didn't like it?"

"I liked it fine."

"So why'd you stop?"

"Well, after that, Zeke and I were together, and…he didn't like it much."

"And he wouldn't let you?"

"Zeke didn't make rules for me. Marijuana just wasn't part of the life we led. Sometimes at parties, but not often. It's true he didn't like me to do it."

"So you're saying Zeke was an old fuddy-duddy even when he was young?"

Without warning, Molly swiveled on the stairs and grabbed Ashley by the wrist. Hard. Ashley was startled, and cried out. Mostly from surprise, although it probably hurt a little too. "Don't *ever* talk about Zeke like that!" Molly hissed.

Ashley recoiled, and, although it wasn't visible in the dark, her face went pale. A second earlier, they'd been having a good-humored conversation. About drugs, always a potential minefield, but it seemed companionable, non-confrontational.

"I was kidding," Ashley stammered.

"That man has been a saint!" Molly said, her voice rising. "He treats you and Livy like his own daughters!" Then she went too far. "He's a better father to you than your real father, and you know it." She real-

288

ized immediately she shouldn't have said it, but she had a full head of steam, she didn't stop, didn't even try to mitigate it. "He's more caring, he's more generous. The time alone, the time he devotes to you... You think he doesn't have a choice? Is that your impression? Believe me, he could do much less and nobody would blame him. Including me. It's *his* choice. You are so lucky to have him—we all are—it's a miracle. He's sensible and fair and responsible, and if you think those are boring qualities, the qualities of an old fuddy-duddy, then I've failed as a mother, I've brought you up wrong, and I...I just despair. I just completely despair."

Ashley was crying. It was probably more from shock than anything else, from the ferocity of Molly's harangue and its coming without warning. "It was a joke," she said, almost blubbering. "I didn't mean anything. Why'd you get so mad?"

As the waves of fury receded, Molly admitted to herself it was a pertinent question. She pulled her daughter close. After a moment of wary resistance, Ashley relaxed into the embrace, but at the same time started sobbing harder.

From the slash of light coming through the open front door above them, they heard Zeke calling. "What's going on down there? Are you two coming or what?"

It was a bright Saturday morning, but Zeke came through the door looking shell-shocked. One glance was enough to tell Molly the visit hadn't gone well.

"Rough?" she asked.

"I think we've turned a corner," Zeke said.

"Not a good corner, I'm guessing."

"There are no good corners left." He proceeded into the kitchen, with Molly following. "Is there coffee?"

"Didn't you have any at the deli?"

"A little. I didn't much feel like lingering."

"It's probably cold."

"At least it'll stop me from pouring a glass of whisky."

"That bad?"

"I suppose it depends on how you look at it." He found the plunger pot on the counter near the sink, and got a mug out of the cupboard, the navy blue one with the KALW logo. "Her mood was okay. Almost jolly, at least until the end. She had a good appetite, ate her matzoh brei. But Jesus she was confused."

"She's always confused."

"She called me 'Sy.'"

Molly frowned.

"Not just that." He poured some coffee into the mug. "She talked to me as if I *was* my father. And as if they were still married. And then she started to get pissed. When could she come home, where did they live, how long had she been away, was I trying to steal her money, why did I let them perform medical experiments on her."

"Oh, Easy. That must have been awful."

"It wasn't fun. I tried to be reassuring. She seemed cheerful until the anger started, but I had the feeling it wouldn't take much to panic her. She sometimes realizes she's getting everything wrong, none of it adds up, and that's almost worse than believing her delusions. Even the paranoid delusions. When she gets upset, you wonder if it's better to correct her or let it be." He took a sip of coffee and grimaced. "This is cold," he said.

"I told you. Should I brew up a new batch?"

"Nah. I've probably had enough caffeine."

"You're not going to pour yourself a glass of whisky, are you?"

"Not till the sun's over the yardarm. Then, stand back."

"Do we need to move her?"

"I don't know. She's going to need more care at some point, and it's not far off. The facility is monitoring her. They'll let us know."

"What are they looking for?"

"I think incontinence is the deal-breaker."

"That goes for our marriage too, Easy."

"I stand warned."

The doorbell rang, that obnoxious *arooga*. For about the millionth time, Zeke reminded himself they should get it changed. He and Molly looked at each other and shrugged almost simultaneously. As he started out of the kitchen, Molly, behind him, said, "If it's Jehovah's Witnesses, don't be rude. They mean well."

"Polite but firm," he said, and headed toward the front door. Through the open blinds covering the glass-panes, he saw two figures, a man and a boy, both African American. He failed to register that they were dressed casually, not with the dark formality of the sect in question. The man, tall and trim, was in crisp khakis and a pink polo shirt, the boy in loose-fitting, knee-length black shorts of some synthetic material, and a broadly-striped, yellow-and-black soccer shirt.

Zeke opened the door, and realized he was face-to-face with Mike Bond. It took him a couple of seconds to place the man, so unexpected was it to find him on his front porch, so contrary to his thought-stream when he opened the door. With the exception of a couple of parties at Stan and Carla's, Zeke had never seen Mike anywhere but their poker games.

"Judge," he said. "Hello."

Mike smiled in a way that conveyed to Zeke he didn't much like being called "judge" outside the courtroom. "Zeke."

"This is a surprise. What can I do for you?" And then, taking a step backwards, "Come on in."

"Thank you," Mike said. As he entered, with his hand on the shoulder of the young man beside him, guiding him along, he said, "This is my nephew, Shawn. Shawn, say hello to Dr. Stern."

Zeke backed up further, making more room for them in the foyer. After closing the door, he extended his hand. "Hello, Shawn."

Shawn shook the hand, but barely made eye-contact. "Hi," he muttered in an undertone that may have suggested surliness, or embarrassment, or merely shyness.

"Can I get you anything?" Zeke offered.

"No, no, thanks," said Mike. "We won't be long. We were just wondering, is Ashley around? Shawn has something he wants to say to her."

Shawn! Of course! The kid who'd punched Ashley! God, so he was Mike Bond's nephew. This was a surprise, although not necessarily a stunning coincidence; in a small town like Berkeley, the black upper middle-class, those African-American parents with the means to send their kids to a pricey private school like College Prep, represented a modest number of households. "She's here," Zeke said, knowing his face betrayed recognition of Shawn's identity before he could control it.

Mike nodded. *His* face betrayed nothing.

"Hi, Shawn," Ashley suddenly called.

Everyone looked up. Ashley and Olivia were both at the top of the stairs, looking down the stairwell into the foyer below.

"Come on up," she said. She sounded comfortable, friendly, unperturbed. Her manner eased the atmosphere considerably.

Shawn hesitated. He was looking down at the floor. Mike suddenly gave him a poke in the ribs, probably not hard enough to hurt, but not gentle enough to be merely encouraging. "Go on," he said. "Get your butt up there."

Shawn started up the stairs, slowly, reluctantly, as if the steepness of the climb were almost beyond his capabilities. Both men watched him go, exchanging a tolerant smile, the smile of people who know what it's like to be fourteen, male, and in deep shit. Meanwhile, Molly appeared from the kitchen. She waited until Zeke and Mike became aware of her presence and turned to face her, and then said hello.

Zeke made the introductions. Then Molly offered Mike a beer. He declined, but asked if he could have a glass of water. The three of them went into the kitchen. While Molly filled a glass from the Alhambra cooler, Mike said, "I feel rotten about this, we should have come by weeks ago. But I just found out. My sister…she's sometimes scared to tell me about Shawn. The bad stuff, anyway. I get the good news promptly. But she finally let it slip, and now he's up there apologizing to your girl. He's actually a good kid. He knows he fucked up."

Molly said, "I think Ashley realizes she fucked up some herself."

She proffered the glass of water. He took it, nodding his thanks, and said, "At that age, fucking up comes with the territory. But if you use your fists on a woman, that takes fucking up to a different level. I made damned sure he understands that."

Zeke saw Molly frown, and knew she was suddenly concerned Mike might have resorted to corporal punishment to teach his nephew that lesson. Zeke silently pleaded with her not to say anything on the subject, not to offer any fashionable, *bien-pensant* child-rearing advice. Even if—even *though*—he agreed with it.

She didn't, although Zeke had a suspicion it was touch-and-go for a couple of seconds there. "I hope it wasn't too traumatic for him," is what she did say.

"For him? Your daughter's the one with the black eye."

"Yes, true. But just being fourteen can be traumatic all by itself."

"We all managed it."

"Fifteen and sixteen weren't a picnic either," Zeke observed.

"Fifty was pretty grim too," said Mike. "It's not like it gets easier."

"Which, speaking professionally, I regard as a boon." Zeke waited for the answering smile, and then added, "I guess every age has its discontents."

"Ah, Easy," Molly said, "was there any age you unequivocally enjoyed?"

Zeke took this in the spirit in which it was offered, and said with a smile, "Maybe nineteen."

The year they had met. Molly caught the reference, and cocked her head.

Mike said, "This guy of yours *is* a natural-born fretter. You should see him at the poker game. Moans like Job. If Job ever drew to an inside straight."

Zeke didn't know how he'd become the goat of this conversation, but the razzing was good-natured. He said, "We Jews embrace suffering with discriminating, finely-calibrated enthusiasm. We know all the gradations. We're connoisseurs."

Molly said, "Would you like some coffee, Mike? I can brew up a pot."

Mike glanced at his watch and said, "Maybe another time. We need to get going. I'm taking the kid to the driving range this afternoon. Teach him to hit something inanimate." He yelled up the stairwell, "Hey, sport! Time!"

There was some sort of answering yell from upstairs.

"I'll take that as an affirmative," Mike said. Then, lowering his voice, he said, "You've both been decent about this. I didn't know what we'd be encountering today. If you'd been harsher, I wouldn't have blamed you. Hell, if the shoe was on the other foot, *I'd* be harsher."

Molly said, "Well, even though I totally agree with you about hitting, no matter what the situation or who's doing it—" managing to sneak it in willy-nilly—"there was blame to go around. We had our own little talk with Ashley."

"Hitting's a deal-breaker for me," Mike said. "With what I see in my courtroom. And I told Shawn today, don't think you can just waltz through this, it isn't a matter of duck, shuck, and jive. He's good at that. Then I had to explain what a waltz is. $20,000 a year tuition and these kids don't know what a fucking waltz is. Anyway, I said he had to really apologize, not just grind out some euphonious B.S. He had to think about it and come to terms with what he'd done and apologize for it and mean it. So I hope that's what's happened."

Ashley and Shawn appeared at the top of the stairs, and started down. Shawn's transformation was striking; he looked looser, more relaxed, less self-conscious, less sullen. He and Ashley were both laughing.

"Everything all right?" Mike asked.

"Yes sir," said Shawn.

He addressed Ashley. "You okay with everything? Anything you want to tell Shawn?" He didn't say, "before I pronounce sentence," but there was something in his manner that reminded you what he did for a living.

"I think we got it straightened out," said Ashley. "We're friends again. Right, Shawn?"

Being put on the spot like that discomfited the boy. He said, "Uh huh," and his dark face flushed.

"You might want to apologize to Prof. Hilliard and Dr. Stern too," said Mike. "I'm sure you put them through some changes."

"Yeah. Okay." You could see what he was thinking: Will this penance ever be over? But you could also see he was determined to suck it up and do what had to be done. He turned to face Zeke and Molly, and a little shudder went through his body as he collected himself. Then he said, "I'm sorry. A guy shouldn't ever use his fists like that. Especially on a girl. I was wrong."

"It's nice of you to come and say so," said Zeke. "We know it wasn't easy."

"Okay, folks," said Mike, "guess that covers it. Thanks again. Zeke, see you at the next poker game."

"Right."

Mike exchanged a quick handshake with Zeke and was out the door with Shawn a few seconds later. After the door was shut, and she was confident the visitors were out of earshot, Molly said, "That was strange."

"Nice, though. I mean, thoughtful. Decent."

"Uh huh. It was more for Shawn than for us, I think."

"Sure. But it wasn't *just* for Shawn. It was for everybody. Including Mike. A matter of honor. Like paying a debt." He turned to Ashley. "To you especially, of course. Was it all right up there? Or mainly awkward?"

"It was okay. Awkward at first and then it was okay. Once he said his piece. I like Shawn. He's a lot nicer when no one else is around."

"I can understand how that might be. He must feel a lot of conflicting pressures. Can't be easy for him."

Suddenly, without warning, Ashley threw her arms around Zeke and nestled her face against his chest. Zeke was startled, even a little perplexed, but he immediately wrapped his arms around the girl's shoulders and pulled her close. "What's this?" he asked, his voice both tender and humorous.

Her lips vibrating ticklingly against the front of his shirt, Ashley mumbled, "I don't know...just, you know, thank you."

When Zeke looked up, Molly was regarding them with a grave smile.

On Mondays, Zeke's final appointment ended at 5:50. There were other days when he had to schedule clients later—clients who couldn't show up until their own business day ended—but he did it reluctantly. It was harder to sustain focus as the day drew to a close; his thoughts began to stray toward home, family, dinner. He preferred to end even earlier, so he could take a short run in the hills before starting his evening; there was something satisfying about decisively demarcating the conclusion of one part of the day and the start of the next, something cleansing. Working up a sweat, clearing his head, not taking his clients home with him. The shower afterward was blissful, as was the vodka martini with a jalapeno-stuffed olive plopped into the chilled martini glass that followed.

His current schedule permitted this luxury only on Tuesdays. A good thing from the point of view of the bottom line, although it rarely felt like it at 5:00 PM, when the final client of the day rang his buzzer and he had to rouse himself out of a gathering torpor. Still, it was churlish to grumble about a thriving practice. And this semester, Molly's seminar didn't begin until 6:30 on Mondays and Fridays, so those evenings began late anyway.

Nowadays, he took a few minutes at the end of each day, before closing up shop, to enter notes on his computer about the day's sessions. A sign of age. A sign of oncoming decrepitude. A way-station en route to his mother's addled wits, unless medical science came up with a cure more quickly than his intellect deteriorated. Once upon a time, the sparse notes he scribbled discreetly on his pad while the client talked were sufficient. When a client entered the office, he could instantly remember not only outstanding issues, but the names of major players. They simply presented themselves, like a slide in a power-point presentation. It never used to seem unusual, it was part of the job. Only now that it was gone could he recognize it as another valuable skill among many he'd taken for granted until they slipped out of reach. It was no longer possible to serve his clients adequately without having something more concrete to consult than the convolutions in his brain. A downward path no doubt lay before him. Who could say what would go next?

He was at his desk, entering notes about Ira Fineman, a professor emeritus in the engineering department who'd lost his wife to cancer. Fineman was a difficult case, a severe, precise man in his sixties who seemed to feel no connection to the physical facts of his existence—who seemed to view his body as an unwieldy vehicle for transporting his brain from place to place—and who had no vocabulary for describing or even acknowledging emotions; he was bewildered to discover he had any, let alone one so overwhelming as grief. While Zeke typed, there was a knock on his door. He started. Fineman's situation was so close to what he himself had gone through with Angie ten years earlier, it was difficult to focus on the case, or rather, to exclude his own feelings, to focus on Fineman's case rather than his own. The effort put him in a trance-like zone of obliviousness. Moreover, knocking was a rarity in this room. Clients rang the outside buzzer to be let into the building, and then sat in a waiting room, leafing through old magazines and avoiding eye-contact with their fellows, until a therapist came to fetch them. It some-times happened that one of the other shrinks in the building dropped in at the end of a day to say hello or discuss a tricky therapeutic quandary, but not often.

"Come in," Zeke called. "It's open."

He shifted his weight in the oversized office chair, turned to face the door, and felt his breath catch as Corin McCabe pushed into the office. Zeke's respiratory system recognized the man before he did. Even after thirty-five years, there was no mistaking him. So here it is at last, he thought, the undistinguished thing.

"How'd you get in?" were the first words out of his mouth. Which was interesting in itself, psychologically speaking. The question certainly didn't reflect any of Zeke's chief concerns. Except, perhaps—the thought occurred to him after a lapse embarrassingly long for any self-respecting therapist—symbolically.

"Slipped through the front door when somebody was leaving," Corin said. He barely bothered to glance at his surroundings before adding, "Nice office."

Zeke stared. Corin was not much changed. Unlike Liam, his good looks hadn't been undone by age and bad habits. The lines were deeper at the corners of his eyes and the corners of his mouth. A little more jowl, a hint of loose flesh at his neck, a slight thickening about the waist. But still lean, still rangy, still ropily muscular. The same enviable posture. The same full head of hair, maybe a lighter shade of sand now. The same etched, virile handsomeness, the sparkling, amused eyes, the confiding, confident smile. If anything, his presence was more vivid than before; you could tell, just by looking at him, he'd seen a lot, had been through a lot. Had *lived*.

"You shouldn't be here," said Zeke. "You're trespassing."

"That's no way to say hello."

"I believe the song goes, 'That's no way to say goodbye.' Which is what I'm trying to do."

"Aw, for the love of God, Zeke, how about letting bygones be bloody bygones? I mean, fucking hell, how much water has to flow over the dam? People have grown old and expired since we last saw each other. Wars have started and ended. Whole galaxies have died a fiery death, while new ones burst into existence. I've changed. We've all changed. Beyond bloody recognition."

Zeke glanced back at his computer screen. Longingly. With nostalgic affection for Professor Fineman and his intractable anguish. He hit the "save" key, a tacit admission there was no way to avoid seeing this through, and turned back to his visitor. "People often tell me they've changed, but I've never heard anyone say, 'I'm not the same guy who got 1600 on my SATs.'"

This got a smile from Corin. Zeke frowned. He didn't want a smile from Corin. "What are you here for? What can you possibly want from me?"

"Therapy?" If he intended irony, his tone didn't betray any.

"Give me a break."

"Why not? It's a difficult time. I'm anxious and depressed. I need help."

More of the old blarney. "You can't afford me."

"I can."

"With the money you borrowed from Stan?" Corin frowned at that; the gift was apparently an embarrassment. "No dice. Besides, we have a history, you and I. It wouldn't be ethical. I can give you a referral."

"Holy shite, were you always this po-faced? I suppose you were." He pointed to the couch, with its crocheted maroon throw. "Your patients lie down here?"

"They can. I don't use it much anymore. Most of my clients prefer eye-contact. They usually sit in a chair."

"This one?"

"No, that's mine. The other one. But like I said—"

"Relax, boyo. I just want to talk to you. As you know perfectly well." Corin eased himself into the chair Zeke had designated as his own.

Zeke's heart was still beating fast, and he knew sweat was all but drenching his armpits; he could smell his own acrid odor. These reactions had begun the moment Corin entered the room. But one valuable skill he had *not* lost over the years—not so far—was the ability to keep his voice steady while those other things were occurring. He sometimes took that one for granted too, but not today. He might be willing to exchange it for the ability, lost years ago, to secure a fresh erection within a few minutes of orgasm, but no one had made the offer, and at the moment, at least, this other ability was more useful.

"What about?" he asked.

Corin smiled easily, not only as if he were amused, but as if Zeke intended to be amusing. "Oh, I don't know. About you and me, why not? And Mols, I suppose. Guilt and redemption. Atonement and forgiveness."

"Not interested."

Corin's smile widened into a grin. No mistaking the genuineness of his amusement, nor, indeed, its warmth. "You people really are stiff-necked and no mistake," he said. And then, "Jesus, man, I'm not even sure what you're being stiff-necked *about*. Is it what happened with Mols, or the robbery, or something else?"

"Wasn't it a robbery-murder?"

If Zeke hoped this would be a some kind of body-blow, he was disappointed; Corin absorbed it without much reaction. "Two people died, a cop and one of the fellas I was with. One of theirs, one of ours. A total cock-up all around. Can't call it a murder, though. Murder is a legal category. The case hasn't been adjudicated."

"That must be a comfort."

"It's no comfort at all. But really, is that what you're pissed about? Is that why you harbor a grudge? If so, fine, it's certainly the worst thing I ever did. And not so much the doing of it…I didn't actually shoot anybody. But I put myself in a position where it could happen, and I convinced myself there was something heroic in it…the weight of that, the sheer fucking arrogance and stupidity…it never leaves me." His voice was growing husky and plaintive. "You can't begin to know what it's like to live with that."

"You've given this speech before," Zeke said. Something in Corin's cadence sounded rehearsed; he was too fluent with the emotions he was expressing and the words he was using, an actor in a long-running play. "Has it helped you get women into bed over the years? The disillusioned idealist on the lam? The sensitive soul tormented by a tender conscience? You must make out like a bandit."

Corin blinked. The flurry of wild punches had, amazingly, connected. After a short pause, he said, "Now see here, when people ask me about it, I tell them. I've no doubt said some of it before. That doesn't mean it's untrue. It doesn't make it less of a burden. It was an awful thing, and I can't just shrug it off."

"And it must really melt the babes."

"You know, Zeke, speaking frankly, with your permission, I don't get the impression it's the bank thing that bothers you. Not so much. If you didn't have another beef with me, I think you'd be willing to accept it's something I regret and can't undo. You might even want to help, like Stan and Liam. Your problem with me isn't armed robbery or even homicide, it's something else."

"The same guy did it all," said Zeke. Not much of a response.

Corin wasn't keeling over from the lucky jabs Zeke had landed. Far from it; he'd rallied, he even seemed to feel he'd regained the initiative. "Think about it for a sec. An event where two people die, one of them the father of two kids. And for what? For a cockamamie caper that was supposed to be political but in reality was nothing of the sort. Just some punks trying to prove something to themselves and each other, make a splash, get some media attention and media cred. As if that made us serious revolutionaries. Grotesque. I can describe it in much harsher terms than you ever could, and believe me, it isn't to melt any babes. But I'd wager you've never given it much thought."

"Are you trying to demonstrate you're even worse than I think?"

"No, I'm trying to demonstrate you're a self-pitying asshole wallowing in your own solipsistic slops." Corin's face was flushed, his voice harsh, his pose of affability gone on the instant. The sudden anger was scary; the man still had plenty of personal force. "The girlfriend of a mediocre, dull guy ups and leaves him for a more exciting guy. Is that so rare? Some vast historical tragedy? Get over it. Get over yourself. There's serious shit and there's trivial shit, and that was trivial shit. I don't have a scintilla of remorse about it. Not a fleeting regret. I'd do it again in a second. It was just...nature. Asserting itself. You should quit whining about it."

"I'm not whining about anything." How had Corin managed to put him on the defensive? "I just don't want to have anything to do with you. It isn't the morality of it. The death of two people exists on a totally different plane, I'm not making comparisons. And I'm sure you've committed other heinous acts over the years, and I have no doubt they were abhorrent too. This has nothing to do with that."

"I didn't do anything to you, you sanctimonious fuck! I liked your girlfriend and she liked me, she liked me better than she liked you. To no one's surprise but yours. You were always punching above your weight. End of story."

"Not quite."

"No, that's true. You got her back, didn't you? So what's your problem? You got her back. Probably much improved by the experience."

"I didn't 'get her back.' Thirty years had gone by. It's a separate life-time."

"You're saying you weren't the same people you'd been before?"

Zeke didn't have a ready answer. It was irrelevant, but still, it was a sharp counter-punch, distracting and on-target at the same time. Zeke was puzzled. "Were you part of that argument?"

"I heard about it from Stan. We were talking about...God, something naff, Lysenkoism, the feasibility of creating socialist man. A couple of wankers, we were. And we moved on to questions of identity and self-hood—we were high, needless to say—and one thing led to another. He said you two always fought about that."

This is getting to be too much like ordinary human conversation, Zeke was thinking. He abruptly snapped it back. "You know what bothers me? I mean, always did, even before the Molly thing. The reason I always mistrusted you? It's... you're a guy who needs tumult, who thrives on chaos, who's offended by order. It isn't political. Not really. Ideology was never more than an excuse. It's a sick need. And it's dangerous, it's destructive, it's...evil. *You're* evil." As he said this, Zeke suddenly became aware he'd felt it from the start. He meant it. "Building something stable and positive is hard, it requires sustained effort, it's a rearguard action against the forces of entropy. If I were a religious guy, I'd say it's God's work. Even building a sand castle on the beach when you know the tide's coming in, that's God's work. But kicking it over can be the mischievous or reckless impulse of a moment. It takes nothing beyond malice. The Vandals can always sack Rome, the Taliban can always dynamite statues of the Buddha. That's easy. It's how impotent people feel competent or in control, by trashing something whose creation is beyond them. Nathuram Godse putting himself on the same level as Gandhi. Sirhan Sirhan and Robert Kennedy. As if knocking something down is equivalent to creating it."

Corin leaned forward in the armchair. Zeke's armchair. There was something eager about his posture, something fierce and almost joyful. "And you, Zeke—since we're apparently leveling with each other—you were a disappointment to me from early on. When we met, I thought you might be interesting. A worthy adversary. You thought for yourself, you had presence, some kind of...I don't know, some kind of *heft*. In a way that Stan, say, didn't. Stan was bright enough, but hell, in a town like Berkeley, people are bright. I thought you had something more. But…" He shrugged. "I was mistaken. I don't usually get such things wrong, but…" He shook his head as if he still felt let down, was still experiencing the disappointment. "You know why Molly left you? Why she threw herself at me, virtually begged me to take her? Not just fuck her—the reasons for that are obvious enough—but actually let her into my life. Did you ever get around to asking her that question? You've had plenty of opportunities over the years. Did you ever ask her?"

"None of your fucking business."

"Weren't you curious?"

"We talked about it." He was suddenly recalling that awful, painful Christmas Eve at Chez Panisse. "When she was first experiencing buyer's remorse. When she decided she'd made a terrible mistake."

"I wonder if she told you what she told me."

The smile accompanying this statement was so malevolent, Zeke felt a premonitory tremor of alarm. He decided not to answer, or ask.

"Don't you want to know?" Corin urged. "You must be curious."

It must be bad. Corin was too eager; no way it could be anything else.

"It's a long time ago," Zeke said. "We all said all sorts of shit back then."

"She thought you were *boring*," Corin said. "In bed and out. We used to laugh about you. A fogey at twenty-three. An old woman. Predictable. Timid. Fearful. She was practically jumping out of her skin, she couldn't take it anymore."

Well. It was harsh, but it didn't alter the picture in any fundamental way. Zeke felt a measure of relief along with the hurt. The hurt largely deriving from her having shared these feelings with Corin. The injury she'd done was already patent; why add insult to it? "She had things to say about you too," Zeke said quietly.

"Go ahead."

"Uh uh. I'm not going over that ground again just to score points."

"You disappoint me." He sat back, getting comfortable in the armchair. Zeke's armchair. Corin was radiating satisfaction all of

303

a sudden. "You know why we broke up, Mols and me? Did you ever discuss that with her?"

"I think this conversation has gone on long enough." Zeke gestured toward his desk. "I have work to do. You're keeping me from it."

"She got scared, that's all. She wanted some adventure, she wanted a little excitement, but safely within bounds. Reality spooked her. At heart, she was just a bourgeois bint who wanted a few thrills under her belt—by which I mean inside her frilly little panties—before she settled down to a boring bourgeois life."

"With someone who punches above his weight?"

"What could be safer than that?"

On some level, Zeke was thinking, this explanation was probably accurate enough. "One person's boredom is another's contentment. We have to make choices, we get only one life apiece. I'm okay with mine. How's yours?"

It was surprising to Zeke that this mild rejoinder seemed to draw blood. A look came into Corin's eyes—it was brief, a mere flicker—of something haunted. But he answered promptly, "I've made mistakes, I don't deny it. But I engaged. My mistakes were big because my aspirations were big. My *soul* is big, forgive the pomposity. And I never became a boring old crock, making my nice money and hunkering down in my nice house and letting the world go to hell while I played with my toys and myself."

"Huh. So I have to wonder: If I'm so boring and useless, why have you been so eager to get hold of me? It feels like you've been stalking me for weeks. What's the attraction?"

There was a pause. And then a slow, reluctant smile started to spread across Corin's face. The anger in him seemed to evaporate. He shrugged good-humoredly. "It's a puzzlement." He raised his eyebrows, inviting Zeke to share the joke. "I don't honestly know. It's one of the things I need to talk to a shrink about."

Molly was approaching the UC parking lot on Channing, two blocks from campus. It didn't panic her, this location, but it was a little dicey after twilight. The days were long at this time of year, but her evening seminar didn't end till 8:00, and by now the light was pretty well gone. The area south of campus had been a hippy-dippy paradise when she first arrived in Berkeley, with record stores, book shops, cheap and often exotic restaurants, clothing shops, head shops (only one still existed, perhaps maintained, like colonial Williamsburg, as a historical curiosity), flocks of street merchants hawking their hand-crafted wares, and a shifting population of vagabond kids strumming guitars and smoking dope right out on the street, some of them panhandling money from, some of them offering flowers or sticks of incense to, passers-by. The Berkeley cops had been permissive as a matter of policy, and that was an indispensable aspect of the scene; cops would stroll past kids sprawled in a tatterdemalion clump, backpacks and guitar cases strewn about them, sharing a joint, and they would smile and say hello, and the kids would smile and say hello back. No threats on the one side, no oinking noises on the other. A remarkable phenomenon in those days, when cops and kids were regarded as natural foes, predators and prey, in almost every other college town in the United States.

Now, though, Berkeley was paying the price for all that tolerance. Some nasty, tight-assed martinet like Rudolf Giuliani would no doubt say "I told you so," and feel smugly confirmed in his authoritarian inflexibility. There were still craftspeople selling their wares from sidewalk stalls during the daytime, but the area wasn't inviting after dusk; it had been decades since a woman could feel comfortable strolling there alone. Marijuana and LSD had given way to junk and crack and crank, and peace, love, and rock and roll had been replaced by disease, crime, and random mayhem. The side streets just off the avenue were more dangerous than the main drag, less populated and less well-lit. The parking lots on these side streets, even darker, with plenty of vehicles for potential malefactors to hide behind, were especially unnerving. And so, although she always managed to keep her anxieties and sense of vulnerability in check, Molly never felt at ease in this lot after dark, not until she was safely behind the wheel and her car doors were securely locked.

Which is why she literally jumped when, as she opened her car door, a voice said, "Hey, Mols." She froze, her heart beating wildly, her body immobile, like a small herbivore in the jaws of a large carnivore on the African savanna.

"Did I startle you?"

Her system still haywire from the adrenaline flooding in, she rounded on Corin angrily. "You son of a bitch! Of course you startled me!"

He took a step backward. "Hey...wait..."

"No, fucker, *you* wait! You don't sneak up on somebody in a parking lot at night! It's stupid and it's dangerous, and, and it's stupid."

"You already said it was stupid."

She didn't smile, although she had the impression he expected her to. "It's worth mentioning twice. A big guy like you may feel safe out here, but...Jesus."

Corin's face bore an unfamiliar hang-dog expression under this assault. Despite her panicky reaction, Molly retained enough presence of mind to expect him to defend himself or attempt a counter-attack. That was his style. And some part of her hoped he would; it would give her an opportunity to renew her harangue, and she wanted to shout at him until her throat was sore, she needed the release. But instead he shrank back, almost cowering, and muttered, "You're right. I'm sorry."

"And anyway..." A new thought occurred to her, a new source of indignation and alarm. "How'd you know to find me here?"

"I knew when your seminar ended."

"And where I parked my car? And what I drive?"

He shrugged, and essayed a half-smile. One of his most appealing looks, a mischievous expression that said, "I was naughty and you caught me red-handed," with his lower lip thrust out and his cheeks puffed and his eyebrows raised. Molly had seen it often enough in the past, and been charmed by it more than once. He'd retained it in his repertoire, and for good reason. It must have come in handy often.

But this time she wasn't buying. "Uh uh. It isn't cute, Corin. What you're doing isn't cute. Frankly, it's creepy. This is the third time you've just, just sprung at me without warning. And now I find you're, I don't know, you're *stalking* me like some kind of crazed fan. You know my teaching schedule, you know what I drive and where I park, you show up at my house without warning. You attend my class, hiding in one of the back rows, you've talked to my kids, you're trying to waylay my husband. I don't know what else you know about my life, I assume there's more, but the point is, it isn't okay. It's unacceptable. It's got to stop."

The expression on Corin's face had been changing as she spoke, metamorphosing from amusement and twinkly charm, an implicit suggestion they could step offstage and appreciate the humor in their situation, into something melancholy and pained, and then, finally, into something affronted. "Aw, Molly..."

"No, this isn't an 'aw Molly' situation. If those exist anymore, which they don't. You're making a pest of yourself. That's the kindest description I can offer."

His face fell even further. The expression he assumed was a new one to her; his face seemed to crumple. It was boyish, yes, but paradoxically, it also made him look older, slack-jawed, careworn, lost. His eyes had dulled. You could descry the old man germinating within, preparing to emerge from the chrysalis of this still handsome, still youthful middle-aged man.

"I saw Zeke today, Mols," he said in an undertone. "I spoke with him."

"You did?"

"That's why I wanted to talk to you. Tell you what happened."

Molly's eyes widened. "What do you mean? What *did* happen?"

"Maybe we shouldn't discuss it here."

Her eyes widened further. "*Did* something happen? Is something wrong?"

"I shouldn't have put it that way. Nothing happened in the sense of, of something *happening*. We just talked. But it feels wrong, discussing it in an open parking lot."

"It's where you chose to accost me."

"There weren't many other opportunities. You're a busy lady. Listen,

307

how about giving me a lift to where I'm staying, we can talk on the way." He noticed the look that greeted this suggestion, a mistrustful, hard glare. He laughed, embarrassed but apparently also amused by his old antics. "It isn't far. On Prince, a block or so below Telegraph. Barely out of your way."

She processed the situation swiftly. It might be the easiest way to deal with him: Take him where he wants, drop him off, go. He was persistent enough so that if she didn't handle this now, it would have to be handled later. Besides, she was curious about what had passed between him and Zeke. That was a confrontation she'd been dreading. "Okay, get in," she said.

"Thanks, Mols."

"Don't regard this as a precedent."

He opened the passenger-side door. "Understood."

"And buckle your seat belt."

"Of course. I can't risk even a trivial infraction. They run an ID check on me, I'm done for."

It felt odd to be sitting next to Corin in a car. Especially after dark; by now the sky was inky black over the hills and a deep lavender toward the bay. This was a far more intimate kind of proximity than when they had drunk coffee a few weeks ago at that café on Bancroft. It felt closer, more private. The most uncomfortable thing about it was that it almost felt comfortable.

When she pressed the ignition button, he said, "How do you like the Prius? These hybrids any good?"

She turned toward him. "You really want to talk about cars?"

"It just seems like a very Berkeley thing to drive."

"It's a sensible and responsible thing to drive."

"Jeez, Molly, relax. You're awfully touchy. For most people, their cars aren't a loaded topic."

She resisted the urge to order him out of her car, but she was annoyed. It pressed a lot of old buttons, the way he maneuvered and distorted a conversation to secure the upper hand. About matters large and matters minuscule. She had watched him win a lot of arguments that way in the past. Sometimes she'd busted him for it and sometimes she sat back and enjoyed his slippery ingenuity.

She backed out of the parking space and headed toward the exit. After making a right turn onto Channing, she said, "How'd you manage to get to Zeke today?"

"I just showed up at his office. After his last patient left."

"How did you know it was his last patient?" Corin didn't answer. "You fucker! You've been spying on him too!"

"Don't be melodramatic, Mols. No spying was involved. It was six o'clock, the work day was over. It was an opportune time to pop in."

"You mean you ambushed him."

"I showed up and knocked on his door. Is that an ambush?"

"It isn't exactly phoning and making an appointment."

"That didn't seem like the most promising approach."

"You've been gunning for him since you got here, haven't you?"

"I've tried to see everybody. The old crowd. Stan, you, Liam, people you know and many you never met, here and in SF. Zeke's been the most elusive."

"You're the last person he ever wants to see."

Silence. Surely this couldn't come as news. She crossed Telegraph Avenue, which was one-way for a half-mile or so south of campus, the wrong way from her point of view tonight. Getting Corin home necessitated a detour, down to Dana, south to Dwight, and then back up to Telegraph. A bother, with stop signs at every corner.

Corin finally answered. "What's he got against me?"

"You're joking."

"I know he was upset when you and I ran off together. But we weren't casual about it. Remember how we discussed it? Sometimes it felt like we didn't talk about much else." His voice sounded raw, emotional, wounded. Molly was taken aback by its intensity. What was at stake for him here? "But good Christ, shit happens. People recover. And so much has happened since. To all of us, and to the human race."

"What can I tell you? Zeke apparently feels differently. I don't think it's your place or mine to argue."

"But damn it, he's forgiven *you*, and you were much more to blame than me."

Which gave her an unpleasant jolt, a nasty tingle along the back of her scalp. It might be true, but it was coarse of him to mention it. Ungentlemanly.

"I'm not sure forgiveness is the point. And I don't know that he *has* forgiven me, I don't know that he hasn't forgiven you. He doesn't think in those terms. You want absolution, re-join your church and talk to a priest."

As if she hadn't spoken at all, Corin resumed, "Aside from everything else, no guy was going to say no to you. Zeke must realize that. You were a luscious piece of ass. How can he blame me for succumbing? I was a lusty young boyo in those days, full of juice. And it's not like I started it."

He really enjoyed reminding her the initiative had been hers. Didn't he know how mortifying this was to her? Or was that the point? "Blame isn't the issue," she said.

"He hates me."

"When he bothers to think about you at all. Which isn't very often."

"But why? Why should he hate me? *You* came after *me*. I didn't start it! *You came after me!*"

"Did you tell him that? That I came after you?"

"Well...sort of."

"Wonderful. I'm sure that made his evening."

"I have the right to defend myself. I didn't give him any details, if that's what's worrying you. I didn't tell him the things you said."

She felt herself coloring, felt her face getting hot. With shame at her brazenness with this undeserving man, and at her own perfidy. There were memories she had managed, over the years, to consign to a dusty, cobwebbed, unvisited storeroom in her mind, and now Corin was shining a flashlight into it. It made her feel as if something deep inside her were writhing. She said, in as measured a tone of voice as she could muster, "Listen, Corin. Before you get carried away. What happened back then...it was like...you were...it was like you were the only bus out of town. I needed to escape, not from Zeke, but from my situation. You were the closest thing to Trailways I could find. That's all there was to it."

"I don't think so, Mols. I don't think that's all there was to it." His voice thickening, he continued, "Don't forget, I was there. You can tell Zeke any shite you want, any palliative you think will help, but damn it, *I was there.* I know the things you said, I know what it was like between us when it was good."

"You know what you *thought* it was like, that's what you know."

"Ah, Mols, I may have been a Leninist, but who's re-writing history now?"

She was furious with herself all of a sudden. How had she let herself be inveigled into this conversation? To let it happen at all handed him a victory. And she knew better. Nothing good could conceivably come of it.

"What are you after, Corin? It isn't 1973. What do you want from us?"

And then a terrible thing happened. She had just turned onto Dwight Way, was changing lanes so that she could make the right onto Telegraph, when Corin started to sob. A strangled sound he was attempting to suppress. Which made it worse, turned it into a painful, gasping, spasmodic rumble, like some intricate machine grinding itself to pieces before one's eyes.

It was unthinkable, Corin crying. Literally unimaginable; of all the men she knew—and this was purely speculative, she had never seen any of them cry except Zeke, at their wedding, which didn't count—she would have figured Corin the least likely. But here he was, seated beside her, his head in his hands, his body wracked by a seemingly unending series of throes. She had no prejudice against grown men weeping, no notion it was unmanly, but she'd never been confronted with it before, and was surprised by her own reaction when it came. Which it did, after a short delay no doubt occasioned primarily by surprise, or incredulity. She suddenly felt waves of compassion washing over her. Solicitude. Maternal tenderness.

Fuck.

"What is it, Corin? What's the matter?"

She kept a box of Kleenex on the floor on the passenger side of the car. Corin, not having noticed it at the time, had stepped on and crushed it when he'd first climbed in. But now he reached down toward the squashed box at his feet and maneuvered a tissue out of it. He blew his nose and said, "God, this is embarrassing."

"No it isn't," she said firmly. "It's human."

"I told Zeke I needed help. He wasn't interested. He didn't care."

"What were you expecting?"

"I didn't expect anything. But I don't want him to be my enemy." He blew his nose again. It was hard to tell whether the crying jag was over, or gathering strength for a second go-round. And then he heaved a mammoth sigh, expelling all the gathered grief. "Where did everything go? How did everything go *wrong*? I'm sixty-one. Ancient! I dedicated my life to something bigger than myself, and maybe I got it wrong, but I cared about something, I wasn't selfish. And now it's 2014—it sounds like a science fiction date, like Jules Verne or Arthur C. Clarke—and I've got nothing to show for my life. The cause I believed in is lost, it was misguided and hopeless all along. I'm a wanted man. I don't have a home. I don't have a family. I'm skint. I have no idea where to go or what to do. *I want my life back.*"

Molly, driving slowly along Telegraph, had no answer. Everything he said was irrefutable; what comfort was there to offer? The bleakness of his current existence was vivid to her for the first time. Funny she had never considered that aspect of things before, seen it from his point of view. Hadn't let herself, probably. Corin always had too much energy, too much life in him for bleakness. But the view from behind his eyes must be looking awfully bleak these days.

"And my so-called friends," he went on. "I thought people here were on my side. But the old Movement people...some are underground, some are in jail, some are capitalists in Silicon Valley, some have become gangsters, no politics to it at all, just violence and greed, and of course some have disappeared, no one's heard from them in years, they're probably dead. And my Berkeley mates…Stan threw me out of his house, did you know that? His astonishing cunt of a wife. He was supposed to be representing me, cutting some kind of deal with the Feds, but he didn't come through, I don't know if he even tried. Now he doesn't return my calls. And Liam, who smiles and acts friendly but doesn't want to give me the time of day, I'm like a zombie menacing his menage. That hostile Chink wife of his, giving me the fish-eye whenever I come around. Why'd all the guys marry harpies? Except Zeke," he hastily put in. "And then there's you. The one that hurts the most."

They were approaching Prince Street. Molly knew how jarring it was at this fragile moment to ask for directions. In her gentlest voice, she said, "Here?"

"Yeah. Hang a right."

She made the turn. He explained, "It's on the next block. A little bungalow on the left, set back from the street."

They were seconds from his destination. How in the name of God could this conversation be brought to anything resembling a graceful conclusion? And even more important, a conclusion that really concluded things, that definitively ended all intercourse between them?

"We shared something," he was saying. "I know it ended badly, and I believe it ended prematurely, you applied to Stanford and everything unraveled and I still don't know why…But we meant something to each other, and now you treat me like a stranger, an importuning stranger. No, worse, like what you said before. A stalker." She could hear it in his voice: He wasn't sobbing, but tears were flowing again.

Why did it have this effect on her? Would she have reacted the same way before the girls were born, or was it a consequence of motherhood, some set of hormones that came with the package? She said gently, soothingly, "You can't just show up after all this time and not expect things to have changed."

"This is it," he said. "Just here." She pulled over and stopped the car. He said, "No, I didn't expect that. I just expected…I don't know. Caring. Friendship."

"Seems to me Stan offered you friendship and help."

"At first. Then he took it back. Anyway, I'm not talking about Stan."

"Do you need money?" She silently cursed herself once the words were out of her mouth. Of course he needed money. Could she possibly write him a check? What would Zeke say if he found out? She'd have to make it out to cash to prevent that, but still…if he ever learned of it, there's no way he'd regard it as anything but a betrayal. And the mere fact she'd made the offer could be a weapon in Corin's hands.

"I don't want money from you, Molly."

She recognized this refusal as gallantry on his part. It couldn't have come easily. He'd already said he was broke, he obviously was destitute beyond what he'd been able to borrow or scrounge, and he had nothing that even resembled prospects.

She heard herself asking, "Then what *do* you want?"

"It's just, I feel…is it only me? I feel we have unfinished business."

"You and me?"

"Yes."

She steeled herself, and said, "It's only you. Our business is very much finished. Completely finished." No softening of her attitude, and no piteousness in Corin, could induce her to acquiesce in such a notion or sugar-coat the answer. That way calamity lay. "It was finished forty years ago. Nothing's changed."

"You got scared, that's why it ended. Otherwise—"

"I did get scared, that's true. But I knew I'd made a mistake before that, I knew it right away. Anyway, this is ancient history. We needn't go over it again."

"You're the only woman I ever cared about, Molly."

"Stop it. Please."

"How did you and Zeke get back together?"

"We're not going to have that conversation."

"Isn't there anything from the old days you remember fondly? Anything about the time you and I had together?"

"We're here, Corin. I gave you a ride home as requested. Let's say good night. Let's say goodbye."

He unclicked his seat belt and turned toward her with a sigh. "All right, Mols. It's not my choice, but we'll say good night." He placed his left hand very gently on the back of her head, and with his right hand, equally gently, he touched her cheek and turned her face to his. She felt oddly entranced, powerless to resist. And then he kissed her, his cheeks wet where the tears had flowed, his lips soft and insinuating against hers, and just slightly parted; he knew what he was about, Corin did, knew when to insist and when merely to suggest.

She would never admit it, but something happened. She felt it happen, deep within. And on the moment remembered things she thought expunged. She pushed him away forcefully as soon as her mind registered what was occurring. "No!" she said. "Stop it! Jesus Christ, what do you think you're doing?"

His hand was still on her cheek. He knew. Some men just know, damn them. "Aw," he said in a quiet, lilting voice, little more than a whisper, "you can't fool me, Molly Hilliard." Even in the darkness, she could see the small triumphant smile on his face. "Never could."

She slapped his hand away. "Get out," she said. "Now. Out of my car." There was nothing gentle in her voice, no vestige of her earlier solicitude.

"Seems we'll always have unfinished business," he said.

The smug bastard. "Go to hell," she said.

The door was open, he was sliding his legs out. "'Night, Mols. Thanks for the lift."

During dinner an hour or so later, the late dinner they ate on her seminar nights, she mentioned to Zeke, as casually as she could, that she'd seen Corin, and that she knew Zeke had too. She even told him about giving Corin a lift. It seemed sensible to include as much of the truth as possible, in case she and Corin had been observed, or in the unlikely event Corin said something to Zeke. Who knew what the man was capable of?

She chose to tell him at the dinner table because of the presence of the girls. Their being there would inhibit Zeke; he'd ask fewer questions, express fewer misgivings, demand fewer reassurances. She

315

wanted to avoid a barrage of questions; something in her manner, some involuntary tic, might reveal something was awry, or even suggest more was awry than actually was awry. Zeke was too observant to be relied on to miss any signals. And he had a shrink's propensity to over-interpret.

"He touched all the bases today, didn't he?" Zeke said.

Pretty mild reaction, she thought. Could that be a result of his own meeting with Corin? Had it settled something for him? Unlikely, but it reminded her she was still pretty damned curious about the meeting and Zeke's reaction to it. Corin had revealed almost nothing, despite having offered to do so. It was his pretext for requesting the ride home.

"How was it to see him, Easy? After all this time?"

"Maybe we should talk about it later."

"Hey, don't mind us," said Ashley.

Olivia said, "Keep out of it, Ash." Rather sharply, for her.

Ashley was offended. "We're sitting right here. We're not pieces of furniture. It's rude. Like whispering."

"That's a fair point," said Molly. "We'll talk about something else."

At which Olivia hissed, "See? Now they won't say anything." When Zeke laughed, she half-smiled in his direction, and, continuing to address Ashley, added, "The trick is to shut up and be invisible. They forget you're there."

Zeke was impressed; knowing when to keep mum was a vital part of his own work, an indispensable way to glean information. Stay mute and recessive and people start discounting your presence. That was one reason Freud used the couch. Out of sight, out of mind.

Which gave him, unbidden, an idea for a *New Yorker* cartoon. A therapist seated in an armchair listening to a patient reclining on a couch; a ribbon above the therapist identifying him as, "Out of sight," one above the patient as, "Out of mind." It had probably been simmering inside him ever since Corin asked about the couch several hours before.

He glanced over at Olivia again. He often wondered whether, hiding behind her determinedly bland exterior, an interesting mind might lurk.

This little exchange seemed evidence not only of an interesting mind, but of a strategy behind the bland exterior. Did she intentionally assume an innocuous veneer as protective coloration?

If so, it was probably because of the divorce. That must have taught her to lie low, stay out of everyone's way, and listen close. Not the worst lesson, but sad to have learned it so young, and so thoroughly.

No kid emerges from a divorce unscathed. He'd had enough clients who were children of divorce to know that. Olivia and Ashley seemed to be doing okay, but we're kidding ourselves if we pretend it's had no impact. Was the same true of himself? By the time his parents separated, he was already in college, his formative years over. But it might have had some influence on how he'd reacted to Molly's absconding. Sensitized him to issues of abandonment, alerted him to and alarmed him about the precariousness of all relationships.

Molly didn't renew her inquiry during the rest of dinner. Zeke expected her to raise it later, once they were alone, but that didn't happen. For an hour or so, while he watched TV and then checked e-mail and desultorily read a few favored blogs, Molly was in Olivia's room, helping her with an English paper due later that week. Then, when he was in bed reading, and she climbed in beside him, she surprised him not by asking about Corin, but by nestling up beside him with her mouth near his ear and her right hand along his thigh. An unambiguous announcement of intent, and a rare mid-week occurrence at this point in their lives. Indeed, it had been a couple of weeks since they'd made love at all, what with one thing and another.

Surprised, he turned to her with a smile, and said, "Are you trying to take advantage of me, lady?"

"Turn out the light, Easy," she murmured. "It's been way too long."

As he stretched away from her to click off his bed-side light, he said, "Does this have anything to do with seeing Corin?"

It was lucky he wasn't looking her way when he asked. It made it easier to say, "Good God, no," without having to worry about the expression on her face.

At which point the light was out, they were in darkness. He shifted his weight back toward her, reached for her, and said, "So this isn't some kind of…I don't know, some kind of statement?"

"What kind of statement would that be?" Her tone gently teasing, to camouflage both her relief and her apprehension. Zeke's antennae were clearly twitching, but he didn't seem to be on high alert. Not, she quickly assured herself, that there were grounds for suspicion: All that had happened was a single, unexpected, uninvited kiss, which she'd immediately repelled.

"I don't want to put words in your mouth," he said.

She was smiling at him in the darkness. Relief had ceded way to affection; she knew what he wanted, she was familiar with the roundabout way he indicated such things, and she suddenly found the whole transaction endearing, found *him* almost unendurably endearing. "Okay, Easy," she said, "you want a statement? Here goes. I love you and I'm so glad we're sharing our lives I can hardly express it and I'm feeling incredibly aroused at the moment. Maybe because today showed me all over again how lucky I am. There's my statement."

"I guess it'll have to do," he said, before leaning down to kiss her.

She laughed, but then grabbed for him. There was no denying her ardor tonight. It took Zeke by surprise. Not that he had any serious complaints about their love-making generally, but a certain level of routine had undeniably crept in over the years. They knew how to satisfy each other and often went about it briskly, without much ceremony. The intimacy lay in the efficiency, not in any particular passion. Tonight, though, was different: Molly was ravenous and aggressive, as if some dormant part of her erotic imagination had been freshly engaged. He felt some niggling misgivings, some gnawing uncertainty about its origins, but giving in seemed wiser than engaging in an inquisition. A mood like this might prove ephemeral. Gather ye goddamn rosebuds.

After she came, quicker than usual, while riding him, she leaned down and whispered, "Can you hold out a little? I don't think I'm done."

"Sure." An advantage of being fifty-something. "As long as you want."

Her excitement inspired him. It was the most adventurous, the most sustained, the most energetic lovemaking they'd shared in years. After-wards, also for the first time in years, they fell asleep in each other's arms.

They were very deeply asleep when the phone jangled them awake. Molly was the first to open her eyes: The clock on Zeke's bedside table said 3:37. Oh Christ, she thought, what now? Not the girls, they're home. Owen? Or…her blood ran cold when she thought, Oh shit, Corin? That thought immediately jerked her into full wakefulness. Was he taking his stalking to a new level? She reached across Zeke—the phone rested on his bedside table—and groped for the receiver. He was stirring, of course. More than stirring. He was awake.

She found the receiver, pulled it over. "Hello?" she said, unable to keep the apprehension out of her voice. A few seconds later, she gasped out an "Oh my God!"

"Who is it?" Zeke said. Not mumbling, not confused. There's some-thing about a telephone ringing in the dead of night; you know it can't be good, you know it isn't trivial, and that knowledge cuts right through the fog of slumber. "Owen?"

She shook her head and held up a hand for silence, and a few moments later said into the receiver, "You don't know yet?" And then, after a few more seconds, "He was? Jesus!" and then, "Okay, hon, hang tight, we'll be right there. Shouldn't take us more than fifteen minutes. Stay calm, it'll be okay."

She hung up. Zeke had already switched on the bedside light, and was looking at her inquisitively. She said, "Get dressed, Easy. Hurry. We're going to the Alta Bates E.R."

The Alta Bates Emergency Room could be bad on weekends, thronged with the injured, the overdosed, the dazed and confused. But this was Monday—or early Tuesday, to be precise—and the waiting area was almost empty. The only people seated there were two uniformed Berkeley police, one a white man, the other a short, swarthy woman of indetermi-nate ethnicity, and several chairs away, Melanie, who spotted Zeke and Molly as soon as they entered, and rose and rushed toward them. Her eyes were dry but bloodshot. She was wearing jeans and a navy-blue sweat shirt, and no make-up. Zeke reflected that it had been decades since he'd seen her so un-gussied-up. She didn't look too different, though.

"Any word?" asked Molly, while embracing her friend.

"They don't think there's a concussion," Melanie answered. "He's going to be okay, it seems like. Lacerations and contusions, but no permanent damage. Thank God for the airbag. He's under arrest, though." She cast her eyes toward the two cops and lowered her voice. "DWI. He's been breathalyzed. They're taking him downtown and booking him as soon as the doctor releases him."

"Christ," said Zeke. And then, "Was anyone else hurt?"

Melanie hesitated before saying, "Well, a tree. And a picket fence. They don't think the fence is going to make it."

"The car?"

"Totaled."

Molly spoke. "Have you seen him?"

"For a minute, when we were waiting for the doctor. And he called from the scene before the cops showed up. He wasn't sure how bad he was hurt, but he was pretty shaken. And completely humiliated. He hasn't been like this since he got sober. It's awful, really. Such a setback. I honestly never expected it would happen again." She sounded distressed but fully in control of herself.

The male cop glanced over at them. Melanie noticed, and said, very quietly, "Let's go outside and talk for a minute."

Which is when Zeke suddenly realized what must have happened. He didn't say anything until they stepped outside, into the chilly darkness. The lights from within the hospital behind them cast long shadows on the sidewalk. A black-and-white police car was parked in the loading zone. The area was otherwise deserted.

After a second, Zeke said in an undertone, "He wasn't alone."

An interesting look, of admiration it seemed, crossed Melanie's face. She said, "No, Zeke."

Molly was puzzled. "Who was he with?" She was wondering, Zeke guessed, whether Liam was with a woman, whether that was the issue.

320

"Corin," he said.

"That fucking bastard," confirmed Melanie with a decisive nod. "I don't know how bad he was hurt, probably not as bad as he deserves, but in any case, he got away before the cops and ambulance arrived. No one seems to suspect anything."

"Oh my God," said Molly.

"Can someone tell me this guy's magic?" Melanie suddenly demanded. "I didn't know him when he was young, so what am I missing? It completely escapes me. Who elected him Pied Piper?"

"Ask Molly," Zeke said curtly, jerking a thumb in her direction. "She's the goddamn expert." It was odd, it surprised him as much as anyone, but he was caught in a rising tide of anger. Almost overwhelmed by it. He wasn't even sure at whom it was primarily directed, but Molly was definitely in the line of fire.

She looked as if she had been slapped. She glared at him, started to say something and then thought better of it.

None of this escaped Melanie, but she may not have understood it. Zeke wasn't sure what she knew of Molly and Corin, that whole saga. She said, "Liam's been sober for...for whatever it's been. He could tell you down to the minute. It was such a point of pride, I never thought he'd take another drink. *He* never thought so either. And now he has to start the counting from zero. The next meeting, he'll have to say his name is Liam and he's been sober for one day. Or a couple of hours, if we can make bail and get him home quick enough. It's going to kill him. Everybody'll be supportive, of course, that's how these things work, but it's an awful defeat." She sighed. "I'm really mystified. What is it with this guy? Hypnosis? Mind control? Dinner and a movie? How does he convince someone as fortified as Liam that it's okay to get loaded?"

"Will you ask him?" Molly asked. She had taken a couple of steps away from Zeke, a way to express her irritation, but she was trying to keep her focus on Melanie, whose needs, after all, were pressing.

Meanwhile, Zeke was pondering his sudden intense anger. The only villain tonight was Corin, inducing Liam to drink, let alone drink and drive, sheer madness. Why should this provoke anger at Molly? If anything, their extravagant lovemaking tonight should be inclining him in the opposite direction. What were the intervening psychic steps, and why was he repressing them? Because it was a reminder of her susceptibility forty years before? Because she gave Corin a lift home, which suggested a vestigial inclination to do his bidding? Or because of the persistence of his own vague misgivings, which he'd been nursing for the past few weeks and was still, despite everything, feeling right now, present tense?

He sensed Molly's reciprocal irritation; ordinarily, that would have driven him to try to find a way to make peace. But instead he was feeling spiteful and indifferent. Which perhaps suggested she was the primary target of his anger after all, regardless of the lovemaking, and regardless of who had gotten Liam drunk.

"I plan to, sure," Melanie was saying. "In time. I'm curious. That's in addition to wanting to wring his neck. I'm curious and furious. How could he have done something so unbelievably stupid? But I know I'll get mad when we talk about it, no way to prevent that, and lots of other stuff has to come first. He's going to need TLC before we get to the tough love."

They all sensed at once that something was happening inside the hospital. Looking in through the glass front, they could see a nurse pushing a wheelchair with Liam in it through the double-doors separating the garishly-lit waiting room from the hospital proper. He was looking to left and right apprehensively, searching for a friendly face. For Melanie's face, hoping it would be friendly.

With Melanie in the lead, the three friends hurried back through the automatic doors into the building. When they entered, the cops were already descending on Liam. One of them had a pair of handcuffs ready.

"Honey!" said Melanie.

Liam glanced up gratefully. He looked pretty beat up; there would be plenty of swelling and bruising tomorrow. "Hi, Mel," he said weakly. He managed a hesitant smile, then grimaced in pain. The pain would also be a lot worse tomorrow.

"Zeke and Molly are here," Melanie said.

"Yeah, I see. Thanks, guys. This is really…Melanie always says you're the ones we'd turn to in a crisis." He faced Melanie. "Mel…I'm so, so sorry."

"I know you are." She said it gently; whatever ire she was feeling, she kept a tight rein on it. She put a hand on his shoulder, and leaned down and kissed the top of his head, where no injuries were apparent. "Anyway…" She glanced at the police officers hovering at her elbow. "Maybe there were extenuating circumstances."

"We need to take him in now," the male cop said. Apologetically. He was trying to be a good guy.

"Yeah," Liam said to him, "no problem."

"We'll get you processed quick. It's a slow night. You'll be home soon."

"Thanks. I appreciate that." He looked at Melanie, slid his eyes toward the cops, and then back to Melanie again. "It's nice of you to say, Mel, but there's no such thing as extenuating circumstances. Only one person is responsible when this happens. So don't go blaming…you know, that other thing. I blew it. Period."

"I blame that other thing too," Melanie said. Grimly. "But that doesn't mean I excuse you."

The policeman nodded to the nurse, who resumed pushing the wheelchair toward the entrance. Melanie, Zeke, Molly followed. "We'll be booking him downtown," the cop said to Melanie. "You know how to get there?"

"Yes," said Melanie. "And I'll be right behind you." She turned to Zeke and Molly. "Go on home. I can take it from here. I shouldn't have bothered you in the first place. I just…I needed moral support. I was in a tizzy."

"Of course," said Zeke. "Anytime."

"Well, I hope there won't be another. But thanks." She gave him a kiss on the cheek, hugged Molly, and headed off to the parking garage across the street, a small, dark, forlorn figure.

After a few silent seconds, Molly grunted, "Just don't say anything, okay? Not a word. Not a single fucking word."

Zeke had been about to say, "This is never going to end, is it?" Relatively non-contentious, he would have thought, given the circumstances. But he said nothing. They drove home in silence. It was too late to go back to bed. Molly went straight into the kitchen to make a pot of coffee. Zeke climbed the stairs to the bedroom, quickly changed into shorts and a tee shirt, and went for a pre-dawn run.

Eleven

1973 – 2002

I wasn't interviewed after the robbery. Corin and I were never close; nobody was going to tell a reporter covering the story, "Talk to Zeke Stern, he'll fill in the picture for you." Same was true for Liam. Stan *was* quoted a couple of times, including in *The New York Times*, a big deal. His parents had the clipping laminated and framed, and it hung proudly ever after in their living room. Not that his contribution amounted to much, just a sentence or two expressing skepticism that Corin could be involved in anything violent. I don't know if he was really skeptical or just politic: The article appeared so soon after the event, maybe there was still room for doubt if one wanted to doubt. But the question was never in real doubt. This was the first time Stan was identified in print as "left-leaning lawyer Stanley Pilnik," although it was far from the last. They had jumped the gun though, since he hadn't finished law school. On the plus side, they spelled his name right.

It was a pretty big story for a while. Whatever regrets Corin might have felt about the crime, he couldn't have felt short-changed by the attention it got locally. I first learned about it the morning after it occurred, from the *Chronicle*. Banner headline, full-page photo of the bank interior after the shoot-out. Very dramatic; it looked Depression-era. I immediately phoned Stan. He was eager to share and explore his confused feelings and complex sense of conflicting obligations—he didn't express any doubts about Corin's participation *then*—but I stopped him. "Wait! What about Molly? Is she involved? Is she in trouble?"

He was startled. "Jeez, Zeke, no. She and Corin broke up months ago."

This was big news too, at least to me. Friends were reluctant to tell me anything about Corin and her, no doubt to spare my feelings, so I was completely ignorant. "They did? Was it acrimonious?"

"It wasn't amicable."

I liked the sound of that.

And then, a couple of days later, I was shocked to see her on TV. A KRON minicam team had waylaid her on the Stanford campus; the locale itself, instantly recognizable, also came as a surprise. I didn't know she was back in school, that she'd had a second change of heart cancelling out her first change of heart.

She looked pretty much the same, of course; less than a year had gone by since I'd seen her. She had impressive poise on camera. "I'm not going to talk about this," she told the reporter, her voice firm but without any perceptible hostile edge. It's the sort of thing she could pull off. If I have to say no to somebody, I sound either pathetically apologetic or like an asshole. When the reporter pressed her, in that way TV reporters do, she said, "Look, Corin and I haven't spoken in months, I don't know anything. And I have nothing further to say."

"Did it come as a surprise?"

"If I answer, that would be something further, wouldn't it?"

"Have the police been in contact with you?"

"Yes." She started walking away.

"Are you worried about him?" The reporter clearly wasn't going to let her slip through his fingers without a struggle. Not while she was still responding.

She reluctantly turned back to face the camera. "Why in the world would I want to share something like that?" she said, her tone still conversational, without a trace of overt testiness. "It's like totally not your business."

They aired the clip, I'd hazard, only because she was pretty.

Nationally, the robbery was a modest story, its shelf-life extended a bit by Corin's having escaped arrest. The fact he was attractive probably played a role as well; we were shown his photograph a lot. Back then when political crime still had a trace of outlaw glamour, even a wisp of moral prestige, at least among some of my more fatuous left-wing brethren, he acquired rock-star status in some circles. Dubious circles, needless to say, and among people who didn't know the guy or bother themselves with the specifics of the case. But this was the era of the SLA and the Baader-Meinhof Gang and the Red Brigades, so there were scatterings of people who were prepared to regard Corin as some sort of renegade hero. I'm sure there must have been teenage girls around the country looking at Corin's photograph and fantasizing about him. That sensitive face, that lively, friendly smile, those crinkly, twinkling eyes. Hunk on the run. Warren Beatty as Clyde Barrow.

It's easier to idealize somebody when you have to fill in a lot of blanks.

Did I want Corin to get caught? From this remove, it's hard to remember *what* I wanted. No doubt my feelings were confused; I abominated the crime on principle—what civilized person could feel otherwise?—and despised Corin himself, but there's still a natural resistance to wanting someone you know, and with whom you have, if nothing else, friends in common, to face a lifetime in prison. Besides, I shared the prevailing skepticism about legally-constituted authority, and a concomitant reluctance to side with it. I probably chose to have no opinion at all. I opted for hostile neutrality, although I couldn't shake an abiding albeit grudging curiosity. I devoured everything published about the crime.

I resented my curiosity, though. And blamed Molly for it. And at the same time wondered how she felt about everything. The one glimpse of her on TV was piquant; her cool self-possession, impossible to decipher, rendered the riddle of her feelings even more intriguing. But asking Stan what he knew would have entailed a loss of face, and I'd managed so far to keep my face largely intact. No point sacrificing it at this late stage. Especially since he probably wouldn't know anything anyway. Not about Molly's state of mind. States of mind weren't Stan's forte.

I did ask him whether he knew anything about the robbery.

"In advance, you mean? Jesus, Corin would never have confided in me. He didn't consider me reliable. And besides, we'd kind of lost touch. He…" Stan laughed. "I guess it won't surprise you to hear he was moving in different circles."

"He didn't keep you apprised?"

"Hardly. He considered me a bourgeois whose radicalism was a hobby, like stamp collecting. A dilettante. Unserious and unsound."

"He told you this?"

"He didn't have to."

I asked, "What would you have done if you'd known what he was up to?"

"Tried to talk him out of it."

"And if you couldn't?"

"I try not to think about that."

"Would you have alerted the authorities?"

"I try not to think about it! Probably. Or, I don't know, maybe not."

"You could have saved a couple of lives."

"That's clear now, but wasn't at the time. And it's no small thing to drop a dime on a friend. It's lucky Corin didn't trust me. Maybe he was right not to."

The robbery story had legs, but not enormously long legs. After a couple of weeks, the second week mostly rehashing the same stories and reiterating that Corin was still at large, the media moved on to other matters. It flared up again, briefly, when the two guys who were caught were sentenced, months later. Both pled guilty, both got life. With an armed robbery resulting in two fatalities, one a cop, and the Nixon Justice Department in charge of the prosecution, clemency wasn't on the cards. Indeed, had a nation-wide moratorium not been in effect, the death penalty would have been all but inevitable. Murder during the commission of a felony qualifies as special circumstances, as does the murder of an on-duty police officer. When the sentences were announced, the media took the opportunity to give us further glimpses of Corin's photo. The guy who got away. The white guy.

By then, I was just starting to pull myself together. I applied to graduate school in clinical psychology—it was the most organized thing I'd done in many a month—and was accepted at a number of places. It wasn't hard to settle on UC Berkeley. I wasn't in any shape to uproot myself.

During that period, I did a foolish thing, and kept it up for a long, long time. I kept a photo of Molly on my dresser. I couldn't bring myself to remove it. Maybe having it removed—unbeknownst to myself, to paraphrase Abraham Lincoln—would have been okay, but actually doing it seemed too premeditated, too deliberate, too cold and final.

In my practice now, when counseling a client with a broken heart— and that's a sizable number—I follow the precepts of cognitive behavioral therapy, techniques I've added to my clinical repertoire in recent years. Among other things, I tell her (more of my clients are hers than his) to stop thinking about the person she's lost. It's within her power. Kick the habit. She should give herself some time to grieve—the soul has its claims, and among those is the need to mourn after a bereavement— but a healthy, functioning psyche has its own legitimate demands, and a return to the ordinary gamut of emotions is one of them. So after a reasonable amount of time, she needs to wrench herself out of the hole she's in and move on. What she's been doing is a form of obsessive-compulsive behavior. There are ways to get past it. They work. She and I will still delve into other issues in her life in time-honored talking-cure fashion, but we can start ameliorating the pain right away. It takes determination and discipline on her part, but the option is available when she's ready.

I didn't know that then. I didn't have a clue. Neither did my shrink; it wasn't in the mainstream therapeutic arsenal yet (in fact, it would have been frowned upon, would have been dismissed as a form of avoidance). And those melancholy, mournful feelings were seductive, they were sweet, they kept murmuring to me and beckoning me back. So I kept the photo on the dresser by my bed for years. Literal years. Sometimes I didn't notice it, but sometimes it caught me unawares and brought me up short, I'd stare at it, and that big smile of Molly's would remind me of the day I'd taken the picture, when the two of us had gone camping in Sonoma County for an idyllic few days. I'd awoken the first morning, just after dawn, and Molly was already up, brewing coffee over a campfire. The sight of her, in jeans and a tight white sleeveless tee, shivering, trying to stay close to the fire to keep warm, was too fetching to resist; her lips were blue and trembling, her hair was disheveled, and because her top was much too thin—we'd generated a lot of heat in the sleeping bag the night before, and so, when she pulled on some clothes before we fell asleep, she'd left off her sweatshirt—I could see her erect nipples poking against the thin cotton. She was a vision; to my lustful eye, she was a David Hamilton model, a paragon of eroticized young womanhood. Without leaving the sleeping bag, making as little noise as possible, I'd reached over, grabbed my camera, and called her name. She turned toward me with a goofy grin on her face, and when she saw the camera, she laughingly protested that her hair was a mess and she hadn't washed and I mustn't, I absolutely mustn't, on pain of death, press that button. But I went ahead and shot the picture anyway. After we got back to town a few days later and the film was developed, she had to admit it was a good shot. She even liked the nipples, although she said because of them she could never show the picture to her dad.

And now she was gone and I'd sometimes look at it and get moony and sad and start thinking about all the joy I had lost and would never get back.

I suspect part of me kept the picture there to protect the sanctity of my bed. I don't mean anything mystical—I don't mean as a talisman—but rather, more prosaically and more insidiously, as a deal-breaker: I may have been acting on an unconscious desire to sabotage a post-Molly love life, seeing that eventuality as a final, dreadful confirmation that the Molly chapter was over for good. In fact, the picture never killed a seduction outright, although it stuck a spoke in a few wheels. "Is that your sister?" a woman might ask, after coming home with me from a party or a bar, when we'd made our way to the bedroom after some preliminary making-out in the living room. As if I could possibly have a sister with blond straight hair and a petite retroussé nose. Or simply, "Who's this?" And I would explain. At length. A disquisition well beyond what the question required or sought. No woman ever upped and left afterward. I suppose, by the time anyone laid eyes on the photo, things had reached the point of no return, the deal was too near to being sealed to be queered. Still, you could usually feel the ardor hissing out of the room. Getting it back wasn't always possible, even if we went through the motions.

There was, you see, an unspoken etiquette of one-night stands, a code of behavior, and I was finally, belatedly, learning it, even while violating it. *By* violating it. One of the most important tenets is, Keep your personal baggage to yourself. And the harsh justification for that is: Even though what you're doing looks and feels like an intimate activity, it *isn't* an intimate activity, and you mustn't make the mistake of treating it like one.

Previously, I had known sex only in intimate contexts. With the girl friends I'd had before Molly, in high school, there had been a putative relationship of some kind. Maybe it was largely a useful fiction to enable sex, but even so, there was conversation, there were confidences, there was time invested. I found it jarring to discover that people did the exact same things, in pretty much the exact same way, for sport. It wasn't surprising as *news*—the culture was positively awash in recreational fucking—and I wasn't so priggish as to have a principled objection, but nonetheless, it was disorienting as a reality experienced first-hand. I had to learn appropriate deportment the hard way, by getting things wrong.

But I was engaged with the world again. Often reluctantly, under duress, but I was doing it. Liam was insistent about my going out with him, and under his tutelage, and in his company, and with his example before me, I discovered I was a salable commodity on the open market. No doubt being in his presence, sitting at his table, helped. Even Liam couldn't accommodate every woman who smiled in his direction during the course of an evening. I got some of the spill-over.

Cocaine helped too. Cocaine was ubiquitous in those days. And possessing it in your twenties was a sign of affluence, an automatic guarantor of…not wealth precisely, but robust participation in the world of grown-ups. It elevated you a notch, differentiated you from other men your age. In addition, it was my somewhat alarming experience that women, respectable, serious women, would fuck for coke. They would never admit it, not even to themselves, they would never think in such terms, but if they discovered you had a little vial in your pocket with a tiny spoon attached, the atmospherics changed. You instantly became more interesting and more attractive. They didn't have to be self-identified coke whores, either. They might work in the Financial District. They might be able to afford their own coke.

Naturally, it was Liam who introduced me to it. There wasn't a mind- or mood-altering substance that Liam was unwilling to ingest. But I never felt in serious danger of getting hooked. I liked it well enough, but I quickly learned the first rush of the evening was the best you were going to get; after that, it was all diminishing returns and clogged sinuses. Most of the people I knew who abused coke—and that emphatically included Liam, who could go through the better part of a gram in an evening—kept vainly pursuing that elusive second rush all night. Maybe it was just my natural timidity, but honestly, moderation felt like a rational response rather than aversion to excess. Still, for a number of years, coke was part of my life. I'm glad Ashley hasn't asked about it. So far.

Later, being a shrink, and even before, when I was studying to be one…that proved to press erotic buttons too. Who knew? I don't mean with my fellow grad students; I had short affairs with a few of them; it sometimes felt as if everyone in the program was sleeping with everyone else in the program, although it probably only looked that way to those of us in the program who were sleeping with one another. But I'm not talking about classmates, I'm talking about civilians.

Somehow, just being a shrink seemed to generate instant transference reactions at parties and in bars and clubs. As soon as they learned what I did, women talked to me freely, disconcertingly freely—I learned more about female orgasms over drinks than I ever did in the bedroom or consulting room—and invested me with a whole host of sterling qualities, many of which I didn't possess and to which I laid no claim. Qualities they happened to regard as especially desirable, rarely embodied in a single individual, and ideally tailored for them alone. I'd had no idea that would be the case when I applied to grad school. All I was after was a degree.

Over time, I recovered my life. One does. I went to grad school, took my classes, passed my orals, wrote my dissertation in jig time, got my doctorate, did a post-doc abroad, hung out my shingle. Along the way, I made a few new friends and kept my more important old ones, and I dated a bit. My life, I was discovering, had been more sheltered than I ever suspected; having a steady girlfriend so early supplied lots of sheltering. Now I was playing the field, and the field had no shelter. There were one or two relationships along the way that seemed to offer promise, but, well, it turned out they didn't. Possibly because—and I don't think this is so rare—Molly, my first love, was imprinted on my mind as the model, the Platonic ideal, of what a lover is supposed to be. And so, more mischievously, anyone who differed from her, and any relationship that differed from that relationship, was, to the extent of the difference, less than ideal.

Maybe that's why so many women accused me of being unwilling or unable to commit. But they had it exactly wrong: I'd already committed so deeply and thoroughly I was *still* committed, even though the person to whom I was committed had long since moved on.

I met Angie in the early '80s. A couple of years after a dank, dreary, indispensible year in London, doing a post-doc in adolescent psychology at the Freud Institute in Hampstead. It was lonely and hard—the winter seemed to last forever—and I wasn't 100% convinced by what I was being taught. But my having survived the year intact may, all by itself, have made it worthwhile. I was getting stronger.

I signed up for the course mostly just to get away—it was past time to do something else anywhere else—but I also had a hard-nosed business instinct that in a university town like Berkeley, certified expertise in adolescent clinical techniques might prove marketable, might attract referrals. To whom do you send a troubled adolescent? Why, to a certified expert in the troubles of adolescence. And the Freud Institute conferred an especially impressive-sounding imprimatur.

By the time I met Angie, my practice was starting to do okay. Not thriving the way it is now, but I had enough clients to make a decent living, and word-of-mouth was steadily bringing me more. Not all of them adolescents and post-adolescents by any means, although freshmen and sophomores with first-time identity crises (and broken hearts, naturally) have been my bread and butter over the years. Nor was I totally dependent on referrals from colleagues; clients more or less my own age seemed to value talking to a shaggy, informal contemporary who understood their referents and intuitively grasped the social context of their issues. So current and former clients started recommending me to friends.

I was enjoying the work, felt I was helping people. I hadn't been entirely confident about that side of things at the beginning, I wasn't a true believer in the efficacy of psychotherapy. Reading Hans Eysenck's 1957 paper on the subject when I was in graduate school, reading it, so to speak, while the horse was on its way out of the barn, shook my confidence further. And the published refutations of that paper always seemed to carry a whiff of special pleading. So I was like a theology student who's started to question his faith. Freud may have been a genius, but that doesn't mean he got it all right. (Hell, Thomas Aquinas was a genius too, and he got almost everything wrong.) I've gone back and forth on these questions ever since, and I still don't buy the theory in its entirety, but theory no longer concerns me much. I've come to believe that giving clients space to vent, and offering common-sense advice when it suggests itself and doesn't break their flow, serve a useful purpose independent of any therapeutic doctrine.

But I'm digressing. I do that when difficult material is on the horizon. Freud didn't get *that* wrong.

My office was on Euclid, a couple of blocks from campus. That stretch of street had the air of a leafy commercial village lane in those days; while most of the shops and restaurants were aimed at students—you passed a dinky two-screen art-house cinema, a pizza parlor (the same one Molly and Stan and I used to frequent in our undergraduate days), a bookstore, an old-fashioned grocery, a burger joint—they seemed subdued, uninsistent. Maybe it was just the prevalence of trees. I used to enjoy taking little walks there whenever I had a free hour. I had more free hours in those days than was good for my balance sheet.

One of the shops I used to browse in was a small down-at-the-heels emporium offering scented massage oils and incense and some artsy-craftsy tchochkes, macramé hangings and hand-dipped candles and so on, plus a smattering of health foods and herbal medicaments. A sort of head shop without drug paraphernalia. Sometimes I'd drop in and pick up a granola bar or some ginseng tea or scented soap. I wasn't exactly keeping the place in business, just justifying my browsing.

It was overseen by a young man and a young woman. The woman, a couple of years younger than I, was very cute, but with the young man in the picture, my flirting was understated to the point of invisibility. Still, the shop was one of the more enjoyable stops in my ramblings, and the woman was the reason. She was pretty and funny, and her buxom peasant's body was sexily novel to me. As a physical type, she was Molly's opposite, and maybe that was part of her appeal. The earthiness, the density. I liked her round Vermeer face and her untamed nut-brown hair. The young man, although his presence was inconvenient, was likable too, fey, irreverent about the shop's wares, clearly, unlike the woman, an agnostic about holistic dogma. She enthusiastically extolled the health-promoting properties of everything they sold.

And then one day the guy let slip that they were siblings. I don't think it was necessarily with ulterior intent; he said something nondescript like, "My sister's at the bank right now, she could explain that product better than me." It was natural-sounding and relevant to whatever we were discussing. But it's also possible he did it on her instructions, because when, the next day, I finally got up the nerve to ask her out, she said, "Finally! I was wondering what you were waiting for." My interest in her was apparently more obvious than I realized.

So I explained, "I thought your brother was your boyfriend or your husband."

"I had a feeling that might be it. Well, Rolly *is* my brother, plus he's gay. So unless you like him better than me, in which case you'd better lay your cards on the table right now, buster, the answer is yes, I'd love to have dinner with you."

Rolly died of AIDS six years later. A terrible tragedy in a terribly tragic decade. It hit Angie and me hard. Especially Angie, of course; they'd been best friends as well as siblings and business partners.

I soon learned it wasn't only as a physical type that Angie was Molly's opposite. Where Molly had always aspired to be rational and analytical, Angie was intuitive and emotional. It wasn't a question of intelligence, this difference; Angie was plenty smart. But her distrust of intellect was virtually a philosophical stance. She didn't believe in psychotherapy either; she made some allowances for Jung, and was tolerant about its being my profession, but she believed it went about its business all wrong. She preferred to read astrological charts, throw the I Ching, or rifle through a tarot deck. She always gravitated toward the exotic and the occult, and was deeply skeptical about Western approaches to almost anything.

This was a girl who'd grown up in San Luis Obispo. Her parents were Baptists, and she and her brother had been church-goers until they went to college. I have no idea where these exotic predilections of hers came from.

So we finally went to dinner, and we successfully navigated the subtle change from flirty customer and proprietor to two people who discover they like each other. It was easy. The easiest, pleasantest date I'd ever been on. Angie made it easy; she was so artless and honest, there was no room for dating strategy, and no need for any.

Well. Not to belabor this. We liked each other, we got serious fast. She was warm and accepting, and that was just what I needed. I didn't know it was what I needed until I was presented with it, but then it was obvious. And I had reached an age where settling down was overdue. Not going tomcatting with Liam every night was a relief. Promiscuity never really agreed with me, not after the novelty wore off.

The second time Angie spent the night at my apartment, she suggested I take the photo of Molly off my bureau. Not angrily, and not because she felt threatened by it. She wasn't competitive that way. She just figured it was time. "Are you even aware of it anymore?"

"Mostly not," I admitted.

"And you probably can't hear her voice in your head, or remember how she smelled, anything important."

"You're right. It was a long time ago."

"Do you think about her every day?"

"Not really."

"'Not really?'"

"Not. Period."

"Do you think about her once a week, would you say?"

"Maybe. That's a reasonable estimate. Maybe less. If you mean actually think about her. Not just have her flit across my mind for a meaningless second."

"She probably doesn't think about you at all. Based on what you've told me."

"I have no idea where she is or what she's doing. It's been ages."

"So give it up. Really. I'm not saying throw the picture in the garbage. Put it in a drawer somewhere. Keep it as a souvenir. Take it out and look at it once a year if you feel the urge. This isn't for me. I don't care whether you have her picture out or not. But you don't want to turn into…what's her name. In that book?"

"I need more information, Angie."

"I read it in college. By Dickens, maybe?"

"Miss Havisham?"

"Right. You don't want to turn into her."

Angie didn't believe in therapy, but she devised her own form of cognitive behavioral therapy years before it achieved any currency within the profession.

"And anyway," she added, as I silently put the photograph away, "it's better she doesn't see what's gonna happen next."

Things moved quickly with Angie, as I've indicated, but I had my misgivings, and I held back a little. I liked her a lot from the first, I enjoyed being with her, I missed her when we were apart. And she had a maternal side, a sweetly nurturing side, the like of which I'd never experienced. But we were so different, I just couldn't see over the horizon with her. Molly and I, despite our disparate backgrounds, had always seemed in sync, had been able to finish each other's sentences, had believed and valued almost all the same things. But Angie felt like an alien creature, simpatico but *other*. There were times it seemed we barely even spoke the same language, when communication between us was not only imperfect but might actually be illusory.

It was Stan, of all people, who set me straight. Stan has sometimes been able to surprise me when I think I've got him pegged.

We were playing ping pong in his garage, at the time the closest thing to physical exertion Stan engaged in. This was years before Dr. Penman told him he was a walking—or waddling—time bomb, and he took her admonition to heart and started getting real exercise. He and Carla were living together in his modest house in the flats in those days—they weren't married, although they seemed happy as clams and it wasn't clear to me what they were waiting for—and the only place where there was room for a ping pong table was his garage. So he parked his car on the street to free up the space. His neighborhood was far from crime-free, but the car he drove back then was so unprepossessing, one quick glance was enough to tell you it didn't have anything in it worth boosting.

He usually beat me—he played a lot of ping pong out there in his garage, and so, despite his lack of coordination, he got pretty good by sheer dint of practice—and he was beating me now. But the game wasn't the point. It was an activity that let us talk the way we used to talk. Stan was still the person I turned to when something troubled me; it isn't that I valued his advice, it's more that I didn't fear his judgment. Talking to him let me to think out loud. And ping pong helped, maybe because eye-contact was impossible. He became my blank screen.

He and Carla had been to a movie with Angie and me the night before, and while we played, he said, casually, "That was fun last night."

It was an odd observation, and possibly a covert invitation for me to unburden myself. (As I've said, I sometimes give Stan too little credit for sensitivity, although it's also true that whenever I think I've underestimated him, he does something so insensitive I conclude I was right the first time.) We'd gone to a movie, but for some reason I no longer recall, hadn't had dinner together. So there hadn't been much socializing; it wasn't the sort of evening where you'd say "that was fun," you'd just say you liked the movie. But I didn't argue.

He went on, "Carla has taken to Angie."

"Has she? That's nice. Angie likes Carla too." At worst, a little white lie. Angie's feelings toward Carla were benign, although not especially warm.

"Says she's clearly nuts about you," Stan went on.

"Carla said that?"

"Uh huh." At which point he bungled his shot. Neither of us was paying much attention to the game. "And says she doesn't think you notice."

I went to fetch the ball, lurking behind some debris in a corner of the garage: A couple of cardboard cartons full of books, a queen-sized mattress on its side, lots of dust. While hunting for it, I said, "I don't know about that." It was beginning to dawn on me he was initiating this conversation at Carla's insistence.

"Which part? The nuts-about-you part or the not-noticing part?"

"Both."

"That's inconsistent. If you question the first, you can't logically reject the second. The second part is contingent on the first."

It's not always easy, being best friends with a skilled litigator.

"Carla says you keep yourself aloof from her, especially when she's being affectionate."

I found the ball. As I was returning to the table, I said, "I'm extremely fond of Angie, okay? Extremely. We're doing great. But…I don't know, we're sort of mismatched, don't you think?"

"Uh uh."

"What?"

"I don't think that."

I was about to serve. "Do you remember the score?"

"Screw the game. I was going to win anyway. Let's just rally."

"Okay." I hit the ball gently over the net. "You don't think we're mismatched?"

"No more than anybody else." He returned the ball without putting any tricky english on it.

"She listens to country music. She believes in astrology."

"She's a great girl who adores you. You adore her too, even though you don't let yourself realize it. As far as I'm concerned, that ain't a mismatch."

"But over the long haul—"

He smashed the return so deep into my backhand that it flicked off the edge of the table. A beautiful shot. No way I could have returned it, not even if I'd been prepared. While I went off to find the ball again, he said, "You think you should be with your clone? People are different from each other. That's how it works."

"It's a question of degree." I scooped up the ball, rolling along the floor.

"Who'd be a better fit?"

"Well," I said, as I believe he knew I was going to, as I believe he was deliberately maneuvering me into saying, "Molly and I were well-matched."

"Oh Christ." His exasperation was a tad theatrical.

I served the ball to him gently. He let it go by, giving it not so much as a passing glance, and went on, "You really need to get over that. It's been a very long time. Maybe you were a perfect match, maybe not. She apparently didn't think so."

That stung. "It's not a question of getting over her. I've recovered. But you asked who'd be a good fit. With Molly, a lot of our tastes and interests were in sync."

"And how'd that work out?"

He put his paddle down. I took my lead from him and did the same. We faced each other across the green table. He said, "I know my experience in this area is meager. Compared to Liam, God knows, and maybe

340

even compared to you. But when it comes to getting dumped, I've been around the block. I sometimes got dumped as a prophylactic measure, before the relationship even began. And here's one thing I learned...the worst mistake you can make is to try to replicate the person you lost. To make her a template. You do that and you're doomed. No one's gonna be her as well as her. You have to abandon that mold and find a new one."

"Can we play ping pong?"

"Is that your way of saying, 'You're right, Stan, thanks for the sage advice?'"

"No, it's my way of saying 'Fuck you.'" He *was* right, of course. And right about being right. And those two positions aren't logically inconsistent.

What he said resonated immediately, but also acted like a Contac, the time-release decongestant I sometimes took in those years; over the next few days, it kept hitting me afresh. By now I'd spent years waiting for a Molly avatar to come along. It was time to stop. If I couldn't see what a godsend Angie was, I didn't deserve her.

What followed was...well, for a while what followed was just life, in all its undramatic normality. Angie and I moved in together, we married about a year later, we bought our house in the hills. She miscarried once, but then, a year later, Owen was born, and his life became the most important thing in ours. We did the boomer parent thing, with progressive pre-school and Camp Kee Tov and play-dates and music lessons and assorted weekend activities to keep him entertained. We watched *Sesame Street* and a small collection of infantile videos, over and over. It's hard to explain the stupefying combination of boredom and delight attendant upon all of that.

My practice grew, and for a while there, I published a few respectable but unspectacular papers in professional journals. Then I stopped seeing the point of it, and didn't bother. Angie had sold the store on Euclid Avenue when her brother got sick, but a couple of years after he died, she opened a similar but less funky store in the Elmwood District, an old-fashioned middle-class area south of campus that looks like the neighborhood where Beaver Cleaver grew up. Angela's Organics, the shop was called. It did okay. Stan and I got our investment back—we were her prime backers—and after a few years the place started generating a steady income.

It was just life. And I was content. Just life suited me just fine. I gloried in the *New York Times* arriving on our front steps every morning, wrapped in its bright blue cover. I didn't much like the news it contained, but I cherished the regularity of its arrival, and the ritual of unwrapping it and settling down with it. I liked my Peet's coffee every morning, felt privileged to live where such a luxury was an unexceptional part of quotidian existence. I liked the ritual of listening to NPR every day, to *Morning Edition* when I shaved and *All Things Considered* on the way home from work. I liked putting the recycling and the garbage out Tuesday night. I liked the slow, gently grinding progress of the seasons, each one somehow a surprise, a modest, predictable surprise. The shortening days of fall, with the subtle bite in the air and the aromatic hint of eucalyptus off the hills. The lengthening days of spring, the pillowy, langorous warmth of those lovely evenings. The inconvenience of rain in winter, the summer lassitude. One year turned into another, and nothing much happened; we kept ourselves busy making a life.

And the people. The insufferably smug, decent people of Berkeley. North Berkeley was like a village. All those familiar faces, including many people whose names I didn't know and with whom I'd never spoken, or spoken only to say hello. Shopkeepers, folks in the neighborhood, other parents in the park, even the panhandlers. It's a town a large number of denizens choose not to leave; to watch a face age over the course of 35 years, a face belonging to a person you don't even know, was compelling, a disturbing reminder of mortality but at the same time a reassuring symbol of continuity and survival. I watched a whole generation start to resemble my parents and their friends, saw familiar racial and physiognomic types emerge from the fresh, youthful faces I first encountered as an undergraduate. My own included, but you stop noticing your own face. If you know what's good for you.

A difficult confession: I never felt passionately in love with Angie. My heart never raced at the prospect of seeing her, I never felt a special sense of completeness in her company. The qualms I expressed to Stan during that life-changing ping pong game never went away. We weren't soul mates, we rarely discussed our deepest concerns (except about Owen). It may even be true I was never altogether in love with her. I loved her, her presence was never less than a comfort, and I gloried in her relationship with our boy—the natural way she took to motherhood was a liberal education in the art of selflessness—but that isn't quite the same as being in love.

That didn't happen, if it happened at all, until after she died; the sense of loss when she died, the keen sense that a certain unique, irreplaceable kind of sweetness was gone from life forever, felt like a gauge of all the feelings I hadn't experienced when she was alive. It had been so easy to take them for granted. By being such an undemanding, generous, nurturing partner, she'd made it too easy. First I felt panic and befuddlement, a numb sense of helpless incompetence, a dazed certainty I'd be unable to cope as a single father or a single man. That feeling of inadequacy was immobilizing; without friends pitching in, without Liam and Melanie coming over and sitting with me silently, without Carla making meals for Owen and me, and Stan occasionally taking Owen to ball games or even picking him up from school when my schedule was crowded and I was at my wits' end, and without the parents of some of Owen's classmates going the extra mile, I'm not sure I could have gotten through it.

And then, as I finally started to adjust to my new reality and the panic began to recede, I at last felt grief. For a long time, there wasn't a night when, after getting Owen to sleep, no small undertaking in itself—he cried for Angie every bedtime for most of that first year—I didn't feel a draining sense of isolation and loss. I was coming to recognize that I needed her, and missed her, as much as he did.

Who needs a soul mate? A soul mate is a luxury. I needed someone who accepted and cared. Someone whose love, unlike my own, was unconditional.

I can't bring myself to go into too much detail about how she died.

It can't matter all that much, surely; it was pointless and needn't have happened. If we hadn't assumed, with the casual, heedless arrogance of youth, that we were immortal, it wouldn't have happened. She had a little discoloration on her cheek neither of us noticed for some time, and then, when we did notice it, neither of us took seriously. Made jokes about acne and prolonged adolescence. And then it got worse, and when she finally went to see Dr. Penman about it, it had already metastasized. Nodular melanoma. We did everything the doctors recommended, the whole awful, debilitating battery of cancer therapies then available, but it was too late. It was a long process, with some ups and downs, some extended periods of false hope followed by bitter, stomach-plunging disappointment. She died at home, holding my hand, making me promise—unnecessarily, as she certainly knew, and as she let me know she knew—to be gentle with Owen.

It was all so dumbfounding, so excruciatingly unfair. An arbitrary, random, needless reminder of our impotence at the hands of fate, and of fate's heedless, impersonal malevolence. Frankly, I still can't get my mind around it. A tiny sore on Angie's cheek is what killed her.

Twelve

NOW

S tan rented a suite at the Oakland Coliseum. He did this several times a season, and no one else was allowed to contribute to the cost. Since he was far and away the richest of them, and seemed to get a lot of pleasure out of the exercise, they had come to accept his largesse with good grace. The baseball game itself wasn't the point. The only serious fans among the six of them were Stan and Liam. An implausible bond between them, but then, everything about their friendship was implausible. It would never have happened without Zeke's mediation; whether it would have continued without his ongoing presence was less clear. Baseball might have provided them with something to talk about if the going got rough.

Stan, unlike Liam, had never played the game, except under coercion, when it was required in PE class. God knows he'd never been any good at it. He'd never been good at any sport except ping pong. Each spring, when baseball season began and the captains chose up teams, he was always the last to be chosen, he was always put ninth in the batting rotation (and when he came to bat, the entire opposing outfield moved in close), and in defense he was usually positioned out in left field where it was hoped the ball would never venture. Zeke couldn't remember him ever snagging a fly hit his way. Not once. The anticipatory groaning of his teammates usually started before the ball began its descent.

But he loved the game. Like many L.A. kids of his generation, Stan got the bug in '59, when the Dodgers, recently-arrived from Brooklyn, had climbed out of the cellar to which they'd been relegated the previous year and won the World Series. It had been exciting enough simply to have a home team after a lifetime (admittedly, a short lifetime) without one; since forever, LA kids had felt like second-class citizens in a second-class city. Besides, since many of the families in the Fairfax section of LA were transplanted Brooklynites, the Dodgers were favorites in the neighborhood even before they arrived. To see them become world champions one short year later, especially given that ignominious first season, was galvanizing. The whole city went nuts, and no one more so than that year's crop of pubescent boys.

Zeke had shared Stan's enthusiasm back then (and it hadn't dampened their zeal that the Dodgers' most promising young pitcher, soon to be acknowledged the best pitcher in baseball, was Jewish; any implausible ethnic fantasy now seemed possible). Zeke and Stan used to go to games together pretty regularly during the summer months, first at the Coliseum downtown, then, when it finally opened, at Dodger Stadium. They always brought their mitts along, although both lived in unacknowledged terror a foul ball might somehow come their way. No chance they wouldn't blow the catch, probably with a painful injury resulting. A concussion, say, or irreparable damage to an optic nerve. But it was humiliation they feared more than maiming. It would be worse than gym class, their incompetence a spectacle witnessed not only by classmates, but a whole stadium full of strangers, plus the two competing teams out on the field, not excluding Sandy Koufax.

Professed enthusiasm for the Dodgers was universal in their crowd, even if the passion might occasionally be feigned by some bookish fellow who down deep couldn't care less. For a male adolescent in Los Angeles in the late '50s and early '60s, you had to share the enthusiasm or be accused of effeminacy, or worse. And there wasn't anything worse.

Stan had remained a baseball fan ever since. Although he didn't command Liam's grasp of the strategic intricacies, and was oblivious to what Liam viewed as the game's aesthetic subtleties and sociopolitical resonance, he read the sports pages first thing every summer morning, stopping once the World Series ended, resuming the following spring. He listened to games on the radio while sitting out on his deck with a glass of claret at hand. He could give you up-to-date news on the league tables with the same casual familiarity he could call upon when citing legal precedent.

A few years before, after much soul-searching, Stan had transferred his loyalty from the Dodgers to the A's. A wrenching decision; it took him decades to feel doing so wasn't tantamount to treason. In fact—and Zeke felt this reflected credit on him—he refused outright to make the switch during the '70s, when the team had been riding high and any fan with an eye on the main chance might have crossed over. It took almost twenty additional years. It was a momentous thing in his life, it had the gravity of a religious conversion.

Zeke was willing to go along, in the interest of amity rather than conviction. He didn't care enough to think anything like principle was involved in deciding what team to root for. He once said, in an ill-advised and slightly inebriated moment, "Caring about the American League is like voting in a Republican primary." This wasn't a popular stance. Stan and Liam told him he was full of shit, and even Molly and Melanie feigned outrage. They didn't really care; it just amused them to see Stan and Zeke argue. Melanie went so far as to claim that when they argued about baseball, they sounded the way they'd sounded when they used to argue with tearful ferocity about the relative merits of Sheriff John and Engineer Bill, two local kids' show hosts when they were little, or, with equal heat, about the appeal of John Kennedy and Adlai Stevenson the year the Democratic convention came to town. Stan worshipped Adlai Stevenson, but Zeke—to the dismay of his parents as well as Stan—thought Kennedy so suave it didn't matter that his father had been a Nazi apologist. Carla, a lifelong Yankees supporter, kept out of the

347

argument altogether. One of the rare controversies she chose to avoid.

Despite the contention—mostly playful—everybody had a good time at these outings. The suites were luxurious, the catered food was fine (Stan's sole complaint being that he wasn't allowed to bring his own wine), the company convivial. The game was only as important as anyone let it be. Neither Stan nor Liam insisted the others pay attention to the goings-on on the field or care about the results. It was an opportunity for old friends to hang out together more than anything else. Stan always made a point of switching off his cell phone, putting on his glasses, and focusing on the play, but there were no demerits for anyone who preferred to chat or read a newspaper or eat and drink himself into a state of stupefaction.

This particular Sunday, though, Zeke was apprehensive. Driving to the stadium, he was conscious of the silence between himself and Molly. It wasn't a comfortable silence. It felt, rather, like two aggrieved internal monologues taking place contrapuntally. They weren't quite feuding over the last several days, but there was an unmistakable wariness and no warmth. Casual conversation had been rare. In the evenings, Molly seemed to make a point of keeping to herself, going to her study to read papers or prepare lectures. They normally got over disagreements more quickly than this; they normally either talked them out within a day or two, or forgot about them amidst life's clamorous demands.

And they hadn't seen Liam since the accident. Who knew what his mood would be like, or how he and Melanie were doing? This could be a tense afternoon. Exactly what it was designed not to be.

When Zeke and Molly got to the suite, Stan and Carla were already there. Carla, in a pink velour warm-up suit, was stretched out on a sofa, sipping a fruit-flavored sparkling water direct from the bottle. Stan was squatting in front of the small refrigerator that came with the suite, examining the snacks it contained. He stood and turned to face Zeke and Molly as they came through the door. "Welcome," he said. And then, "Carla and I are having a tiff."

Oh great, Zeke thought. Perfect. The one thing the day lacked.

But it turned out Stan was being facetious. Carla said, "Honestly,

Stanley." She made a sort of snorting noise, then faced Zeke. "He's trying to be funny. The A's are playing the Yankees, he and I are on opposite sides."

"I take it personally," Stan said. "A man expects support from his wife in these matters."

"Maybe a wife expects support from her husband," said Carla. "Have you considered that possibility?"

"Uh uh."

"Have you seen Liam?" Molly asked, cutting off the banter. It wasn't especially amusing to her, and she thought she detected a hint of real contention just under the ostensibly good-natured surface.

"Since the accident?" said Stan. "Nope. I phoned the other day, he seemed okay. Subdued, but okay. Haven't seen him, though. You?"

"Only on the night." She risked a glance at Zeke. No obvious reaction.

"How'd he look?" Carla asked.

"Bad."

"I never thought he'd be such a jerk," said Carla.

No one said anything to that. Stan returned his attention to the refrigerator, studying the cheese and fruit platters, Molly fished in her purse for glasses or Kleenex or nothing at all, and Zeke strolled over to the front of the suite and looked through the windows at the baseball field, where grass was being hosed down.

Carla, aware on some level she'd said the wrong thing, tried to redeem herself by digging in deeper. "No one here's going to defend him, are they? Or say he didn't know better. Or that we all make mistakes and to err is human."

"Okay, Carla."

"No, Stanley, I mean it."

"No one doubts that."

At that moment, the door to the suite opened and Melanie entered, followed a moment later by Liam. "Hey, guys!" she said. Her good cheer sounded effortful.

Liam, following after, looked terrible; his left eye was purple, puffy, and half-shut, his lower lip swollen, and there was bruising on much of his face. He looked like he'd spent some quality time with a couple of Mob enforcers.

General shock. Carla gasped so audibly that everyone turned to her. "Liam!" she exclaimed. It seemed to Zeke an implicit expression of regret for her earlier callousness, even though Liam hadn't been privy to it.

"You should see the other guy," Liam said.

Which might have defused the situation, however slightly, except that Carla misunderstood and said, "Corin?"

Her gaffe was so appalling it actually saved the day. After a moment of speechless consternation, everybody but Carla burst out laughing. The sheer tone-deafness of the response, the way it stumbled into every carefully-sidestepped nexus of awkwardness, produced a great gust of general hilarity. And a second or so later, Carla laughed too, probably just so as not to be left out.

"Since Carla's mentioned it," Zeke said, after the laughter finally subsided, "I never thought to ask, but was Corin hurt?"

He felt rather than saw Molly shoot him a sharp glance. He wasn't certain what it conveyed. Maybe only that she'd been wondering the same thing but had been leery about asking.

"I don't know," Liam answered. "I was in no shape to tell. I was busy trying to figure out if I was dead, that sort of thing. He probably wasn't hurt *too* bad. He managed to hightail it out of there pretty quick."

"Just like thirty years ago," Stan said. "More lives than a cat."

"A tomcat," said Carla.

"Maybe we should talk about something else," Melanie suggested.

Words almost guaranteed to stop conversation in its tracks. Melanie wasn't so maladroit, ordinarily; it was evidence of extreme discomfort. The earlier laughter hadn't dissipated it. This was shaping up to be a rough afternoon.

It was Liam who broke the silence. "Can we get one thing straight? I fucked up big time, but I'm okay now, even though I look like hell, and I'd really prefer not to tiptoe around it. I fell off the wagon—I didn't know I could, and then I did—but now I'm back and I feel fine.

Embarrassed, and bad for Mel, and it literally hurts when I laugh. But I'm not fragile and you don't have to walk on eggshells."

"Is the pain bad?" asked Carla.

"Nothing a little Percodan can't fix."

It was a sign of how much tension they were under that the ensuing laughter felt strained. The air never did quite clear that afternoon. It wasn't just Liam's situation. Everyone was hyper-aware of the tension between him and Melanie, and most were at least subliminally aware of the abiding tension between Zeke and Molly. And since the game was boring, one of those pitchers' battles where not much happens on the field, diversion from that quarter wasn't forthcoming. Also, everyone was feeling a little awkward about drinking—alcohol might have eased the self-consciousness, even for those who didn't drink—despite Liam's insistence he was fine and that the last thing in the world he wanted was for people to feel inhibited. Zeke nursed a single beer through three innings before permitting himself a second; Stan stuck with one glass of red wine, and Molly did the same with white.

At least no one had to worry about designating a driver.

Zeke would have been happy to leave after that first beer, but it wasn't an option. One of those awkward situations where you felt trapped, where extricating yourself early might provide momentary relief, but would ultimately make things worse. By the end of the seventh inning neither team had scored, so the specter of extra innings was adding to the general anxiety. Carla wasn't the only one celebrating when the Yankees got a run in the eighth, although she was the only one to do so out loud. After that, the pitching held, and the game was over fairly quickly.

As they were leaving the suite, everyone thanking Stan for his hospitality and trying not to make too mad a dash for it, Stan pulled Zeke aside and said, sotto voce, "Listen...was this so bad we'll never do it again?"

"Nah," Zeke said. He was slightly surprised Stan was aware it had been as bad as it was. You never knew with Stan. "Just a tough day. All circumstantial."

"'Cause I remember in my dating days...sometimes..." He blushed, but went on, "…a bad night in the sack, that would be that. No repeats. One strike and you're out. I hope it's not going to be like that."

Zeke chose not to say what he suspected was the case: Those "bad nights in the sack" were a pretext to end something already perceived to be deficient.

"It won't be," he said. "I promise."

After he and Molly were in their car, and he was inching toward the exit, calibrating which cars had to be allowed to cut in and which could be dissuaded by a show of determined forward motion—a tricky business at slow speed—he suddenly felt so oppressed by the pervasive tension with Molly, he said, "Look—"

And before he could say anything further, she said, "I know, Easy." Her voice was gentle. It hadn't sounded like that for days. She must have been doing some thinking during the game. "I understand. How could I have been so…not just stupid, stupid is self-evident…but so unoriginal, so oblivious, so obtuse and mediocre? What I did was demeaning to you, but equally bad—and I mean in my eyes, not just yours—it was demeaning to *me*. I was like some credulous, clueless bimbo dazzled by bling. I do get it, Easy. And I understand how it's all come flooding back, and how, even after forty years, how much and in how many different ways it hurts. I won't waste my breath saying I was a different person, I know your feelings about that. I can explain some of what happened, and I can tell you the ways his being dangerous and, and genuinely *awful*, were actually part of the attraction in some horrific way, but you know that already, and you hate that part too, so my saying it won't help."

He started to speak, but she cut him off again. "And I realize it'll always be there, despite everything that's happened since. I accept that. I have to live with it. My being sorry only takes us so far. It isn't just a question of forgiveness."

"It's not a question of forgiveness at all," Zeke said. "And it's not always there. It mostly *isn't* there. But lately, with his coming back…"

"I realize. And what happened with Liam the other day…I get that

352

too. Why you got mad at me. It's like…why can't we show a little class? Liam *and* me. If we have to be tempted by a serpent, it shouldn't be some slimy little snake in the grass."

That wasn't quite fair, Zeke thought. Corin was despicable, and no one was more immune to his charms than Zeke. But he wasn't dismissible, he wasn't negligible. There was something undeniably galvanic about him, he took big chances, he had some odd sort of stature. As he'd said of himself, his was a big soul. But Zeke certainly wasn't tempted to defend the man now. "It doesn't matter," he said. And then, aware this sounded dismissive, that it foreclosed discussion, he added, "But it's good to know you get it."

"I get you completely, Easy." She smiled at him.

He nodded. "I know. And I like it. I used to think that no one who truly understood me would put up with me."

That got a laugh out of her, even though he was in earnest.

They had almost reached the exit. Traffic was flowing smoothly, at least by the standards of post-game Coliseum parking. Drivers were being civilized about alternating into the exit lane. Within minutes, Zeke was out of the stadium and in a queue of cars inching along the freeway on-ramp. He switched on the car radio. The weekend *All Things Considered* was on. It was a few minutes past the hour, so they caught the local news feed in medias res, read by smooth-voiced Matt Elmore: "--- acting on a tip, apprehended the suspect near the Berkeley campus. Sources report McCabe was unarmed and offered no resistance, but appeared to be seriously injured." Zeke stiffened. Beside him, he felt rather than saw Molly do the same. "The suspect is now at UC Medical Center, receiving care while awaiting arraignment."

Zeke exhaled and muttered, "Holy shit."

Molly was wide-eyed. "I don't even know how I'm supposed to feel," she said after a few seconds.

The next day, Monday, Zeke met Stan for lunch at Café Rouge, a short stroll from Stan's offices. They had arranged the lunch the previous evening, during the flurry of phone calls that had gone back and forth amongst the three households. Everyone had heard the same news report on the radio during the drive home.

Stan arrived first. It was a beautiful mid-summer noon hour, and, being a regular, he managed to snag an outside table. He had a glass of white wine in front of him when Zeke arrived. Stan occasionally permitted himself one glass of wine with lunch on a work day. Only if the meal and the setting seemed to justify it, and never more than a single glass.

When the waiter came to take their orders, Stan asked for a small Caesar salad, followed by mussels mariniere. Gesturing toward his wine glass, he explained to Zeke, almost apologetically, that to eat such a lunch on such a day without a glass of something nice would qualify as a crime against nature.

Zeke, with clients all afternoon, regretfully committed a crime against nature. He ordered the same food as Stan, and an iced herbal tea. Which might have been acceptable, except that he was going to be staring at Stan's glass of wine throughout the meal, and worse, witnessing the pleasure Stan derived from each sip.

After ordering, they didn't waste time teasing themselves and each other with irrelevancies. Zeke immediately broached the topic on both their minds. "Did you see the front page of the *Chron*?"

Stan nodded. "Same old glam shot. A mere forty years out of date."

"I guess he hasn't been posing for many new ones lately."

"Just one," Stan said, his tone dry. And then, "But I gotta say, the bastard doesn't look so different."

"Well, I wouldn't be feeling too envious right now."

"No. Point taken. When I turned my cell phone on after the game, there was a message from him. His one call. He sounded pretty desperate."

"I imagine."

"I managed to connect with him after we got home. Took some doing. I had to warn him the call was being monitored...he wasn't inclined to be discreet. It was kind of an intense conversation. I let him know I wouldn't represent him."

"You did?"

Zeke couldn't recall Stan ever turning down a direct request from Corin. But now that he thought about it, Stan had been acting un-Stan-like in a number of ways since the news broke. Keeping his cards hidden. With Zeke now, he seemed willing to permit himself a little more leeway.

"I told him it was impossible. He argued. You know Corin. That mix of charm and bluster. Holding a gun to your head while sucking your dick. Said I was the best, I have a proven track record defending radicals."

"All true."

"All beside the point."

"Did he sound scared?"

"In the way Corin would sound scared. Tough. Hard-nosed. Cynical and existential and resigned. Rick Blaine on the tarmac with the propellers spinning in the fog. Like this was an eventuality he was always prepared for. But you could hear the fear. He's…I mean, let's face it, this isn't going to turn out okay."

"No? You're sure?"

"I can't imagine a positive outcome. He's going away for good."

Upon uttering these chilling words, Stan suddenly looked up from the table and met Zeke's eye. The look he gave him was unwavering, and startlingly hard. Almost a glare. It was meant to convey something, no question, although Zeke had no idea what.

"Not even with good representation?" Zeke asked. He was feeling a little put off by the way Stan was looking at him, but he didn't know how to address it directly.

"The lawyering won't make any difference," Stan answered, breaking the stare and taking another sip of wine. "I didn't tell him that, of course. I just told him I wouldn't represent him, but I'd give him the names of some good lawyers."

"Can he afford them?"

"Certainly not."

"Did you offer to help?"

"Financially? Uh uh. But it may not be necessary. A bunch of lefties'll probably start a defense fund, as if some grand principle is at stake. And a case like this…some lawyers will handle it gratis, for the publicity. Or the challenge, maybe. Or some sort of residual, sentimental attachment to the cause."

"So why not you?"

"Because I'm fucking done with him." He said it flatly, and then looked up at Zeke again, giving him another peculiar, searching look. And then went on, as if the look hadn't happened, "Plus…" He glanced around their table, lowered his voice. "See, I've got some jeopardy here myself. The guy was hiding out in my house. I was harboring a fugitive. I need to keep my distance from the whole business."

"That's why?"

"Isn't it enough? You sound skeptical."

"Just curious. I mean, you already knew the risks when you were negotiating on his behalf. And—" He hesitated, then finished the sentence, hoping Stan wouldn't find it offensive, "—you've never been great at saying no to Corin."

"I'm not alone in that," Stan said. Pointedly. And smoothly went on, "As for the risks, they seem a lot more concrete now he's in custody."

"I can see that."

"And also…" Stan sighed. "Like I said, I'm just fed up. This is not a good guy." Could Stan really believe this would come as news to Zeke? More likely, he was processing his own thoughts. "What happened with Liam…Would a decent human being do that? To an old friend? And then…" He hesitated, considered for a second, and went on, "He always treated me like crap. So there's that. Like he was doing me a favor hanging with me. Like I was some sort of mascot. I swallowed it in the old days, no doubt for morbid psychological reasons of my own, but…who the fuck is Corin McCabe to judge me? A bank robber and a killer, and he thinks he has the right to assess the value of my life? Not so much."

"You just noticed? He's always been a shithead to you."

"Maybe after all these years, despite never seeing a shrink—and I'm not knocking your profession, therapy might have helped—maybe I'm

356

finally recovering from my childhood, from growing up feeling ugly and ungainly and unworthy. Better late than never." Another small hesitation, and then, "And there's something else. The fucker hit on Carla. While being sheltered under my roof. Can you believe it?"

Zeke played dumb. "You sure?"

"Well, she says so. I doubt he grabbed her ass or forced his tongue down her throat. But you know Corin. He has ways of making his desires known. Of getting his agenda on the table so you're forced to deal with it."

"At least she rebuffed him," Zeke said.

"Yes, that's a comfort." A twisted smile, acknowledging Zeke's own painful history. Followed by another one of those disconcerting hard looks.

"What?" Zeke asked. Enough already with the searching looks.

Stan reacted as if he'd been caught doing something naughty. "What?" The pretense of incomprehension was transparently fake. He resumed a little too quickly, "There are lots of reasons for me to stay out of it. Including Carla killing me if I don't. With luck, I've washed my hands of him permanently."

"Back up a second. Why do you keep looking at me like that?"

"Like what?"

"Oh, please, buddy, we've known each other too long for bullshit."

Stanley's head bobbed up and down once or twice—it wasn't clear if he was nodding in agreement or twitching nervously—and then a sound resembling a giggle escaped him. He said, "Yeah, okay, it's just... Please don't take this the wrong way, Easy, and don't feel you need to say anything in response. It's just...that news report yesterday?...on the radio?...it said the police were acting on a tip."

Zeke's first client of the afternoon wasn't due till three, so he took a walk along Fourth St. before returning to his office. The neighborhood had changed radically over the years. Old shops had closed, new shops opened...intimations of mortality wherever you looked. Every building Zeke passed housed ghosts.

357

Approaching Spenger's, he experienced another *memento mori*; the place had recently re-opened after being shut for more than a year. But it wasn't the same place he and Stan had spent election night 1972. That restaurant was gone, reportedly a casualty of a family feud. A chain had taken over the property and kept the name, but this Spenger's was no longer part of Zeke's history. Oh, a glance toward the parking lot still reminded him of kissing Melanie before they got into her Porsche and drove off to their night of frenzied coupling. But the memory was attenuated, compromised.

Was it the lunch with Stan? Was it guilt? He was feeling deeply morose.

As he was nearing the Apple Store, he came to a sudden halt. He had spotted his son, about half a block ahead, strolling beside a slender but arrestingly busty Asian girl. His arm was draped proprietarily around her shoulders. He seemed absorbed in her company. He hadn't noticed Zeke. Not yet.

Zeke felt sure the boy wouldn't appreciate being observed right now, let alone accosted. He quickly ducked into the closest shop, a cosmetics store, and waited until the two had gone past. It was reassuring to see Owen with a girl. And with his arm around her, evidence his heart was on the road to recovery.

During the following days, it was clear the kids had intuited that something was amiss. Cathexis was interesting that way: You don't need to believe in the occult, you don't need to give credence to those eerie things Angie had taken seriously, to recognize emotional energy can travel along non-verbal pathways. The pathways needn't be supernatural or paranormal. They can exist in nature.

With Olivia and Ashley, the process wasn't mysterious. Leaving aside the fact they'd already been living with a certain level of tension in the house for several days, their awareness was triggered by something immediate and concrete. When Olivia, gulping down a few swallows of coffee before leaving for school on Monday morning, saw the *San Francisco Chronicle* on the kitchen table, she reached for it, and exclaimed, "Hey!

Isn't that your friend? The one who wanted a glass of water?"

Ashley grabbed at the paper and peered at the photograph. "It looks like him. But this guy's a lot younger." And then, with a smile, "And a major babe!" Only then did she notice the headline beside the picture. "Oh. Oops."

"It's an old picture," Molly said, without evincing much emotion. She was in a housecoat, standing by the sink, sipping coffee from a mug. Maybe it was the absence of emotion that tipped them off, the dog that didn't bark. When an old friend is arrested for a number of Class-A felonies, you're supposed to have a reaction.

"So it *is* the guy?" Olivia pressed.

"It's the guy," said Zeke. He was the only one actually eating. A bowl of granola. His insistence on breakfast every morning was a family joke; anyone uttering the phrase "the most important meal of the day" was guaranteed to provoke gales of fond hilarity in the Stern-Hilliard household.

"Did you know?" Ashley asked, pointing to the paper.

"We heard yesterday," he said.

"You seem to be taking it in stride," Olivia observed.

"We were shocked when we first got the news," Molly said.

"Did you know about the bank thing?"

"Yeah," Zeke answered. "It was a big deal back in the day."

"And is he guilty?" Ashley asked. "Or is this like some sort of government frame-up?"

Before either Molly or Zeke could answer, Olivia, typically, told Ashley they were running late and needed to get going. Typically because, in Zeke's estimation, she could already discern the gathering tension; it was like her both to perceive a source of potential strife before anyone else and to shy away from it as fast as possible. She was phobic about contention.

Neither of the girls mentioned it again that evening—had Olivia cautioned Ashley not to?—but the subject inevitably arose a few times over the next several days. Stories appeared on the front page of the *Chron* and once or twice led the local TV news, even though the national

359

press barely gave it any space. Each instance prompted Ashley to ask again about Corin, and about their friendship with him. Hesitantly, and always with an uncertain glance toward Olivia. She could tell there was an interesting story behind all this, and was certain something was being withheld. It didn't require x-ray vision. How many of your parents' friends, after all, are bank robbers and murderers? And why would they become so taciturn when the subject arose, and answer her queries in a minimal, gnomic fashion?

So the girls, who shared the house, and had actually met Corin, were less surprising to Zeke than Owen was. Four or five days after the arrest, Owen showed up unannounced at Zeke's office at noon. Zeke never scheduled clients during the lunch hour, and Owen was aware of that, so, although not expected, he wasn't worried about intruding. When the bell rang, Zeke, knowing it wasn't a client, thought, "Oh shit, not Corin again," before recalling Corin was in custody. Cognitive dissonance.

He was always delighted to see Owen. It was a surprise, but a pleasant surprise. He embraced his son at the building's front door and led him back into his office. "This is unexpected," he said. "Sit down, sit down. What brings you here?"

"Is the couch okay?"

"Sure."

"It isn't moist with tears?"

Zeke smiled. "No, it's been a rather nondescript morning. The usual quantity of kvetching, but no tears. So...to what do I owe the pleasure?"

Owen looked a trifle uncertain as he handed a small, gift-wrapped package over to Zeke. "The thing is, dad...well, first, here. Happy birthday."

Puzzled, Zeke accepted the package. His birthday was still a few days away.

"I, uh, see, I'm not going to be around on the day itself. Unless you really need me to be, in which case, of course I can change my plans, no problem."

He seemed self-conscious. Was it because he was skipping Zeke's birthday party, or was it the plans he could change if necessary?

"What plans?" Zeke asked with an encouraging smile. He had no intention of playing a guilt card. The boy had a right to make his own decisions. And knowing Owen, Zeke was sure he wouldn't choose such a course for trivial reasons.

"Oh, I..." He smiled uncertainly. "I was going to go camping this weekend. I don't have to, though."

"With a girl?"

"Well...yeah."

"Good for you."

"You don't mind? I really can change it."

"Absolutely no need, Owen."

"It's just—"

"No need to explain, either. I'm glad you have something like that to look forward to."

Owen smiled back. "Aren't you going to open your present?"

"Maybe I'll wait for the day. Who's the girl?"

"Well, that's kind of funny, actually. My roommate's cousin."

Ah hah! That explained the Asian girl with whom Owen had been strolling down Fourth Street. "The famous Korean grind?"

"We're getting along much better. The start of freshman year kind of freaked him out. Once I got some beer into him, he loosened up. And his cousin is terrific."

"Is this serious?"

"We're not engaged or anything."

"Right. I wasn't marching you down the aisle."

"Or maybe you meant, are we *doing it*?" Owen's smile widened mischievously.

"No, Owen, I wasn't asking that." Zeke returned the smile, but his mind was calculating rapidly: If a dutiful and loving son like Owen was prepared to miss a family celebration, it probably meant the big event—their *doing it*—was in fact on the schedule this weekend. Zeke couldn't find it in his heart to fault the boy's priorities.

"I'll tell you if you ask," Owen said.

"No, I believe in a zone of privacy in these matters. Unless you *want* to talk about it. In that case, I'm available."

"Nope, all is well. It's still early days, but...so far so good."

"Terrific. Say, wanna grab a bite?"

"I can't, dad. I have a class at one. Just wanted to drop off the present and say a premature happy birthday."

Owen stood up. Zeke followed suit. As they headed toward the door, Owen suddenly said, "Oh, I almost forgot. That guy on the news? McCabe somebody?"

"Corin McCabe."

"Right, right. Am I wrong? Didn't you know him?"

"Yeah, we did. A long time ago"

"Must've been a shock."

"Well, a surprise, anyway."

Owen was staring at him closely, with a quizzical look. Primates pick up subtle cues, no question about it. "You don't sound devastated," he finally observed.

"No, well...devastated? I'm not sure *how* I feel." Other than uncomfortable talking about it.

"You aren't?" And then, with a shrewdness that may have been instinctive and unconscious, "What about Molly?"

"Neither of us is happy to see someone we know go to jail for the rest of their life, if that's what you're asking."

Owen frowned. "There's something odd going on here, dad."

"What do you mean?"

"I don't know what I mean. But something in your attitude is...what? Out of whack. Is he guilty? Is that the reason?"

"That might be part of it."

"Boy. The inscrutable Dr. Stern. Maybe you'll tell me the whole story someday." He grinned. "Maybe after I tell you if Paula and I are doing it."

"Might take a little more than that." And then, "Listen, Owen? I'm glad things are looking up for you again." He suddenly grabbed him in a bear hug.

"Thanks, dad," Owen said, laughing at the spontaneous ferocity of Zeke's affection, and resisting a little, but not so forcefully as to slip from his grasp.

The state of Liam's face could be construed as symbolizing the group's mood. It was healing, although it wasn't altogether back to normal. Still some discoloration, still a bit of swelling. Much improved nevertheless.

Similarly, during this birthday dinner, there might be some residual tension among the six friends, but on the whole the evening seemed to be going well. No awkwardness about drinks, for example, that first potential hurdle. Zeke had no intention of allowing his birthday to pass without a martini before dinner and claret during. He hoped the others were on the same page. He felt pretty confident that resuming normal social drinking would put Liam at his ease more effectively than ritual hesitation, or self-conscious pussy-footing. Or worse still, asking permission.

Liam and Melanie seemed to have been doing some repair work of their own in recent days. They arrived at the restaurant laughing, a welcome sight in itself, and Zeke noticed they were touching each other more than usual; Liam's hand was on Melanie's shoulder as they approached the table, and she gave her husband's hand a squeeze before they took their seats.

Liam made the process easier when the waitress handed Stan a wine list. He said, "I expect you to splurge, Stan. Don't you dare cut corners. We're celebrating. And the better the wine, the more impressed you'll be by my indifference."

Melanie, nodding, added, "Plus, I intend to do my share of the damage. My designated driver is guaranteed."

They must have discussed this in advance; it felt choreographed. But it was the right approach, getting it out there.

Nevertheless, the subject of Corin remained fraught. Unavoidable, but hazardous. Zeke, all too aware of the unspoken constraint it was placing on everyone, tried to adopt Liam's gambit and face it head-on. During a lull, he asked Stan if he'd heard from Corin. It was a noble attempt, but it was a gamble, and it failed. Carla tensed. Molly frowned and looked down at her bread plate. There was a short silence before Stan said, "Not directly. I don't take his calls. I shot a couple of names to him through a back-channel. It's out of my hands."

A silence ensued. It threatened to become oppressive. Melanie coughed nervously. Molly busied herself buttering a piece of bread, although Zeke knew she made a fetish of not eating bread in restaurants. Liam finally broke the silence by saying, "It's been quite a saga."

At which Carla exploded, "Some saga! Like WWII was a saga. I just thank God it's over." And then, mortifyingly, she gave Zeke a brief, tight, conspiratorial smile. Zeke pretended not to see it.

It took a few minutes to recover. But they did manage, another sign things were mending. A couple of attempted conversational bids sputtered out and the second spoiled get-together in a row seemed to be looming. But then Bob Klein, one of the restaurant's owners, bearded and genial, glided up to their table, welcomed them—he knew them all socially, not merely in his role as restaurateur—pulled a seat over to their table, sat down, accepted a glass of wine, and started describing the night's specials. By the time he moved away again, conversation was flowing, and the damage was undone. Kids, movies, books, the scathing review of Liam's book by Michiko Kukitani, Obama, Hillary...there was plenty to talk about.

After they'd eaten, Zeke opened presents. He had already opened Molly's, a Bose SoundDock for his iPod, at the family celebration at breakfast that morning, along with presents from Owen and Olivia and Ashley. Tonight there were contraband Cohiba robustos from Stan and Carla. Very nice, although Zeke doubted Molly would see it that way. He also doubted Carla saw it that way. Liam and Melanie gave him a boxed set of John Wayne/John Ford DVDs, part of Liam's ongoing campaign to convince Zeke to get past his political prejudices and recognize these films as epochal works of art. This was one of the innumerable bees constantly buzzing within Liam's capacious bonnet. Melanie laughingly distanced herself from the gift while Liam assured Zeke he had unimagined pleasures in store.

And then, after coffee and tea were delivered, Stan stood up, abruptly and unsteadily. Rattling but fortunately not upending glassware en route. He had drunk a lot of wine, and was feeling it. "My friends, I'd like to say a few words," he announced. His speech was slightly slurred.

"Oh God," Zeke groaned. The others laughed, but his discomfort was unfeigned. He disliked toasts regardless of the occasion, who was delivering them, and who the recipient. But he especially disliked it when the toast was directed his way; the public display of raillery or affection, the obligation to react, the universal although universally unacknowledged desire for the operation to end as quickly as possible, it was all close to intolerable. In addition, he was uneasy tonight about what Stan might say. It was an occasion riddled with hazards, and Stan, never the most sensitive guy, was pretty thoroughly anaesthetized right now.

"Listen, buddy, you're just going to have to endure this," he said to Zeke. And then, turning to the table at large, he went on, "Okay. So." He cleared his throat theatrically. "I won't claim to know Easy better than anyone else—not with Molly among us—but I *have* known him longer. Longer even than Melanie, by a year. An eventful year, known forever after as kindergarten. Which isn't to say I've always known him as *well* as Melanie—"

Oh Christ, thought Zeke, please please please, at least don't leer! He'd never spoken to Stan about his night with Melanie, but Stan had been present for enough of it to have guessed the rest. To have guessed it before it happened.

Fortunately, Stan didn't leer, or even pause. And Liam didn't seem to have caught the implication in Stan's words. Stan went on, "...but we've been close friends all of our sentient lives. That's not a trivial thing. I don't deny we've had our share of disagreements during that time, some of them pretty heated. Life and death disagreements, it sometimes seemed. From whose Davy Crockett hat was better—that one got ugly—to whether Superman or Batman was the superior superhero, to who was the cutest Mouseketeer. Zeke thought it was Cubby, which still strikes me as totally gay. Who was the cooler Hardy Boy? Adlai versus JFK. Was Soupy Sales hilarious or just funny in an infantile way, which actually, now that I think of it, should interest Liam, it's right up his alley, it was an argument about how meta Soupy was, whether he was doing comedy about getting hit with a pie or doing comedy about the idea that getting hit with a pie is funny. But I'm digressing. Almost like Zeke. Let's see…we fought about whether Rod Serling or Max Schulman was the greatest writer in the history of the English language. We had a lively exchange at my bar mitzvah about whether blow jobs really exist or are an overheated, impossible figment of the adolescent imagination." He glanced over at Carla, visibly thought better of what he was about to say next, and went on, "A year or two later we differed over whether Bob Dylan was a great poet or a pretentious poser—sorry, Liam, but in our circle that was considered a legitimate area of controversy—about whether our only hope for justice was Marxist revolution, about whether Hubert Humphrey was as evil as Richard Nixon, and not so long ago we fought about whether the first Gulf War was justified or was, rather, an exercise in petro-imperialism. And so on. I'm leaving out a lot. These are but a few scattered highlights."

He paused to take a sip of wine—the last thing in the world he needed—and Zeke noticed that Carla was regarding her husband with an approving smile. Will wonders never cease? Stan went on, "So from this privileged position, from knowing Easy so long and so well, I want to say two things about him tonight. Things we don't say to each other nearly enough. Like, ever. We're either too embarrassed or we take them for granted.

"The first is—" He shifted his body again and looked down at Zeke, seated to his left. "The first is, Easy, listen, you've been a real friend. Always. There are times when friendship can be an uphill struggle, especially friendship with me, but you never acted like it was. You managed your side of this friendship with true grace. Don't think I haven't noticed. Your loyalty over the years has been a gift. I always knew I could count on it, and I never felt I had to prove myself worthy of it."

An approving sort of murmur could be heard from around the table, an unarticulated equivalent of "Hear, hear." Even Zeke, discomfited by the raw sentiment, recognized this as a touching tribute. Now, if only

Stan knew enough to shut up, they would all get off lightly.

But of course he didn't. He was drunk, and he had a head of steam. "The other thing I want to say...and holy shit, this one is hard for me... the other thing is, when I look back at all our disagreements over the years...it almost feels right to say 'over the centuries'...and on that score, by the way, I'm glad it's your birthday and not mine...the thing that occurs to me is, when I consider our various disagreements, what strikes me is how many times you were right. How effectively your bullshit detector functioned, how often your hard common sense has withstood the test.

"Those disagreements followed a pattern, I can see that now. While I kept getting swept up in the latest irrational enthusiasm, you stayed tough-minded and skeptical, you were moderate, temperate, judicious. There were times I thought you were close-minded. And old, way *too* old, old before your time. But now that we both actually *are* old, just plain-old old, I can appreciate your...God, you can't imagine how it pains me to say this...your wisdom. And if I ever catch you quoting these words back to me when we're sober, I'll never speak to you again."

There was laughter around the table, and it was affectionate, even approving laughter, but Zeke had a vague sense there was something uneasy in it as well. Or was he projecting his own apprehensions onto the others?

"So," Stan continued, "nowadays, I'm slower to judge, slower to condemn. Slower even to disagree. I realize you always have reasons, and they're usually sound reasons, and even if you say something or do some-thing that seems...surprising, or out of character, I stop and consider it from your point of view. And realize you've seen deeper than I, and examined things more closely.

"So in conclusion, I'll just say you're still close-minded, but now I see that's got its good points.

"Oh, one last thing. Despite all this, I don't want to leave the impres-sion you're *always* right. Far from it! For example, I'll go to my grave insisting my coonskin cap was the real fucking article and yours was just some crappy imitation.

"Happy birthday, Easy!"

Stan raised his glass, saluted Zeke, took a sip, and then sat down to appreciative laughter and applause. Zeke forced himself to join in. His burning cheeks could easily be ascribed to pleasure, amusement, and too much cabernet.

Molly was the driver that night. Some nights he might protest his sobriety and insist on taking the wheel, but tonight, as they approached their car, parked around the corner from the restaurant, he wordlessly headed for the passenger side. And didn't say a word for the first five minutes of the drive.

Finally, hesitantly, Molly said, "That was nice." It wasn't a real observation, it was an invitation for him to unburden himself. Something was eating at him.

He grunted. Molly knew him well enough to assay the emotion behind the grunt: Not anger. Or not, at least, anger directed her way. But something was definitely eating him. So, as a kind of probe, she said, "Stan's toast… he was shit-faced, obviously, but it was sweet. Even loving. Didn't you think?"

That did the trick. Zeke exploded. "Are you nuts? You deconstruct texts for a living! Didn't you get it?"

She waited, driving carefully, keeping her eyes on the road. After a few seconds, he cried, "He thinks I ratted out Corin! Everybody does! That's what that toast was about! When did I become the certified fink? Why me? It could have been anyone. Anyone at the table, and probably hundreds of others. The world must be crawling with people who have a beef against Corin."

"Why didn't you say something?"

"Oh yeah, what's more convincing than some guy shouting, 'It wasn't me!' when no one's breathed a word except by innuendo. Meanwhile winking and nodding to convey the message, It's okay, we don't hold it against you. There's nothing more incriminating than insisting on your innocence. Like Queen Gertrude, every shrink's Exhibit A." He put his hand over his forehead and pressed hard. "What's the use? There's nothing I can do. Silence seems like acquiescence and defending myself just digs me in deeper."

"I didn't get the impression Stan was *blaming* you."

"No, no, the opposite, Stan was, he was basically saying *no one* blames me. And then they all applauded. The whole damned group offering me absolution. Like, hey, we understand, you had a score to settle."

"No, it wasn't absolution, I don't think. It was more like…like gratitude. For having the guts to do a nasty job that everyone knew needed doing."

"So you believe it too?"

She was startled. "Me?"

"You do, don't you? Christ. If I can't even convince *you*…"

"You don't have to convince me, Easy."

"Because you don't think it matters?"

"No, no, because I know it wasn't you. I don't just think it, I know it."

"How are you so certain?"

There was a long pause. Then she said, "Because it was me. I made the call."

She waited for him to say something. He didn't; after a sharp intake of breath, he just sat there frozen. So she went on, "The day after Liam's crash. Just before class. I walked from my office to a pay phone on Hearst—one of the few left—and told them where Corin was staying. Hung up when they asked my name."

"Holy crap."

"I decided on the way home from the hospital." Her voice was muted, almost monotonous, her eyes didn't leave the road. "Someone had to do something. This thing had gone on too long. It had done enough damage. It needed to be stopped."

There was a long silence. She could practically hear the wheels turning inside Zeke's head. An old, familiar sound to her.

After what seemed an eternity, he finally said, "Was it because you—"

She cut him off gently, saying, "Aw, Easy, don't therap this. Please. I implore you. You'll make yourself crazy." She was smiling all of a sudden, a warm loving smile apparently directed at the windshield. "There's no call for you to therap this. I did it for us, okay? That's all you should care about. That's all that matters. I did it for us."

She reached over and took his hand.

2003

I t's possible Liam could have warned me. I've never asked him if he
knew in advance.

Several years had passed since Angie died, and I was no longer in
mourning in any strict sense. There was nothing more to get through.
The grief that still endured was part of who I was. Who I am.

But I was living a fairly reclusive life all the same. It was primarily
a matter of practicality; solo-fathering morning and night, and seeing
clients all day, I had neither the time nor the energy to be sociable. Nor
much inclination. I dated occasionally, and I maintained my ties with
old friends—I wasn't hibernating—but I wasn't getting out much, I
wasn't making an effort to get out much. Not from depression, honestly;
it was more a matter of finding Owen's company fulfilling, and disliking
leaving him with babysitters too often. He'd experienced enough abandonment for one childhood.

But sometimes I could be persuaded to venture out. This particular
night, Liam convinced me to meet up with him and Melanie at a party
given by a friend of his from the English Department. Liam's group of

friends combined people from the university and from Bay Area film, music, and theater circles. A Bohemian crowd. For whatever reason, he put enough pressure on me that I said yes.

Then, when he got around to telling me our host's name, I realized the guy had once been a client of mine, and that gave me pause. But not enough to back out; if you're a shrink in a small town, you occasionally encounter clients and former clients in social settings, and you roll with it. If they're current clients, the experience gives you something to work with in subsequent sessions. If they're former clients, it can be awkward, but it's not the end of the world. I shake hands as if we're meeting for the first time and leave it up to them whether or not to acknowledge our therapeutic relationship. No biggie either way.

This night, the former client—his name was David—was covering his embarrassment with a great show of sociability. After offering me a drink, he introduced me to everyone his eye fell on, including both his wife and the woman I knew to be (or at least to have been) his mistress, and he insisted on taking me all around his house. As if giving me an illustrated tour of the life he had described in such detail over the course of several years.

And then we were in his kitchen, and I was already starting to wonder how to shake free of him without hurting his feelings—but hell, he'd terminated therapy, maybe it was his turn to experience rejection—when he suddenly said in an undertone, "Oh, here's someone you should meet. New hire. We lured her away from Stanford, quite a coup. Usually goes the other way, they have the cash. We were lucky, she was eager to flee Palo Alto. Messy divorce." And then, in a conversational tone, while pulling me along, "Zeke, say hello to Molly Hilliard."

Hearing her name—or maybe hearing mine—she turned our way. And there she was. It was the first time I'd laid eyes on her in about 30 years. The look on my face must have mirrored the one on hers: She was staring at me in ashen, open-mouthed stupefaction. Meanwhile, I felt something momentous happening somewhere within my thorax. I couldn't speak.

She hadn't changed a lot. Or maybe she *had* changed a lot, but she was still recognizably Molly. She seemed solider, although still slender. Her face had more definition, her features seemed stronger. Her hair was shorter. She was still lovely.

"Molly," I finally managed to croak out.

Before she said anything, David said, "Come this way, I want you to meet my daughter, she's in her room doing her homework. She's heard all about you." He was literally pulling on my arm.

I had no will of my own, I let myself be yanked away. Maybe I was being sensitive to a former client's feelings, or maybe I didn't want him to glimpse mine. Or maybe I was stumped about what to say or how to behave. I looked back at Molly, and held up a hand to signify, I'll be back. But I had no idea if she understood, let alone cared.

A few minutes later, after greeting David's eleven-year-old daughter, who, upon our being introduced, uttered the dumbfounding words, "Thank you for making my daddy happier"—Berkeley!—I finally managed to extricate myself from David more or less gracefully, and headed back toward the kitchen. Molly wasn't there. Lots of other people were, but not Molly. I started moving through the house looking for her. I bumped into Liam and Melanie once, and exchanged greetings with them, but continued on. She wasn't in the family room, she wasn't in the living room, she wasn't in the dining room, she didn't appear to be anywhere downstairs. Could she have gone home?

I went up to the second floor, trying to look like a man with a full bladder rather than someone in search of his lost love. Not an impossible challenge for someone my age. I knew which room belonged to David's daughter and passed that one by. I looked into a hall bathroom; the door was open, the room was dark, the old-fashioned creamy tile reflected moonlight. Then I stopped outside the master bedroom and peeked through the doorway.

Dark. Coats piled on the bed. And a figure seated at the far end. Her.

I murmured her name. Her silhouette, across the room, at the far end of the bed, turned in my direction, but there was no reply.

"Howdy, stranger," I said, and took a tentative step into the room. My

373

voice, as usual, was steadier than I was. "Long time no see."

"Zeke," she said. Even on that one syllable, her voice was tremulous.

"Isn't this something?"

"I…I just can't believe it. I'm in shock."

"What are you doing up here? I've been looking all over the house for you."

"I needed to get a grip on myself."

By now, I was beside her. Her voice was so shaky, I suddenly felt this unexpected, overwhelming tenderness wash over me. It was emollient, somehow: My heartbeat began to moderate, my agitation turned into something softer, less jangly. "Molly—" I willed myself to reach out and touch her hand. "I can't even begin to tell you—"

Which is when she started crying. Just buried her face in her hands and sobbed. My heart began to swell. I sat beside her on the bed and put my arm around her. She collapsed against me. Her face was wet where it touched my neck. Her body was shaking, great seismic heaves. She finally stammered out, "I've…this moment…I've pictured it so many times…and now…" She laughed self-consciously. "Oh God, I'm completely fucking this up, aren't I?"

"It's okay. For one thing, no, you aren't. And besides, it doesn't matter, it doesn't have to happen all at once."

"But…I mean…this is crazy. It's insane. I'm…I'm crying for something that was lost a thousand years ago. I don't even know you anymore."

"Sure you do," I said. "Of course you do. I'm the same person I always was."

CPSIA information can be obtained at www.ICGtesting.com
Printed in the USA
LVOW04s2343250814

400916LV00014B/436/P